THE COVE

GREGG DUNNETT

Ebook ISBN: 978-1-80508-372-6
Paperback ISBN: 978-1-80508-374-0

Cover design: Emma Graves
Cover images: Arcangel, Shutterstock

Published by Storm Publishing.
For further information, visit:
www.stormpublishing.co

ALSO BY GREGG DUNNETT

Little Ghosts

The Rockpools Series

1. *The Things You Find in Rockpools*

2. *The Lornea Island Detective Agency*

3. *The Appearance of Mystery*

4. *The Island of Dragons*

Standalone thrillers

The Wave at Hanging Rock

The Glass Tower

The Girl on the Burning Boat

The Desert Run

PROLOGUE

Date: November 5th (fireworks night).
Time: 10:32pm (Mummy thinks I'm asleep!)
Age: eight years, five months, thirteen days (nearly exactly eight and a half!)

Daddy did something weird again. I mean, worse than weird. I shouldn't even write it down here in case he finds this diary. But I feel I need to tell someone. Only I can't, so this is the next best thing.

He's killed another dog.

This one is smaller than the last time, with short brown hair and little legs. I know it too. It wears this pink collar, and it always runs off when the lady lets it off the lead. It comes and barks at the swings. Maybe that's why Daddy killed it, although it doesn't seem a very good reason.

I only know because of fireworks night. There was this big bonfire on the green, and Daddy said we could go, and he'd been storing up wood from all the building works to burn. I don't know why, but I wanted to look at the wood before it got burned. I just think it's weird to how it's there one minute, and not there afterwards. Like it just – disappears. Where does it go? It's kind of the same with the dogs, one minute they're alive, and they fetch balls, and wag their tails, and woof at the swings, and then Daddy does something that takes the alive bit away, and then there's not really there anymore and they go all stiff.

So I sneaked into the garage, where Daddy was keeping the wood, even though he told me not to. And that's when I found it. First it was this weird smell, like a dead-dog smell I suppose, and then I saw the blanket, and straight away I knew what I'd find. This one was sort of wedged underneath some of the wood, at the bottom of the trailer where he'd stored it all. I couldn't un-wedge it without moving the wood, but I could unwrap it a bit to have a look.

It had its eyes open, like it was awake, but the eyes didn't move. When I opened the blanket a bit more there were all bits of it – the inside bits I mean – coming out through where it had been cut open. It was so gross.

I don't know what to do. Maybe I should tell someone, because it's wrong to kill. But it's not like I *can* tell anyone. I'm only eight. No one's going to believe me.

Anyway, I didn't have long to think about it, because Daddy said he had to take the wood to put it on the bonfire before they lit it. I think he wanted to go alone, but Mummy had to go to the doctors, so Daddy had to take me too. He hitched up the trailer and we drove to where they had the bonfire built, but this was before anyone else was there. Daddy drove right up to it, and told me to stay in the car because it was dangerous and the wood might fall, but he only said that so I wouldn't see what he was doing. I was watching anyway, through the window.

He loaded half the wood on the outside of the bonfire, and then he took the dead dog, still wrapped up in the blanket, and he put it right in the middle of the wood pile. Then he put the rest of the wood on the outside, so you couldn't see the blanket.

Then, when he got back in the car, he was whistling the tune from *The Simpsons*.

When we went back later on there was this massive fire, bigger than anything I've seen before. After it died down a bit they let off the fireworks. Normally I'd have been excited by fireworks, but I wasn't this time. Instead I was thinking about the dog, and what will happen if one day Daddy does what he does with the dogs, but he does it with people instead?

What if one day he wants to do it with *me*?

PART 1

ERICA SANDS

ONE

Detective Chief Inspector Erica Sands was reading at her desk while the Murder Investigation Department emptied around her.

It wasn't uncommon for those who worked in the department, known as MID, to stay late, especially if there was a high profile or priority case, but that night there was little to do. The day had seen two birthdays – one of the junior detectives, and DI Lindham, second-in-command of the unit, and Sands' deputy. It was also a Friday night, and most people were looking forward to a rare opportunity to unwind. But the relaxed chatter about which pub they were going to (The George Inn on Poole Quay was favourite) went quiet as the team passed by Sands' desk.

By eight pm she was alone in MID, trying to focus on the details of the case in front of her, but her mind kept shifting to the telephones that sat on her desk, neither of which had rung.

She checked her mobile, then her eyes scanned the desk phone in case she'd missed a message there. She hadn't.

She passed a hand through her hair – dark, mid-length, straight – then drummed her fingers on the desk. She took a deeper breath in an attempt to quell the anxiety, but it didn't help. She picked up the paperwork this time, annoyed at her inability to focus on it. Her fingernails were unpainted, short and neat. As usual, she wore no make-up. It took time to apply and maintain, and time was what she valued most.

Suddenly, the quiet of the room was broken, a telephone ringing – but not one of those on her desk. She glowered and punched a button on her phone to direct the call to her. It was nothing, a request from a nearby morgue that one of her officers should have handled before they left. It wasn't a case she was working directly but she was able to respond to the pathologist's questions, speaking in a clipped, impatient tone. He was still thanking her as she hung up the phone.

She turned back to the file. It was a summary of evidence collected twenty-five years previously regarding the drowning of a twelve-year-old boy. The boy's father claimed it was a swimming accident at a quarry lake, but marks found on the body raised doubts. They could have been the normal bumps and scrapes that any adventurous twelve-year-old might pick up. Or they could have been signs of abuse. However, with no other witnesses, and nothing else to go on, the death had been ruled an accident, with no charges brought. Sands' job – entirely self-appointed, no one had requested she review the file, nor even knew she was reading it – was to check whether the father's name subsequently came up in any other suspicious deaths or complaints in the intervening years, or if there were any other aspects of the case that could be re-examined using the advances in crime detection technology. After half an hour she had found nothing and was considering moving onto the next file, a stack that towered on one side of her desk. But then her mobile rang.

Instead of snatching it up like before, she looked at the screen, and felt a hollowness appear in her stomach. She picked up the phone and accepted the call.

"Detective Sands? This is Dr Hannigan."

"Go on."

"Chief Superintendent Yorke has asked me to keep you informed, I believe you're aware..."

"Yes. Go on."

The man on the other end of the line hesitated. "I'm afraid it's not good news."

This time Sands said nothing. Her mouth felt dry.

"I understand he's explained the situation with your father? I'm sorry to say his condition has deteriorated further, and he's been moved into the intensive care ward." The doctor paused again.

"And?"

The doctor seemed to choose his next words carefully. "We hoped that would bring about an improvement in his condition, but I'm afraid that hasn't happened. Indeed, we've actually seen a continued worsening." This time the hesitation was accompanied by a sigh. "I think we're now at the stage where there's only one outcome. I'm sorry."

"What outcome?"

The doctor hesitated again. "What I mean is, his body is shutting down. Detective Sands, I'm sorry to tell you your father is dying."

There was a silence, but just as the doctor went to break it, Sands spoke. "How long?"

There was another hesitation, shorter this time. "We're looking at a number of hours rather than days." He gave a sigh. "He was fit for his age, but with this virus, we're seeing such a rapid decline. I wanted to let you know, if you wanted to say goodbye in person, you should come now. At once."

If the doctor said anything else after that it was lost to Sands. The room around her began to swim and blur.

"Thank you, Dr Hannigan," she said, interrupting him a few moments later, when she realised he was still talking, giving details of how she could visit. She hung up the phone and stared out in front of her.

She gazed out at the familiar view of the office, not seeing the banks of computers, the walls of filing cabinets, the room dividers that doubled as pin boards for photographs and newspaper cuttings. Then she turned and looked again at the folder open in front of her, the photographs of the dead boy, the injuries highlighted and ordered like a shopping list. Suddenly, she felt a strong desire to get out of there, this place where she spent her life. Breathing hard, she swept the papers together and returned them to the file, then bundled that and two other cases into her bag – some light reading for the weekend. Then she checked her desk, shut down her computer and walked quickly away.

She took the stairs. The cleaning team, two ladies from Venezuela, glanced at each other. They were surprised but grateful that she was leaving early for once. They'd learned long ago the need to vacuum the office around Sands' schedule and not interfere with it. She strode out past the security on the front desk, not saying a word, for once not even nodding to the guard who'd be there the whole night.

She strode out into the car park, unlocked her car, a rosso-red Alfa Romeo, and got in. But she didn't start the engine. Instead, she sat there. Staring out again with unseeing eyes.

Although Sands had known she would one day face the death of her father, she had been caught out by the suddenness of his decline. It was just three days since she'd been contacted about his illness, and only today that the doctors had given any indication it might be life-threatening. It was too fast; she didn't know how to feel. For her entire adult life she'd lived with two certainties about her family: firstly, there was only her father – and second, that he was safely locked away. But now, without the time she needed to adjust, that was all changing, as the minutes slipped away.

Her hand went to her chest, finding the locket that hung there, the only piece of jewellery she wore. Her fingers stroked the metal, tracing a pattern so familiar it was worn into the white gold itself. She felt an urge to open it, but automatically resisted. Even here, in the privacy of her car, it still wouldn't be safe.

There were people who would celebrate her father's death, she knew. It would merit a mention in the press, even this long after his conviction, and they would bid him good riddance. Others though would mourn. He had his supporters, even after what he'd done. But how did she feel? She wasn't sure. Whatever he'd done, he was her last remaining family member. And when he was gone, she would be truly alone.

Suddenly, she dropped the locket and leaned forwards. She punched the address of the hospital into the car's GPS and drummed her fingers in irritation while it calculated. The screen changed, telling her that in one hour and seventeen minutes she could be arriving at the hospital where her father lay breathing his last. Hannigan had made the arrangements so that she'd be allowed access. Her hand went to the ignition key, almost turning it. But she stopped. It was like her body and mind were being pulled apart, driven both to go, and not to.

She touched the locket again, her fingers tracing the same pattern. She wished she could speak to someone, but there was no one. Her colleagues held her police work in the highest regard – she made sure of that – but she wasn't close to anyone. How could she be?

And then without really thinking at all, she pulled the key out and pushed open the door. She took her bag, locked the Alfa and walked. She had no idea where she was going. She just walked. At first in no particular direction, but soon vaguely towards the town centre, and then towards the quay, where she lived in an apartment overlooking the harbour. She realised at one point that this was the first night, in five years of working at MID, that she'd walked home. It gave her a purpose to cling to.

There seemed to be some sort of festival on, a winter-lighting event aimed at rejuvenating the town centre, a flyer pinned to a tree told her. She passed a church illuminated with different colours, and the town's small fountain was rising and falling to music and lights. Above it a sliver of the moon was visible for a moment, before it was hidden behind scudding clouds. Small throngs of people stood about watching, while mobile stalls sold plastic light-up toys to eager children. She passed through it all, unseen and unseeing. Her mind – if it was anywhere – was on another child, a girl, years ago now, who would never play again because strong hands squeezing around her neck had choked the life out of her.

She came to an open doorway, a building used as an arts space. She'd never been inside before, never even noticed it, but tonight the light and sounds drew her in. Downstairs, black and white photographs of the town and the quay had been enlarged and hung on the wall. A handful of people milled around, grateful to get out of the cold. She stood in front of the displays and saw nothing of the life they represented. She climbed the stairs to a busier room and stood in front of a canvas, a black and blue mush of what looked to her like a close-up of the bruises and tangled hair of a scene-of-crime photograph. But she didn't really see it. That night she just needed to be somewhere other than her life.

"It's the brush strokes, isn't it?" A voice cut in from her left and she swung her head around sharply to see a man smiling at her. He was a few years younger than her, and even through the daze that was her mind, she registered he was handsome.

"They really do capture the spirit of..." He leaned in to read the caption underneath the artwork in a voice heavy with sarcasm: "*The wind in the leaves.* So original and..." He shook his head, pretending to be rendered speechless by the skill of the artist. "Just brilliant."

Sands offered nothing in return and turned back to the painting. But the man didn't give up.

"You must be a real connoisseur. Are you buying?" he asked suddenly, as if the idea had only just occurred to him. "All the artwork here is for sale, and I have a list of guide prices if you're interested? I can get you a drink and we can discuss..."

"No."

"I don't blame you," the man continued without a moment's hesitation. "Looks more like spaghetti than leaves to me. Or maybe seaweed. I can see seaweed in there, what do you think?" He turned his head onto one side, as if studying the art, then turned to her with a smile. He seemed confident that this would win her over. "You know she's asking *twelve thousand pounds* for this? The artist, I mean, which I think is daylight robbery. And I say that as her brother, her very loving brother. Say, you're not with the police are you, not working undercover?"

Even though she had no official reason to be there, the question still made Sands' heart thud in her chest.

"It's just I thought you might be here to investigate daylight robbery, though it's not daylight is it?" He glanced at the window, then turned back and tried again. "Or crimes against art. Is that a thing?" He looked questioningly, but she turned away again, realising it was only a joke. He went on, undeterred. "Seriously, she ought to be arrested for what she's charging for this tat. Even worse, the commission I'm getting." He paused, suddenly seeming to notice he was getting nowhere with his current approach. "Say, would you like a drink anyway? We've rather over-catered to be fair. Expecting a rush."

"No." Sands started to move away, wanting to be alone, when in a flash she saw what that meant tonight. A lonely walk home to her empty flat. No one to call. The whole weekend alone with only her thoughts, and her case files of those who'd died long ago. And perhaps, hidden within the pages, the proof that cold, predatory men were still out there, somewhere. Doing what they did in the darkness. For once, she just didn't want to face it. She needed to spend just a little longer in the light.

"I'm not here for the art," she heard her voice say, and it set the man off again. She felt compelled to watch as his wide mouth split into another generous smile.

"*No one's* here for the art." He rolled his eyes, deep blue in colour. "It's all about the free booze and the canapés..."

"My father's dying."

She didn't say it to stop him. She said it because it was true, and because she needed to say it to someone instead of repeating the words over and over inside her head. But it did stop him. Cold.

"Oh – shit." He frowned but didn't turn away. "Hell, I'm sorry. I'm being an arse. What does he have?"

Sands shook her head. "They don't know exactly. Some sort of virus. They just say he'll die tonight. He'll be dead by the morning." Again she felt hollow at the thought of it.

At that moment a young waitress walked by carrying a tray of drinks, flutes of what looked like champagne but almost certainly wasn't. The man took two, smiling his thanks at the girl, who kept her eyes on him far longer than she needed to. He didn't respond, turning right back to Sands. "Drink up. You look like you need this."

Sands rarely drank, but she accepted the glass and took a mouthful of the fizzy liquid. Before she knew it, she'd drunk half the glass.

"You wanna talk about it?" the man asked, and Sands considered the question. She thought of the times she had talked about it before. In police interviews, with child psychologists, social workers, the few high-ranking men at work – always men – who knew about her father. And she looked at *this* man now, this friendly stranger, and she knew she couldn't tell him anything. She shook her head and took another sip from her glass.

"You don't have to if you don't want to. I can talk and you just listen. I can explain the motivation behind each of my sister's works here. That's her over there." He pointed towards a dark-haired woman in an emerald-green gown that looked too elegant for the occasion. She straightened as she saw the man pointing at her, as if pretending she hadn't noticed. "You can just listen and laugh at how ridiculously pretentious she is." He paused and watched her for a moment. "It might take your mind off things."

Sands thought about this too. And she found herself nodding. "OK."

The man led her around the room. In front of each of the exhibits he read in a louder voice from the labels underneath the paintings, and then in a lower voice told Sands how his sister was a terrible artist with almost no talent or commitment, only here because she was supported by their wealthy parents. He said nothing about himself, and how he presumably would have benefited in a similar way. But he spoke with humour, about how she spent much more of her time setting up images for Instagram than painting. A couple of times he even drew a smile. Whenever her glass was empty he found a way to offer her another. Eventually, when they reached the quietest corner of the room, he returned to the subject that was so obviously on her mind.

"This is none of my business, but I can't help but notice you're getting drunk in a terrible art gallery and not at hospital saying goodbye. Are you sure that's what you want?"

Sands stiffened. She wanted to explain to this man – this random stranger she'd never see again – but she knew she couldn't, not really.

"You want to talk about it?"

She shook her head.

"I don't mean with me. I meant with friends. Or your family, or someone from work? I can take you somewhere." He looked at her, open concern on his face.

"No." She screwed her eyes shut. "I don't have any family." She swallowed. "Or friends. And no one at work knows about my father. They can't."

He had no answer to that, and stayed silent, and she knew she'd said too much.

"I want to go home," Sands went on.

"Sure." He glanced around the room, then back at her. "You live nearby? Are you driving? On foot?"

"I walked here," Sands answered, almost as if she were reminding herself.

"Let me call you a cab, although," – he stopped, seeming to have come up against a snag – "With this festival, they're busy... Hey, look, let me give you a lift home."

"No..."

"Come on. I've been imprisoned here all evening against my will. I get a commission if I sell something, but I'd also never forgive myself. Come on. Give me an excuse to get outta here. Please? You'd be doing me a huge favour."

Sands nodded, grateful, and the man left at once to inform his sister. Sands saw the woman frowning in disappointment. Then he came back.

"I'm off the hook." He smiled that smile again. "I'm Luke, by the way. Luke Golding."

"Erica," Sands replied.

"Hi Erica. Well, come with me. I'm parked right outside."

They went back out into the night. It was later now and the streets were quieter, the air sharply cold. He unlocked a nondescript Vauxhall and they both climbed in. She gave her address and he said he knew where it was. The engine was quiet – gutless, she would normally have described it – but tonight all she cared about was that the cabin was filled with warm air that made her feel sleepy. But sooner than she would have liked, they were outside the door of her apartment block.

"Well. Here we are." He seemed a little anxious now, like he wasn't sure what to do next. "Say, do you have a flatmate or anything? Or is there anyone I can call for you? A girlfriend? Just so you're not alone?" He gave her a smile that she realised later was probably supposed to be compassionate. But he was good looking, he'd been kind, and with the weird swirl of emotions flowing through her brain she misread it.

"No," she replied. And, like earlier, she made a decision without thinking. "But you can come up if you like."

He stiffened, and although Sands was well used to her own poor judgement in these matters, his reaction caught her by surprise. For a second, she thought he might not have understood. And so she made an awkward situation far worse by trying to clarify.

"I don't mean to look after me. I mean... you know, if you want to come upstairs to have sex." She heard herself say the words and looked away, a pained expression on her face. When she looked back, his eyes and mouth were slightly open. A smile somehow found its way to his lips as he recovered.

"Whoa – I didn't see that coming." He broke off, and Sands felt a sudden surge of shame. This man was only being kind to her; he had no interest in getting into her bed. She turned towards the door now, only partially hearing his words.

"I'm flattered. Really I am, but I don't think that's a great idea," he began, "under the circumstances."

"It's fine." She began to fumble with the door handle, cursing her stupidity for downing so much of the champagne.

The man tried to calm her. "Hey, Erica... It's fine." But already she was gone. She marched up to the door and punched in the code to access into the lobby. When she turned round, the car was still there. Through the glass of the doorway and the car windscreen she caught a glimpse of his face.

TWO

She slept fitfully, dreaming several times that the call had come through; so that when she woke she thought her father was already dead. But there were no messages on her mobile, no missed calls. She made coffee and waited, and finally, just before nine, the phone rang.

"Erica, this is Chief Superintendent Yorke." She steeled herself.

"Is he dead?"

There was a silence. "Actually no. He's not."

Sands' world twisted again.

"What do you mean?"

There was a change to Yorke's tone. "Apparently he responded unusually well to the treatment. They're calling it a miraculous recovery."

Sands rubbed her face. "That's not possible. They told me it was certain, he was dying."

This time Yorke stayed quiet, and Sands caught up. "A miraculous recovery? He was faking?"

Another pause. "I don't know how he managed it, but I'd guess so."

Sands pressed her eyes shut for a few moments, then forced her brain to concentrate. "Why? What would he get out of it? Is he secure?"

"Absolutely. There's no need to be concerned about that. He's physically restrained, arms and legs, and there's a guard outside his door. He'll be transferred back to his cell this morning. I can let you know when he's there."

Sands didn't answer.

Yorke went on. "Erica, I should apologise for getting you involved in this. We ought to have waited until it was absolutely certain, but I thought you had a right to know."

"This isn't your fault. I asked you to be my intermediary."

"Yes, well, anyway. Things should go back to normal now. You won't need to hear from him again."

"Thank you, sir."

There was a silence, before Yorke went on.

"There is actually another reason why I'm calling. I know how you've not had a major case to run, since taking over the department. I think I might have one."

"What's happened?"

"I can get John Lindham to run it, if this stuff with your father is..."

"I'll take it. What's happened?"

Yorke paused again, but just for a moment.

"Someone came across a body this morning. On a beach. Young girl."

"How young?"

"Don't know yet, I'm told about seven or eight."

"We don't know? We haven't found the parents?"

"Not yet, no."

Sands glanced at her watch, frowned. "When was she killed?"

"I don't know. There's not much we *do* know yet, and Lindham is the senior officer on-call. But I also know you've been hanging out for a big case. And this looks big."

"I already said I want it. Which beach?"

Again Yorke hesitated, as if perhaps he was second guessing his decision. "It's at Lulworth Cove. How quickly can you be there?"

Sands thought. It was at least forty minutes to Lulworth from Poole. "Thirty-five minutes, sir."

"Good. I'll see you when you get there. I'm on my way too." He paused. "Oh, Erica? There's something else."

"Yes, sir?"

"Actually, never mind. I'll tell you in person. A Sergeant Sinclair is acting as CSM. If you patch yourself through to control as you're driving, they'll bring you up to date on what we know so far."

Yorke rang off and at once the fog began to lift from Sands' mind. Her father was almost forgotten, the empty, drifting weekend had been replaced with something active. She moved quickly now, going to the kitchen to eat and make more coffee while she dressed. But just as she thought she was ready, she remembered how she'd left the Alfa at the office the night before. She swore out loud.

It wasn't a huge problem. Moments later a taxi was on its way to take her back to the station, but the minutes spent waiting for it were an irritation. She used the time to check through her murder bag, which she kept packed with the basics: forensic protective clothing, maps, torch and police radio – batteries charged. She also had overnight essentials and a change of clothes. Everything was in order. Finally the cab arrived and she hurried downstairs.

Reunited with her car, she waited until the Bluetooth on her phone connected, then pressed the button to access the Force Control Room, identifying herself to the operator. She asked first for the GPS location and plugged it into the car. While she drove – fast – she ordered the operator to read out all the information logged against the case so far. When he finished, she told him to read it again. Then a third time.

Thirty-seven minutes later, she slowed as she dropped down the hill into Lulworth. Quaint stone cottages appeared on either side, most with thickly thatched roofs. A little further down, the large car park – built to accommodate the summer crowds – stretched nearly empty to her right. Just past it, a small roundabout was blocked by a police car, its blue light revolving slowly but the siren off. She angled as if to drive past and lowered her window, as the officer in the other car did the same.

"DCI Erica Sands." She showed her identification.

"Morning, ma'am. It's just down here." The officer started his engine and backed up to let her past. She followed the track another fifty metres down until the way ahead was blocked by a line of vehicles, both marked police cars and SOCO – Scene of Crime – vans. She left the Alfa at the back of the line and went on foot the rest of the way.

The little lane ended where it met the bay. A short, steep beach of pebbles and rocks, which served as the bed of a stream, and then the silver-blue water of the sea. Steep hills rose up on both sides, and the crests wound around in front of her, nearly enclosing a complete circle of calm water perhaps half a kilometre across at its widest point. Ahead of her was the entrance to the sea beyond. A couple of small fishing boats tugged at their mooring buoys, and many more empty pink and orange buoys suggested the cove would be far busier in the summer. It was already noisy though: the stream, engorged by recent rains, roaring as it dropped the final few feet before meeting the sea.

She looked around, at first not spotting the blue forensic tent where the body lay, but that was because it was still almost half a mile away, nearly all the way around the horseshoe-shaped bay. Much nearer, a tape had been pulled across the beach, restricting access.

"Erica!" a voice called out behind her, and she turned to see Yorke, dressed in civilian clothes. Another man stood next to him, in sergeant's uniform.

"Sergeant Sinclair, this is DCI Erica Sands. She's one of our best from MID." He smiled at her and touched the small of her back. "Erica, your Crime Scene Manager." The sergeant stiffened as he reached out a hand, which she shook briefly.

Yorke turned to Sands. "Did you manage to patch through?"

"Yes, sir."

"Then you know as much we do. But it looks like a nasty one. Not the sort of thing you'd think could happen in a place like this." Almost as if driven by his comment they all took a moment to glance around at the cove, but then there was something almost other-worldly in its beauty, despite the circumstances.

"Actually, Erica, there was that other thing. Might I have a quick word, in private?"

"Yes, sir."

Sands followed Yorke to where two small rowing boats were pulled up on the pebbles. In one of them a pair of yellow rubber gloves lay discarded or abandoned, smeared with blood and fish scales.

"What is it, sir?"

He watched her but didn't answer immediately. "They're saying he might have stored up his medication, then taken it all at once. That might explain how he tricked the doctors."

Sands didn't reply.

"Either way, he's already back in his cell. He's completely secure."

"Anything to mess us around." Sands pushed a strand of hair that had come loose behind her ear.

Their eyes met for a moment. "Was that everything, sir? I should get started."

"Actually, no." Yorke gave a half smile, then hesitated. Sands waited.

"Yes, sir?"

"You can probably tell from my fetching attire that I was supposed to be playing golf this morning. With the regional commander." He pulled back a corner of his coat to show off a red golfing jumper. "He's asked me a little favour, which I'm about to pass on to you."

"Sure." Sands nodded without concern. "What is it?"

But Yorke hesitated, and gave her a look of apology. "There's a young lad whose father is a friend of his – I'm not sure of the connection exactly. But he recently passed his detective exam, and I've been asked if this lad might shadow you for a few weeks. I know it's a pain in the arse..."

Sands shook her head. "I prefer to work alone."

"I know you do," Yorke sighed. "And I get it. It's blatant nepotism, or whatever the correct term is. And normally I'd call him out for it, but..." He grimaced and lowered his voice further. "In this case I don't think it's such a terrible idea."

"Why not?"

"Look, Erica..." Yorke sighed, while Sands frowned at him. "You're the most talented detective this force has seen in years. Certainly the most dedicated. Doubtless that's why this lad has asked for you, your reputation is starting to precede you." Yorke tried a smile, but Sands' expression didn't change.

"But?"

"Well let's be honest. You can be abrupt."

"Abrupt?"

"Abrasive even. And I know this lad: he's local, he's a promising detective and a very personable character too. I think you might find it helpful having him around."

"I very much doubt that, sir."

"Even so, you don't have a choice." Yorke's voice suddenly tightened and Sands realised this wasn't going to be negotiable. She stood, her lips thin.

"He'll either help you or he won't, but I've been asked, and the Commander is in charge of my departmental budget. This appears to be the price of a much-needed increase. I'm sorry you're the one paying it."

Sands settled the idea in her mind, then nodded at the Chief Superintendent. It wasn't a huge deal. "Yes, sir."

"Good. And you know it might not be a bad thing. We all need a little help now and then. Even you, Erica."

Sands nodded. "What's his name?"

Yorke didn't answer, as at that moment a young man in a suit stepped onto the beach near where Sergeant Sinclair was waiting for them.

"Here he comes now. I gave him a lift down and had him move the car. Didn't want to get stuck in the traffic chaos here."

Sands felt her heart pump harder as she recognised his handsome face. He recognised her at exactly the same time.

"His name's Golding. Detective Luke Golding."

THREE

Golding stopped in his tracks a few steps away from Sinclair. As Yorke walked over to introduce them Sands also stopped, then swore under her breath. There wasn't time to do much more.

"Detective Golding, this is DCI Erica Sands. She's agreed to let you shadow her in this case."

Golding hesitated but then managed to answer. "Thank you, sir." For a second he stood fixed to the spot, but then seemed to remember his manners and stepped forward to offer his hand.

Sands shook it, and glanced into those deep blue eyes, wide open now, his nostrils flared.

"Thank you, ma'am," he said, dropping his head down.

"Detective Golding." Sands heard how stiff her own voice was.

"You're lucky to get this chance, Golding," Yorke went on, oblivious to the tension between the two of them. "DCI Sands is one of the best detectives of her generation. You'd better make sure you do what she says."

"Absolutely, sir." He was looking away now, unable to meet

her eyes. For her part she was now glaring at him, as if he'd planned this.

There was a moment's silence, with Yorke perhaps looking a little confused at how the introduction had gone, but it wasn't enough for him to enquire further.

"Well, I'll let you get on with it." Yorke held out his hand, and after a second Golding realised he wanted his car keys back. Yorke took them, flashed a final brief smile then walked away.

Sands hesitated, but there was nothing for it but to begin. She turned to Sinclair. "Give me your number, you'll need to coordinate with DI John Lindham from MID. He's setting up an incident room at the closest police station, which I understand is Dorchester?"

"Yes, ma'am, that's right." The man held up his phone, the number showing. Sands copied it into her contacts.

"The control room said no children have been reported missing yet, is that still the case?"

"That's correct, ma'am. None yet."

Sands glanced at Golding, then away again, remembering the awful moment that she'd so clumsily propositioned this man the night before. She tried to swallow the bitter taste in her mouth.

"That probably indicates we're dealing with a child who's either homeless or in the care system. But I'll need to know the moment a child is reported missing, particularly locally." She tried to think. "The woman who found the body, she was a swimmer, correct? A wild swimmer?"

"Yes, ma'am. Crazy what people get up..."

"I'd like to speak to her first."

The sergeant looked awkward. "I'm afraid she's been taken to hospital, ma'am. I know you asked to see her, but the paramedics insisted. She was suffering from exposure..."

Sands interrupted the excuse to swear again under her breath. "You got a statement from her?"

"Yes."

"Did she see anyone? Hear anyone? Apart from the victim?"

"No, ma'am."

"Did she see anything unusual?"

"No, ma'am." Sinclair checked his notebook. "She swims here most mornings, along the shoreline. As she was out towards the headland she noticed something on the beach, got out of the water to have a look and discovered the body."

Sands didn't reply but looked up the beach to where the blue tent was pitched, a dot of unnatural colour against the browns and greens. "Pathologist is on site already?"

"Yes, ma'am."

"OK. That's all for now..." Sands stopped and thought. "Actually, no. There's a pair of bloodied gloves in that boat over there." She pointed at the rowing boat beside which she'd talked to Yorke. "It's probably fish blood, but I want it checked just in case."

"Yes, ma'am."

There was no way to avoid addressing him any longer. She turned to Golding and breathed out slowly. "Detective Golding." She fixed her eyes on his and refused to look away. "I'm going to see the body. If you're shadowing me, you'll need to suit up. Meet me here in five minutes." She turned away, aware of Sinclair and Golding's eyes on her back, and feeling quite sick.

She put her own coveralls on at the car, trying to stop her mind taking her back again to the night before, and her words to Golding. But the effort of doing so distracted her, so that she caught the white forensic suit on a corner, tearing a hole in the leg. She swore out loud at the delay, before pushing the suit off, screwing it up in disgust and opening a fresh one. This time she lined it up carefully with her legs before stepping in, then stood and shuffled it up over her hips. When she was done, she gathered her hair up into a net, pulled the hood over her head and tightened the ties. Next, she looped a pair of coverings over her shoes and drew them tight over the bottom of her coveralls. Finally, she snapped a pair of blue nitrile gloves onto her hands. Then she swung the boot closed, swore again and locked the car.

Back down at the beach, she found Detective Golding waiting for her, dressed in a similar outfit. He greeted her with a wary smile.

"Turn around please," she ordered him, her voice cold. She checked his suit.

"And again."

He turned again and she checked for issues, feeling almost annoyed when there were none.

"OK. Let's go."

They walked together in silence, soon arriving at the point where the beach had been sealed off on Sinclair's orders. The scene guard, a young female PC, stood looking cold by the line of blue-and-white tape.

"Morning Sarah," Golding greeted her as they arrived.

"Hi Luke," the woman replied, lifting the tape. She seemed unable to keep her eyes off him, despite the unflattering forensic suit. Sands glared at her as she ducked under.

"Ma'am," the girl said, respectfully, giving Sands a nod. Sands replied by checking her watch. "It's 10:21, make sure you note it in the scene log." Sands walked on.

It was still some way from the tape to where the body had been found, and they walked side by side, the rustle from their legs the only sound. Until Golding finally opened his mouth. "Listen, about last night..."

"You work out of Dorchester?" Sands cut him off, her voice much sharper. He hesitated before replying. "Er, yeah."

"Yes, ma'am," she corrected him, and he apologised at once.

"Yes, ma'am. But the Dorchester nick is pretty small, and

there's no dedicated murder team, which is why I asked to shadow someone from MID. And with your reputation, you were the obvious choice. But even though I've heard all about you, I didn't know what you looked like."

Sands nodded but didn't reply. A few steps later he spoke again. "Listen, ma'am, I just wanted..."

"What?" This time Sands stopped and turned to face him. "You just wanted to what?"

He stopped and swallowed. "I just wanted to say, about last night. There's no need to feel... I don't know. I get that you were upset, with your father..." For most of the time he was looking anywhere but her face, but then he managed to hold her gaze for a moment.

"How is he, by the way? Did he...?"

"No," Sands replied, and then turned away suddenly as her sense of control threatened to dissolve. She looked back. "No, he pulled through. They think he might make it after all."

"Oh, well, that's great!" Suddenly he sounded happier. "That's fantastic, I'm really pleased to hear..."

"It's not great."

Golding looked confused, but after a while she simply started walking again. He scrambled to catch back up. "I don't really understand."

"You don't need to understand. It's not relevant to this case, and it's not relevant to your life."

Golding was silent for a moment, then he nodded. "OK. I get that. It's your business, it's private. I won't ask any more."

"You'd better not."

They walked on in silence for a while until Golding spoke again. "But there is something else," he persisted. Instead of stopping, Sands picked up the pace, nearly forcing him into a run to keep up with her.

"I just wanted to say you shouldn't... that it should..." He gave a nervous laugh. "That it should be me who feels embarrassed about... what happened. Or didn't happen."

Sands stopped again suddenly, and stared at him. He took the opportunity to meet her gaze again.

"You had family issues, which are none of my business, and maybe they affected you. But as far as I'm concerned it was nothing. It's already forgotten." He smiled, the same one he'd used the night before. The same smile that had make her think he wanted to sleep with her.

She opened her mouth to reply, but then simply turned and carried on walking.

They drew closer to the blue forensic tent, its entrance facing away from them. Sands stepped around without hesitation to see what it concealed.

It was a gruesome sight. Laid out on the larger stones that made up this end of the beach was a young girl's body. She was naked apart from her underwear, and her bare frame was battered and twisted. Her chest had been hacked open so that her entire front was a vivid red mess. The upper part was confusing, but towards the bottom Sands could recognise the intestines, her stomach and kidneys. Sands felt her own stomach begin to spasm, and rapidly shifted her gaze.

For a moment she stared at the pathologist's curved back. He was kneeling beside the body, almost as if he were praying in some form of depraved ritual. Sands kept her eyes on him a moment, but then she looked again, more closely, forcing herself to take in the details. Details mattered.

The hair was blonde but darkened almost all over by blood – there must be a head injury that wasn't immediately visible. In parts it was matted with half-congealed blood, but elsewhere it fanned out behind her. Arranged that way? She moved closer to see the girl's chest, to see what it was that wasn't right there.

"Jesus." Sands swung abruptly to see Golding staring at the body, his face screwed up in distaste. Sands watched him long enough to see if he was going to throw up, but he seemed under control so she turned back.

Sands looked around at the wider scene. A few other SOCOs were working quietly, photographing and videoing, searching or carefully measuring distances. Apart from the body, nothing appeared obviously out of place.

She stepped forward, watching where she put her feet, and murmured, "Doctor Bhatt," as she reached the body and crouched down next to the pathologist. There was a smell of meat in the air, like a butcher's shop.

"DCI Sands," he replied, briefly turning to her and raising his eyebrows over the silver frames of his glasses. He took in Golding's presence but didn't ask his name. "I'd say it's nice to see you, but..." Dr Bhatt was of Indian descent and his voice still had the accent.

Sands didn't reply.

"We've finished with photographs, so I'm just beginning my physical examination. Would you like me to talk through what there is so far?"

"Yes." Sands reached into her pocket for a digital voice recorder. "Go ahead."

Dr Bhatt returned to his task, his gloved fingers now touching the girl's face, probing the smooth skin, manipulating the muscles, as if expertly identifying and checking each one. As he did so, the expression on the girl's face seemed to change. For a second, Sands had a flash of how the girl might have looked in life, smiling or frowning. But the expression never looked complete – there was something missing, some light in the eyes.

Bhatt stopped what he was doing and rocked back on his heels. He took a breath.

"There are three major elements to the injuries," his melodic voice began. "She's been strangled. And we have significant wounds to the back of the head, here." He pulled the head forward slightly to show them. "And there's the stomach and chest." He pointed again, the tip of his gloved finger glistening with fluid. "Which is all really one wound, or a series of wounds. These are both stabbing and slashing in motion, and they go deep." He pointed out fragments of white, broken bone. "Several of her ribs are broken, and there's significant damage to all major organs." He paused, then went on. "And then there's *this*." He pointed at something pink, not a natural part of the girl's insides.

"What is that?" Sands leaned forward.

"I'm not going to remove it here, but it looks very much like a doll."

"A *doll*?"

"That's right. If you look here, you can see an arm. That's a leg. The head appears to have been forced right into the chest cavity."

Now that she could see it, Sands couldn't *un*see it. It looked grotesque, but also almost comical, as if the doll were burrowing its way headfirst into the child's body.

"It's the type you can heat up," Golding interrupted suddenly, and Sands looked across at him in surprise. "The doll. They've got some sort of beans in them. You put them in the microwave and they stay hot."

"Thank you." His interruption had surprised her. She should have noticed that. She turned back. "How would it have got there?" she asked the pathologist.

"Hard to say. It appears undamaged, so was probably pushed into the body after the stab wounds were made."

Sands studied it for a few seconds. Despite the horror of the scene, it helped to break down what she was looking at into its constituent parts. A body. A child's doll. A puzzle as to how they came together.

"Could it have been pressed up against the wound and then forced in?"

The pathologist turned to her, not understanding the question.

"Like a compress? An attempt to stop the bleeding? Either by the girl or someone else?"

Dr Bhatt hesitated. "I suppose it's possible. But not by her, not with those wounds. And it would have been far too late by then to save her."

"And there's no way she could have done it herself?" Sands pressed. "Hugged the doll tightly after she'd been stabbed?"

This time the pathologist firmly shook his head. "Not with that level of tissue damage."

Sands leaned in still closer to examine the dark hole in the girl's small chest, the doll half buried inside. Her nostrils filled with the scent of it and she pulled back a little.

"These injuries, did they happen here? Or was she moved?"

"From the amount of blood spilled at the scene, it's highly likely she died here."

Sands didn't question this and moved on. "What about her age?"

The pathologist took another breath before answering. "I'd say..." he began, but then leaned in close and pushed the dead girl's lower jaw down, using his thumb to press the tongue out of the way. That way he was able to gently insert his other fingers inside.

"She has both lateral incisors in the lower jaw." He paused and shifted lower so he could look upwards more easily into her mouth. "But she's lost the upper ones. Based on that, and her size, I'd estimate her age to be between seven and nine."

"Time of death?"

The pathologist removed his hands but didn't reply. He looked uncomfortable. "It's going to be a bigger range than you're happy with."

"Why?"

"The hole in her abdomen. She's still above ambient

temperature, which means she died less than twenty-four hours ago, but to narrow it much further..." He stopped and thought. "With the chest open she'll have cooled faster than normal, but how much? It's difficult to say. Plus she's young. Normal temperature is more varied in children." He shrugged.

"How about lividity?"

"It's advanced, in both her face and limbs, but again we're looking at a wide range, for similar reasons."

"What sort of range?"

The pathologist looking pained. He thought for a while then sighed. "The best I can do is to say she's been dead between ten to seventeen hours."

Sands flashed a glance at her watch and calculated. "That would give us a time of death between six pm yesterday and midnight?"

Bhatt hesitated. "If you say so; your maths is better than mine."

Sands ignored the comment and looked around. Six pm. In February. The beach would have been dark by then, perhaps just a little light left as the sun set into the sea. Was there moonlight? She thought back to her walk home the night before; it had been cloudy, barely a sliver of moon. She glanced at Golding, not meaning anything by it, but he surprised her by seeming to read her thoughts. "A little light from the village spills onto the beach, but not this far round."

She nodded and seemed about to turn away before changing her mind. "How popular is this place?"

Again Golding seemed to know what she meant. "In the daytime it gets busy. But at night... the only way here is to walk along the beach like we did, or climb down from the hills behind. I'd guess that whoever brought her here would have had the place to themselves."

Sands nodded thoughtfully and turned back to the pathologist. "What was she was stabbed with?"

Bhatt shook his head. "A single blade of some description. Some sort of knife I'd guess. The wounds look relatively clean, with no obvious debris pushed inside. Except for the doll. But we'll know more when I get her back to the lab."

"Is there any sign of sexual abuse?"

"Yes."

Sands barely reacted. "Before or after she died?"

"Both."

"Semen?"

The pathologist shook his head. "Nope. Sorry. And I don't think we're going to find any either. It's early days, but I'd say whoever did this was careful."

Sands sighed. "OK," she said at last. Her legs were burning from squatting down. "Is there anything else?"

"Not yet. But I'll let you know." Bhatt sighed. "Oh yes, I forgot one thing. She has a birthmark." He leaned in again, this time showing them a small blemish on the girl's cheek. "It should help in identifying her."

Sands studied it in silence, then pulled out her phone and snapped a close-up photograph of the mark before thanking the doctor and standing up. She stepped away from the body and Golding followed her.

For a few moments, she stared around the beautiful curve of the cove. The few stone houses visible from where the village met the bay were now across the water, far away from them.

"What are you thinking?" Golding's voice interrupted her.

"Excuse me?"

"What are you thinking?" he repeated. His voice was still serious, his face white. She remembered he was supposed to be shadowing her, and even though the interruption irritated her, she answered anyway.

"I'm wondering why we haven't heard from the parents yet," Sands replied. "She doesn't look like a runaway. Her hair's clean, and apart from her injuries she looks well cared for. So why haven't we heard from them? What kind of parents don't notice that their child is missing?"

Golding was prevented from answering by Sands' phone. It was Sergeant Sinclair.

"Yes."

"We've just had a report come in, ma'am. A missing girl."

Sands glanced at Golding meaningfully. "Age and description?"

"Eight years old." There was a pause. "Slight build, blonde hair."

"Any identifying features?"

"Yes, she has a birthmark on her left cheek."

Sands felt an odd coldness crawling over her face. She glanced over at the dead girl, still close enough to see the empty look in her eyes.

"What's her name?" she asked, her own voice lifeless.

"Slaughter, ma'am. Emily Slaughter."

Hello Emily, Sands thought. *I'm sorry this has happened to you.* She was silent for a few seconds. "OK. Who called it in?"

"The parents, ma'am. They say they woke up this morning and the girl wasn't in her bed."

"How come they took so long to call it in?" Sands asked, but she quickly decided it wasn't a question worth asking. At least not yet. "Never mind. Is anyone with them?"

"No, ma'am. You said I should tell you right away. Should I send someone?"

"Are they nearby? I'd prefer to see their reaction first hand."

"Actually, yes ma'am. If you look back towards this end of the beach..." Sands nearly shouted at Sinclair to just give her the address.

"Yes?"

"You see the little cliff that rises up, to the left of where we met?"

"Yes."

"There're some houses up there."

"I can see that."

"It's one of those. It's the last one, ma'am. The square one."

Sands stared at it, far enough away that it was the size of a matchbox, and yet within sight of where the body lay. She wondered if they were watching now, if they could make out the blue of the pathologist's tent, and knew the horrors it signified.

"It's the mother who called," Sinclair went on. "Name of Janet Slaughter. She's there with her husband, Rodney. Apparently she's in a real state. Should I send someone?"

"No." Sands signalled to the pathologist that they were leaving and beckoned Golding to follow her. "No, we're on our way."

Sands ended the call and was about to tell Golding what had been said when he asked, "Did he say Rodney Slaughter?"

Sands glanced across. "You know him?"

"I know *of* him." Golding turned now to look at the distant cliff-top houses. Despite the distance, it was clear the house was different from its neighbours. A modern building. It looked somehow out of place.

"Everyone here does," Golding continued. "There're all sorts of rules against any new buildings going up around here, but then this guy gets permission to build this huge house. The suspicion is that money changed hands. A lot of it."

When Sands said nothing, Golding went on. "The locals have a name for it. On account of the house being so ugly it kills the view. Well, sort of. It's more to do with the family's surname I suppose..." He paused, and though Sands knew what was coming, it still sent a chill down her neck.

"People call it the *Slaughter House*."

FOUR

They stripped off their coveralls together while they sat in the open boot of the Alfa.

"How many death visits have you done?" Sands asked, breaking a near silence that had lasted since they'd left the site of the body.

"Quite a few," he nodded. "You might not believe it, but I have a sensitive side." He smiled grimly. She reacted by snapping at him.

"You're a detective, not a therapist. When children below the age of ten are found murdered, fifty-eight percent of the time they're killed by their parents, almost always by the father. It rises to sixty-six percent for female victims. I want you to observe everything you see in there. I want you to be suspicious as hell. There's nearly a seventy percent chance you're going to meet that girl's killer." She pushed the last of the overalls off her feet and reached down to ball them up.

"Sure." He nodded quickly. "Sorry ma'am."

The younger detective ran his fingers through his hair, now the net had been removed. Sands ignored hers and got in the car. When Golding did the same, she waited, watching him, ready to start the ignition.

"What?"

"Seatbelt."

Golding glanced out through the windscreen. The turnoff to the house was up ahead, it was clear the car wouldn't get above ten miles per hour.

"Apologies, ma'am." He buckled up.

Sands drove slowly and parked the car carefully inside an enclosed area in front of the big house; then they waited a moment, looking up at the impressive building. Most of the houses in the village, and indeed the wider area, were traditional in style. If they weren't as old as the hills around them, they at least looked like they'd been there for a century or more. But not the Slaughters' house. It was completely modern, an imposing rectangular block, almost absurdly wide. It was so plain it almost resembled a cube rising out of the ground. It was also clearly brand new – indeed not even quite finished. The parking area was cluttered with building materials, a pallet of bricks and a parked-up mini-digger. Before they had time to take in any more, the large, grey front door burst open. A middle-aged woman came running towards them, a pair of fluffy slippers on her feet. Sands pushed open the car door, but before she got out she issued a warning. "Remember, everything you're about to see could be an act." Then she got out and raised her voice: "Mrs Slaughter?"

The woman reached them, her arms now wrapped around her body, her face streaked with tears. "Have you found her? Please tell me you've found her? They wouldn't tell me anything on the phone." She spoke fast. She wore a dressing gown which she'd wrapped tightly around herself.

"I'm Detective Chief Inspector Erica Sands, this is my colleague Detective Luke Golding." She guided the woman towards a temporary path of stone-chips that cut through the unfinished driveway. "We should speak inside."

There was enough in her tone for the woman to fall silent, and then to clamp her hand over her mouth. A few moments later she started to make small sobbing noises. Sands watched her impassively.

"Mrs Slaughter?" Sands indicated the still-open front door. The woman looked up.

"What have you...?" she began, but Sands cut her off.

"Please, we need to go inside."

Janet Slaughter's lips quivered and she began to cry again, but she nodded and led them into a cool, white-painted hallway where the house's secret was dramatically revealed. Inside it wasn't a box, but was formed of two distinct wings, like a squared U-shape, with a generous courtyard between each wing. Beyond the two arms of the building, the plot fell away to the cliff edge, with the ocean below. Janet Slaughter led them towards the left side of the house, which opened into a dramatic open-plan kitchen-living space. Its front walls of plate-glass gave such breath-taking views of the sea that it was almost impossible for Sands not to be distracted for a moment. A second later she noticed the room wasn't empty. There was a man, dressed in black jeans and a black shirt, matching his hair.

"Mr Slaughter?" Sands turned her back on the view to examine him more closely. While the mother seemed on the verge of full-blown panic, he seemed calm and reserved. Unnaturally so, Sands thought. She shot a glance at Golding. She began to introduce herself and Golding, but was interrupted by Janet Slaughter's pleading.

"Have you found her? Please tell me you have her?" The rising panic in her voice made Sands turn back to her. The woman looked ready to collapse.

"I think it might be best if we sit down," Sands said, glancing around and then moving towards a dining table. Its green-glass top, with tiny imperfections and bubbles trapped in the material, made it look like the surface of a calm sea. Sands took the lead, pulling out a heavy chair, feeling how it glided across the marble floor on thick felt pads. Janet Slaughter sat obediently on the chair and Sands pulled out another for the father. As Rodney Slaughter sat, she noticed further details about him. The signet ring on his finger, made from thick, heavy gold, the Rolex on his wrist. He still hadn't spoken.

Before she went on, Sands took a deep breath. She knew this moment would stay with the couple for the rest of their lives. But then, she knew their daughter's life had already ended, brutally. She sat down and did her job. "I have to tell you a discovery has been made this morning," she began. "And a murder investigation has been started."

An awful whining noise escaped from Janet Slaughter's lips. Rodney Slaughter sat completely rigid, though the muscles of his neck began to tremble.

"The victim is a young female, and we estimate her age to be between seven and nine..."

She was stopped by Janet Slaughter's whine rising in pitch and volume, as if she were trying to drown out Sands' voice. Trying to make her words not real.

But Sands pressed on. There was no advantage in delaying. "Do either of you have a recent photograph of your daughter, one that clearly shows the left side of her face..." She allowed her eyes to rest on the mother, clearly seeing the significance of her request hit home.Janet screwed her eyes shut, and Sands had to ask again. "Mrs Slaughter?"

Slowly and clumsily, the woman fumbled in the pocket of her dressing gown and pulled out an iPhone. Her hands were shaking so much it took a while for her to pull up an image, and when she finally managed it, she seemed reluctant to hand the phone over. Sands held out her hand to speed things up.

In the photograph the girl was standing on the beach below

the house. She was wrapped up warm in a winter coat and part-grinning, part-squinting into the sun. She looked happy. Well-fed and full of the life she still had to lead. Sands blanked her mind and zoomed into the image, so that the face filled the screen. She tried to ignore the look on the girl's face, and instead focused on the left side, the slight blemish of the birthmark. The odd, cold feeling came over her again. The detached hollowness of another person's grief. She tried to separate herself from what she was about to say so she could better study Janet and Rodney Slaughter's response.

"I'll need one of you to make a formal identification. But the victim we found this morning has a birthmark that exactly matches what you've just shown me."

The whine, which had never stopped coming from Janet Slaughter, now exploded into a full-blown wail of horror. Seconds later she was taking in big gasps, but seemingly unable to get any air inside her. She turned to her husband and for a second Sands thought she was about to hug him, but instead she began beating at his chest with her fists, until he finally caught her arms and gripped them hard, pulling her into a tight embrace. He was breathless too, but he squeezed the panic out of her rather more forcefully and expertly than Sands expected to see. But then he relaxed his grip. Janet continued to moan loudly, but at least she was still.

"There must be some mistake." He spoke for the first time. His voice was deep. "It's not possible..."

Sands waited to see if he would finish the sentence, and only answered when it was clear he wasn't going to. "I also recognised her from the photograph. I'm afraid there's no doubt."

Janet Slaughter's wailing rose up again, silencing Sands. It seemed directed at her, but when she didn't respond, Janet turned instead to Golding, who was still standing. Her eyes seemed to plead with him, until he very slightly shook his head.

"I'm very sorry Mrs Slaughter," he said, then turned to the husband and nodded.

Sands watched as he did so, frowning slightly. Then she looked back at Janet Slaughter and her husband. The woman's eyes were unfocused, but Rodney looked right back at Sands, as if he expected to be able to observe her without being noticed. He soon flicked his gaze away, but not before she noticed his eyes were nearly pure black.

For a few moments the only sounds were the moans of pain that came from Janet Slaughter. Despite its size, her cries filled the room, and Sands was left in no doubt that her agony was genuinely felt. But that didn't mean she hadn't killed her daughter, only that the reality of the girl's death upset her.

Sands waited until they were ready to go on, using the time to look again around the room. She noticed the decoration – or lack of it. It was painted white, the furniture minimalist in style and clearly expensive. There were no family photographs on display. No toys on the floor. It didn't look much like a child lived there.

"Mr Slaughter, Mrs Slaughter," Sands said, when the mother's moaning had subsided a little. "I know this is difficult, but I need to ask you some questions, and I do have to ask them now. Whoever has harmed your daughter, the sooner we can begin to look for them, the better chance we have of finding them." She set her voice recorder on the table and pulled out a notebook, then clicked her pen ready, signs that they had no choice in this.

Janet Slaughter moaned again, but she also nodded, seeming to latch onto the words as something to focus on. Rodney Slaughter's face was expressionless, his black eyes impossible to read.

"I'm confused that we found your daughter before you reported her missing. Could you explain to me when you last saw her?"

Janet Slaughter answered. "Last night." Her voice was tiny,

and cracked with every word. "She was feeling poorly, and we had guests over, so I put her to bed early. And then this morning... I thought she was up, watching TV in her room, but she... wasn't. And then I assumed she was playing outside, but I couldn't find her... that's when I..." She broke down again into little sobs. "That's when I called." When fat tears ran down her cheeks, she did nothing to rub them away.

Sands noted her answer before getting up and heading to the window which looked out over the courtyard between the two wings of the house.

"The house is upside down, correct? The living area is on the first floor, with the bedrooms beneath?"

"That's right," Rodney Slaughter answered.

"So Emily's bedroom is on the ground floor?"

"Yes."

Sands sat down again.

"You had guests?" She kept her eyes on Janet; it took a while for her to register, but eventually she nodded.

"OK, we'll come to that in a moment." Sands spoke slowly and clearly. "I need to know the last time you saw Emily. What were you doing?"

"It was when I put her to bed."

"And what time was that?"

Again, she had to wait for an answer.

"We had guests coming at seven-thirty," Janet Slaughter said eventually. "I had to cook. Emy wanted to help, but she... well you know what children are like..." She looked up, and her eyes swam. For a second it seemed she might hyperventilate again, but she made an effort to control herself. "I gave her a bath and I... I put her to bed."

"At what time, Mrs Slaughter?"

"I don't know. About seven I think."

"Could you be more precise? It might be relevant."

The mother hesitated. "It was definitely close to seven. Maybe a few minutes after."

Sands turned to the husband. "Mr Slaughter? When did you last see her?" But he shook his head, almost as if he were dismissing the question.

"I... I didn't. I was... working all afternoon." When he glanced at his wife, she was too deep in her misery to notice, but Sands wasn't.

"Where were you working?"

"I have an office. In Dorchester."

"I didn't ask what you have, I asked where you were."

Rodney Slaughter's face flushed, as if he might challenge her tone, but he backed down. "In my office. In Dorchester."

"And you came back here straight after work?"

"Yes."

"What time?"

He shook his head. "About seven-thirty. Emily had already gone to bed."

"Again, it's helpful if you can be as precise as possible. What time exactly did you arrive here?"

Rodney Slaughter drew in a deep breath, then let it out. "I don't know *exactly*. It was about half past seven. I think." He gave a very slight shrug.

Sands watched him a moment. "We can check with your mobile phone data." She said it as a warning, but there was no reaction on his face. She went on. "And you didn't go in to see your daughter when you arrived home? Is that normal for you?"

Rodney Slaughter stiffened again, clenching his jaw. "She was already asleep when I got back. And we had guests coming. I needed to prepare." He lifted a hand to smooth down his gelled-back hair. Sands noticed how the hand shook a little, how he touched it with the other hand to quieten it. She looked into his eyes, searching for the reason. He surprised her by meeting her gaze.

"OK." Sands was the first to look away, a little unsettled. She turned back to Janet Slaughter, but had to check her notebook to prompt her next question.

"Once you'd put her to bed, did you hear or see anything of her after that?" Her voice became brisk again, Janet Slaughter's reply stilted and weak.

"No."

"Did you see or hear anything unusual? Noises? Lights outside you wouldn't normally see?"

"No."

"Either of you?" She turned to Rodney Slaughter again.

"Nothing I can recall."

Sands tapped her fingers on the glass of the table, feeling its glossy smoothness.

"Who were your guests?" She changed tack. "You said you were entertaining?" She didn't aim the question at either one of them, but Rodney Slaughter answered.

"Stephen Wade, and his wife Dorothy." He seemed to recognise that the names alone hadn't registered. "That's Mayor Wade. We've become friendly since we moved here. They were interested in seeing the house, now that we've moved in."

"I'll need their number."

Rodney Slaughter pulled out a phone from his jeans pocket. He consulted it, then held the screen up to Sands.

"What time did the Wades arrive?"

"Just before eight. They rang to say they'd be late."

"And what time did they leave?"

Rodney thought for a moment. "Late, but not too late. A bit before midnight."

"Did the Wades see Emily at all?"

"No. She was in bed."

"What did you do while they were here?"

Rodney Slaughter stared as if this question were crazy. "We had dinner. We talked."

"What about?"

"The usual things. Whatever people talk about at dinner parties."

"I don't go to dinner parties, and I certainly wasn't at this one. So what did you talk about?"

Slaughter glared at her, then sighed. "We talked about the house. And about... politics. Mayor Wade is a prominent member of the local Conservative Party. We discussed the possibility of my making a donation to party funds."

Sands remembered what Golding had told her and thought about asking if the donation was linked to their planning permission, but decided against it.

"Did you show the Wades around?"

"Excuse me?"

"You said they were interested in seeing the house, now that you've moved in. Yet they came after dark. Did you show it to them?"

"Not as such. Once we got talking, the time slipped by."

"Did they go downstairs?"

"No, they only came... in here."

"Did they use the bathroom?"

"Excuse me?"

"They were here for nearly four hours. They didn't need to urinate?"

"I imagine they did, I can't remember. We have a bathroom upstairs, in the hallway." He pointed, and Sands noted the location.

"What did you drink?" she asked next.

Rodney Slaughter frowned, but answered. "We had a couple of bottles of red, but I don't drink much these days. The girls were on the chardonnay."

Sands got up now and moved towards the kitchen area, where the empty bottles were neatly stacked, as if ready to be taken out to be recycled.

"That's from last night?"

"Not all of it."

Sands examined the bottles, then returned to the table and sat back down. "What did you do after the Wades left?"

The question was aimed at Janet Slaughter, but she was in no state to answer, so Rodney spoke again. "My wife went to bed right away. I cleaned up a little, loaded the dishwasher. Then I went to bed as well."

Sands persisted with Janet. "You didn't check on your daughter?"

The woman seemed to plumb new depths within herself to answer. When she lifted her head, her face was a mask of misery. "I normally do... but..." She seemed unable to go on.

"But what?" Sands pressed, almost impatient.

"I don't know. I was... tired. I usually check but it was late..."

Janet Slaughter broke down again into tears, and again Rodney just stared at his wife, his face white, his breathing hard.

Sands turned to him. "How long were you cleaning for?"

"I don't know. Forty minutes?"

"Then you went to bed as well? Also without checking Emily?"

"That's right."

Sands considered. "Was your wife asleep? When you went to bed?"

"Yes." Rodney Slaughter hesitated a second. "Actually, no. She woke briefly. I remember she looked at her phone, I think to see the time."

Sands glanced at Janet, who didn't seem to have heard. "Did you wake? When your husband came to bed?"

She looked uninterested in the question, totally preoccupied by grief, but eventually she half-shrugged, half-nodded.

"What time was it?"

She answered in a weak voice, "I think it was just past one."

Sands reviewed what she'd written so far, then got up again from the table and walked to the window at the front of the room, far enough away that the couple couldn't hear her. Here she pulled out her mobile phone and dialled, speaking quietly for about a minute before slipping the phone away and looking back. Janet was again sobbing quietly. Rodney sat stock still, his face a mask. Golding stood almost as stiffly by the table. Sands considered them all for a moment, then walked back. "I'd like to take a look at Emily's bedroom now," she said.

Neither of the Slaughters moved, so Sands spoke again. "I'd like us all to go, please," she insisted, and waited until the couple pulled themselves to their feet. "It's extremely important that neither of you touch anything. Nothing at all. Please just show me where the room is."

Rodney Slaughter led the way, back out into the hallway to a large staircase that led downwards. Sands followed him down the wide, highly polished concrete steps, noting how large he was, his broad, powerful back almost filling the whole space. Janet Slaughter came after Sands, with Golding bringing up the rear. Downstairs the house was less dramatic, just a corridor running along the back wall with several rooms leading off it, and a door at the end that appeared to lead outside. Rodney Slaughter moved along the corridor and stopped at one of the rooms. He reached out. "This is Emy's..."

Sands' arm shot out to restrain him. "Touch nothing please." She let her hand stay on his arm long enough to guide it away from the door handle, but also to get a sense of how solid the muscles were. The answer surprised her. Then she reached into her pocket for another pair of gloves. "Wait here please." Sands snapped the gloves onto her hands, but still used her pen to push the door open.

Emily Slaughter's bedroom didn't look unusual for an eight-year-old girl's room. It was of generous size, but not exceptionally large. The bed, chest of drawers and wardrobe looked new, of good quality, but again were nothing out of the ordinary. Down here the walls were of a light shade of pink, and a few toys were scattered across the floor, but most were resting neatly on shelves. There were no signs of a struggle, much less a murder. Sands moved over to the bed, noting that the duvet was pulled back, as if the girl had just got up. Or as if someone had pulled it back to pick her up. She sensed Golding standing beside her and glanced at him, their eyes meeting. Then they both moved next to the window.

It wasn't actually a window, but a sliding glass door giving access to the courtyard outside. She noted the lock, and then the key hanging on a hook beside the door. Then Sands crouched down low, studying the carpet, pulling a flashlight from her pocket and shining it on the ground. There were a few marks here, tiny spots of mud, but it would be impossible to say when they'd got there. She stood and looked out into the courtyard. Beyond the door was a walkway; beyond that the courtyard had been landscaped as a garden. On the other side of the garden, the opposite wing of the property stood unfinished and empty. The building didn't reach all the way to the cliff edge, so that it was open to the left, where steps led up and out of sight.

"Where does that go?" she asked, turning to the Slaughters, who were still waiting in the bedroom doorway.

"Nowhere," answered Rodney. "Just out onto the cliff path. It'll be walled off when the house is finished."

Sands nodded, then turned back to the door. She tested it with the edge of her pen and found she was able to slide it open without applying much pressure. It moved almost silently. "Was the door locked last night?"

"Of course," Rodney answered, but Sands reacted as if she hadn't heard. She asked the question again, this time to Janet. She sobbed an answer.

"Yes."

"Are you sure?"

"Yes. I'm certain."

"My wife is extremely security conscious," Rodney Slaughter said. "We both are."

"And how about this morning? Was the door still locked?"

"I think so." Janet sniffed. "I unlocked it to check the courtyard. But she wasn't there."

Sands turned again to Golding and frowned, then stepped outside. Here again she inspected the ground carefully, but saw nothing. Then she bent down and inspected the outside of the lock. She shone the light from her mobile at it and noticed the faintest of scratch marks on the lock's white-metal surround. It could have been something, or it could have been nothing.

Sands thought again for a minute, then came back inside and closed the door. She turned to Janet Slaughter. "Are there any clothes missing? Or shoes? Coats? Anything like that?"

After a while the woman shook her head in reply.

Sands considered this. "How about a doll? Have you noticed a doll that's missing? Specifically the type that you can put in the microwave to heat up?"

Janet Slaughter's head jerked up at this, and she nodded at once. "Buddy – I don't know if he's here..."

"Was this doll special for her in any way?"

"She's her favourite. She usually keeps it under her pillow." Janet Slaughter was about to enter the room but Golding stopped her. "Thank you, Mrs Slaughter. It's better you don't touch."

Sands turned to look at the bed. Even wearing her gloves, she still didn't want to pull back the pillow. After all, she already knew the doll wouldn't be there. She took a last look around but decided she'd seen enough. Whatever evidence was left in this room was best discovered by the forensic investigators. She stepped back into the hallway. "Would you follow me back upstairs please?"

She led the way this time, back to the main room. As they got there, the doorbell rang. Sands nodded at Golding to answer it.

A few moments later Golding came back into the room, followed by another woman, whom Sands introduced. "This is Detective Constable Carol Bookman. She's a specialist family liaison officer." The Slaughters looked at the new arrival mutely. It was as if control of their house was just a natural next step.

"I'm so sorry for your loss," Bookman said, her voice as soft as her expression.

"Detective Bookman will act as the point of contact between us and you over the next hours and days." Sands watched as Bookman approached Janet Slaughter, took her hand and covered it with her own.

"I'd like you to go with DC Bookman to the police station, where we can ask you some more questions," Sands went on, waiting only a beat before continuing. "I've also applied for, and been granted, a warrant to search this house for the purposes of preservation and recovery of evidence. We'll be starting immediately." She kept her eyes on Rodney Slaughter as she spoke, registering how they widened slightly at the news.

"It's completely standard in the circumstances, but I have to warn you it's likely to take a number of days. DC Bookman can arrange a hotel for you, though if you'd prefer you can arrange something yourselves. If so, please ensure it's nearby." She stopped, her face still expressionless.

"A hotel?" Rodney Slaughter replied, and Sands nodded, still watching closely.

"Yes. If you like."

"I don't like—" He stopped himself before finishing the word. When he spoke again, he chose a different one. "I don't *understand*. A warrant? Are you suggesting...? Are you suggesting that Janet or I had anything...? That's..."

Sands didn't reply at once but considered her words. Eventually she spoke. "I'm not suggesting anything at this point. Other than we search the house thoroughly in order to recover as much evidence as possible, to help us catch whoever killed your daughter. I trust you don't have a problem with that?"

Rodney Slaughter glared at her again with his black eyes. But then he nodded, and dropped his gaze to the floor.

FIVE

Sands allowed Janet Slaughter to get dressed, although she had to do so in the discreet but watchful company of DC Bookman, before the couple were driven away to the police station in Dorchester. The two detectives then waited in the Alfa until a pair of uniformed officers arrived. Their job was to guard the house until the forensic teams got there.

"What did you think?" Golding asked after they'd been sitting in the car a while.

Sands continued to stare silently into space.

"I mean, she looked genuine to me. Him? I'm not so sure."

She still didn't answer. Instead she pulled out her phone and dialled the number Rodney Slaughter had given her for the Wades. When a man's voice answered, she identified herself and got his address, mouthing the words *how far* at Golding in the passenger seat.

"Twenty minutes?" he replied quietly. As he spoke, a marked police car pulled into the drive and a uniformed officer approached the window.

"Don't go anywhere please, we'll be with you in fifteen

minutes." Sands finished the call. Then she wound down the window, gave her orders to the officer and started the engine.

"Well?" Golding tried again, once they were on the way. "What did you think?"

She considered continuing to ignore him, but remembered the promise she'd made, or been forced to make, to Yorke. "What do *you* think?" she asked in the end. Golding seemed encouraged by this, and launched into an explanation. "I thought she seemed genuine. But his reaction seemed weird."

They were leaving the village now and Sands accelerated hard, gripping the corners of the twisty lane that led back to the main road. It became clear she wasn't planning on replying.

"I don't understand how she gets down there," Golding continued. "Onto the beach I mean. After dark on a winter's night."

Sands angled her eyes left but said nothing.

"The last time they saw the girl alive was at seven last night. The house is all locked up, there's no obvious signs of a break-in. So how does she end up dead at the far end of the beach the next morning?" He shook his head in frustration.

"Clearly there's a limited list of possible scenarios. Why don't you start by listing those?"

"OK. Alright, sure." He sat back. "The way I see it, there's three main ways. One, she leaves the house by herself. She goes to the beach, and someone attacks her there..." He stopped, and Sands waited. "But it's the middle of winter. It's hard to imagine an eight-year-old going that far from home. Not on her own. In the dark."

"Alright," Sands said. "So what can you imagine?"

"She might have left the house. She could have left a toy or something outside, and gone out just to get it. And someone grabbed her then."

"It'd be a coincidence though, someone just happening to be waiting for her."

"So maybe she was lured out by something? By someone?"

Sands shrugged.

Golding screwed up his face and looked away.

"What else is possible?"

"Alright. Two. She didn't leave the house. Someone came in and took her."

"How did they get in? All the doors were locked."

"They broke in. You showed me that scratch on the lock..."

"I showed you something that *might* be a scratch. We'll get it checked, but surely there's an easier explanation, that doesn't require a break-in."

Golding thought for a moment. "They did it. *He* did it."

"Why Rodney Slaughter, and not Janet? Why not both of them?"

"She seemed more upset."

Sands took a corner fast, clipping a bramble bush and flicking the wing of the car. "It could be an act." Then she changed the subject. "There's a junction up ahead, which way?"

Golding glanced outside, as if surprised to find himself in a vehicle. "Uh, left." He looked at Sands again. "He had the time. He could have sneaked into her room while Janet was cooking, after she'd put the girl to bed. He could have killed her then, and then waited until after the dinner party to take her down to the cove."

"It's risky, what if she checked the child when she went to bed?"

"She didn't though. Maybe that's normal for them?"

"Or maybe it's not. And surely she had more opportunity. She could have been lying about putting her to bed, and killed her then instead."

"And sat through a whole dinner party? Knowing she'd just killed her child?"

Sands shrugged. "Why not? Whoever did it is almost

certainly a psychopath anyway. We've seen what they're capable of."

"So you think it was her, not him?"

"I don't know what I think. But I told you to list the possible scenarios. You're not finished."

Golding sat back, thinking once again. "OK. The Wades? They could have done it..."

"Maybe," Sands replied, taking a roundabout fast. Then she slowed rapidly as they reached the outskirts of the little town of Wareham. She glanced at the clock. Seventeen minutes had passed.

"Perhaps we're about to find out."

SIX

The Alfa coasted to a halt opposite the white-painted cottage of Steven and Dorothy Wade. From inside, a woman peeked out behind floral curtains, then shrank back out of sight when she saw she'd been spotted. Sands kept staring until the woman risked a second peek, this time disappearing for good. Then she opened the car door.

The front garden of the Wade's cottage was guarded by a cast-iron gate, a sign on it warning that the household didn't accept unsolicited mail or takeaway menus. The hinges squeaked as Sands swung it open.

She led the way up the path, bordered on one side by a neatly cropped lawn, and on the other by a driveway and a large, pristine burgundy-red Jaguar.

There was no need to ring the bell, since the door was opened as they arrived by a short man in his late fifties. He was dressed in ill-fitting jeans and a rugby top, but he wore them like he didn't feel comfortable in casual clothing.

"Detective Sands?"

"Detective Chief Inspector Sands," she corrected him.

"This is my colleague Detective Golding. You must be Steven Wade?"

The mayor hesitated, as if he might insist on his official title, but something about Sands' manner stopped him. "That's right."

"We should do this inside."

He again hesitated, but then stood back to allow the two detectives into a thickly carpeted hallway. The walls were patterned with floral print. The air smelt of flowers too, but the chemical tang of a plug-in diffuser.

"We could go through to my office..." the mayor began, before Sands interrupted him.

"No. We'll speak with your wife as well. I saw she was in."

"Oh yes, of course. She's uh... She's in the conservatory."

He led them through a small living room cluttered with figurines of animals and tiny porcelain thimbles. Bland water-colours hung on the wall, while pride of place was given to a large photograph of Wade in his ceremonial mayoral robes.

Dorothy Wade – the woman who had been at the window – was pretending to read the *Mail on Sunday.* She put down the paper when they came in, feigning surprise. When she stood, it became obvious she was even shorter than her husband, and the two detectives towered over her. Perhaps sensitive to this, the mayor quickly waved them to sit on floral-printed sofas.

"So, what's this all about?" he asked.

"It's bad news," Sands said, focusing on the mayor. "The body of a child was found this morning on the beach at Lulworth Cove."

The man's eyes widened, his eyebrows rising. Dorothy Wade gasped and her hand flew to her mouth.

"The identity is unconfirmed at this time," Sands went on. "But we believe the victim is Emily Slaughter, the daughter of Rodney and Janet Slaughter."

A horrified squeak escaped from Dorothy Wade. Her

husband turned to look at her but said nothing, just blinked repeatedly.

"I understand you were at the Slaughters' house last night?" Sands went on, still keeping her attention on Steven Wade.

"I... we... we were there for dinner but..."

"But what?" Sands asked.

When he finally replied, Steven Wade shook his head. "But nothing. I don't... I don't know what to say, that's unbelievable. That's awful. Truly awful."

Sands allowed a moment of silence to settle on the room before she went on. "Yes." She leaned forwards, closer to the mayor. "Do you know the Slaughters well?"

"Yes... no... well..." He sounded panicked. "Actually, not really. Not at all. Only since they bought the plot up above the cove. But Rodney, he's... Well they both seem like... the sort of people one would want to attract to the area. If you know what I mean."

Sands was silent, remembering again the rumours of dodgy payments in exchange for planning permission. Steven Wade apparently took the silence to mean she hadn't understood.

"We have a lot of out-of-towners who buy property but don't actually live here. Holiday homes. At least the Slaughters intend to live here full time."

"I see," Sands said. "Had you been to the house before?"

"No. Well, I visited as it was being built of course, in my official capacity, I sit on the planning committee, but last night was..."

"Was what?"

"Was our first time as guests."

"OK." Sands paused and took a moment to watch Dorothy Wade. She had almost frozen since hearing the news.

"What happened?" Stephen Wade asked. "Was it an accident?"

"No. We've opened a murder investigation."

"Oh my *gosh*," he said, his breathing now light. "*Murder?* But... how..."

"We don't have any information we're able to share at this stage."

Dorothy Wade's hand was over her mouth again. Her husband glanced at her before turning back to Sands. "But we were with them just last night!"

"Quite. So you'll appreciate that we need to ask you some questions."

He looked bewildered as Sands pulled out her notebook and recorder.

"What time did you arrive?"

"Erm..." The colour had mostly bleached from Wade's face, except his nose, which stayed red. "Last night? I don't know. I think about eight." He turned to his wife, but she just stared back at him, her hands still covering her mouth. "Yes, it was just before eight. We were due at seven-thirty but were running late."

"And what time did you leave?"

"Around midnight I think. I'm not quite... Yes, yes, it was just after twelve that we got back. I noticed on the kitchen clock. So it would have been just before..."

"Did you see Emily Slaughter when you were there?"

"*No.* I suppose she was in bed. I mean I *supposed.*" Steven Wade turned to his wife. "We've never even met the girl, have we dear?" Dorothy Wade stiffly shook her head. Her husband went on. "This is such a shock. Such a terrible shock."

"Indeed. Did they mention their daughter to you? Last night?"

"No." Wade looked to his wife, who shook her head, but then spoke, her voice tremulous. "Janet told me she was feeling poorly. That there was something going around."

"Just that? Nothing more?"

"She talked about schools."

"Can we at least know what happened to her?" Steven Wade interrupted suddenly. "Surely we have a right..."

"We'll release information as soon as we can," Sands cut him off firmly. She took her time before addressing the next question to the mayor. "Did you notice anything unusual during the evening?"

He shook his head. "No. Nothing at all."

"What did you talk about?"

"I... um... you know. We talked about the house. How he'd have the second wing finished by the spring. And then, issues affecting the area. And nationally. Just ordinary dinner-party conversation."

"You spoke mostly with Rodney Slaughter?"

"Well, yes... I suppose so."

"How did he come across? Did he seem relaxed? Anxious? Distracted?"

"No. He was... relaxed. He was fine. He was explaining about his business in Japan. Apparently, they lived out there for several years."

"Was there anything about the evening that struck you as unusual?"

"Such as?"

"I don't know. I wasn't there."

The man looked confused and Golding stepped in to clarify. "Noises outside, lights perhaps? Anything you can remember?"

"No. Nothing like that." Wade looked from one detective to the other. He seemed genuinely stunned.

"Did you have a tour of the house?"

"No, no we wanted to, but it was dark, and they suggested we come back another time."

"Did you go downstairs at all?"

"No."

Sands read back everything she'd written, and then

proceeded to repeat the questions she had asked at the Slaughter's house before, checking whether their answers matched up. There was nothing that jumped out at her. Finally she turned back to the mayor. "Do you have anything else to add?" she asked.

"Excuse me?"

"Anything else to add, to what you've already said?"

The mayor looked at his wife, then back at Sands. "I don't think we've really said anything yet. Nothing happened..."

"Something happened," Sands corrected him. "At some point last night Emily Slaughter was murdered, either while you were there or around that time." She stared at them both, making Dorothy Wade whimper. "Are you sure you didn't see or hear *anything* out of the ordinary? Think carefully, it might be important." She looked back at the mayor, waiting until he shook his head. Then she turned to Dorothy Wade, who whimpered again, her head shivering rather than shaking.

Sands sighed. She looked to Golding, inclined her head then rose to her feet. "I'll have someone come round to take your statements. Please don't leave the house or talk to anybody in the meantime."

"Statements?" the mayor asked. "We've just told you everything..."

"And you'll need to tell us again. If you'd prefer you can attend the police station and give formal interviews there, but I thought you'd appreciate the opportunity to keep things discreet, given your status." She flashed a cold smile, and the mayor looked flustered, and then flattered. What Sands had said wasn't true, the reality was that Dorchester police station simply wasn't big enough to send every witness there while keeping them isolated. The mayor began to nod, self-importantly.

"Yes, yes, well thank you for that."

Sands regarded him coolly. "If you do think of anything we

haven't discussed in the meantime, you shouldn't wait." She handed him her card. "Contact me at once. Is that understood?"

The mayor nodded.

"Of course. I'll see you out."

"Thank you."

They walked back through the living room and into the hallway. Somehow, the decor of the house seemed to help the mayor regain some of his self-confidence. He spoke when they reached the front door. "Of course, it's obvious where you should be looking."

Sands looked at him in surprise. "It is?"

"Yes. It's that bloody St Austells. I always said something like this would happen." He shook his head as if the subject were something they both regularly moaned about. Sands stared back at him, openly confused.

"What is St Austells?"

"You don't know?" Wade was incredulous. "It's the homeless shelter, just up the road from Lulworth..." He shook his head. "I've been warning about that place for years. It's a menace to the whole area, filled with violent and dangerous people." He looked at Sands encouragingly. "I've been campaigning to have it shut for years, haven't I dear?" He glanced at his wife, who'd joined them in the hallway. "It'll certainly be closed down after this." The colour was returning to his cheeks now and he nodded enthusiastically.

After a moment of silence, Sands said, "OK," and nodded too, but just once. "Thank you for your time Mr Wade, Mrs Wade. We'll look into that."

Back in the Alfa, they sat for a while, both still watching the little cottage, but Golding occasionally watching Sands.

"Are we waiting for anything?" he asked after a while.

"No," she replied, not moving. Golding tried again. "So what do you think? Were they involved?"

She turned to face him. "You tell me."

"I don't think so," he said carefully. "They didn't seem to have any idea about it. They seemed genuinely surprised."

Sands didn't reply, she didn't even seem interested. Instead she suddenly pulled out her phone, dialled Lindham and told him to get a pair of detectives to take a statement from the Wades as soon as possible. When she hung up, she stared out of the windscreen for a while, before finally turned to Golding.

"Tell me about this homeless shelter. St Austells. Do you know it?"

Golding looked surprised, but nodded. "Yeah. Everyone here knows about it."

"Why?"

A shadow of a frown appeared on Golding's face. "It's kind of notorious."

"In what way?"

Golding didn't reply, he seemed to be pondering how to respond. "OK." He drew a deep breath. "It's some sort of charity hospital place, to help homeless people – recovering alcoholics, drug users – that sort of thing. The idea is to hide them away in a rural location where they can break their addictions without temptation."

"Does it work?"

Golding didn't appear to anticipate the question. He hesitated. "I suppose it might, sometimes..."

"So that's a no?"

He glanced at her, and finally shrugged. "Not so much. In my experience..." He seemed to consider. "The residents there aren't allowed to bring anything inside the refuge – drink or drugs I mean. But that means they just go into the nearby towns to do it. There's a lot of begging too, and shoplifting from local stores. When I was in uniform, I had to deal with it all the time."

Sands listened thoughtfully. "Ever see anything violent?"

Golding shook his head. "A few fights. Between the residents, when they'd had too much, or with some of the teenagers from the towns who took issue with them. But that's it. Never anything like this."

Sands drummed her fingers on the wheel. "Where is it?"

"A few miles back down the road. There're some woods. It's kind of hidden away in there."

"Down this road?"

"Yeah."

"So not that far from the body?"

"No."

Sands sat a while longer, thinking. "OK," she said in the end. "We should go and check it out then." She turned the key and fired the engine into life.

SEVEN

This time Sands made calls the entire way, following Golding's pointed finger when they came up to junctions. The operation was increasing rapidly in size and complexity, pulling in officers and staff from MID and other branches, and, as the lead detective, she was responsible for directing it. She was barely done when they arrived at the refuge, a tall red-brick building surrounded by mature trees. She guided the car through a narrow entrance between two high brick walls and swung into a parking space next to a battered minibus with the words *St Austells* stencilled on the side. Sands got out and looked around, quickly followed by Golding. There were only a few other cars, one resting on bricks with its wheels removed. A bike rack built against the rear wall housed a few battered bicycles.

Sands glanced around carefully as she led the way to the door.

She rapped hard with her knuckles, while simultaneously searching for a doorbell. When no one answered, she tried turning the handle, discovered it was unlocked so pushed it open and went inside. There was a smell, institutional, like sour food. Another bike stood against the wall in a hallway, its back tyre deflated. The whole place needed redecorating. There was no reception area, but a woman came hurrying to meet them, looking anxious.

"Hello? Can I help you?" She looked even more worried when Sands said, "I'm DCI Sands from the South West Murder Investigation Department. This is my colleague Detective Golding. We're investigating a serious incident that took place this morning at Lulworth Cove. Who are you, please?"

The blood drained from the woman's face. "You'd better see Julian. He's in his office."

"OK."

The woman stood wringing her hands for a moment before Sands' expectant look prompted her to move. She led them quickly down a hallway. Sands glanced into the rooms they passed. There was a kitchen, where the foul smell was stronger, and a communal area where a TV blared loudly, showing some panel show. A figure in a wheelchair sat watching it, while two young men quietly played pool on an undersized table. The detectives came to a closed wooden door, which the woman meekly knocked on. When nothing happened, her eyes darted to Sands, and she quickly knocked again.

"What is it?" A man's voice from inside rang out, he sounded irritated, but the woman nervously opened the door a crack and whispered inside. Thirty seconds later she still hadn't been given access, so Sands took over, pushing on the door to open it wide. Inside, a man with long, greasy hair looked up from his desk in astonishment.

"I'm DCI Sands, and this is Detective Golding, South West Murder Squad." She held open her badge. "I apologise for the intrusion but this is a time-sensitive investigation. Are you in charge here, Mr...?"

The man stood up. He was in his early forties, tall and dressed in jeans and a Hawaiian shirt. His long hair was tied in a ponytail. He'd been watching a small TV on his desk. He didn't turn it off but turned down the volume. "Pink. Julian Pink. I'm the manager here. And most people make an appointment rather than barging in."

"We just have a few questions." Sands walked into the office, found a chair, moved it closer to the desk and sat down.

Pink forced a smile, then gestured to the chair sarcastically. "OK. Well, have a seat. Anything for the police." He also sat, and waited, arms folded now. There were no other chairs, so Golding stood just inside the door.

"We're investigating the murder of a child whose body was discovered this morning less than three miles from here," Sands began, but she didn't get the chance to finish.

"Well, that didn't take long."

Surprised at the interruption, she frowned. "What does that mean? Do you know something about it?"

He sighed. "It's just that bad news travels fast down here. And usually in one direction."

Sands continued to frown, and glanced back at Golding, who very slightly rolled his eyes. She turned back. "Can you explain that comment, Mr Pink? I'm afraid I don't understand."

Pink smiled disingenuously. "Whenever there's any trouble, we're always the first point of call for the local boys in blue. Or girls in blue." He offered a nasty smile.

Sands felt her eyes narrowing, but tried to ignore the attitude. "It's been suggested to us that a resident of your institution may be involved."

He almost laughed. "I'm sure it has, Detective. I'm sure it has. It doesn't make it *true* though, does it?" His eyes flicked to the TV, which showed a news channel, something about an infection in China, people dressed in orange Hazmat suits with enormous hoods, looking like explorers on the surface of Mars. Pink looked back at Sands, still smirking.

"I don't think you quite understand me, Mr Pink," Sands said. "A girl has been *murdered*. This conversation is going to happen; it's your choice whether we do it here or at the station."

The smirk dropped away. "I'm sorry, Detective. One does get rather tired of the persecution."

Sands stared at him. "Would you mind turning that off?" Pink picked up the remote control with an audible sigh and muted the volume. But when he looked back at Sands she was glaring at him. He switched it off.

"You're quite right. What can I do to help?"

"We're going to need a full list of everyone staying or working here. But it might save time if you can tell me if there's anyone we should look at first. Anyone with a history of violence, specifically violence towards children, anyone on the sex offenders' register."

Pink blanched a little at this. When he answered, it was clear he was choosing his words carefully. "I'm sure... I don't have that information to hand, but I would expect several of our residents have a background of that nature. It's inevitable with the type of people we try to help."

"No doubt. Is there anyone that comes specifically to mind?"

Sands saw from the man's eyes how he was mentally scrolling through names. "No," he said a moment later. "There isn't."

"How many residents do you have at the centre at the moment?"

Pink didn't answer at once, but this time it was clear he knew this without thinking that hard. "Fifteen."

She was about to move on when Golding surprised her by asking a question of his own. "Fifteen? So you have a room empty?"

Sands turned to look at Golding, her eyebrows raised.

"There were sixteen beds here," he explained to her. "At

least there were when I was in uniform, bringing them back to sober up."

Julian Pink frowned a little as he responded. "We have space for sixteen residents. One man decided to leave this morning."

"Is that normal?" Sands turned back to him, suddenly interested. "For people to leave? Don't you offer free accommodation? To people who are otherwise homeless? Why would anyone choose to go back out on the streets?"

The man smiled again, back on more familiar ground. "Detective, as much as we try to help people here, it can be a difficult place to do so. The local population," – he smiled and looked up at Golding, – "the local police too, can be rather lacking in compassion and tolerance."

"Why did this man leave?" Sands ignored the lecture to press the point.

Pink seemed irritated at the deflection, but opened his hands and explained. "This is a refuge, not a prison. No one is forced to stay."

Sands turned to Golding to see if he understood better than she did. Then she turned back to Pink. "Does that mean you don't know?"

Pink smiled again. Just when it looked like he wasn't going to answer, he said, "People do leave from time to time. Sometimes they decide to move back closer to where they come from. To live with family. Sometimes people just decide to leave. The people we help here suffer from a range of complicated issues. They can be unpredictable."

Sands sat back, looking at the computer on the man's desk. She shrugged. "OK. In that case you'd better give me that list." She waited, but the man didn't move. It irritated her further. "Mr Pink, do you still not understand the seriousness of this situation? I need a list of all your current, and recently departed residents, plus the names and addresses of all your staff. And I need it now."

Julian Pink swallowed carefully. Then he picked up a mobile phone on his desk and spoke to a lady named Wendy, asking her to come to his office. A few moments later there was a knock on the door and the woman they'd met earlier opened it. Pink repeated the request Sands had made and told her to get the list at once. She left, looking doubtfully at the two detectives.

Another long silence descended. It had the feel of a stand-off, as if Pink were challenging Sands to see who could maintain it the longest. It was childish, but Sands wasn't going to be the one to back down. She simply sat, staring at him as he adjusted the pile of papers on his desk, then picked up his pen, inspected it, and put it down again. She was disappointed when her own mobile rang, breaking the awkwardness. Walking to the back of the office before answering it, she listened, pressing the phone into her ear to stop the sound leaking from the earpiece. When the call was done, she ended it with a curt: "Call me if you find anything else." She strode back to the desk and sat back down, no longer willing to play games.

"How did you find out about the murder this morning? You didn't seem surprised at the news."

He looked up, caught out by her change in tactics. "I told you, bad news travels fast."

"That doesn't answer my question. What did you hear? How? Be specific."

Pink squirmed a little. "We're not far from the main road. There must have been a hundred police cars coming past. We could hear the sirens."

"Sirens don't tell you *what* happened. You knew a child had been found. Who told you?"

Pink looked away for a few seconds, as if working out how

to get out of this without answering her, but in the end he shrugged. "There was a row in the centre this morning."

"What row?"

"Between a couple of the residents. Nothing serious, but they were talking about it."

Sands sighed impatiently. "Which residents?"

Again, Pink was hesitant. He shook his head, as if this were nothing more than a distraction, a waste of his and the detectives' time. "A couple of the guys were having an argument in the common room. They threatened each other. It happens from time to time. I went along to break it up, and they were talking about how a kid had been killed. One of them was blaming the other. I was called to break it up. It was nothing."

"*What*?" Sands didn't even bother to hide the astonishment in her voice. "One of them *blamed* the other?"

"Don't get excited. These guys, they're... You don't necessarily want to believe them when they say things like that. They'll have heard about it from someone in town. Or seen the police cars and put two and two together. I mean, what else could it have been? With that many cars?"

Sands ignored this. "Who are these people? Who blamed who?"

Pink hesitated again, not wanting to reveal the names, but soon realising he had no choice. "The two men arguing were Michael Sopley and Arthur Josephs. Arthur started the argument. He was accusing Michael. But Arthur is a troublemaker. A liar. I assure you there's nothing in it."

Sands ignored this. "Are they still here?"

"Arthur is. Michael left. I already told you that."

For a second, Sands didn't follow, then it made sense. "You're saying Michael Sopley was the man who left his accommodation here this morning?"

"Yes."

Sands stared at the man in disbelief, trying to decide if she should arrest him right now, simply for pissing her off.

"Where is he? Arthur Josephs? Can you take us to him?"

Pink looked at both detectives, as if he were hoping Golding might be able to re-route the conversation, calm the woman down. But Golding just watched.

"He's here. But you won't get much out of him..." Sands was already up, nearly at the door. "Not now he's had his medication."

"We'll be the judge of that. Show us where he is. *Right now,* please." She held the door open.

Once away from his desk, Sands noticed that Pink wore a pair of yellow flip-flops, which squeaked with every footstep he took. He led them out of the office and back into the centre's communal areas. For some reason Pink slipped into the persona of a proud host showing guests around. "Most of the people here are just like you and me, totally ordinary, but down on their luck. That's why it's important places like this exist," he said, as if Sands hadn't just been on the verge of slapping him in cuffs. "Even if the local plod don't understand that."

"Spare us," Sands snapped, after a while, and this stopped him. They passed the common room again; it looked empty, but then Pink led them inside and they saw the man in the wheelchair was still there, slumped in his chair, looking almost unconscious. Someone had turned the TV down low. Probably not him.

"Arthur Josephs," Pink said, gesturing elaborately towards him.

The man smelt, not just the stale smell of body odour and grime, but something worse; not even the institutional smell all around them could cover it up. The reason for the chair was immediately obvious: he had just one leg, the other had been amputated halfway up the thigh. The remains of his trousers were cut and ragged just below the amputation, leaving parts of the stump visible, the wound lumpy and deep purple in colour. He looked in such a bad state that even Sands briefly hesitated before approaching him, but then crouched down in front of him.

"Mr Josephs?" she asked, and then identified herself.

Josephs barely moved, but one of his eyes opened and he briefly examined the three people clustered around him. Then it closed again.

Sands tried again, but this time the only response was an irritated grunt.

"Arthur usually sleeps for most of the afternoon," Pink explained. "You get a bit more out of him in the mornings, before the medication kicks in. That'll be why he was arguing today. It won't be anything serious."

"Mr Josephs, you spoke with a man named Michael Sopley this morning. You accused him of having something to do with a child who was found dead this morning. Can you tell me about it?" Sands persevered.

"Fuck off," Arthur replied.

Pink made no attempt to hide his satisfaction. Sands glanced at him, annoyed she'd even checked, then moved to a more comfortable position squatting down. She realised it wasn't just her muscles that protested at the awkward position, it was the foulness of the smell as well.

"Arthur has strong opinions," Pink began again. "And that smell, like rotting meat? It's gangrene. It's coming from his leg. The one he has left, I mean. If it's not amputated, he'll die. But he won't let the doctors touch it. He still blames them for cutting the other one off."

No one asked why they'd cut it off, but Pink continued as if they had. "He'd run out of veins in his arms, you see. So he was injecting into his feet, his thighs, wherever he could get a needle in. Problem was, he was using dirty needles. So his first leg got infected and turned gangrenous, and they had to cut it off to save his life. But it didn't stop him. He kept injecting." Pink shook his head. "Now he's got gangrene again, in the other leg, and if they don't remove that too, he'll be dead in a month. But if they do cut it off, Arthur says he's as good as dead anyway. Isn't that right, Arthur?"

This time both eyes opened and the man stared at Pink with clear hatred. Sands continued to ignore the manager. "Mr Josephs, what can you tell us about the man you argued with this morning? Do you know something?" she asked again, but still Arthur said nothing. "Michael Sopley? After you argued, he left the centre. Why did he go? Do you know?"

"Sopley's a prick," Arthur said suddenly.

Pink smiled in mock apology. "Now, now..." he began, but Sands cut him off.

"Mr Pink, if you do not stay quiet I will arrest you for obstruction of justice." She moved closer to the man's chair, forcing herself to ignore the gagging smell. "Why is he a prick?" As she repeated the word she kept her voice soft and neutral. Arthur Josephs kept his eyes open this time, considering her.

"He's a prick *and* a poofter."

"OK. Anything else?"

"And a... a what-you-call it?"

"I don't know, Arthur. A what?"

"A... a nonce, that's what. A dirty nonce."

"Why do you say that, Arthur? Did he tell you something? Did you *see* something? Something we should know about?"

"Why would I tell you?" The man screwed up his face and scratched at the stump of his left leg. His trousers lifted up, revealing blotched and purple skin. When he saw them looking, Josephs continued to scratch.

"Because I can get him into trouble," Sands replied, her eyes back on the man's face. "And you don't like him."

Josephs thought about that for a moment, then half shrugged. "He was acting weird about it. Scared-weird."

"Acting weird about what, Arthur?"

"What you found. Down in the cove. You found a body. A kid's body."

"How did you know about it, Arthur?"

"It was on the radio station, the local one. They said how the whole village had been closed because of it. Sopley started looking worried. I knew why."

"Why?"

"I knew him way back. He was *always* dirty like that. Always liked kids. He as good as told me he did it."

"What exactly did he tell you, Arthur?"

"I just told you that."

Sands slipped out her digital recorder. She showed it to him and lifted her eyebrows in a question. "You mind?"

"Don't bother me." Josephs shrugged.

"What exactly did Michael Sopley say, Arthur? His actual words. It's important."

"It ain't *important* to me."

"But it might help get Michael Sopley arrested and convicted. You'd like that, wouldn't you? Because you don't like him very much."

"He's a prick. An' a nonce."

"So tell us what he said."

Arthur Josephs shifted in his chair before answering. He looked at the recorder, then at Sands. Then he glanced at Pink again, malevolence in his eyes. Then he started speaking.

"Said he did something bad didn't he? Wouldn't tell me what, just it was *bad*. Worser than anything he'd ever done before. And he was nervous. Proper nervous. Sweating. Scared. So I knew it were 'im. You should check 'im out, 'stead of hassling me." Arthur opened his eyes wider and pulled his features into a sneer. "And why else would he do a runner? Huh? Not unless he did it. Nonce."

After that he dropped his head onto his chest, seemingly

exhausted from the effort of talking. Sands tried to press him for more information, but he refused to do any more than grunt non-committal answers. After a full five minutes of persevering, she gave up, stared at Pink, as if the whole thing were his fault, then led Golding over to the other side of the room.

"See if we have anything on this Sopley." She whispered so that only he could hear. "This could all be total bullshit, but if so it's one hell of a coincidence." He nodded and pulled out his phone while she returned to her crouching position in front of the wheelchair. But it seemed that the medication had now kicked in properly. Josephs was semi-comatose. A few moments later she felt a tap on her shoulder and turned to see Golding holding his phone in front of her, a scanned police file displayed on it. She scanned it quickly.

"Oh shit." She took the phone from his outstretched hand.

EIGHT

She read it again to herself, then summarised it out loud.

February 2009, arrested on suspicion of a string of breaking and entering offences. Nothing was taken so charges dropped. Given an official warning.
July 2010, arrested for assault. Convicted and fined.
September 2010, arrested for drunk and disorderly. Charges dropped.
March 2011, arrested for assault. Arresting officers found he was in possession of indecent images of children. Placed on the sex offenders' register.
October 2013, arrested again for breaking and entering. Again, nothing taken. Charges dropped for lack of evidence.
June 2015, arrested again. This time caught inside a house when the owners were on holiday. The family had young kids. He was found inside the girl's bedroom. Playing with her toys. Specifically arranging dolls on the bed.

She looked up at Pink, whose demeanour had changed as she read this out. Her voice was tight with rage. "I asked if you had anyone staying here we should look at for the murder of a child. Instead of telling me about Sopley, you tried to downplay him."

Pink opened his mouth, then closed it again.

"He's on the sex offenders' register. You must have known we'd find that out, but you chose to waste our time." She returned Golding's phone to him. "We need to find Sopley." She wheeled back to Pink. "Where did he go?"

The centre's manager seemed shamed into silence.

"Mr Pink, you've done enough this morning to get yourself arrested. If you'd like to add having this centre shut down, then by all means don't answer me. We'll find him either way."

"I don't know," he replied.

"Did he have transport? A car?"

"No. Very few of our residents do."

"So how did he leave?"

"I don't know."

"He had a bike," Josephs interrupted. "He knows that."

Sands turned to the man in the wheelchair, who had clearly been faking his stupor. She considered trying again to get him to speak, but then didn't need to.

"A mount'un bike," Josephs confirmed, sneering. "Yellow mount'un bike. That's what he left on. I saw him. Dirty nonce." He glanced towards the window, which looked out on the parking area.

Sands turned back to Pink, who briefly hesitated, before seeming to come to a decision. He nodded unhappily. "He was going to the train station. Over in Wareham."

"How do you know?"

"Because I gave him a ticket. That's how."

Sands looked like she wanted to hit him. She took a deep breath. "Where to? What time was the train?"

"London. An open ticket. I often give residents the cost of their onward travel. I saw no reason not to with Michael."

"What time?"

"What?"

"What time did he leave?"

Pink thought for a moment, then shrugged. "The argument was just after breakfast. He packed up and cleared up straight after that. I guess about ten. Ten-thirty..."

Sands spun round to Golding. "How often do the trains to London run?"

"Every hour. On the hour."

"Alright, and it's... what, two to three miles to the station?" Golding nodded and she turned back to Pink, who shrugged again.

"What sort of shape is Sopley in? He anything like Arthur here?"

"No, he's... He's all in one piece."

Golding tapped his mobile screen and showed an image from Sopley's police file. A white man in his forties with sullen eyes, wearing a grubby white T-shirt. He had soft, doughy features, but looked fit enough to ride three miles.

Sands found herself staring at Sopley for a few seconds, asking herself whether this was the face of a child killer, before telling herself that it was an utterly stupid question.

"OK, so he's probably already on the train." She looked at Golding, still calculating. "Get onto control. Let's get someone at the station looking over the CCTV. If we can find out which train he's on, we can still have him picked up at the other end. Call them now."

"Yes, ma'am."

"Then meet me outside. I'm going to take a look at his room." She turned to Pink. "Has it been cleaned?"

He shook his head.

"Well that's something. Come on."

Pink seemed to take a moment to work out that he was supposed to take her there, but then headed off without complaining. He led her back along a corridor, before climbing some stairs and walking down a corridor with doors to the left and right. Pink stopped by the final door, which had the number sixteen stencilled on it.

"This is it." Pink seemed to know not to touch the door, or try to enter himself, and Sands took a look around. An emergency exit door next to Sopley's room led out onto an iron fire escape. She inspected it, noting that it would have to be kept unlocked day and night.

"Is this alarmed?"

Pink shook his head, and Sands nudged at the bar with her elbow. The door opened, sucking in a draft of cool February air. At least it helped with the smell. She stepped out for a second, noting that the stairs led down to the parking area. You could go down here and leave the building without being seen. She stepped back in, letting the door swing shut, fished in her pocket and snapped a pair of gloves over her hands.

Then she pushed open the door into Sopley's room.

There was a new smell in here, still unpleasant, but different to the institutional smell in the hallway. This one was mustier – stale and masculine. It was obvious that Sopley had left in a hurry. The blankets had slipped from the single bed and lay crumpled on the floor. She poked through the clothes left in the wardrobe, feeling inside the pockets. Then she went to a desk standing beneath the window. It was an untidy mess. Dozens of empty instant noodle packets were strewn around, and from the electric kettle and two mugs half filled with the dried spirals, it was obvious he cooked them here in the room. She pulled open the desk drawer to find more noodles, an empty packet of medication which she photographed, and finally a tabloid newspaper. She was about to shut the drawer when she saw something lying underneath. She nudged the paper out the way to see a magazine, and swore quietly to herself when she saw the title. *Antique Doll Collector*. The cover image was a creepy-looking doll with a soft body and a painted porcelain head.

"Oh Christ."

She was about to let the newspaper fall back when she saw something else, something written on the cover, scrawled in blue biro. She stared in confusion. It was clearly a telephone number, but beside it someone – presumably Sopley – had written a word in messy capitals:

HELP!

Sands poked around but found nothing else of interest. She pulled out her phone and typed the number into the keypad. She was about to dial, but remembering Pink was still outside, she slipped the phone back into her pocket.

She had a last look around, then walked out.

"This room is now sealed," she said to Pink, who nodded. "I'll have officers here in ten minutes. Until then, no one goes in, do you understand me?"

Pink nodded again and this time Sands led the way back down the corridor and down the stairs.

Outside the centre she dialled Lindham and arranged the forensic team. Not enough personnel were available for both the Slaughter house and Sopley's room, so she was forced to prioritise, telling him to focus on Sopley first. Then, since Golding still wasn't there, she paced impatiently up and down the compound before remembering the number she'd taken from the front of the magazine. She dialled, but it just rang and rang. And after twenty or so times the line suddenly disconnected. Sands wasn't sure what that meant, so she tried again. But exactly the same thing happened. At that moment, Golding walked out of the centre, his phone outstretched.

"It's the pathologist, ma'am. He couldn't get through on your line. He's found something."

She took his phone as she climbed into the car, then punched the button to put it on speaker. "This is Sands, what do you have?"

"I think you're going to like this, Detective." Dr Bhatt's voice sounded excited. "He made a mistake."

"What?"

He coughed to clear his throat. "You remember I mentioned the lack of obvious physical evidence from the perpetrator. That he seemed to have been careful?"

"Yes."

"Well he wasn't quite as careful as I first thought. He left a hair."

Sands felt the news running through her body. Without realising, she clenched a hand into a fist.

"Go on."

"A very black, and very obviously *pubic* hair – so clearly not hers. It was actually protruding from the underwear the victim was wearing, half inside, half out. Otherwise I wouldn't have found it before getting her back to the lab."

"There's enough to get a DNA profile?"

"Oh, more than enough."

"OK. I need it fast tracked."

"It's already happening. We'll have the results in two to three hours. If he's on the database he'll come up."

Sands stared at the mobile. She felt a thrill at how everything was suddenly slotting into place, but then a twinge of guilt at herself, giving what had happened to the victim. She resolved the tension by telling herself to calm down, there was a way to go yet.

"Thank you, Dr Bhatt."

NINE

Sands used the quiet in the car to evaluate the case so far. Every investigation, at every stage – but especially during the critical first few hours – was about choosing where to concentrate extremely limited resources against a potentially infinite lack of knowledge. Get it right and you sent the inquiry in the right direction. Get it wrong and it could give the perpetrator the time and space to invent distractions and bed-in lies. Investigations that went badly wrong, almost always did so in the first few hours or days. The result was that many of them were never solved at all.

There were already many strands to consider in this case. Too many. There was the forensic examination of the body and the site where it had been found. Dr Bhatt was thorough, and Sinclair seemed at least competent. There was the Slaughters' house, which would now have to wait, because she had already ordered that Sopley's room in St Austells should be prioritised.

She felt a moment of dizziness, from the pressure to get it right. Rodney Slaughter was a clear suspect, but he was contained, for now. There was no risk he could abscond. If there was evidence in the house that pointed to him, it shouldn't be time-sensitive. There would be a chance to find it.

She shook her head sharply to refocus her thoughts. There was also Janet Slaughter and the Wades – had she overlooked anything there? It was hard to see what motive any of them could have for the girl's murder, but that meant very little. She understood that motive often meant nothing in child killings such as this. At least, not in the traditional sense of the word. Not to those who didn't understand the psychopathic mindset.

No. It was a judgement call, but it was her job to make it. With everything she knew at that moment, going after Sopley felt right. He had motive, if that really meant anything, and he was on the run, and they had to know why. But her approach had to be balanced: Sopley was the priority, but she still had to consider other possibilities.

These thoughts didn't ease her anxiety. She still felt like a gambler who had bet it all on red, and was standing at the roulette wheel, watching the ball spin around, jumping from one black number to another.

They reached the train station in Wareham in less than five minutes. It was a little way out of the town, and a pair of police cars were already parked outside. Sands pulled up behind. She led the way inside the ticket office, which was cold and draughty. Only one of the three ticket windows was open, and the woman sitting behind it was the only person in sight.

"CCTV room?" Sands asked, flipping open her identification.

"I'll let you in," the woman replied. "There's two of your lot in there already." She led them into a tiny, dark room where two men were already working through CCTV images on a bank of monitors. They glanced up at the interruption, murmured respectful hellos to Sands and ignored Golding. The ticket seller left them to it.

"You got anything?"

"Nothing yet, ma'am." The man operating the system pointed at the monitors. "We've got a camera at each end of the two platforms and then two covering the two entrances. This last one's in the ticket office. We're taking time stamps every time we see an IC1 male, but nothing so far matches the description."

"OK. We need this quick. You're able to replay all the screens at once?"

"Yes, ma'am. And we're replaying at quadruple speed. We need to cover four hours, so it shouldn't take too long. Plus, we've got Lukas and Willoughby outside on each platform just in case he turns up now."

"Good. Keep going." Sands stood back, watching as the screens started rolling again, the only source of light in the darkened little room. Even at quadruple speed, it was clear there was very little happening. Wareham wasn't a big town, and on a weekend in February there wasn't a lot to capture on CCTV. The detective controlled the feed using a large ball set into the desk, rolling it to slow the footage every time a person appeared in one of the shots, but none of them was Michael Sopley. At one point a train flicked into view, coming in comically fast. The detective rewound the tape so that it arrived at something approaching normal speed. A woman alighted, carrying shopping bags, followed by two teenagers with skateboards that they immediately jumped on to cruise down the empty platform. Another woman, older than the first, walked down the platform and boarded the train, her actions sped up so that she waddled like a cartoon penguin. A few seconds later – a few minutes in real time – the train pulled out again, with no other passengers.

"Which train was that?" Sands asked.

"The eleven o'clock."

"That's the one he should have been on," Golding said.

The screens reverted to an empty station, with no trains or people in view. Then a few minutes later, the time stamp at the bottom of the main screen passed the time the other detectives had arrived at the station. The man operating the machine shook his head. "Doesn't look like he got on any train, ma'am."

Sands stood in the darkness, deep in thought. "What time did you start from?" she asked.

"Ten-thirty, ma'am. Same time Sopley is supposed to have left the refuge."

"Do it again. Start earlier this time, and go slower."

The man hesitated for a moment, as if aware of the futility of this, but he did what she asked. And though she waited while he spooled the machine back to 9am, she watched the footage again, this time knowing he wouldn't appear.

"So he runs away with a train ticket but doesn't use it. Why not?" Sands meant it as a rhetorical question, but when Golding answered she didn't object.

"Maybe he thought he'd be too easy to track on the train?"

"Which means he must have thought we'd come after him."

They waited until the time stamp at the bottom of the screen had spun through twelve o'clock a second time before Sands pushed back out of the booth and pulled out her phone. This time she ordered a wider review of the CCTV that covered the whole town, and from other towns nearby. Then she and Golding got back in the car and drove to the newly set-up incident room.

TEN

The DI she had placed in charge of setting up the incident room, John Lindham, was directing a couple of IT guys as they hooked up computers and phones. A number of other officers from MID were already using them, alongside more from the South West Police Force. Sands got Lindham's attention, pointed to an empty cubicle, then sent Golding to fetch coffees.

When Lindham came in she told him to wait. She needed a moment to clear her thoughts. Golding returned with three cardboard cups of coffee. He set them down on the desk and shut the door.

"OK." Sands nodded to Lindham. "Where are we with the Slaughters?"

"We're talking to the mother now," he replied. "I sat in for a bit. She says she put the girl to bed around seven last night, then went in this morning and found her gone. She claims she didn't hear a thing. She's a mess though, don't know if she even knows what she's saying."

Sands sipped her coffee.

"What about the father?"

"We've kept him isolated. I figured you'd want to be the one to speak to him."

Sands considered, then nodded. "But he'll have to wait. What else is there?"

Lindham glanced down at a hastily scrawled list on his notepad. "Forensics are inside Sopley's room now. Nothing yet. But we got lucky with the locks on the Slaughters' house. There's a forensic locksmith, a good one, who happened to be nearby. He's on the scene now, but he called to say he agreed with you: there are signs the lock on the bedroom door might have been picked."

"*Might* have been?"

"He's taking the locks back to the lab to be sure. But he thinks so."

"OK. Good. How about the hair? The one the pathologist found? Anything more on that?"

Lindham shook his head. "Not yet, but they've dropped everything to work this one. It would be a minor miracle, but we might even hear within the next hour. If the owner of the hair is on the database, that is."

"If it belongs to Sopley it will be," Sands replied, thinking. "We're also going to need a swab from Rodney Slaughter."

"Already done, ma'am. He didn't object."

"And Stephen Wade."

"Yes, ma'am."

Sands still looked dissatisfied, and for a few moments she drummed her fingers on the desk. "OK." She pointed to a computer. "Can we get Sopley's record up on that? He was into burglary, what was his MO?"

Within a few seconds Golding had logged into the terminal. His fingers moved quickly over the keys to bring Sopley's record onto the screen in front of them. Sands and Lindham looked over his shoulders for a better view. "He breaks in..." Golding read aloud, scanning the relevant text. "He doesn't take anything, just plays with the toys... with the dolls." He stopped.

"But how? How does he get in?"

Golding clicked the mouse to a different part of the file. "Here." He pointed with his finger. "Oh shit."

Sands read the text he pointed to out loud: "While there were no visible signs of damage to doors or windows in the property, a subsequent inspection by forensic locksmiths showed the use of picks and a tension wrench. Sopley's work history shows he spent almost ten years as a commercial locksmith." She drummed her fingers again until she was interrupted by the ringing of her phone. It was the pathologist. Sands put the call on speaker. "Dr Bhatt, you're on speakerphone. What have you got?"

There was a hesitation. When he spoke, Bhatt's voice was breathless, fast.

"We got a hit on the results from the DNA on the hair."

"You've got the results?"

"Yes, and we've run them. We've got a name."

Sands kept her eyes unfocused. She was aware of the two men in the room holding their breath. "Uh huh?"

"Lit up on the sexual offenders' register. It's a forty-three-year-old man by the name of Michael Sopley. That's Sierra, Oscar..."

"We know it. We already have his file on the screen in front of us," Sands interrupted.

"Oh. Well, I wanted to let you know as soon as possible."

"Thank you, Dr Bhatt. Thank you very much." She killed the call.

Sands said nothing for a moment, but she felt her heart beating fast. She turned to Lindham. The time for balance was over. "I want everyone we've got out looking for Sopley. Everything else takes a back seat. Search out-buildings, barns, any derelict houses. Call in any CCTV you can get." She paused, thought. "Better alert any sports clubs where there are children gathering, as well. Especially those of an age that play with dolls. He knows we're onto him, and he knows he'll never get another chance once we catch him. He may try to kill again before we do so."

ELEVEN

Sands paced around for an hour, fielding questions and trying to work out where she could get hold of more manpower. Even Golding's shadowing had been suspended: she had more CCTV coming in than officers to view it, and he was going through the feed from Wareham's high street. But it wasn't from here that the breakthrough came. It was Lindham, who came jogging into the office where Sands was working.

"We've got him, ma'am. Sopley. A farmer's just called it in."

A few moments later Sands blitzed to the front of the incident room, snapping her fingers in annoyance at an officer who was still looking at his monitor. Everyone stopped what they were doing to face her. Her eyes scanned the room, counting heads.

"As you know, we have DNA evidence linking Michael Sopley to the body of Emily Slaughter, and his record closely matches the crime." She paused briefly. "We now have a farmer who's called in to say that a man answering Sopley's description has threatened him with a shotgun. Armed response is en-route now. We're gonna meet them there. I want everyone please, so let's go. Right now."

She led the way out of the building and into the car park, climbing into the driver's side of her car before spotting Golding and leaning over to push open the passenger side. Then she fronted the convoy, driving fast out of the town and into the countryside.

Fifteen minutes later they reached a short lane leading to a collection of farm buildings. Parked up before the turning was a lone police car, its blue roof light turning silently and a solitary officer sitting in the driving seat. He met Sands' eye as she pulled up in front of him. He looked nervous.

She turned to study the location. The lane led to a pretty, stone-built farmhouse; opposite it sat an ugly, metal-roofed cowshed. Beyond that were several other farm buildings of various sizes, nestling beneath the fringe of a green-sloped hill, veined with drystone walls. Parked up between the buildings were two minibuses in the deep blue of the Armed Response Unit. A dozen officers, already dressed in their full uniform of body armour, helmets and face shields, stood waiting to be deployed.

Sands drove on down the lane and parked a short way back from the minibuses, using the radio to instruct her officers to stay behind her vehicle until they were given clearance to act otherwise. She stepped out to find the ground an inch deep in near-liquid mud. She swore under her breath, but climbed out anyway, picking her way through the mud to where a tall, blond man in body armour was talking to a civilian. From his wellington boots and tatty red jumper there was no doubt he was the farmer.

"DCI Sands." She introduced herself to the Commander of the ARU. "I'm in charge of the investigation."

"Commander Mike Roper." The man nodded and offered his hand.

"I'm ceding command of the situation until you declare it safe to continue," Sands continued, and he nodded again.

"Thank you." Roper turned to the farmer. "This is Mr Jackson. He owns the farm and witnessed the suspect entering the barn."

Sands looked at the farmer but didn't speak to him. "Do you have the subject's location identified?" she asked the commander.

"We're still trying to establish that..." he began to reply, but the farmer interrupted him. "He's holed up in that barn." He pointed to a row of low buildings a short distance from the farmhouse. "Took my bloody shotgun he did."

"*Which* barn, Mr Jackson?" the commander asked, apparently not for the first time. The reason for his question was obvious. The long, low building the farmer was pointing towards had four separate entrances, each one large enough to drive a tractor in. There were no doors, the entrances just black holes into the darkened interior. Outside the barn stood a green Land Rover, its front passenger door left wide open.

"I already told your man on the phone. He's in the barn."

"*Which* of the barns?"

"Well, that's the one he went into, with my gun, but actually it don't much matter. They're all linked on the inside, see."

"OK." Roper looked as if he'd finally got clarity on the question. But he checked again. "You're quite sure he's in that building there?"

"'Course I'm bloody sure. I've been watching the doors since I called you. Took your bloody time too."

Roper ignored this. "Are there any back doors? Any other ways out? Windows, cellars? Anything like that?"

"Nope. You can get from one barn to another inside, like I said. But those four doors are the only way in and out."

"OK." Roper seemed satisfied. He picked up his radio and quietly issued a series of orders, manoeuvring his men around the farmyard so they fanned out around the entrances to the barn. Once they were in place, he turned back to the farmer. "How long's he been in there?"

The man glanced at the sky, and Sands noticed his wrist. He wasn't wearing a watch. "An hour? Maybe more. Like I said, the woman on the 999 number wouldn't stop asking me bloody questions so I..."

"OK. We'll have plenty of time for settling complaints later. Let's get him out of there first." The commander squinted at the building. It looked as though his men had it well covered, but he still wasn't happy. He picked up his radio again and made adjustments, pulling some men nearer and others a little further back for a better angle into the four wide entrances. They moved quickly and quietly, but they weren't silent, slightly encumbered by their rifles and body armour. Finally satisfied, Roper turned again to the farmer.

"You say he's armed with at least one shotgun. What can you tell me about it?"

"It's like I told your lady on the phone. I had it next to me in the Land Rover, but I had to get out and open the gate. Then while I was doing *that* my phone rings, so I answers it, and it's my daughter, my Clara. She's having a baby next week, you see, and I was telling her not to worry, it's just like when the lambs come. Then I see this geezer on his bike, and I tells him this is private land – that's it over there." He broke off from his explanation and pointed to a yellow mountain bike, abandoned in the mud.

"I don't know, there looks something wrong about him, so I just wave him away, because I'm still on the phone with Clara... the next thing I know the bugger's grabbed my shotgun from the Land Rover..."

"Did he threaten you with it?"

"Not at first he didn't. We both stared at each other, like we was both as surprised as each other. Then he just ducks right inside the barn there." The farmer pointed at the building again. "I started to go in after him, and he starts screaming blue murder, don't come in here or I'll shoot... I tell you, he's a wrong 'un."

"OK." The commander considered a moment. "What can you tell me about the gun itself? You know the make and model?"

"'Course I do. Browning 525 Hunter Classic."

"Double barrelled? Under and over?"

"Uh huh. Best hunter for less than a thousand quid."

"Was it loaded?"

"In the Landie? What you think I am? It were broken down."

"Cartridges? Slug or shot?"

The farmer hesitated at this. "Shot. But big 'uns. Triple Os."

A shadow of a wince registered on the commander's face.

"I know that's a bit much, but I was going after foxes."

"You must have some big bloody foxes round here," Roper muttered under his breath, then added: "How many cartridges?"

"Whole box. I packed 'em up myself. Cheaper that way."

"How many in the box?"

"Twenty? Thirty? Oh, I got a speed loader an' all. Had it on the seat next to the gun."

Roper took a breath this time. "And he took that too?"

"Wouldn't be so worried if he hadn't, would I?" The farmer seemed to think this counted as a joke, but the ARU commander didn't laugh, wincing slightly as he stroked the chin strap of his helmet. "How about other weapons in the barn? Anything else we should know about in there?"

"Nope, there's nothing in there. It's just me tractor shed. I got an old Massey Ferguson waiting on some parts – been waiting a while if you must know. And the far end is full of straw bales." The farmer glanced at Sands, but when she stared blankly back, he turned back to Roper: "So what happens now?

You gonna blow it up? I'll get compensation if you do, right?" He looked hopeful, but again Roper ignored him, instead leading Sands a few yards away to brief her in private.

"OK. We're looking at a very powerful gun at close range – that's anything less than fifty metres. Beyond that it'll be inaccurate, but I still wouldn't want to get in the way of it. The cartridges are filled with large-diameter shot, maybe eight projectiles per discharge. With the speed loader he has the ability to fire four shots in very quick succession. So I'm going to need your officers kept behind these vehicles until I give the all-clear."

"Understood," Sands replied. Roper paused, his eyes reading her up and down. "We'll try and make contact with him now. Since you know what he's supposed to have done, it makes sense for you to initiate that. If you agree, that is?"

"I agree," Sands confirmed.

He nodded. "Right. I'll get the loudhailer."

"Michael Sopley?" Sands heard her voice echo around the farmyard, weirdly boosted electronically through the device. She settled her nerves, and carried on. "You are surrounded by armed police. Put down the weapon and come out with your arms raised high." The sound bounced off the farmhouse, but when it died away there was only silence, the rustle of wind in a nearby stand of trees. She noticed, surprised at how suddenly it had happened, that the light was dying. She had to strain to see the entrances clearly, inside the barn it was pitch-black.

Sands tried again, repeating the same words twice more, but each time there was no response.

"We're going to light it up," Roper said, and Sands nodded.

From the shelter provided by the Land Rover, one of the ARU officers aimed a mobile lighting unit into the first of the entrances. Even from thirty metres away, the beam easily cut through the darkness and illuminated the building's back wall. The man carefully played the beam across the entire space, but there was nothing to see. He shifted to the next entrance and repeated the procedure. This time, the light illuminated an old tractor, casting a giant shadow on the back wall. The third and fourth entrances showed only bales of hay. Since the entrances were large, they'd seen most of the interior.

"He could be hiding behind the tractor," Sands muttered, with the loudhailer switched off. and Roper nodded, as if he'd been thinking the same thing.

"Try to raise him again."

Twice more Sands repeated her demand. Twice more her words were met with empty silence.

"OK," the commander said, "we're going to need better visibility in there." He looked around, assessing his team's deployment again. This time he jabbed towards the building opposite with his radio. It was slightly higher and had a small window at the top. "What's up there?"

The farmer squinted. "Fuel store."

"Up there. Above it." The commander pointed to the higher part of the building.

"It's got a little raised floor. That's my workshop."

Roper nodded and brought the radio to his lips again. "Evans, Jones. Can you get into that building opposite and get upstairs? You might be able to see over the tractor into the second door."

Again, his men reacted, working skilfully and carefully to cover each other's movements, and for a few moments there was just the soft clattering of the officers changing their position. It was strangely calming. But then the quiet was blown apart.

BOOM!

The noise came first, but almost simultaneously the officer who'd begun to enter the fuel store was thrown violently backwards out of the entrance. He landed with a crash in the mud of the farmyard.

Then there was chaos. Shouts from all around as the commander and eighteen ARU officers grasped the horrible reality that now confronted them. Somehow, they had been facing the wrong building. For many of them, the positions of cover they had adopted instantaneously turned into the exact opposite, traps where they were completely exposed. As they ran, undirected, to protect themselves, the man who'd been shot began trying to push himself up from the mud where he lay.

BOOM!

With the second explosion, the man jerked back down in the mud. This time he didn't move.

To Sands, it was as if seconds were passing in slow motion. The ARU commander was yelling, both into his radio and across the farmyard, screaming at his men to find new positions, but she couldn't make out the words. Then the effect stopped, and time flowed normally again. A shout came out from the second building where the shots had come from.

"*Keep away.*" The panic in the words was clear. "*Get away or I'll shoot him again.*"

The ARU officers were still scrambling. One approached the man in the mud.

"*Back off or I'll finish him!*" Sopley screamed now. "*I'll do it!*"

And now Sands saw him for the first time. Or at least she glimpsed him, scrabbling to load the shotgun again, then quickly holding it to his shoulder and aiming it at the approaching officer. She saw him long enough to confirm he was the same man she'd seen in the file, Michael Sopley. Then he backed away so the stone wall of the building hid him from view.

The commander ordered the second man to fall back.

"Don't move. I'll shoot!" Sopley shouted again, but the

officer had already sprinted to the left, throwing himself behind a car, his chest heaving up and down. Sands realised she still had the loudhailer in her hand.

"Don't shoot." She spoke on instinct. "We're moving back. We're doing what you say."

It might have been the additional volume from the loudhailer, or perhaps the moment had just passed, but for a few seconds nothing happened. It seemed everyone was trying to come to terms with this sudden new situation.

The only officer left in the open was the man who'd been shot. He lay alone just outside the doorway of the building where Sopley was hiding. But he *was* moving, attempting to crawl his way backwards. Sands could see the pain on his face. The fear, too.

"Michael Sopley? Is that you, Michael?" Sands asked through the loudhailer. "Can you hear me?"

There was no reply from Sopley.

"He's injured, Michael. He's not dead, the man you shot is *not* dead. You need to let us come and get him." Just twenty metres away the injured man continued his slow attempts to drag himself out of range of Sopley's weapon.

"I didn't want to shoot him!" Sopley shouted suddenly. "I had no choice. The bastard came running right at me. He came right at me with a massive gun. What was I supposed to do?" A howl came out of the barn. Filled with self-pity.

"He didn't mean to, Michael. He didn't know you were there."

"*Fuck you.* It was a set up. This whole thing is a set up. Coming after me. Sending him running in there with a massive gun." The words were delivered between choking sobs.

Sands glanced at Roper, checking he still wanted her to try to communicate. His face was white and he was breathing hard, but he nodded his assent.

"No, Michael. It was an accident. We thought you were in

the building opposite." Sands felt suddenly sick; a man had been shot. He might be dying right in front of them. "You need to let us recover that man you've shot. Don't make your situation worse."

"How can my situation be worse? I've killed a cop. I'm screwed."

"He's not dead. Look at him, Michael. You have to let us come and get him."

"Stay away. Anyone comes near him I'll shoot them."

Sands clicked the loudhailer to speak but changed her mind. She lowered it and stared at the ARU commander, her eyes questioning what the hell they were supposed to do now.

TWELVE

When the firing had started, the farmer had ducked down and moved backwards until he was hiding behind a wall, but the police officers now moved over to him to find out more about the barn Sopley was holed up in. It wasn't good news. It was a small stone room with no other entrances, and used mainly to store fuel for the farm's machinery. There were several fifty-gallon drums of agricultural diesel as well as one nearly full of petroleum for the Land Rover. Worse, it also contained a small, raised platform, accessed by steps at the rear, which led to a small workshop. This was where, the farmer sheepishly admitted, he refilled his own shotgun cartridges, keeping the gunpowder in Tupperware boxes. Whatever they did to get Sopley out, they'd better not be firing into the building.

While Roper considered this, Sands made repeated attempts to talk Sopley into allowing someone to come and recover the man who'd been shot. But each attempt was met with screams and abuse.

"*Shit!*" Sands said, giving up for a moment. She looked out at the mess the situation had become. The wounded man had managed to drag himself a couple of metres from where he'd first landed, but his progress was slowing, and now he was barely moving at all. Yet he was still wildly exposed if Sopley fired again. There was a thick trail through the mud behind him, and even in the half-light it looked ominously filled with blood.

"Let me try." The ARU commander interrupted her thoughts, and Sands let him take the loudhailer. Roper took several deep breaths before pressing the button. "Michael? Can you hear me?" He stopped and waited, but there was no reply. He tried again. "Is it Michael, or do you prefer Mike?" he asked. "You wanna know something funny? My name is Michael too. Commander Michael Roper of the South West Police Armed Response Unit. But I'm a Mike really. What are the chances huh? Two Mikes." He paused, but just for a second. "And the man out there in the mud. He's called Dean."

There was still no reply, but Commander Roper didn't seem to expect one.

"His name is Dean Jones. He's twenty-nine-years old. Mike? He's just a kid. And he's a nice kid too. He's got a wife and a baby who's six months old. As things stand, you've shot a police officer by accident. We all understand that. He went running in, he startled you. That wasn't your fault. But that won't help you if you won't let us get to him. He's going to die, Mike. If you don't let us come get him, he's going to die, and that *will* be on you." Commander Roper clicked off the loudhailer. There was silence while they all waited to see if anything would happen.

Nothing did.

"Come on, Mike. If we all keep calm here, we can fix this. No one has to die here."

Suddenly, there was a reply. "I don't want to die. I didn't do anything that bad."

Sands suddenly noticed they'd been joined by a paramedic, a grey-haired man in the uniform of the Air Ambulance. The helicopter had landed in the field behind them. She hadn't even heard it arrive. The paramedic nodded and leaned out to get a better view of the wounded man. The commander noticed and handed him a large pair of binoculars.

"What can you see?" Roper asked a few moments later.

The paramedic dropped the binoculars and shook his head. His face was grim. "Enough. He's wearing a bullet-proof vest?"

"Yeah."

"Then perhaps the pellets won't have hit any major organs. But the wounds in his limbs still look serious enough for him to bleed out. We need to get him to hospital. Right now." No one answered for a second, and the paramedic went on. "I'm sorry. I do mean *right now*. If we can't get compression on those wounds within... minutes, it's going to be too late."

The commander screwed up his face, then took the binoculars back and scanned the scene in front of him, both the injured man and the entrance to the building where Sopley was hiding. Then he dropped the binoculars and picked up the loudhailer again.

"Mike." His voice was calm, but it sounded different now, twisted by tension. "The man you've shot is bleeding out. He's dying. Whatever else happens now, we need you to let us come and get him. He'll die if you don't."

Silence.

"Did you hear that, Mike? We can't spend time talking this over. Dean will die if we do. So let me get him, Mike. Let me come get him. You don't have to come out."

Both the paramedic and Sands turned to Roper in surprise, but he ignored them.

"Mike? Are you listening, Mike? I can come out and get him. We have a helicopter here. We can get him, compress the wounds and get him to hospital. Then we can discuss what you want to do. Dean doesn't have to die. Isn't it better that way?"

"You can't go out there until he's disarmed," Sands said to him, but Roper spun round, suddenly angry.

"What choice do I have?"

"What if he panics? What if he shoots you?"

"I don't think he will. He's seen what he's up against. And I'm not standing here and leaving one of my men to die." He put the loudhailer to his lips again, shutting off any further protest. "I'm going to come out now. I'm not coming for you, Mike. Just for Dean. Do you understand me? I'm just coming to help Dean. I'm just coming so he doesn't have to die."

"Just you. No one else." Perhaps Sopley's voice had lost some of the earlier panic.

Sands watched the commander, holding her breath. Their eyes met as she silently took the loudhailer.

"Just me, Mike," he shouted, unaided.

"And no guns," Sopley yelled. "If I see a gun, any gun, I'm going to shoot."

Roper shouted back. "No guns." He spoke quietly into his radio, instructing his men to fall back far enough that they couldn't be seen. Then he unclipped the handgun strapped to a holster on his belt. He pulled the slider back, ejecting the cartridge before handing it to one of his men.

He shouted again. "No guns, Michael. That's a promise." He went to take a step forward but Sands' hand on his arm slowed him. She opened her mouth to speak, meaning to remind him of the protocol he worked under, they both worked under, which might not have been written for this exact situation, but which nevertheless clearly forbade what he was about to do. But then she relaxed her grip, saying nothing.

Roper met her eyes and seemed to read her thoughts. They stayed on her a beat, before flicking first to the paramedic and then to his officer, dying in the mud in front of them.

"He's dead if I don't."

Sands let her hand drop away. Two other ARU officers

hurried up behind them ready to help their injured colleague the moment he was behind cover. Sands heard the thump thump of the helicopter. Then, slowly, Roper stood up and walked forward. As he did so, Sands' phone lit up. She moved at once to shut it off, but then noticed the number, the same number she'd seen written on the cover of the *Doll Collector* magazine in Sopley's desk. Her memory provided a near-perfect copy of the spidery handwriting, and the word scratched out below: HELP! She hesitated for a fraction of a second, before accepting the call.

"Who is this?" she asked quietly as soon as the line connected. Her eyes were still on Roper, creeping forward through the mud to reach the wounded officer.

"Hello?" A man's voice, sounding confused but also strangely gentle.

"This is the police," Sands replied. "I called this number earlier and no one answered. Who am I speaking to?"

Another pause, longer this time, then: "This is *Help*. We offer support to people who are experiencing suicidal thoughts." Again the man hesitated. "Can I ask what this is about?"

Sands looked up. Commander Roper was nearly at the dying man, completely exposed.

"Shit!" she muttered. Then, without realising she was still on the call, she went on speaking her thoughts out loud: "He's suicidal. Sopley's suicidal." Her voice grew louder. "He wants this. He wants to die in a blaze of glory."

And then the situation exploded out of control.

THIRTEEN

"I'm nearly there, Mike," Roper called out, as he reached his wounded colleague. From the shelter of the Land Rover, Sands watched as he bent down, rapidly scanning the man's injuries. Both men were now directly in front of the dark doorway where Sopley was hidden.

Sands looked around in near panic. From her position she could see a dozen armed officers, their weapons trained on the entrance to the barn. But their positions were poor. They had no lights trained onto the building, and their angles were all wrong. Sands could see inside better than they could.

"He wants this," Sands said again. But no one was listening. "He wants to die." She looked at Roper's second-in-command, the man he'd given his gun to, but though – to his credit – he seemed to understand what she meant, he looked back helplessly. Sands spun around to see Roper trying to pull his wounded colleague back towards them. But there was a problem, the mud was too slippery, Roper's body armour and helmet were hindering him and he couldn't get a purchase on the ground. As she watched, he slipped and fell over onto his knees.

"He's going to be killed." The second-in-command seemed

to understand her, but was frozen, unable to act. Then he looked away, refusing even to make eye contact. Sands looked back at Roper, struggling back to his feet in the thick mud. Then, inside the door of the barn, she saw movement.

Time slowed again as Sopley went for the doorway, pulling the shotgun up into a firing position as he did so. There was a noise, a crazed scream from somewhere deep within him. Sands was already on the move, leaving the cover of the minibus and sprinting across the mud towards the commander...

BOOM!

The orange blast from the doorway lit up Sopley's figure for a split second, and the man on the floor jerked backwards. Sands collided into Commander Roper, sending him down, too, but there was no time...

BOOM!

As Sands tried to get him to the ground, she saw the side of Commander Roper's head detach, helmet and all, as if half of it were simply removable and could be taken off at will. And as he fell, and noise exploded all around her, she felt as if a bomb had detonated on her right-hand side. Her body cracked and she went careering sideways, off her feet and down towards the mud. At the same time, the barn where Sopley had been standing lit up in yellows and oranges and noise and heat. But he was gone. He hadn't moved: he was just nowhere to be seen.

The impact was so extreme that nothing else cut through. The breath was gone from Sands' body, and no more would coming in. Then she was in the mud. It covered her eyes and blocked her nose and filled her mouth with gritty, gagging slime, and still she couldn't breathe. The need to do so grew and grew and grew, and every moment that she failed to fill her lungs, a horrific pain grew with it, so she was screaming, but screaming silently. The pain filled her head and she needed to breathe and it was impossible, it was *impossible* to do so. And there was a moment. A final moment of clarity, where the need to breathe actually stopped growing, and then stopped mattering at all. It became as irrelevant to Sands as what she'd eaten for lunch that day. And she remembered that she hadn't eaten at all. And then, the blackness of the mud closed, an almost-peaceful dark around her, even as her real surroundings were illuminated brighter and louder by the still-exploding fuel store.

The final thought that passed through the mind of Detective Chief Superintendent Erica Sands as she lay on her side in the mud was the irony of it. It wasn't supposed to be her that died that cold February day. It was supposed to be her evil bastard of a father.

PART 2

CHRISTINE HARVEY, SIX MONTHS LATER

FOURTEEN

"Come on, Ryan, get in the car please, the lorry has to go." Christine Harvey tried to keep the anxiety from her voice, but it was difficult – perhaps the most difficult challenge in a day that had tested her almost to breaking point.

"I just want to have a last look round," her son replied, his long teenage limbs somehow unable to prevent his feet from dragging on the ground. "Don't want to forget anything. If I'm never coming back." The way he said it made clear this was another dig, and she gave in, wondering yet again if this were a terrible mistake. Her daughter Molly, who was already clutching her hand, seemed to sense how upset her mother was, and squeezed more tightly.

"Am I really never going to see my bedroom again, Mummy?" Molly asked, for at least the third time that day.

"You're going to get a new bedroom." Christine turned and crouched down to her. "A brilliant, brand-new bedroom, with views of the sea and everything."

"But it'll be in a different house." Molly refused to be pacified by the sea view this time. Christine tried to smile, but they'd been over this so many times.

"It *will* be a different house, but a house is just bricks and mortar. What's important is who's *in* that house. And we'll all be there, your brother and me and you."

"But Daddy won't be," Molly said. "And even though he's dead now, he *was* alive, he *was* in this house, and he'll never be in the *new* house. So shouldn't we stay here? Because here we're closer to where he was?"

The logic of this was too much for Christine. She stood up, as great choking sobs threatened to burst out of her chest. She wanted to sit down, but all the furniture had been loaded into the removals lorry, so she had to lean up against a wall instead, the one they'd used to measure the height of the children as they grew. She'd photographed it, but what she really wanted was to take the wall with her.

She closed her eyes. This had seemed such a great idea, the fresh start they needed –

after the shock of Evan's sudden illness, the worry and frustration that they couldn't see him because of the virus, and then the horrific moment the hospital called to say that her husband was dead. Just like that. After the funeral, which they'd streamed into the living room because they weren't allowed to leave the house, it had seemed imperative to get out. Out of the house, out of London, start again – somewhere cleaner, away from the city. But perhaps it *wasn't* the right thing to do? Perhaps it was just a case of action feeling better than inaction? Perhaps tearing the children away from *everything* they knew, so soon after the loss of their father, wasn't for the best after all, but instead the worst *possible* thing she could do? She squeezed her eyes tight, feeling the tears fill up behind. The horrible truth was she had no idea.

She opened her eyes to see her daughter staring at her with her mournful expression, and in her son's face that familiar glare of teenage anger and resentment. It brought her back to the present, and the enormous responsibility that now lay upon her alone. Whether she'd made the right choice or not, it was too late now. The decision had been made. There were contracts, solicitors. A new family had bought this house and were due to arrive at any moment. And they – her family, or what remained of it – would start their new life in a new house. A new chapter. For better or for worse.

"Come here kids. Please." She let the tears flow and held out her arms to gather them to her. Molly came at once and Christine kissed the silky-smooth hair on the top of her head, feeling how it absorbed her tears. Surprisingly, Ryan came too, shying away from his mother when she went to kiss him, but as he did so, she saw his own eyes were red from tears, and she realised he was just scared. Like they all were. She squeezed him, and for a moment the three of them embraced, in the empty house that had been their home, their everything. Until *everything* changed.

A few months previously Christine had never even heard of "Coronavirus". As far as she knew, Evan hadn't either, even though he was a Fellow of the Royal College of Anaesthetists, and had been working as a medical psychotherapist, so might have been expected to know about these things. She was just living her life, with no idea of the chaos that would soon engulf her.

It had been a good life too. They'd had their ups and downs, like any couple, but Evan had earned a good salary, and once Ryan came along Christine hadn't needed to work. Instead, she'd embraced motherhood and child-raising, and quickly convinced Evan to have a second child. But no second baby came. They tried and tried, and when nothing worked, turned to IVF for help. But that didn't work either. Over time it became – to Christine at least – a full-blown obsession, her only focus. And then finally, on the third and final round of IVF –

the very last chance – she fell pregnant with Molly. It felt like a miracle. A precious, fragile gift that had to be protected at any cost. Since Molly's birth she had continued to treat her in the same way.

The gap between the children's ages meant they didn't really play together, not in the way she remembered doing with her own sister. But that was OK, because, with Evan working long hours, and Ryan already at school, Christine herself was able to shower the infant Molly with love. It was a good life, better than good. She had her boy, and she had the most beautiful, perfect little girl that anyone could ask for. Christine was happy. Right up until that day when Evan came home with a troubled look on his face. When she asked what was bothering him, he told her about a virus in China, a new virus, one the world hadn't seen before and from which no one was immune. A virus he feared would rip through the populations of the entire world, and come here, to their country. But even he didn't foresee how quickly it would rip their family apart.

Soon, the virus was in the news. It was still seen as a problem for other countries – but when Italy began reporting infection, hospitalisation and death rates higher than in Asia, it was clear it was coming closer. And then the doomsday prophesies appeared. This thing was like the plague, like the pandemic of 1918. Christine had never heard of the pandemic of 1918 either and initially refused to believe it had killed more people than the First World War, but Evan assured her this was true, and that terrified her. Some boffins somewhere came out with a computer model which suggested the new virus, Covid-19, could kill up to a million people in the UK. The National Health Service would be overwhelmed, hospitals reduced to plague-morgues, corridors choked with the dead and dying. Late – too late it seemed – the government (which was new and had been preoccupied with its Brexit project) tried to react. Emergency field hospitals were hurriedly built, and doctors from all disciplines ordered to staff them. Schools were closed. A national lockdown was imposed. Christine found herself trying to home-educate Molly, while Ryan sulked in his room because he wasn't allowed to meet up with his friends. And in a way, Evan was gone even before he died, so committed was he to his sudden new role on the Covid wards and the dying patients that filled them.

In the few weeks before his death, Evan wouldn't talk about what he saw there. When he did come home, after stripping to his underwear in the porch, dumping his clothes into a black refuse bag and going straight to the bathroom for a long shower, he was usually too exhausted to speak at all. But Christine saw plenty. On Facebook mostly, but on the TV news too, she saw the patients lined up in the corridors, coughing and spluttering, the deadly disease flying anywhere and everywhere in droplets. She saw the lack of personal protective equipment, the doctors wearing black refuse bags as makeshift aprons. She saw the ICU wards, filling up fast with patients on ventilators, the panic that vital pieces of equipment would soon run out. She saw her neighbours coming out to clap and bang their pots and pans every Thursday night as a so-called show of support. And she joined them, of course, glaring with disbelieving anger at those doors which didn't open. And then she saw the deaths begin. Not the patients, not the elderly – but the medical workers. The nurses, the doctors, the anaesthetists. People like Evan, who were so needed to intubate patients on the ICU wards. It was just a few at first, but then a steady stream. A terrifying *daily* death-toll of medical staff who were not ill, not sick, but just there to do their jobs. She pleaded with Evan to stop – by text, mostly, since she hardly saw him in person. She begged him to come home; he didn't need to be there, he'd volunteered to transfer back to his old speciality and staff the wards of the sick and the dying. But he wouldn't listen. It was like he felt driven, had chosen to be with these people as they coughed and spluttered their last deadly breaths. She discovered, after he'd died, that he had volunteered to work on the very front line, in the intensive care ward that had the highest fatality rate.

That piece of news had horrified Christine perhaps more than anything. Why? When he had children at home who needed him. *Why* would he put himself at risk like that? He'd tried to reassure her. The hospitals were probably the safest place he could be, he claimed. He brushed aside her protests about the lack of protective equipment. They were being careful, he claimed. And working there gave him the best chance of helping to find out what this virus was, and how it could be defeated. He wanted to help. People were dying and he wanted to help.

And then came the phone call. Not from Evan, but another doctor, whom Christine didn't know. She told her that Evan had fallen sick, and that from the symptoms it was likely to be Covid. At once, Christine snatched up her car keys, saying she'd come in, but the doctor told her she couldn't. Evan was being isolated. She could only see him on a computer screen, and even then only for short periods, because someone needed to be there to help him operate his phone, and with so many off sick, they were desperately short of staff. But Evan was strong. For thirty-six hours it seemed likely he would shrug it off, this invisible killer, but when Christine next spoke to her husband, she saw a dramatic decline. The shock of it was written clearly on his face.

That very night he was taken into the ICU ward where he himself had been working, placed into a medically induced coma and connected to a ventilator. At least they had one for him. For a week there was little change. Another doctor, a man with a reassuring, kindly voice, called her every day to give her updates. And though there was little change, that in itself was a cause for hope. But then his vital signs crashed, and seven days after being admitted to the ICU, the same doctor called her again. This time his voice sounded hoarse, as if he'd spent a week in hell itself. He told her that Evan had just passed away.

Christine hadn't been allowed to see his body. There was no proper funeral, no real goodbye at all. There was just madness. A science-fiction-like descent into unreality.

All around the world, and right into the heart of her family.

FIFTEEN

In the car it was better. She had something to take her mind off it. Christine wasn't used to driving long distances – Evan always did that – but she could follow the removal lorry, which helped. Although after a while on the motorway, and limited to sixty miles per hour, she decided to overtake it. They would stop somewhere for lunch and probably both arrive at the new house at about the same time.

Both Molly and Ryan sat with their headphones on. They kept their old places in the back seats, leaving the passenger seat vacant, as if Dad might decide he wasn't dead after all and jump in with them. Molly was listening to one of her audiobooks, a funny story about dragons, and every now and then she would giggle out loud. Christine didn't know what Ryan was listening to, she rarely did these days. For her part, she drove in silence, letting the hum of the tyres on the road and the burr of the engine wash over her.

They headed southwest. Down the M3 until Southampton, then turning west through the New Forest with its purple heathlands and stands of trees. Evan had once told her it was actually ancient, despite the name. And then – nearly there –

they turned south once more towards the coast. Evan had introduced her to this part of the world. He'd suggested a holiday, so that Ryan could try kayaking and Molly could spend a few days as a palaeontologist, finding fossils in the Jurassic-era cliffs. And it had been wonderful, even Evan had seemed surprised by how beautiful the coastline was, how restorative the fresh sea air felt when they sucked it into lungs so habituated to the smoky fumes of London. How much *space* there was. One evening, probably after a little too much wine, she and Evan had talked about how wonderful it would be to move down permanently, to let Molly grow up by this wild coast with its sweeping views and rolling hills. Neither of them meant it as anything real, it was more a holiday romance with an idea – an idea that didn't have to face the hard practicalities of real life. Where would Evan work? What about Molly's school? The friends she'd made? No, their *lives* were in London. Back then it was just a flirtation with a dream. But when the reality of their real lives changed to a nightmare – when Evan lost his life – well, the dream seemed like the only way to bring them all back together. How quickly the impossible became possible.

It was just a month after Evan's death, a time when the country was emerging from the first lockdown, and no one was sure whether this thing was over, or if the country was in a lull before it came roaring back. The papers were full of articles about how property prices in London were plummeting as people rushed to move out to the countryside and the coasts. It was safer there, fewer people crowding dangerously together. And with millions of office workers across the capital now working from home – for the foreseeable future – it seemed demand was about to explode outside London, and implode within it. This ignited a kind of panic in Christine. It seemed almost as if the idea belonged to Evan himself, his parting wish for the family, yet if she didn't move fast it would be too late for her to do it for him. She and the children would be stuck in a worthless, and potentially lethal, London house, priced out of the countryside where Evan had envisaged them carrying on. The holes in her logic were big enough for her to sense them, even through her grief. But with no one there to discuss it with properly, and some unexpected support from Ryan, she'd started looking on property websites. She'd scoured maps, wandered around quaint villages and towns via Google's Street View, catching tantalising glimpses of a sparkling sea in the background. And then she'd come across a truly spectacular property. A unique opportunity, but only if she could move fast.

In one sense she had little choice. With Evan gone, and the couple having only modest savings, suddenly Christine had no way to meet their mortgage payments. Their London house was comfortable, and though not large, it commanded a high value due to its position, giving easy access to the city. And even with the falling prices, it was still worth what to her sounded like a huge amount of money when the estate agent valued it. Enough, in fact, to buy outright the amazing coastal property she'd found.

She moved faster than was probably wise, given her mental state and the disorientation caused by her bereavement. But all the while she felt propelled, driven by the sense that, if she didn't get out *now*, she would be trapped, in a dirty, dangerous, virus-laden city, while the lucky people, the smart people, were already gone. Those who were left behind, she thought, in what felt like a horror-movie plot, would probably simply die, succumbing one by one to the inevitable creeping death of the hated virus.

Other than the children, she only ever discussed the idea with her sister Sarah, who lived up in York. Sarah had agreed, tentatively, that getting out of London was a good idea, but not with Christine's plans to move south rather than north. There was beautiful countryside around her, she pleaded, a stunning coastline too, and the houses up there were even cheaper than the one Christine was looking at. But Christine had a stubborn streak. It had been evident when she'd married Evan, nearly fifteen years her senior, and when she'd insisted upon having Molly, even when it seemed like the universe didn't want it. That streak appeared again now. The southwest was what Evan had liked. It was where Evan had *wanted* to be. Moving there would be like moving closer to him.

The discussion turned into an argument, widening a gap between them that had been growing for years, and which this time had put a stop to them talking at all. This only made Christine more determined. The decision made, she put their house on the market. She priced it low, on the advice of the estate agent, to ensure she didn't fall behind the market – whatever that actually meant. As a result she had viewings the very next day, and two asking-price offers within forty-eight hours. The way the estate agent framed it was, *which* of the offers did she want to choose? Not whether she really wanted to go through with it at all. And so the whole idea, which was in truth still only part-real at that point, took on a momentum she wasn't able to stop. Now there were professionals doing their jobs, people she would be letting down if she pulled out. The family who wanted to buy the London house; the couple who were selling in Dorset.

And so she had researched the schools in the area. She found an idyllic primary school in a nearby village where the headteacher seemed genuinely delighted at the idea of Molly joining. Nothing like in London, where Christine had needed to fight for her children's places. For Ryan, the nearest secondary school was perhaps less impressive academically than the one he'd been attending, but he'd be off to university soon, and for the time being it looked likely most schooling would take place online anyway.

Ryan did worry her, though, more so than Molly. But then he always had in a way. When Evan was alive the family had split naturally along its gender lines, her and Molly, Ryan and Evan. She smiled at the sudden thought of them, thick as thieves, in a way that few fathers and sons really were these days. Astronomy had been the latest craze, before Evan's death. He'd bought Ryan a telescope for his sixteenth birthday, and they'd take it out together on clear nights, filled with an excitement she couldn't fathom. They'd be out there for hours, exactly where she didn't even know, just staring up at the stars. Of course, that was all over now. Ryan hadn't touched his telescope since Evan's death. But surely he would benefit the most from the move? From the fresh air, the opportunity to spend time in nature? The chance to be closer to where Evan's spirit truly lay? Besides, despite his teenage surliness, he seemed consistently in favour of the idea. At least until that morning. But then perhaps that was when the reality of it finally hit him.

And how about her? Was the move really what *she* wanted? She had barely even begun to consider that, much less what she would do when she got there. At least there wasn't any massive financial pressure on them. The maths of the sale was simple enough: once the London house was sold, the Dorset house bought, a little money would be left over for settling in, but there would be no onerous monthly bills, no mortgage to pay. After a while she'd need to find a job. Surely there would be something? But was it really what she *wanted*? As she drove, allowing her mind finally to consider this question, she felt, not an answer, but a cold sense of panic creeping up her body. Was it what she wanted? Ripping her family away from everything they had ever known? Responsible alone for successfully replanting them?

"Mummy, I'm hungry," Molly's voice interrupted, allowing her to push the panic back down. She turned around to project a beaming false smile at her daughter.

"I know, darling. There're services coming up." The smile became real, though, at the sight of her beautiful girl. Because suddenly she knew. Wherever Molly was, *that* was home. That was the truth of it. The reality of the strange life she lived.

"Would you prod your brother and tell him we'll stop?"

Christine watched in the rear-view mirror as Molly did just this, and even found pleasure in the predictable look of annoyance on Ryan's face.

SIXTEEN

The last part of the journey took longer than she thought, and by then they were all tired from packing up the old house and spending so many hours in the car. Yet, at last, their destination began to appear on the road signs – the tiny village of Lulworth with its world-famous cove. And then they crested a final hill and there it was, spread out before them. The ocean, blue-grey and shimmering in the day's dying light. They got a glimpse of the scallop-shaped cove, cut from the chalk cliffs. Christine wanted to stop, to study it in wonder, but there was nowhere to do so. Even so, she noted how both children slipped off their headphones and stared at it too.

"Doesn't that look wonderful?" she asked. "Can you believe this is going to be our home?" She shouldn't have said that, she realised at once, since it risked sending Ryan back into his sulk. But he seemed to have risen out of it. Instead, he just stared at the water, and as they all joined in, the sun was revealed by a gap in the cloud cover. The world below responded, the silvery ocean turned to deep blue, and the hills above it glowed an almost luminous green, until the clouds rearranged themselves to cover the sun once more. In the moment that beam of sunlight had shone down, Christine felt – perhaps for the first time – that this *was* the right choice. A crazy choice, no doubt, and one which would come to define the rest of their lives. But the right choice, nonetheless.

They drove down through the picture-perfect village, with its stone houses and thatched roofs, and Christine's mobile beeped to tell them the removals lorry had arrived at the house – they were only a couple of minutes behind. What was that if not a good omen? She carried on almost to the cove itself, and then turned right, up a tiny road that threaded behind the village and a small hill the locals called Dungy Head. The house soon came into view. Christine had never been there in person, though Ryan had sworn he remembered it, and why not? The house was certainly striking enough.

Because of the virus, the sale had been conducted via video conference. Plus the couple selling had put together a promotional video showing the house in great detail. It was enough to make clear just what an opportunity it was. One not to be missed.

It was a highly unusual house in several ways. For one, she wasn't buying the entire house. The couple (the estate agent had told her he was actually an internationally famous architect) had explained how their original plan was to build a single house on the clifftop, but the pandemic had led to a significant downturn in their business, and as a result they had been faced with the choice of either dividing the house into two halves, and selling one, or the bank foreclosing on them, and losing everything. Christine had listened as the wife had explained all this on her computer screen, but she'd had almost zero compassion for the couple's bad luck. With everything her family had been through she was due a bit of good fortune.

As they approached from the road, the house looked huge, even though it was shielded by banks of earth and newly planted vegetation. It looked almost – and Christine felt a stab of concern at the thought – boxy. But it was abundantly clear the position, right on the edge of the steep, rocky cliff, was something quite exceptional. She pulled up to the property in a kind of trance, seeing the lorry parked up there – small by comparison – and the men who'd emptied her London house so easily that morning smoking roll-up cigarettes as they waited. The sun was low now, and discreet lighting illuminated aspects of the house. It had very few windows at the back – Christine knew from the video tour how the front walls of the building were very different, made almost entirely of glass, and she felt dizzy now at the thought she'd soon be able to stare through them, not at a London street and her tightly packed neighbours, but at the wide, cool Atlantic ocean. She opened the car door and stepped out, at once tasting the salt on her breath. Her feet crunched on the fine gravel. She looked down, as if surprised it was real. Then the front door opened and the woman she'd seen on the computer screen came towards her, followed by someone who presumably was the architect. The removals men flicked away the stubs of their roll-ups, and, before she could take a few breaths to compose herself, her new life rushed up to meet her.

"You must be Christine! I'm Janet, this is my husband Rodney." Janet Slaughter reached out a hand before pulling it back with a rueful smile. "Sorry, old habits! Welcome, welcome."

The man's smile was considerably less effusive. He wore all black, and his hair was black too with just a few strands of grey. He stood back while Janet made a play of air-kissing her from far enough away to pay lip service to social-distancing rules.

"How was your trip? Would you like tea? A glass of wine?" Janet asked. And then as Molly disentangled herself from her headphones and emerged from the back of the car, her face changed, as if the sight of the child broke Janet Slaughter's heart, just as it broke Christine's each and every day.

Janet pulled herself together. "And *you* must be young

Molly. I've been *so* looking forward to meeting you." Janet crouched down until it became clear Molly was too shy to go up to her. Then Janet stood up again, clearly trying to hide her disappointment. Christine thought she caught a brief, odd look between the couple, but there was so much going on it was instantly forgotten.

"We start getting the stuff in?" The moment was interrupted by one of the removals men, an incredibly tall man who despite being in charge wasn't a big talker. Even though it was now quite cool outside, he wore a filthy T-shirt, revealing long, toned arms, nearly completely covered in tattoos.

"Wanna get done before it's too late yeah?" he sniffed, and Christine was reminded of her plan to disinfect everything once it was inside the house.

"Yes please," Christine replied; when she then realised she didn't have the key, Rodney stepped forward and held it out to her. For a split second he seemed reluctant to let it slip from his fingers; perhaps Christine only imagined it.

"Welcome. We'll leave you to it for now," Rodney said firmly, glancing at his wife who flashed a guilty smile.

"Yes, of course. You're busy." Janet nodded effusively. "We can introduce ourselves properly later on."

Christine felt relieved at the suggestion. She'd expected to meet the estate agent there, but he'd said it was easier to deal directly with the couple since they literally lived next door. Somehow, she hadn't expected him to mean *this* literally.

Rodney took his wife's arm to lead her away.

"Oh, but..." Janet Slaughter only got a few steps before turning back. "I cooked you a lasagne. I'll drop it around with some plates. I don't suppose you'll have time to make anything." She gave Christine a brief smile before her eyes drifted to Molly.

"Well, come on, you two!"

Christine walked up to her new front door, Molly and Ryan

close behind her, and the removals guys a few paces back, carrying a sofa between them as if it were nothing. Christine fitted the key into the lock of the great, grey door and pushed it open. It was dark inside and she felt around for a light switch. LEDs lit up high in the ceiling. A stairway to their left led down rather than up, and a second door ahead of them led to the open-plan living area. Glancing at Molly, she led the way into the most incredible room she'd ever seen.

It was one thing to see it on videos and photographs, but quite another to experience it first-hand. The estate agent had called it an upside-down house, but Christine was quite certain it was the perfect way round for this location and that Rodney Slaughter must be a very good architect indeed. The living area was on the first floor, giving the large room extra height above its clifftop position. The walls of the back part of the room were of bare, polished concrete with just a few, tiny imperfections, so that Christine felt she had to run her hand along them to feel how smooth they were. But it was the front of the room that really stood out. The entire front wall, and large sections of the side walls too, were made of floor-to-ceiling glass. The effect was astonishing. The sea felt so *close*. She found herself reminded of one of her favourite films, the moment when Leonardo Di Caprio and Kate Winslet – Jack and Rose – embraced as if flying on the bow of the Titanic. Although whenever she watched that movie she got so caught up in the love story, she always forgot the ship was going to hit an iceberg and sink.

She turned to look over the kitchen area – open plan, and obviously expensive, even better than the one Evan had insisted on having fitted in London. The entire house was far, far more beautiful than anywhere she had ever imagined herself living in. But one thing she hadn't expected – and which hadn't been shown on the video –was just how near the other half of the house was, the part still owned by the Slaughters. The original plan was for the entire plot to be one house, that her half would be additional bedrooms and some kind of studio, she wasn't sure what exactly. And in that scenario perhaps it wouldn't have seemed odd that one half of the building overlooked the other so starkly. But now that it was *two* houses, lived in by two *separate* families, well, it was striking just how much of the Slaughters' living space was visible from Christine's half of the house. And how much of her space would be visible to them.

"They don't have no curtains," Ryan said, obviously thinking the same thing.

"Any curtains," Christine corrected automatically.

"What?"

"They don't have *any* curtains."

He gave her a surly look. "That's what I said."

It was Molly who rescued the moment. She seemed oblivious to the overlooking issue and was staring out of the front window in excited amazement. "Look at the sea, Mummy, look how close it is!"

Christine went to join her and held her close while watching the wind blow dark lines of waves into Lulworth Cove's narrow entrance. Far out at sea a ship, probably full of containers from China, twinkled on the horizon. A pair of seabirds, gliding on outstretched wings, cruised past the front of the house. Weather was pushing in from the west, where the arrowhead shape of the Isle of Portland was a faint shadow on the horizon. When Ryan joined them, she glanced at him to see his face had softened. She thought for a second he was going to say something, to drop his teenage guard for a moment, but though his eyes were red with tears, he didn't say a word.

They explored downstairs, choosing which rooms each of them would have. There was less of a dramatic view of the ocean here. Instead, the rooms opened onto a kind of courtyard between the two sides of the building. The overlooking was less of an issue here: the Slaughters had installed curtains in both houses to provide the bedrooms with some privacy. The rooms were large, each with their own bathroom. Molly loved hers, and even Ryan seemed awed by the scale of the house. Christine realised she was too. All this while the removals men were working, first filling the huge upstairs area with furniture and boxes, then moving to the bedrooms. It would be days before the house was in anything resembling order, but they had beds, and a roof over their head. And Janet Slaughter's lasagne, which she handed over on the doorstep.

And as they ate the food, the weather arrived, sending rivulets of water running down the walls of glass and turning the late summer day into a wet, autumnal-feeling night.

SEVENTEEN

The first few days passed in a blur. A visit to Molly's school, where in under a week's time she would begin Year Four. Buying a bus pass for Ryan, so he could get himself to the college where he would be completing his A-levels. A visit to the supermarket in nearby Dorchester to stock the fridge and freezer with brands they knew, a chance to keep something familiar in all their lives. And walks. Down the lane to the cove and along its curving beach. Down the cliffs to the much less-visited beach on the other side of them, which led eventually to the world-famous rock arch of Durdle Door. Molly had insisted on climbing up to the top, although the path looked worse than it actually was. Ryan had scared her with reckless talk about jumping in, if only the day was warmer. They walked miles along the cliff path one day, east towards Kimmeridge Bay, and then, when Molly became a little sullen and withdrawn from hunger, they found a café with the most wonderful garden. And then they walked back, up and down over the steep green hills, until they were exhausted. And that was a day spent perhaps more soulfully than any they'd ever spent in London.

They only saw the Slaughters in those first few days enough

to exchange a few words, but no more. It seemed the couple were cautious not to impinge on Christine's process of settling in. However, that wasn't to say that Christine and the children didn't see them inside their house. During the day it was easier to forget just how clear a view they had into the Slaughters' living space, and vice-versa. After all, Christine found her eyes naturally drawn to the ocean, and its ever-changing patterns of waves. But at night, when the ocean became just an expanse of empty blackness (especially if there was no moon), it was very different. It was then impossible not to notice what the Slaughters did – or didn't do. Unlike the Harveys, who owned a large TV and had subscribed to various satellite and streaming services, the Slaughters didn't even seem to own a TV. Instead, they spent their evenings reading, and – judging by the way Janet Slaughter sometimes seemed to dance a few steps when moving around – listening to music, although it wasn't possible to hear anything through the triple-glazed glass. It made Christine feel somewhat inadequate as she tuned almost automatically into the soaps and the distinctly low-brow entertainment she was used to. She pledged to make curtains a priority, though looking at the wall of glass, it was hard to see how you could even *get* ones to fit it.

And thus it was a full six days after the Harveys had moved in, on the night before Molly's first day at school, that Christine saw the lasagne dish still resting on the kitchen work surface. It hadn't been the easiest bedtime. Molly had admitted she had worries about the big day ahead, and Christine had laid down with her, stroking her hair, until the girl finally fell asleep. And when she came back upstairs and saw the empty dish, Christine felt a flash of guilt. She decided she would return it right away.

"Christine!" Janet Slaughter began speaking before she'd even opened the door, giving Christine the impression she already knew she was there. Perhaps they had one of those video doorbells. "Oh, you didn't need to do that." Janet saw the glass dish and waved at it as if she hadn't expected it back, only making Christine feel even more inadequate. She wished she'd prepared something in return.

"It was delicious, and a lovely idea. Thank you."

The two women looked at each other for a moment.

"Come in, won't you?" Janet smiled. "After all, we're neighbours now."

Christine hesitated.

"Oh – you don't want to leave the children?"

"No, no it's fine. Molly's in bed and Ryan – well, I don't know what Ryan's doing, but he's in his room." It occurred to her that if any problems did arise, and Molly came upstairs to find her, then she'd be able to see her from the Slaughters' living room.

"OK. Just for a moment."

Janet smiled, letting Christine into a hallway area that matched her own, except its layout was the exact opposite.

"Kids, huh?" said Janet with a knowing look, adding, when Christine didn't seem to understand, "Your boy. He's quite the teenager."

"Oh, yes. Well, he's not too bad." she replied at once, suddenly worried. Was this a problem for them? Were they worried he might be planning some wild parties? Because that wasn't Ryan at all.

"Can I get you a coffee? Something stronger?" Janet asked as she guided Christine into the kitchen area, patting a seat at the breakfast bar. "If you don't mind, I'm on the white wine."

Christine glanced at her house across the courtyard. The light was on, and neither of the children were upstairs looking for her. If they did appear, she could be back there in seconds. "Why not? Thank you."

She watched as Janet poured her a large glass and sat down across from her.

"Cheers," Janet said, raising her own glass and taking a large gulp. "How are you settling in?"

Christine took her time to reply. "It's lovely," she said at last, hearing how subdued she sounded. She felt a need to make more of an effort. "More than that. It's incredible. When you've been cooped up in London for so many years. I can't quite believe we live here now."

"I know. I'm not used to it either. We've only had the house finished for..." She checked herself, giving a smile. "The *houses* I mean. It's only been a month or so since the builders finally moved out."

The comment washed over Christine. "Where were you before?"

Janet sighed. "Well, London originally, like you. Then a few years overseas, in the Far East, but when we had..." She stopped, suddenly smiling. "Well, we decided if we didn't come back when we did, we'd stay out there for ever. So we came back to the UK, but to somewhere beautiful, like this." She smiled again, but there was a sadness to it. "We, um..." Her voice suddenly became serious, and she looked Christine full in the face again. "We heard from the estate agent about what happened to your husband. I'm so sorry."

For a second Christine wondered how her body would force her to react. Sometimes, when people brought it up, she lost control, but this time she stayed almost calm.

"Such a sacrifice." Janet laid a hand over Christine's. Christine looked at it. She felt confused.

"Yes. It's... It's going to be quite a change for us all."

"I think you're very brave, but it's a lovely village. And the school's fantastic. For Molly I mean."

Again, Christine didn't reply. But Janet went on. "Do you know which teacher she's going to have?"

Christine felt herself unable to answer. Tomorrow morning she'd drop Molly off and leave her there the whole day. They'd been down to see the teacher twice, not only to prepare Molly, but probably Christine as well. And yet, for a second, she couldn't remember her name.

"Is it Mrs Donnelly?"

"That's right!" Christine flashed a smile of relief.

"Oh. She's lovely," Janet smiled back, but there was an insincerity there, or perhaps something else. Christine frowned a little.

"Do you know her?" she asked, still in the same conversational tone, perhaps expecting that Janet had a niece or nephew at the school, or that the village was so close-knit that everyone knew everyone else. But that didn't seem to be it: to her surprise Janet Slaughter visibly winced and turned away for a few seconds. When she looked back, there were tears in her eyes. Christine looked away herself, around the room, to give Janet time, but also – suddenly – because she wanted to check something. She'd already seen – from glances sneaked across from her own house – that the Slaughters had only the bare minimum of designer furniture, but she looked now for any photographs, any clues to their family situation. Had their kids moved away? They were old enough. Or had they been unable to have kids, as so nearly happened to her? Only one photograph gave a clue, a black and white photograph of a child. A beautiful little girl. But it wasn't a family shot, it was clearly a piece of expensive artwork.

"Do you have...?" She stopped herself. "I'm sorry, I don't mean to pry."

"No." Janet blinked rapidly. She forced a smile "It's OK. What were you going to ask?"

Christine continued. Actually, she *was* interested. She did want to pry. "I was just, you seem so natural with Molly... I just wondered why you don't have children of your own?"

The smile on Janet's face froze and a silence stretched out between them. "Oh, I..." Janet stopped, covering her lower lip with her hand when it began to quiver. "I... we... Oh, gosh. We assumed you would have heard..."

Christine felt the ground beneath her shift. She was missing something. Something huge, but she had no idea what. "Heard what?"

Janet's hand slipped from her face and fell onto Christine's arm. "We do have a child, Rodney and I. We did, I mean. She... she passed away."

"Oh, I'm so sorry." Christine felt terrible, Janet's words triggering a thought of what it would be like to lose Molly. But at the same time there was a hint of something else, relief perhaps, because, whatever the circumstances of this woman's loss, it couldn't be that bad. Perhaps it had been during childbirth, or just after; perhaps the child had been very ill, and it was at least history by now. Realising what such a callous thought said about her, she tried to erase it from her mind.

"I'm so, so sorry," she said again. But now she needed to know. "Was she ill? What happened?" Janet said nothing. "I'm so sorry – do you mind me asking?"

But instead of answering, a procession of different expressions moved across Janet's face. Confusion, uncertainty. Pain. "Oh dear," Janet said eventually. "This is... I really thought you would have known about this?"

Christine said nothing, but the confusion spread to her face too. There was something more here.

"No, she wasn't ill. She was..." Janet looked away, her eyes blinking rapidly. "Erm... Look, this... There's no easy way to say this..." She suddenly fixed Christine full in the face. "Emy was murdered."

Something suddenly sparked in Christine's mind. A connection to a memory that was only half-heard in the first place. "Oh my gosh. That's awful, that's..." She felt her own eyes fill with tears. "I'm so sorry, Janet. I had no idea."

"Yes, I see that," Janet replied, her face now also free-flowing with tears. "I had no idea either. That *you* had no idea, I mean. We assumed, with all the stories in the media... Or that..." She hesitated, wiping her face. "You know, the estate agent would have told you."

Christine felt her blood run colder. *The estate agent?*

"Our daughter, Emy..." Her tears were coming so fast that Janet seemed to be finding it difficult to talk. "She was... taken. And she was murdered."

Janet Slaughter looked Christine full in the face, her expression one of pure pain. A flood of compassion within her had met an equal-sized flood of... what? Something else. Concern? She looked across the darkened courtyard between the two houses, into the empty, illuminated lounge of her new home.

Fear?

"*Taken*? *The estate agent*? Why would...?"

Details about the purchase of the house appeared in her mind. The pushy manner the young estate agent had, how he'd repeatedly shown her price comparisons between her new house and other similar-sized and similarly located properties. His insistence that she'd need to act fast if she really wanted it. And then, once she had made her offer – for the full asking price – how he'd been so keen for her to use the solicitor he recommended. She'd assumed at the time it was probably so she could be overcharged, but since she didn't know any other solicitors, it had seemed the easiest option. But why should he have told her about...?

Her attention focused on the look of pain on Janet Slaughter's face, and compassion won her over. What was she doing? What was she thinking? This was awful news, but it didn't affect *her*. This poor woman had lost a child in terrible circumstances. Presumably it had been some years before, but still, Christine could imagine how terrible that must be. She really could. In a strange way, she had lived the whole of her own children's lives imagining it.

Her face began to melt into an expression of concern. But it never quite got there. "When...? When did...?" Christine couldn't bring herself to finish the question.

Janet composed herself, as if her tears were too silly for something as trivial as this. "Just about six months ago. Just before this whole Covid thing appeared."

Six months? Christine felt her heart fluttering, her breath coming fast. "*Six months?*" This wasn't – wasn't the *past*, this was still... happening. Suddenly, fragments of details came back to her. Awful details. "It happened... here?"

Janet nodded and Christine swallowed. She looked across at her empty house again. Below the illuminated lounge was Molly's room, the sliding door window dark and invisible.

"Did they catch... whoever did it?"

"Yes. Oh yes. *Yes.* You mustn't worry. It's all – resolved in that sense. It was a homeless man. The police tracked him to a nearby farmyard, where he was... well, he blew himself up. He was shot. Two police officers died as well. I guess that's why we assumed you must have known. It was all in the news."

Christine was silent. She did remember now. The details had almost completely passed her by, but she'd still heard them on the TV. Perhaps if the pandemic hadn't been hitting just then, it would have made more of a story. She'd thought it happened somewhere up north. But no. It was here. Not just near here. But *here. Right here.*

And quite unwittingly, she'd moved next door.

"I'm so sorry, Christine," Janet went on after blowing her nose. "We honestly thought you knew about this. We thought that was one of the reasons you were so keen to move in. To be close to people who understood loss as well."

No, Christine wanted to say – actually, she wanted to scream it. That wasn't why she moved here.

Not why she'd moved here at all.

EIGHTEEN

Christine stayed only a few minutes more, just long enough to not appear too rude, before she hurried back to her own house where she went at once to Molly's room, as if fearing that instead of finding her sleeping there, the bed would be empty and cold. But of course there she was, breathing lightly and perfectly in the low lighting from the hallway. Christine checked on Ryan too, then returned to her daughter, just waiting with her, stroking her hair. And then she went to the sliding door that led to the courtyard outside. She checked it was properly shut and locked before removing the key. She slipped it into her pocket. This door would not open.

Perhaps an hour later she slipped upstairs, collected her tablet from the lounge and took it to her own room downstairs, next to Molly's. She hadn't opened the curtains in there since moving in. She sat on her bed and typed "*Emily Slaughter*" into the browser, gasping at the hundreds of results. Each headline was like something from a horror film. "*Local Girl snatched from clifftop house.*" "*Blood on the beach.*" "*Butchered body found at Lulworth Cove.*"

Christine learned how the Slaughters' little girl had been

found at the far end of the cove, raped and then horribly butchered. How the killer had broken into the Slaughters' house while they were entertaining upstairs. She learned how the man was a serial paedophile, already known to the police, and how there'd been a terrible breakdown in the way these people were supposed to be monitored. Though why they were monitored at all, and not simply locked up, with the key thrown away, she couldn't understand. She learned how he'd died, the same day the girl's body was discovered, in a firefight with the police, while hiding at a nearby farm. The case would have been impossible to miss at any other time, especially for Christine. But with Covid tearing her world apart, she'd only been dimly aware of it.

She lay back, but it was impossible to even slightly relax. She felt the need to check again on her sleeping daughter next door. Before she knew it, Christine had dragged her own duvet into Molly's room and wrapped herself up on the floor beneath her bed.

It wasn't the hardness of the floor that stopped her from sleeping. It was the sudden uncertainty of what this all meant. Although the news had – on the surface – nothing to do with her own family, it still seemed to completely upend her fledgling new life, and her brain fizzed with the implications of what she'd just learned. A question kept rising to the top. Should she – could she – keep the discovery from the children? Presumably Emily Slaughter would have attended the same school where Molly was starting the very next day – there was only one primary school in the village – and didn't that explain why Janet Slaughter had known the name of her teacher? And surely that meant the other girls and boys would know about it? Maybe not the more gruesome details, but they would have known Emily. And the other parents *must* know.

Her blood ran cold at the thought of this. The truth was that even before Evan's death, she'd never been comfortable with the social scene at the school gate. Evan had been fifteen years her senior, which made him older than most of the other dads, and her considerably younger than the other mums, who'd mostly had careers before children. Some had given up their jobs, but most were still working, their lives now a dizzying schedule of drop-offs and pick-ups and apparently incredibly important work meetings. The ones that didn't work seemed to fill their lives with gossiping about each other, rather than devoting their love to the children still under their care, unlike her with Molly. She'd had a fantasy that perhaps it'd be different down here in Dorset, a world far away from the rat race of London. A simpler world, where there was nothing to gossip about. But now a new thought hit her. If one of their children's classmates had been murdered – worse, *abducted* and murdered – then clearly *everyone* would know about it. Gossip about it. And here she was, sending Molly into such a world. Taking the dead girl's empty place in the class. And not just that. She'd literally moved Molly into the dead girl's *house*.

Suddenly, Christine felt herself violently overheating. Realising her duvet was soaked with sweat, she threw it off, laying there briefly unsure where she was, staring at the painted wooden legs of Molly's bed, the only familiar thing in an unfamiliar room. She fixed her eyes on them, as if wishing she could transport the bed and the child back to their old life. To London, with Evan to protect them both. But the wishing didn't work.

A minute or so later she got up and walked upstairs to a small control panel. The estate agent had told her lots about the house, how it wasn't like a normal building, it was designed to be warm in winter and cool in summer. He'd promised it was completely self-regulating, so that you didn't need to do anything; but if you did, it was possible to set the temperature via a control panel on the wall. She stared at it now, its LED controls glowing steadily back at her in the dark. The controls, like most other things designed or chosen by Rodney Slaughter, were as minimal as possible. There were no labels on the buttons and she stabbed randomly at them, angry at how they didn't seem to do anything at all. The unit's display showed the time – 03:14 – then the colour changed from cool white to vivid blue. But nothing else happened. When the display told her it was eighteen minutes past three, Christine gave up.

As she poured herself a drink from the kitchen tap, she noticed a light was still on in the Slaughters' house, across the darkened courtyard. Not the main lights – that would have been obvious – instead, a small sidelight. For a second Christine supposed they must have left it on by accident, or perhaps they left a light burning each night for security. But then Rodney Slaughter walked into view wearing blue check pyjama bottoms, his top bare.

Even though her lights were off and she couldn't be seen, she was glad she'd pulled a dressing gown around her before heading upstairs. She cinched it tighter around her waist before finishing her drink. Then she glanced up again, casually, just in case Rodney might be able to see her after all. But if he could, he certainly wasn't looking. His actions had a bizarre, almost sinister, look to them. Rodney Slaughter was in his lounge, standing very still and facing the ocean. Then, after a while, he began very slowly and deliberately to move his arms from one position to another. Christine stared, and slowly began to recognise it. It was some kind of martial art perhaps, or – what was that thing people used to do in the park opposite their London house – Pilates, Tai Chi? She didn't really know the difference, but thought it had something to do with worshipping the sun. Rodney Slaughter, however, was doing it in the dark. Christine continued to stare at her new neighbour, taking in the sheer size of him, barrel-shaped, his chest thickly matted with black hair.

Suddenly he exploded into movement, slashing his arms through the air in strikes and lunges. It felt eerie watching from her own darkened house. She felt somehow dirty, but there was something almost erotic about it as well. The dark hair of his chest thinned over his stomach, but thickened again as her eye tracked lower.

With a jerk, she stopped herself, nearly cracking her empty glass on the work surface. She would head downstairs and go back to sleep. Molly had her first day at school tomorrow morning; Christine had to be fresh, ready to give her every support she could. Perhaps Rodney Slaughter had turned to some Eastern, Buddhist nonsense as a way of coping with what had happened? If so, what business was that of hers?

She certainly couldn't blame him for it.

NINETEEN

She woke before Molly, giving her time to move her duvet back to her own bedroom before Molly asked what she was doing there. Then, since the world outside was now light, and the fear of Molly being snatched in the night seemed almost ridiculous, she hurried upstairs to put her plan for Molly's first day at school into action.

She quickly made up a pancake mixture, only occasionally glancing across at the Slaughters' house as she beat the batter. The couple were not yet up. She made a decision. She would tell Ryan about Emily's death as casually as she could, as he'd surely hear about it at college, but she wouldn't tell Molly. She felt sure the teachers would be careful not to allow any talk of murder in their classes. And as for the other mums – well, if they wanted to gossip about it, they wouldn't be the type she'd want to make friends with anyway. Besides – another thought had occurred to her – perhaps she'd over-thought how important the murder would have been to the other parents. Or not *over*-thought – of course it would have been a huge and terrible shock for any parent, but at the same time, Lulworth hadn't escaped Covid, and the virus had the effect of eclipsing everything else. Molly's first day at school was also the first day that the school had even been open for nearly six months. Surely that's what the other parents would be talking about? The difficulties of lockdown? Home schooling. Christine had been nearly overwhelmed with emails from the headteacher outlining their Covid-secure rules for reopening, the staggered start times and one-way systems.

"Hi Mummy." Molly wandered upstairs in her nightdress, tugging at it where it was now a little too small. Her mouth was turned down. Her demeanour subdued.

"Hello darling!" Christine hid her concern with the biggest smile she could muster. "How are you?" The child responded with a noticeable quiver of her lips, and Christine felt instantly overcome by love and the more familiar fears that had plagued her since even considering moving house – Molly's first day in a new school. She fixed her false smile more securely in place. "Are you ready for the big day? I'm making pancakes."

Molly nodded bravely, but her lip wobbled again.

"Oh, you'll be fine. I know you'll be fine." Christine crouched down and enveloped her daughter in a hug. She would have given everything to never ever let her go.

They ate their pancakes far too quickly. There hadn't really been enough time for them in the first place. It was bizarre, really. Despite her love for Molly, she'd felt throughout lockdown that it was a little overwhelming and suffocating to spend *every* day with her and Ryan, to be responsible for Molly's education, when she also had to arrange a funeral, finalise Evan's affairs and then move house. But now she suddenly felt the exact opposite. It wasn't nearly time enough, and she wanted it back, to spend it again. To spend it better. But that wasn't possible. The best Christine could do now was to savour every second of the minutes they did have together, helping her daughter get dressed in her new school uniform, fixing up her hair just the way she liked it and keeping that false smile fixed in place at all times, not letting even a hint of the terror she felt on the inside appear on her face.

Christine had hoped that Ryan would join them for breakfast, and she made enough pancakes for him too. It was also his first day at his college, but his classes didn't start until eleven, and he stayed in bed, groaning in protest when Christine tried to rouse him. By the time Christine and Molly had to leave, they still hadn't seen him. In a way, it was better like that, just the two of them.

It was breezy outside, blowing strands of Molly's hair loose as they climbed into the car. The Slaughters' front door opened and Janet came running out, her hand raised to tell them to wait for her.

"Hello!" she said to Molly, her voice a little breathless. "I just wanted to catch you this morning to wish you luck." She beamed at Molly, who regarded her cautiously.

"Thank you," Molly said in her most polite voice. She turned to climb into the car.

"It's such a lovely school," Janet went on. "I know you're probably a bit worried because you don't know anyone there. But you really shouldn't be. Emy was worried when she started, but right from the very first day, all the other children just wanted to be friends with the new girl, and she really enjoyed it." Janet smiled widely. "And I'm sure the same will happen to you."

Molly looked at her, a small frown creasing her forehead. "Who's Emy?"

Christine's heart skipped a beat, but Janet was unfazed. "My daughter." She beamed again, then reached out to tuck a loose strand of Molly's hair behind her ear.

"I didn't know you had a daughter," Molly said, looking

around as if she might have been hiding somewhere and was now about to reveal herself. "Where is she?"

Janet didn't answer. Instead, she stood up and smiled weakly at Christine. "You mustn't worry either. It's a lovely, lovely school. And Mrs Donnelly is so nice. I'm sure Molly will be happy there." Christine said nothing, glancing at her daughter when she asked, "Mummy, will Emy be at school?"

Christine tried to give her a reassuring look, but her fake smile failed her this time. "Come on Molly, we don't want to be late."

Molly asked twice more in the car who Emy Slaughter was, and whether she'd see her at the school. Twice, Christine awkwardly changed the subject, leaving it eventually as a "maybe". It was only when they arrived at the gates that Molly changed the subject. "Have you got your mask, Mummy?"

Christine stopped. One of the many rules instigated by the headteacher to enable the school to reopen "safely" was that all parents had to wear a face covering when they dropped their child off or picked them up. A handful of other parents were walking in now, the children unmasked, but all the parents wearing some variety of mask. Christine swore under her breath. She had already bought several masks – you needed them to visit the shops by then, and she had experimented to see which type looked the least horrible and felt the least unpleasant on her face – but they were all in the house. She parked and dug around in her handbag. The best she could do was unfold a tissue and hold it to her nose, almost like she was gagging herself.

"Come on darling."

The headteacher of Lulworth Primary School was waiting by the gates, a clipboard in his hands. A few parents looked lost, and it seemed it was his job to send them on the correct route to their child's classroom. Christine couldn't help but fear he was also there to enforce the mask rule, and she tried to rush past without him noticing her. Fortunately, he said nothing. It would be better in the classroom itself, Christine thought. Molly gripped her hand tightly as they walked, staring nervously at the other girls. Christine tried to examine the parents too, but they were hard to read, made more distant by the Covid security measures, literally and metaphorically. Despite her intention to speak with at least one other mum on the way in – and ideally to find another little girl who could be a first friend to Molly – it proved impossible, and she reached the classroom doorway without speaking to anyone. A young woman waiting just outside held a pump bottle of disinfectant. It wasn't Mrs Donnelly, but the teaching assistant Christine had been told would be helping with the class.

"Hello!" Christine said, trying for a bright tone, but not quite succeeding. "It's Miss Juniper, isn't it? This is Molly. It's her first day!"

The teaching assistant glanced back at her but didn't hold eye contact. "Hello Molly." She smiled briefly at Molly, but did nothing else. And there was something missing from the way she spoke. There was no concern. No enthusiasm.

"It's her first day," Christine heard herself say a second time.

"OK," Miss Juniper replied. "Can I just do her hands please?" She looked down at Molly, as if the sight of her hiding behind Christine's legs was nothing more than an annoyance.

"She doesn't know anybody yet," Christine went on. She tried to get the teaching assistant to look at her, to emphasise the obvious significance of this, but she continued to look evasive. Awkward. Maybe even bored.

A voice behind her made her turn around to see a tall man, dressed smartly in a dark suit, approaching along with a boy in uniform. Clearly a father and his child. The man wore a mask over his face, but when he crouched down to embrace his son he pulled it down for a moment, showing off a rather attractive face. She felt it was wrong somehow to notice, but as she turned back, she saw how openly Miss Juniper's attention was now directed on the man. It might have been enough to make Christine gather up her daughter and lead her away from this terrible place, but at that moment, Mrs Donnelly appeared. At once she crouched down to match Molly's height.

"Hello Molly! I've been *so* looking forward to getting to know you." She held out her hand, and though Molly didn't rush to hug her, Christine could sense her beginning to relax.

"Now I hear you used to go to a very exciting school in London. In a place called Wimbledon? Is that right?" Mrs Donnelly waited until Molly finally nodded. "Well, I'd so love you to tell me about it." Her face split into a beautiful smile. "Would you do that?"

Both she and Christine watched Molly's face until she finally nodded again. She was still holding Christine's hand, but at least no longer hiding behind her legs. Mrs Donnelly stayed crouched down but looked up.

"Normally we'd ask if you wanted to come inside to help settle her in, but with Covid..." She grimaced, then turned to Molly again. "But I promise we'll take very good care of you, won't we, Miss Juniper?"

"Yeah." Everything about Miss Juniper reeked of inauthenticity, but Mrs Donnelly didn't seem to notice. She mouthed to Molly, "*The very best care.*"

Then she pushed herself back up and turned to Christine. "Don't worry, she'll be fine. It's a lovely class and I'm going to put her with a kind girl called Daisy. She's lovely."

"Do you want to say a quick goodbye to your mum?" Mrs Donnelly smiled when Molly nodded. She waited while Molly did so, then held out her hands for a blob of liquid disinfectant. A moment later Mrs Donnelly put her arm around Molly and led her inside the classroom. Christine was able to watch as the teacher appeared to introduce her daughter to a girl with dark hair. She saw Molly say something but couldn't hear what.

"You have to wear a mask next time," Miss Juniper interrupted her.

"I'm sorry?"

"At drop off. And pick up. All parents have to wear masks."

"Yes, I forgot..."

Miss Juniper said nothing. As she backed away from the classroom door, Christine tried to catch her daughter's eye. The two little girls were talking, but then Molly turned around, perhaps suddenly sensing her mother wasn't there. She glanced to the left and right, then spotted Christine through the door, just as Miss Juniper was closing it.

"You'll be fine. You'll have a great day," Christine called out before the door closed.

For a moment she even believed it.

TWENTY

Christine hurried back to her car, suddenly desperate to reach it before she broke down into the flood of tears she knew was coming. She sat there blubbering with her head bowed, not caring who saw her. But after fifteen minutes had passed, and she finally felt empty enough to carry on, she drove home, hoping perhaps to catch Ryan before he left. But he'd already gone, leaving his dirty pancake plate unwashed, and an odd sort of emptiness within the walls.

She cleaned up, then waited a while; she wasn't sure what for. Eventually she forced herself outside for a walk. As soon as she was outside, with fresh sea air filling her lungs, she felt better. She headed west, following the coastal path up and down the steep green hills that rolled from inland and sank into the sea. Once she'd warmed up, she felt like she wanted to walk forever, to leave her problems behind, but before she went too far she turned around, so that there was no danger of being late collecting Molly. It was harder coming back though. A strong wind she hadn't noticed on the way was now blowing into her face.

As she passed the stone arch of Durdle Door, she was faced

with a choice. Climb up again several hundred metres to the top of the hill before the final descent into Lulworth, or follow the beach of St Oswald's Bay for a flatter route home. She chose the latter, enjoying the feel of her feet crunching through the shingle. About halfway along she saw something colourful dancing above the waves ahead of her. It was a kite, the horseshoe-shaped type, controlled by a man on a surfboard. Following the lines downward she saw him, and found herself enjoying watching him tack in and out, sometimes falling into the water, but mostly skipping expertly along on top of it.

As she drew closer, the man came ashore onto the beach at the foot of the cliff just below where the path led up to her house. For a while he kept the kite flying in the air above him, then he feathered it into the wind until it came to rest on the shore, where he gathered it up and began to walk up the beach towards the cliff path. She saw to her surprise that she recognised something about the barrel-like shape of him. A little nearer and it was obvious. It was Rodney Slaughter, wearing a black wetsuit, his black hair slicked back against his head. They were the only two people this end of the beach and their paths would soon cross at almost exactly the same point.

Christine wondered what would be appropriate to say in such a situation, and even practised a couple of polite greetings in her mind. But then something about his body language stopped her. He was visibly angry, talking to himself, and though she couldn't hear much of what he was saying, she caught several swear words. She felt herself withdrawing into herself, wishing she wasn't there. She wondered whether she could pretend to be taking a different route, so that their paths wouldn't intersect. But then he reached a bag she hadn't noticed lying on the beach and busied himself rooting around in it. He wasn't headed for the cliff path after all. She took the opportunity to alter her course, heading to the very top of the beach. He didn't notice her at all, for which she felt a strong sense of relief.

Once back at the house she checked to see if Ryan was back yet – he wasn't – and then on impulse ducked back out the front door and rang the Slaughters' doorbell. She could see from the colourful kite flying over the water that Rodney had gone back out on his surfboard, and she wanted to speak to Janet.

"I just wanted to say how sorry I was," Christine said as Janet started trying to fix a coffee from a furiously complicated-looking machine. "I should have said something last night, but it was a bit of a shock. It must have been just the most awful thing, to lose a daughter."

Janet looked relieved. "Thank you. And yes. It still is." She fiddled absently with the machine. "You read about these things in the paper. But they always happen to other people. You never really think it could happen to your own child." She stopped. "And while we're doing this, I think I owe *you* an apology."

"What for?"

"I shouldn't have mentioned Emy to Molly like that. I wasn't thinking. I mean I *was* thinking... but about Emy's first day at school. It was inappropriate. You need time to tell her what happened. To help her understand that nothing like that is ever going to happen to her."

The two women looked at each other. And without thinking Christine walked over, her arms held open. "I'm so sorry for your loss. I really am."

Janet abandoned the coffee machine. She took Christine in her arms and they pulled each other tight. As Christine felt Janet in her arms, she realised she hadn't touched another human being, not properly, and with the exception of Molly, since Evan had died. The pandemic had made it socially unacceptable, even illegal.

"I'm so glad someone nice has moved in," Janet said a moment later when they'd pulled back. "I'm sure we're going to be great friends."

Janet tried again with the complex coffee machine but soon gave up, throwing part of it down in mock disgust.

"It's Rodney's," she complained. "Everything has to be the absolute best, you know? I've got some wine in the fridge?"

Christine almost agreed, but then remembered and shook her head. "I have to pick Molly up at three."

"Of course." Janet's smile grew distant again, but she rummaged around in a cupboard by the sink until she pulled out an old-style plunger coffee pot. "Ta-daa!"

They chatted. Christine told her about how the drop-off had gone, and they even laughed together about the way the headteacher had stood with his clipboard. Christine almost told her how cold Miss Juniper had been, but it felt somehow disloyal to Molly, who'd be sharing a classroom with the woman. Even so, she almost felt she was enjoying herself. And then Janet surprised her.

"We really must welcome you properly," she said, tilting her head onto one side.

"You have," Christine replied, a little confused.

"Come over for dinner," Janet said. "Bring the children, it'd be lovely to meet them properly too. Come this Saturday?"

TWENTY-ONE

The rest of the week came and went, and a routine emerged. Christine would drop Molly off for school, then pass the day attending to the many little jobs that still remained – unloading boxes and setting up the rooms. She measured up the windows for curtains, then discovered that the size and shape of the glazing made it a more complicated job than she'd imagined, and curtains were completely unsuitable for them. In the end, she was able to order a set of blinds, ten times more expensive than she'd expected. But the real downside was they had to be specially made, and there'd be a six-week wait until they could be manufactured and fitted.

She also managed to spend some time with Ryan and explain to him about the Slaughters' murdered child. To her relief, he took it almost in his stride. Or at least, if he saw it as a big deal, he kept it to himself. It was at least some relief to Christine that her oldest child seemed to be coping with the move so well.

Christine waited until Saturday morning before taking Molly to the large Waitrose in Dorchester. Pushing the trolley around the aisles felt comfortingly familiar – they had used the same supermarket back in London – so for a while it was almost like they'd never left. Except that Christine was wearing her mask, and Molly was chatting about her new school.

"Have you made friends then?" Christine asked, accepting that Molly didn't want to engage in pretending they were still in London.

"Yeah!" the girl answered enthusiastically. "There's this one girl called Daisy who's really kind. And she's got a horse."

"Really?"

"Yeah, and she actually rides it. Like they do on TV."

"That's nice."

"I know. It's amazing. I wish I could ride a horse."

"I expect it's quite dangerous."

"It isn't. Not really. Daisy says so. She says she wears a helmet. It's just like riding a bike."

"That can be dangerous too, darling."

"Mmmm." Molly was quiet for a moment and Christine felt a pulse of concern. Was she being smothering again? It was one of her faults.

"Maybe we could get a horse?" Molly said suddenly. "Then we could get to know it, like with Humphrey?" Humphrey was her hamster, a timid animal that had become quite tame before it died. "Horses last a lot longer than hamsters too."

"Well, I'd hope so. But we don't have room for a horse, I'm afraid. Maybe we could find somewhere that offers lessons. We're in the countryside now. There might be somewhere."

"Do you think?" Molly turned to her mother, her little face so earnest and hopeful that Christine would have done anything for her.

"Well. We'll have to see." She fixed her fake smile.

Molly returned it, but then let it fade away, perhaps a little too used to promises that weren't kept.

"How about your teacher?" Christine asked. "Is she as nice as she seems?"

"Yeah she's nice," Molly nodded, but her mind was clearly still on horses.

Christine looked around. She'd intended to have this conversation at home, but then she'd put it off, time and time again. And though that was her default way of dealing with difficult problems, there were some issues so vital that she had to face them. And maybe this one was better in public. Away from the house. And there were no other shoppers in earshot.

"Actually, Molly –" Christine steeled herself. She almost felt like she was floating outside her body, watching herself. "There is something I need to tell you. Something important." She swallowed, stifling the doubts.

"What?" Molly looked earnest again, an interested frown creasing her forehead. There was no easy way to back out now.

"It's about Emy Slaughter," Christine began, already wondering if this was wise.

"The girl who got killed?" Molly asked at once.

Christine stopped, stunned. "Yes. How did you know?" But she knew the answer even before Molly replied. *Of course* someone would have mentioned it. She'd been at the school a whole week.

"Daisy told me. She said she was *murdered*. And Daisy was in her class last year."

"Oh." Christine felt her heart racing. "I see."

"But the man who did it, he's dead too. He got blowed up, so he can't do it to anyone else." A look of satisfaction came onto Molly's face at this.

"No. That's right," Christine heard herself reply. "He can't. He was a bad man, Molly. A very bad man, but he's gone. You understand that?"

Molly shrugged carelessly. "Yeah, I understand."

Christine marvelled at the resilience of both her children and squeezed Molly tight – too tight really – as they stood together in the empty supermarket aisle.

There was a queue at each of the three open tills, but for once Christine chose the quickest one, and they packed the groceries together. As they turned to leave the store, Christine recognised the broad back of a man who was just leaving the till nearest the door. It was Rodney Slaughter again, a plastic bag hanging from each of his arms. Christine smiled to herself at the smallness of the world she now inhabited, and then the smile deepened as she wondered if Janet had sent him to buy food for this evening. They were an odd couple, she decided. On the face of it, Rodney was clearly the dominant half of the partnership, but she wondered if Janet was really in charge. In a strange way she'd felt the same about her marriage.

Even so, she made no effort to catch up with Rodney Slaughter. For one thing they were both still wearing their masks, which made conversation difficult, at least with strangers. But there was something about him that made her just a little uncomfortable – actually, *quite* uncomfortable, she realised now, dwelling on the thought for the first time. Perhaps it was because they hadn't really talked, not yet. But on top of that, there was something else. He had an *anger*. At first she'd thought it had to do with his disappointment at having to divide up the house. But now of course she knew better. Of course he was angry. He was angry at a world which has so cruelly taken his daughter. But it didn't make him any easier to approach.

She spent a few moments pretending to look for loyalty tokens in her purse that she knew weren't there. In the car park Rodney turned right and she turned left, and she soon forgot about him altogether. Instead, she began thinking about how she should try to make other friends, besides Janet, now the children were getting settled. And by the time she'd loaded the shopping and checked Molly had fixed her seatbelt correctly, Christine had built herself an entirely new fantasy-friendship group, formed from local mums' groups and coffee mornings. But then, as she was waiting to leave the car park, a large white

Audi four-by-four swept past her. Rodney was driving, but there was a second person in the passenger seat. Christine found herself trying to make eye contact, assuming it was Janet Slaughter. But it was a much younger woman. With a shock, Christine realised she recognised her: it was Molly's teaching assistant Miss Juniper, still wearing the same slightly bored sneer she'd worn at the door to Molly's classroom.

Before she could even think about it, Christine found herself on the road behind them – not following, they were simply going the same way. But now her mind was racing. Why would Rodney Slaughter have Miss Juniper in his car? Christine knew by then that Emy Slaughter had attended the same school as Molly, but she didn't know which teachers she'd had. Then she remembered what her daughter had said back in the supermarket.

"Did you say your friend Daisy was in the same class as Emy Slaughter?" she asked, as casually as she could.

From the back Molly answered. "Yeah. That's what she said."

"Do you know who their teaching assistant was? Last year? Was it Miss Juniper?"

Molly looked stumped by this. She looked to her left and right and frowned while she thought about it. "I *think* so," she said slowly. "I think she's really good friends with Mrs Donnelly, so they're always in the same class." She looked doubtful of the logic for a moment, but then nodded firmly.

Christine half turned to give her daughter a smile.

"Why?" Molly asked. She hadn't noticed Rodney Slaughter or Miss Juniper in the car in front of them, and Christine didn't want to draw attention to them.

"I was just wondering." She gave her daughter a vague smile and turned back to the road. The Audi was still a few cars in front, and they were on the road that led back towards Lulworth and the house. Perhaps she was coming for a visit?

Perhaps she had struck up a friendship with the couple, following their loss? After all, Christine considered, it would be a huge shock to the teaching staff as well – to have a child in her class murdered. Perhaps the innocent explanation was that the three of them were supporting each other through a terribly difficult time. Christine even felt briefly guilty that she'd contemplated other, less innocent, possibilities, but then the Audi suddenly indicated and turned off into a small cul-de-sac. Christine didn't follow but craned her neck as she drove past, just enough to see the red brake lights on Rodney Slaughter's car as he pulled up outside a small, ordinary-looking home. Very much the sort of house you might expect a young teaching assistant to live in.

It played on her mind the rest of the day, and by seven o'clock – when they were due at the Slaughters' for dinner – Christine was exhausted from even thinking about it, and would gladly have cancelled the whole event. But she could see across the courtyard that Janet had laid their great glass table, even putting out silver candle holders. She had at least used the excuse of Molly needing to get to bed to keep the evening as short as possible. As to whether she'd mention Rodney Slaughter having Miss Juniper in his car that morning, she decided to play that by ear.

"Oh. Aren't you dressed yet?" she said to Ryan, who had just walked upstairs in his tracksuit trousers. He stopped, as if she'd just paid him a terrible insult.

"What's wrong with this?"

"Don't you have a shirt or something smart?" She forced a smile, trying to keep the tension from her voice.

Fuck's sake Mum. He didn't quite say it to her, but she caught the words nonetheless as he turned on his heel and went back down the stairs, leaving Christine alone in the living room. For the hundredth time that day she glanced up, and wished the blinds had already been fitted.

TWENTY-TWO

"I hope you like salmon?" Janet Slaughter said as she opened the door wide and beamed at Christine. "You look fantastic by the way." She gave Christine two air kisses and smiled at the children, Molly more so than Ryan. "And so do you, my darling. I *love* that dress."

"Thank you," said Molly and pressed out her little chest with pride. Janet led them in, talking to Molly the whole time.

"I hope you like the table. I put candles on it, just because I thought you'd like them."

Molly looked impressed. "I know," she said. "I saw them from our house."

Janet pulled what Christine thought was a rather confused expression, as if it hadn't occurred to her that this might be possible. "And that's a rather smart shirt, Ryan." Her smile to him was cooler, but he smiled back politely nonetheless.

"Thank you, Mrs Slaughter."

"Janet. Call me Janet, please."

"OK. Thank you, Janet." Ryan smiled again.

"Well? Drinks everyone?" Janet swung round. "Christine – you'll have some wine?"

She nodded as Janet poured her a large glass.

"Now, I've got squash for young Molly, but – is Ryan allowed a glass of wine too? A small one?"

"I guess a little bit won't hurt."

Janet smiled. "Excellent. Now do you like white or red? Rodney has a very expensive bottle of red on the go," – she winked at Ryan – "and he isn't supposed to be drinking too much, so I'm sure he'd love to find someone to share it with."

"Yes please, Janet," Ryan said, looking awkward. "That would be nice."

Janet reached into a cupboard for a second glass, and turned to Christine as she set it down, mouthing that she had *such polite children.*

At that moment Rodney Slaughter walked in the room. He was wearing black jeans and a crisp white shirt with the sleeves rolled up, a stark contrast between the dark black of the hair on his arms. He said a quiet good evening, but beyond that, made no effort at conversation. When Christine glanced at him, she noticed his eyes were fixed on Molly, which she didn't like.

"Could you pour Ryan a glass from that nice bottle you have open?" Janet prompted him. As the bottle was nearly empty, Rodney reached into a glass-fronted cabinet and pulled out another one.

They took their drinks over to the lounge area, sitting on white sofas facing each other by the front windows. A glass coffee table divided them, a smaller version of the dining table, set with bowls of nibbles. Some sort of classical music played from invisible speakers. Rodney said little, occasionally feeding himself peanuts in a way that made Christine think of an alpha-male gorilla in a TV documentary. In the meantime Janet Slaughter gently interrogated Ryan about how he was finding his new school. To Christine's surprise he opened up, and she found herself listening with interest as he compared his new school with his London college. He had – she noticed now –

even combed his hair after she'd sent him downstairs for a shirt, so that he looked and sounded smart and intelligent. Handsome too. Christine felt a pang of pride, and then guilt that she'd shouted at him earlier. Janet excused herself after a while to tend to dinner, leaving Rodney Slaughter feeding peanuts into his mouth with slow deliberateness. An awkward silence stretched.

"How are you finding the house?" he asked, finally.

Rather than being an innocent question, Christine thought she caught a hint of an accusation hidden somewhere in his words. As if she'd somehow stolen her new home from him, rather than paying him an enormous sum of money for it and rescuing his own finances.

"It's fine thanks." she said briefly, not wanting to pay the architect any compliments.

Rodney's lips curled briefly, then straightened out. He took another sip of his wine from the large, goblet-like glass. "And how about young..." he looked to Molly and waved a hand, as if airily suggesting he'd forgotten her name.

"Molly." Christine helped him out, her voice a little thin.

"Yes, Molly. How's she settling in?"

Christine suddenly had the sense that this man was insulting her, even though on the surface he was pretending to be polite. She struggled on. "She's already made a friend, a lovely girl named Daisy."

Perhaps she hoped this would have been of interest to Rodney, but he simply nodded, then fed himself more peanuts. Although it felt as though Christine and her family were being belittled, she persisted. "Yes, and she's in a nice class. With Mrs Donnelly, who's lovely. Oh, and she has a really nice teaching assistant too. Very *young*." Christine beamed at him, full in the face. She caught his eyes narrowing and flicking back to hers.

He hesitated for a second, then glanced towards his wife at

the other end of the room. "Really?" he asked. "Which teaching assistant does she... er, does she have?"

"Miss Juniper."

And in that instant, Christine knew. The bastard was having an affair. It was obvious, written all over his face for the half second before he managed to regain control of himself. But it was still there, in the way he slipped a finger inside the neck of his shirt, in the way he glanced up at his wife and then hurriedly looked away when it was clear she'd heard too. In the awkward half smile he gave to Christine before he turned away. What a scumbag. He was having *an affair*. An affair with one of the teachers from his dead child's school.

But as soon as this thought seemed solidify in her mind, Christine began to second guess it. *Of course* she would see a reaction. Miss Juniper was the same teaching assistant who'd taught his daughter, the daughter who'd been brutally murdered not six months before. Of course he would glance at his wife. It meant just as much to her. Christine briefly considering going on, mentioning as innocently as she could how she'd noticed them together that morning in the supermarket car park. But the opportunity had passed. Instead, they fell into silence again.

They sat down to eat. Janet had baked a whole salmon side with pickled cranberries, parsley and pistachio, a selection of tiny vegetables carefully arranged around huge white plates. She made a fuss about not remembering to ask whether Molly had any sort of nut allergy, but once Christine had forcefully confirmed that she didn't, they ate, the conversation still stilted.

"So what will you do with yourself?" Janet asked. "Now that you're here. Do you work?"

"No. I mean, yes. I used to work, before the children. I'm actually thinking of looking for something. Just part time."

"Oh really? What sort of work?"

Christine felt herself sink a little. "Oh, you know. Admin. I don't really have any technical skills." She hated admitting that she'd never actually needed a career because Evan had had one for her.

"We might be able to help. We have an office up in Dorchester, on a little business park. I know some of the people there. I'll ask around."

"Oh. Thank you."

They ate for a while, before Janet began asking Ryan more questions about school.

"What are you studying?" she asked, seemingly genuinely interested.

"Sociology, psychology and..." He paused to wipe his lips with his napkin, something Christine had never seen him do before without prompting. "Politics."

"Politics?" Janet eyed her husband, who gave a little snort. "Now there's a dangerous dinner-party topic these days." But she failed to take her own advice. "Tell me, what are your views on everything that's going on?"

Ryan still looked confident. "What things?"

"Oh, you know – Brexit. And Mr Trump over in America. I suppose you're against them all, being so young?"

Christine felt uncomfortable as she sensed Rodney Slaughter's attention shift onto her son. Ryan seemed to feel the pressure too, reluctant to express his own view. "The politics teacher I had before," Ryan began, "he used to go on about Brexit all the time. That it was this giant con." He stopped, smiling, but this wasn't enough for Rodney Slaughter.

"I hope you're smart enough to make up your own mind?"

"I think so."

"Because the real con was where unelected Euro bureaucrats tricked us into giving up our sovereignty, when we'd only signed up for a loose trade deal."

There was silence.

"You don't believe me?" He turned, and for some reason began talking directly to Christine.

"I didn't say..."

"But that's what's you *think*. It's rather obvious from your face."

Christine was shocked. She tried to reset whatever expression she was wearing.

"Oh, come now. They talk about the snowflake generation. But surely you can't be offended by simply learning the truth?"

Christine felt herself becoming a little angry. "I'm not offended. I'm just surprised you've assumed what my views are."

"Oh? Am I wrong?" He smiled. "What are your views?" He leaned back in his chair.

Feeling attacked, Christine drew herself taller in her seat. "Well, I don't think we ever did lose our sovereignty, if you really must know."

"What about the euro?" Rodney fired back without hesitation. "If you lot had your way, we'd have joined in 2000 and then the country would be bankrupt. We'd be just like the Greeks."

Christine hesitated. Although she had been able to parrot the gist of her husband's strongly held view that leaving the European Union was the height of stupidity, she didn't really understand the complexities of it herself. The truth was, she didn't really care. "Well, the Germans have the euro. They seem to do all right."

"Hear, hear!" Janet Slaughter raised her glass. "Well said, Christine. But maybe this is a topic for another day?" She stared meaningfully at her husband. He bristled visibly but turned back to Ryan.

"Well, I hope they'll teach you more sense down here. That's all." He went back to eating his food in moody silence.

. . .

Half an hour later they'd finished both the main course, and dessert: chocolate pie, specially chosen for Molly, apparently. The conversation had never recovered, and by now Molly was yawning. It gave Christine the excuse she needed to take her daughter back next door to bed.

As soon as they were inside, Ryan took himself to his room and Christine heard his games console switching on. She put Molly to bed, staying with her while she cleaned her teeth. When she came back upstairs, she deliberately left the lights off.

Opposite her, in the Slaughters' house, it was obvious an argument was going on. Janet was angrily waving her arms at Rodney, who was standing still, only occasionally answering her back. Finally he shrugged off his wife's anger and poured himself another glass of wine before carrying it downstairs and out of view, leaving Janet yelling silently at his departing back.

Janet turned to the window and her eyes looked directly towards where Christine was standing, hiding in the dark. Christine sucked in her breath in shock and horror, until she realised Janet couldn't see her after all. She was only staring into the darkness outside, her eyes heavy with tears.

TWENTY-THREE

On the Sunday, Christine took the children on a day out, leaving early with the hope of getting to know the area where they now lived. She buried any thought there might be another reason, that she simply didn't feel comfortable in her own house while it was so overlooked by the Slaughters. But she wondered about the obvious tension in the couple's marriage. It was understandable, given all they'd been through. She made a mental note that she would search Google later on to find out how often couples stayed together after the loss of a child.

It felt good to get away. They drove west, breakfasting in one of the roadside diners that cater to the flow of tourists in the area, then stopped at Weymouth, where there seemed no danger of seeing anyone they knew from Lulworth. The weather was good and they walked on the sandy beach, watching a fleet of windsurfers zooming in and out. Later on they ate fish and chips, Molly throwing the scraps to a gang of seagulls who got so close to her that she ended up shrieking and running away. For a day they had, perhaps, the kind of time that Christine had imagined when she'd pictured the Lulworth cliff-top house, back when it had only been an idea on a computer screen.

But then, all too soon, they had to return there.

When they got back it was getting dark, not just outside but in the Slaughters' house too, at least allowing Christine into her living room without feeling that her every move was being watched. She put Molly to bed, knocked on Ryan's door and warned him not to stay up too late, then flicked through the TV channels until she found something undemanding. Then she pulled her laptop in front of her and began to search.

As she typed, the computer's auto-complete accurately guessed her question, giving her that alarming but not unfamiliar sensation that technology was somehow tapping into her thoughts.

How many parents stay together after the death of a child?

When the first result claimed the figure was just sixteen percent, Christine's heart bucked, but she soon realised she was reading it wrong. It was the reverse: just sixteen percent of parents actually separated, citing the death of their child as the reason. The article was titled: *The myth of divorce following the death of a child.* This comforted Christine a little, although she wasn't sure why it suddenly seemed to matter to her.

But what about after a *violent* death, she wondered. Surely that made a difference? She replaced the word *death* in her search with *murder* but ended up with nearly the same set of results: it appeared there weren't any specific webpages that looked at divorce rates following the murder of a child. Well – perhaps it simply wasn't common enough. That was a good thing, surely? But then she scanned further down and found that a couple of pages *were* different. They weren't about murder specifically, but talked about a child's death where one parent was to blame. She began reading a story of a man who'd lost his son. She quickly knew she shouldn't carry on, but by then it was too late.

He'd been with his ten-year-old boy while his wife was at the hospital for a routine check-up. About to cross a road, the boy had run out without looking, stepping into the path of a car. The man described that what happened next was the most horrible sound he'd ever heard. The screech of the brakes, the scream from his son, the crunch of the impact, and then the silence, before more screaming from his son which at first he took to mean that the child was only injured. But then the article described how the man had picked him up, only for the boy to go limp and quiet as he died in his arms.

Christine had to look away, her eyes filling with tears. She composed herself and read on. The man had told his wife at the hospital what had happened, and expected, what? Sympathy? It wasn't clear, but he hadn't been prepared for the tsunami of rage and hatred she threw at him. He hadn't only suffered a bereavement, but he'd been blamed for it. His conclusion, which Christine read through full-blown tears, was that a couple separating after the death of a child in such circumstances wasn't an inevitability, but it was very likely, unless their relationship was unusually strong.

Christine broke away and wiped her eyes. She glanced through the window at the still-dark house opposite and was again grateful the Slaughters weren't home. She wondered whether either of them had been in any way to blame. She realised she still didn't know the full details of what had actually happened. For a few seconds the idea of googling it felt distasteful. But only for a few seconds. She typed another search.

The murder of...

Again, Google knew her mind before her fingers could type it out, auto-filling *Emily Slaughter*. Christine wondered which computer boffin was responsible for this – did they somehow know she lived next to a murder victim? Did so many neighbours in her position end up searching for details of the murder next door that her computer was able to guess what she was searching for just from the word *murder*? She was distracted from pursuing this thought by the search results, mostly newspaper articles, many from the local paper, but also plenty from the nationals. She picked the *Guardian,* Evan had always said it was the most trustworthy.

Suspect and Two Officers Die in Lulworth Cove Murder Shootout

Two police officers were killed on Saturday night, along with a man suspected of being involved in the abduction and murder of an eight-year-old girl, in an explosion and gun battle near the Dorset village of Lulworth. Another police officer also injured.

The incident, which is under investigation by the Independent Office for Police Conduct (IOPC), followed a short stand-off with the man who is believed to be responsible for the murder of eight-year-old Emily Slaughter.

The cause of the explosion is not yet known, but it's believed the suspect first opened fire on one armed officer, and then attempted to do the same when a second officer went to assist his colleague, leading to a barrage of gunfire which killed the suspect, but also triggered a large explosion.

Police suspect the man, a 43-year-old named Michael Sopley who was living in sheltered accommodation at a nearby refuge, was responsible for the abduction of the girl, known locally as Emy, from her home, and her subsequent murder. Emy Slaughter's body was found on the beach in the popular visitor spot of Lulworth Cove.

Detective Inspector John Lindham of the South West Murder Investigation Unit said in a statement that the suspect was being sought following strong evidence of his involvement in the murder. "He was located in a nearby farmyard where he had

stolen a firearm. Despite attempts to talk him down, he opened fire first and officers had no choice but to respond."
The officers who died have not yet been named.

Christine found many more about the farmyard incident, but frustratingly there was little about what happened at the house. The reason, she decided, was down to the timing. The murder happened just days before the country was thrown into chaos by the pandemic outbreak. The police had issued statements about what happened at the farmyard – the names of the dead police officers and so on – but they hadn't released much about the murder of the girl. And with the pandemic consuming everything, the papers hadn't given it the attention it would normally have deserved.

There were still plenty of articles about the murder, but the details were sparse. She still felt like she needed more information. Then she saw the comments open under an article from the local newspaper's website. She felt a strong temptation to continue down the page and look through them, but then a stronger pang of guilt for feeling tempted. It was because of Evan. One of his pet hates was the comments below newspaper articles. It was a strange obsession for a man who was usually so calm and in control, but it was there nonetheless. He would often rail loudly about the "idiots" who commented, and he condemned the people who read them as no better than those who'd written them in the first place. Christine's standard reaction was to avoid them.

But then Evan was dead.

Still feeling his disapproving eyes watching over her, she scrolled through the messages without really reading them properly. They were mostly expressions of sympathy. Christine felt a wash of relief – what else had she been expecting? But as she scrolled further down, another theme slowly became apparent. Criticism of the parents. Firstly, for how they'd failed to secure the house properly – as if their daughter being taken from the house while they were in it was somehow proof that they were to blame. But more than that, there was a clear idea circulating in the comments space that there was something more to it. A lot of people thought the Slaughters weren't telling the whole story. The final comment, before she had to click to a new page, summed it up:

I don't believe that homeless guy could have broken into a brand-new house like that. No way. I reckon Rodney Slaughter did it.

TWENTY-FOUR

The next day, soon after Christine had arrived home after dropping Molly at school, the doorbell rang. It was Janet Slaughter, a large bunch of flowers in her arms.

"I tried to catch you yesterday but you were out," she said.

"Oh. Yes, we had a day out. In Weymouth."

"Oh, it's lovely there." For a moment it seemed like Janet might launch into a long discussion on the pros and cons of the nearby town, but she steeled herself, holding out the flowers. "These are for you. To apologise."

"Whatever for?"

"For Saturday night. It was awkward. Rodney was in a bad mood. He gets like that sometimes."

Christine considered saying that she hadn't noticed. But in the end she stayed quiet.

"May I come in?"

She wanted to say no, but she couldn't, not after the effort Janet had made. She forced a smile and opened the door wider. "I'll put some coffee on."

"Bloody Brexit, hey?" Janet sighed once they were settled in Christine's kitchen. "Something about it seems to appeal to men of a certain age. Gammons, isn't it? What they say? I think it connects with their fear of impotency."

Christine smiled weakly.

"But it was completely wrong of him to speak to you like that. And I want to apologise because *he* probably won't. He's so used to arguing with me."

"You don't agree with him?"

Janet shrugged. "One die-hard Remainer, one fervent Brexiteer. You wouldn't think it possible that a couple could have opposing views and still live together. But there you are."

Christine relaxed a little at this. She opened the cupboard where her vases were kept.

"He's actually not one of the crazy ones," Janet went on. "The problem is, at work, we have to comply with a load of regulations that come from Brussels, and many of them genuinely don't make much sense for British buildings." She raised her eyebrows. "In my view the benefits of getting rid of them have been outdone by the chaos that's been unleashed over the past three years. But I do understand the argument at least." She paused, and her tone changed. She glanced at Christine. "But actually, I think there was more to his mood than politics."

Christine was setting the flowers in the vase by now, cutting each stem one by one. She stopped.

"You've probably gathered that he wasn't exactly one hundred percent keen on the idea of splitting up the house? He's still getting used to it. Evidently."

Christine frowned. "How do you mean?"

"I don't want to make you feel guilty," Janet continued. "This is your home, and you're totally welcome here. I'm just trying to explain. Here, let me..." Janet moved past Christine before she had a chance to object and took over the job of filling the vase. Christine turned to make coffee.

"You see, this house has been his project, his passion. For

years," Janet said, frowning as she worked. "We first bought the plot ten years ago, and now he knows every... every brick, every screw that's gone into it. Not that anyone's allowed to see the bricks." She turned and smiled. "And we put everything into it, financially I mean. We put it all on the line. And then to get so close to bloody finishing it, only for there to be a global pandemic that crashed the economy. I mean, what are the chances?" She gave an airy laugh. "There!" She stood back from the completed vase, as if expecting Christine to praise her.

"What actually happened?" Christine said after a few moments of quiet. "With the house. If you don't mind me asking?"

"No. No I don't mind at all." Janet took a sip of the coffee that Christine handed to her. "Mmmm. Thank you." She set the cup down on the table. "It's a simple case of greed really. The money for this place was all dependent on other projects that Rodney had invested in. In normal times they would have worked, but with Covid they were all cancelled. And when they failed, the bank demanded repayment on the loans we had on this house. If we didn't pay, they'd take it." She shrugged. "We had a choice. It was either sell half the house or lose the whole thing."

"Did they not...?" Christine hesitated. "I mean your daughter had just... just *died*. Did they not take that into consideration?"

"You'd think so, wouldn't you? But no. It's all done by computers these days. No humans involved to apply compassion or any understanding of exceptional circumstances. No. We did try to argue that, but there wasn't a box to put it in. It didn't fit the forms."

"That's awful," Christine said.

"It is. But that's what I'm saying. You saved us where the bank didn't. And I'm sure Rodney will come to understand that in the end. It might just take him a little time."

Christine thought for a moment. She saw Rodney Slaughter in his car, Miss Juniper sitting primly and smugly in the passenger seat. She blinked the image away. That was none of her business. "What did happen with Emy? Do you mind me asking that?"

Janet was slower to answer this. "There's not that much to say really. She was a beautiful and kind girl. She always will be. She was just in the wrong place at the wrong time. We all were."

"She was taken from the house?" Christine took a sip of her drink, carefully watching the other woman as she replied.

"Yes." Janet drew in a breath. "I know I owe it to you to explain." She spent a few moments composing herself before going on. "It was a Friday evening, and we'd just moved in, even though the house was only half finished. There was a politician friend of Rodney's – I think he's the mayor of somewhere – he'd helped with some of the paperwork for the planning application, and we were having him and his wife to dinner. Just as a thank you. And Emy was a little poorly, so I put her to bed early." She stopped and Christine could see that her words were bringing that awful night flooding back.

"The police don't think we'll ever get the full details. Not now the man is dead. But it seems he had a history of breaking into houses. They think he'd been watching the house for days. He broke in through Emy's bedroom door. He used chloroform, which means she was unconscious – that's something. They think she might never have woken up at all. They think he probably broke in after we'd gone to bed. He was a locksmith, an expert at picking locks, it was just..." She stopped suddenly and Christine saw that her hands were shaking.

"I feel like a terrible, terrible mother. And Rodney too. He feels he failed to protect her."

"Oh, but you're not," Christine said at once. "It was..." She wasn't sure how she intended to finish the sentence. "There was nothing you could have done." She didn't know if she believed that.

"Thank you.". Janet held up her shaking hands "The police were understanding. They said it's just awful, terrible luck. A one-in-a-million case. But I still wake up some days and feel like killing myself."

The suddenness and starkness of the admission stunned Christine into silence. She had no doubt that Janet meant it literally.

"I won't, I won't. You don't have to worry about that." Janet smiled now. "It's not what Emy would have wanted. She loved life." Janet suddenly shuddered. "Oh. This is too morbid. Let's talk of happier things?" But then before she followed her own advice she went on. "You do know he's gone, don't you? You do understand that? The man who killed Emy is dead and gone and he can't do anything like this ever again. We'd never have let you move in here if that wasn't the case. You wouldn't be here if there was the slightest risk to Molly. She's quite safe here."

"Yes, of course," Christine said a moment later. But the conversation left her feeling just a little dizzy. Until that very moment, it hadn't really occurred to her that Molly might be in danger. Without meaning to, however, Janet Slaughter had just planted that seed. Not so much that it was in plain sight and impossible to ignore, but deep enough that it would inevitably take root.

TWENTY-FIVE

Christine didn't sleep well again. Her mind dwelled on the hand she'd been dealt in life and the choices she'd made with it. Eventually she reached for her phone, and the screen – too bright in the darkness – told her it was 2am. She flicked it off and tried to sleep again, but only grew wider awake. Eventually she gave up and got out of bed.

She padded up the stairs in the darkness so as not to risk waking Molly and Ryan by turning on the light. The house was cool and the night clear, with a bright moon. When she reached the main room she saw it, hanging again above the water, its reflection almost perfect below. She quickly checked the Slaughters' house to ensure that Rodney wasn't lurking opposite, and then stood at the huge window looking out over the ocean. She drank in the beauty of it all.

After a while she was drawn to her laptop. She returned to the local newspaper articles about the crime, this time reading every one of the hundreds of comments. The ghost of Evan might still have been watching over her shoulder, but now it was easier to ignore.

A detailed reading revealed a more complex range of opinions. Many had posted to leave their condolences for the two policemen who'd died in the shootout. Many expressed their horror that such a young girl had been killed with her whole life ahead of her. But again, it didn't take too long to find other ideas. The refuge where the killer – Michael Sopley – had been living was a place called St Austells. Christine was shocked to learn it was just a few miles away. It was singled out again and again as a destination for dangerous criminals who were being brought into the area at great risk to local residents. But once again it wasn't hard to find a thread that blamed the parents.

Christine got the sense that many of the anonymous authors had had a problem with the Slaughters even before their daughter was killed. They talked of corruption in obtaining planning permission and their arrogance in building such a house. Many criticised them for allowing Sopley access to their daughter – how could they not have heard this murdering madman breaking in? Only a few blamed the Slaughters more directly, a mere handful of posters doubting the official police explanation for the killing, and accusing Rodney Slaughter instead.

It would have been easier to dismiss them as the rantings of thoughtless idiots in the bright light of day, but far harder at three in the morning in the knowledge that Rodney Slaughter was sleeping just a dozen or so metres from where she sat. It was even more difficult when she suddenly realised he wasn't asleep at all, for at that moment a light suddenly went on in the Slaughters' living room and Rodney was padding barefoot across the floor.

When she saw him, Christine thought for a second she was only imagining it, or hallucinating. Particularly because, this time, Rodney Slaughter was naked. She stared for a second, too shocked to react, then quickly slammed shut her laptop so the light from its screen wouldn't alert Rodney to the fact that she was up. There she stayed, crouching low on the sofa and watching her neighbour through the glass.

He drank a glass of tap water – his lower half thankfully hidden from view – but then walked over to the window as Christine had done earlier. He stayed there a while, side on, just watching the water. The thick darkness of his pubic hair was just visible. Then he began stretching, reaching up towards the tall ceiling and turning towards her. Suddenly, his penis was impossible to ignore. Although it was flaccid and flopped rather pathetically from side to side, it was still large.

When he'd finished stretching, he turned away and pulled out several items from a cabinet. He unrolled a mat on the floor, then – mercifully – he dressed in white robes, tying a black knotted belt around his waist. Then he picked up a third item. Christine gasped as she saw that it was a sword, an actual *sword*, housed in a scabbard. He stood with his feet wide apart, and very slowly withdrew the blade from its cover. Christine was completely unfamiliar with weapons, but to her it looked Eastern in origin, its curved blade gleaming and almost glowing in the dim light. He handled it reverentially, both hands wrapped around its elaborate handle. He stood carefully on his mat, holding the sword out in front of him. Then he slowly drew it behind him, and, in a sudden movement, rendered silent by the glass between them, he slashed the blade through the air.

For twenty minutes, Rodney Slaughter barely stopped. He was clearly expert at whatever sport or art-form this was, and his arms and the silver blade barely slowed down. He performed thrust after thrust, parry after defensive block as he stepped back and forth across the mat, and ducked up and down with the sword. It looked like something between fighting an invisible army and performing some kind of dance. But even though he seemed expert, there was something about his movement, a stiffness and an expression on his face, that gave the impression he wasn't entirely satisfied.

After a while, it occurred to Christine that she ought to take a photograph – evidence – and that triggered her into considering just *what* it was she was watching. It was the middle of the night, and he was fighting with a sword, less than a year after his daughter had been brutally murdered. Was that evidence? Christine searched her mind for how Emy had been killed – what weapon had been used? In the end she didn't dare to take a photo in case the phone operated the flash.

Finally, Rodney Slaughter bowed to the window – which gave Christine the unnerving sense that he was bowing at her. Then he returned to the table where he'd left the scabbard and carefully slid the sword back into it. He drank more water, then left, turning off the lights in the living room. For a second the house opposite was dark, and then a new light went on downstairs, in a room which – assuming the Slaughters' house was arranged similarly to Christine's – must be one of the bathrooms.

If Christine found it hard to sleep before, it was impossible now.

TWENTY-SIX

The rest of that night Christine sunk into a state of semi-sleep where the same ideas chased round and round her head. The first was that she would sell the house. As soon as she awoke, she would put it on the market. It would sell, surely it would sell. After all, when she'd bought it the estate agent had been adamant that if she didn't agree to pay the asking price at once, she'd certainly lose her chance. And yet she now suspected this had been a lie. Indeed, she'd probably known at the time, but she'd wanted the house anyway. She'd wanted to believe it was true. But surely it *was* true up to a point? *She'd* wanted to buy the house therefore, surely *someone else* would. Even if she had to sell at a loss?

But then she worried about how it would look. How would she explain to Sarah, her sister up in York, that her crazy plan had failed – just as Sarah had said it would? And how would she explain to any potential buyers that she was selling just weeks after moving in? Worse still, what would she say to Janet? That she couldn't live next to a Brexiteer? She certainly couldn't tell her that she suspected her husband was responsible for Emy's murder.

But was that *really* what she was thinking? Could that be true? Could a father do such a thing? She'd read enough stories in the newspaper to know he could.

By the time she finally fell asleep she'd decided the house had been a mistake. Just because they had enjoyed one holiday there as a family, it didn't mean they could live there. The very idea was crazy. She would sell. She would make some excuse about how the children weren't settling in properly and get away as fast as she could. She didn't know where they'd go. She didn't much care. Only that they would get away. They had to get away.

Her alarm woke her, and for a few moments she was unaware of the churning of her exhausted mind and just craved more sleep. But then it all came back to her – the sight of Rodney Slaughter padding around naked with his weird exercise with the sword; her plan to move. And despite a terrible weariness, she pushed herself up. She would get started right away. She would break the news to the children and then it would be done. She dressed quickly and went upstairs.

Unusually, both Molly and Ryan were up in the kitchen helping themselves to breakfast. As Christine came up the stairs, she heard the beautiful sound of her daughter laughing.

"What's up?" she asked without thinking, then regretted it, since it cut the laughter off at once.

"Ryan's telling me jokes," Molly said, giving him a knowing look.

"What jokes?" Christine asked.

Molly didn't answer but bit her lip.

"Jokes he's not supposed to tell you? Grown-up jokes?"

Molly giggled. "No," she said, but then she nodded as well. She risked a glance at her brother, but then broke down in a fit of mirth that sent cereal and milk dribbling down her chin. Christine turned to Ryan. "Nice to see you up this early."

He shrugged. "I've got early classes. I made you a coffee though. I was about to take it down to you." He stepped back from the worktop to reveal a mug full of creamy foam which he held out to her. Christine took it from him, almost speechless.

"Oh, Mum," Ryan added, his voice casual now. "I kind of need some money."

She felt herself being led almost automatically down a path that was well-trodden for both of them. "What for?"

"It's nothing *bad*." He read her face. "It's just there're a couple of guys at the school. They do surfing. After school and stuff. They said I should join them. One of them's even got a board I can borrow, and he's gonna teach me. But I need a wetsuit."

A prickle of memory crept into Christine's mind. *How did this fit with selling the house?* She took a breath, about to tell him, but it was like they were on a pre-set course. She couldn't alter the direction of the conversation. "Well, how much are we talking?"

"That's the problem. You can get cheap ones, but Mark said it's not worth it, they don't keep you warm properly. You need to spend at least..." He paused, and Christine waited. "Two hundred quid?"

"Who's Mark?" Christine asked, and her son looked at her curiously. "He's a friend. I told you about him."

Christine felt thoughts and emotions scrambling together inside her tired mind. Should she tell them now she was going to sell the house? Should she tell them at all? In the light of day, with her children so relaxed and happy in front of her, she realised this was one part of the plan she hadn't really decided on. Maybe in her head she had got as far as taking them to her sister's. But, in reality, she was a long way from that.

"I've still got some savings left from my job..." Ryan continued, oblivious to the chaos in his mother's mind. He had worked part-time in a coffee shop before the pandemic, before his father's death. Before she had dragged him here to start a new life. He had already started looking for a job, but there wasn't anything nearby.

"It is why we came down here in the first place," Ryan went on. He looked confused now, perhaps not understanding his mother's silence. "To make the most of the outdoors and everything." He waited.

"Of course," Christine suddenly heard herself saying. "Of course we can get you a wetsuit."

"Cool." He spoke with rare enthusiasm in his voice, and it was a beautiful sound. She took a sip from her coffee, only now understanding it was a bribe. But she smiled inwardly. There was no doubt she loved her son. She would forgive him anything.

"Thanks, Mum," he said. And, for the first time in ages, Christine and her son smiled together. The idea of selling the house, or at least its immediacy, melted away.

"We can go over to Poole at the weekend. I saw there's a couple of surf shops there. I expect they'll have something." She warmed to the idea as she spoke. They could grab lunch too. Maybe get something for Molly.

"No, it's cool. I've already found one online. I just need your card and stuff, to pay for it."

"Oh." Christine blinked, but she kept her smile. That was how things happened these days.

TWENTY-SEVEN

The Slaughter House – or Houses – were not the only buildings on the small bluff that overlooked Lulworth Cove. A dozen older and more traditional homes were also spread out along the clifftop, many part-hidden behind high walls and obscured by tree cover. When Christine had first arrived, she'd assumed most were let out as holiday homes, but since moving in she'd noticed that the cars parked outside a few of them didn't change, suggesting they had more settled residents. A few days later – when Molly was safely in school and Ryan away in college – Christine felt driven to investigate further.

She pulled open the front door carefully, just a crack at first, to see whether there was any risk of bumping into either of the Slaughters, particularly Rodney. But when she saw his Audi wasn't in their parking lot, she relaxed a little, but still hurried to get out of view of the house.

The next building along from the Slaughters' was a large but traditional building. The garden was well tended and a pair of expensive cars stood in the driveway. She tried to peer in the windows for a glimpse of who might live there, but though presumably someone was at home, she couldn't see anything. She kept walking.

The next two properties had the look of holiday homes. They were both smaller, and neither had any cars in attendance. She walked past, gazing at them curiously and wishing she had bought one of these instead, giving her just a little more space to get out of the Slaughters' shadow. Then she saw a figure in the next house along, working in the garden. It was a woman, elderly, her back slightly stooped. She was doing something to a rose bush; Christine didn't know what since she knew nothing of gardening. But it made it clear she lived there rather than being a guest. Christine decided to be brave. She had to introduce herself. She moved closer.

There was a long-distance footpath, the South West Coast path, that ran around Dorset's coastline. All Christine knew about it was that the Slaughters' and her plot blocked the path from hugging the cliff edge itself; instead, it followed the road she was now walking on. And clearly this woman was used to seeing walkers following the path, and was equally used to ignoring them or pretending they didn't exist. When Christine approached with what she hoped was a casual introduction ready on her lips, the woman abruptly turned her back and started hacking at some greenery. The words that Christine had prepared froze in her mouth, and as she turned away her face begin to glow hot with humiliation. She found herself pretending she hadn't been about to stop, in case anyone else was watching, But then, thinking how ridiculous that was, she turned around again. "Excuse me!" she called in a cheery voice.

The woman turned, as if caught out. She frowned at Christine. "Yes?"

"Oh hello!" Christine forced a smile. "I've just moved in down the road and I wanted to say hi." The words came out a little fast, but at least she'd said them. She felt a moment's worry that she might have misjudged the woman after all, as she continued to frown at the interruption. But then her expression changed to one of suspicious interest.

"The second of the Slaughter Houses?"

Christine brightened. "Yes. That's right."

"Oh." The old woman still looked far from friendly. "I saw the removals lorry back in the summer. I supposed someone had moved in."

"That's right."

A shadow crossed the woman's face, but then she begrudgingly softened her expression. "I'm Agnes. Welcome to Dungy Head."

"Christine," said Christine. "And if you see my children, they're Molly and Ryan. Eight and seventeen."

Agnes went back to frowning, as if she didn't approve of children, not near her house anyway. "Well, I haven't seen them. But if I do, I suppose I'll know who they are."

Christine smiled at Agnes. She wondered about inviting her for coffee, a neighbourly chat, but didn't dare. And before she could speak again the woman beat her to it.

"I say, since you're here, you haven't come across my cat have you?"

The change of tack caught Christine by surprise. "No."

"She's normally very reliable but..." Agnes seemed much more interested in this topic than in the fact she had a new near-neighbour. "She's a bit of an explorer you see. She didn't come in last night and it just occurred to me that maybe she was investigating new people." There was a clear, disapproving edge to the way she said "new people", but Christine pushed this thought away. Not least because she *had* seen a cat, in the courtyard between her house and the Slaughters.

"A tabby cat?"

"A mackerel tabby?" The old woman stood up straighter. "With a blue collar? Yes, that's Luna. Have you seen her?"

"Oh." Christine had no idea what a mackerel tabby was,

and now she tried to think about it she couldn't remember seeing a collar at all. "I think so. I definitely saw a cat, but it was a couple of days ago."

There was disappointment on Agnes' face. She bent over again. "A couple of days ago? Well, that's no good. She was here yesterday morning."

Christine wasn't sure how to react to what sounded like criticism, so she stayed quiet. The old woman seemed too caught up in her own concerns to be aware of the offence she'd caused.

"Oh dear. Well, I'm sure she'll turn up."

Agnes let the frown on her face fade slowly away. There was a long silence. "You know, some of the people around here aren't entirely delighted with what they've built," she said eventually. "The Slaughters, I mean."

Christine didn't know how to reply to this either, but she felt pressure to say something. "Why not?"

"Well, it's rather large, isn't it?" Agnes said, as if Christine had somehow not noticed. "But I don't suppose that's your fault. It was meant to be all one house. I suppose that would have been slightly better..."

Christine didn't like the direction the conversation was going, and decided to change it. "What are the other neighbours like?" she asked, trying to not lace the question with the implication that Agnes herself wasn't rating too highly so far. At the same time, she still hoped Agnes might tell her that the neighbours often got together, popping in and out of each other's homes like they were the best of friends.

"Oh, you know. Most of them are second homes. There are only a few of us along here now. And with Covid..." She stopped, then took a step back, as if just remembering. "I have health conditions. I'm shielding. I don't mean to seem unfriendly." She gave a grim-faced look and it crossed Christine's mind that she very much *did* mean it. Agnes was clearly using Covid as cover for her general predisposition to dislike other people.

When she turned to prune the bush again – or whatever it was she was doing – it was clear the conversation was over. Christine smiled a lukewarm goodbye then went on her way. But only a few more houses were spread out along the clifftop before the road ended, and she didn't see anyone in the windows or gardens. The route continued only as the cliff-top walk, which she followed, taken in again by the majesty of the view. It was a beautiful walk, with the late-summer sun softened by mist over a lazy sea, and the bramble bushes heavy with berries. The path stayed high but showed glimpses down the slipping cliff-face to the beach below. There were sections of it, ledges, that looked impossible to reach, and were probably untouched by humanity. In fact, the whole landscape looked entirely natural, except for a few signs here and there that proved otherwise – bright orange fishing buoys, tumbledown stone walls. It was so different from the environment that surrounded her in London, and for a while she was able to lose herself within it – as if her troubles had been left at the point where the collection of cliff-top houses stopped and the cliff path began.

It was over an hour later when she walked back past Agnes' house, and by then her legs were tired and she was hungry. The old woman had finished whatever she was doing to the rose bushes and was nowhere to be seen. But there was one change. A telegraph pole that stuck up from the grass verge in front of her house now had a small white poster on it, the sort printed out on a home computer. There was a photograph of a grey tabby cat with a blue collar, with the word LOST written in bold above it.

TWENTY-EIGHT

"We found blood! Lots of blood!" Molly and her new friend Daisy came rushing back into the house where Christine was talking with Daisy's mother. The two women looked at each other, instant alarm written across their faces. They both got up.

The playdate had been unexpected. Christine had been on Facebook when a message came in from a name she didn't recognise – Katie Rogers. She soon realised she was the mother of the girl Molly had talked about in her class, Daisy. And very kindly, she was inviting Molly – and Christine too – for a playdate after school. Christine had eagerly accepted, but then Katie's husband had unexpectedly needed to work from home and needed peace and quiet to do so – not two eight-year-olds running around yelling. Hence Katie had asked, sounding a little abashed, if they could possibly move the location to Christine's new house. This wasn't quite as good for Christine, for reasons she didn't want to admit to her new potential friend. But without an obvious better option, she agreed.

It had gone well up to the point when the girls ran in yelling about blood. It had turned out that Katie was a "fly-in" too, the term she used to describe people who had moved to the

Purbecks rather than being born and bred here. And from the way she talked, she well understood the difficulty the fly-ins had making friends, particularly in the craziness of these Covid times. But there was a nosiness in Katie's chat which made Christine suspicious that it had been her plan all along to get an invite to her home and see what it was like.

"Blood?" Katie Rogers repeated. Christine found she couldn't speak. The girls had been playing downstairs in Molly's room. How could there be blood?

"*Yes,* Mummy. It's outside." Daisy Rogers grabbed her mother's hand and dragged her towards the door. Christine followed behind, anxious and uncertain. And as they descended the stairs, she realised that Molly had opened the sliding door in her bedroom. She immediately blamed Ryan: he'd complained of a lack of air in his bedroom and Christine had reluctantly shown him where she'd hidden the keys to all the downstairs doors. He must have told Molly. When they got outside, the two girls led them to the low wall that bordered the Slaughters' side of the property and the slope that led down to the cove, a mix of bramble patches and grass kept short by the rabbits.

"Here!" Daisy and Molly stood proudly back as their mothers inspected the patch of grass. It did look as though they were right. A small area of the ground was stained black-red with a substance that couldn't really be anything other than blood.

"Oh," Katie Rogers said. "Well, it's probably a fox."

"Where?" said Daisy. "I can't see a fox."

"I mean it's probably a fox that's..." She glanced at Christine as if this were an unfortunate but inevitable aspect of parenting with inquisitive children. "A fox that's eaten something. It's what foxes do. But anyway, you should leave it alone."

"And Molly, I told you to stay in the house." Molly interrupted her to say it had been Daisy's idea, leaving Christine lost for words. "Well," she went on, after an awkward second or two. "Well. *Now* can you stay inside the house, please? You've got plenty of toys." She led them all away, glancing back at the patch of blood and noting how close it was to the door that led through into the Slaughters' half of the courtyard. It probably was just a fox, she told herself, but she wasn't entirely convinced.

It played on her mind as the playdate dragged on. And when the Rogers went home, with promises that they must do it all again, but at Katie's home next time, it was still playing on Christine's mind. Molly had a mild tantrum, part over-tiredness, part disappointment, that Daisy's suggestion of extending the playdate into a sleepover had been rebuffed so comprehensively. She'd never had a sleepover, but Daisy, it seemed, enjoyed them regularly, and Daisy's mother had seemed open to the idea. But the problem – Christine decided – was that *if* the blood was from a fox's kill, then where was the victim? Would a fox have eaten the whole thing, leaving nothing left? Or did foxes drag their meals back to their lairs? It occurred to Christine that the only real source of information she had on fox behaviour was from half-watched children's TV programmes. And since the foxes she visualised from these wore trousers and a waistcoat, she doubted it was an accurate impression.

Later on, she again found it hard to sleep. She had a nagging suspicion that the patch of blood outside wasn't something she should simply ignore, and might be some sort of clue to explain Rodney Slaughter's behaviour. And from there, it wasn't much of a leap to realise that, as a potentially valuable piece of evidence, it should be preserved. Once this idea had become established, she found herself visualising how she was going to achieve it – by photographing the patch with her mobile phone, even by taking a sample of the blood. She could do this by wearing washing-up gloves and scraping some of the blood-soaked earth into a plastic bag. It wouldn't be pleasant, but she could do it, though her courage didn't stretch to going outside in the dark. She would do it first thing in the morning.

There was an advantage to finding it hard to drop off to sleep. When she did finally drift away, she didn't wake in the early hours as she'd done so often in recent nights. Indeed, she actually slept in a little, so the next morning was a rush to get everything ready. Finally she had Molly strapped into the car, wearing her school shoes and carrying her bag with her break-time snack, reading book and water bottle. She pressed the button to start the ignition, at which point Christine realised she'd quite forgotten her plan to capture the evidence.

And her mind made a sudden connection.

Waiting by the open gates to the shared parking area was a large plastic wheelie bin which belonged to the Slaughters. She knew this was the day the council came to collect the rubbish, but when she'd left her own bin out the night before, the Slaughters' bin hadn't been there. Now it was, and Christine *knew* she had to check it. She *knew* it was connected in some way to the patch of blood that Molly had found.

She checked Molly was still strapped in and told her to wait where she was before getting out of the car and quietly closing the door. As she was about to lift up the bin's lid, she heard the Slaughters' front door opening. She snatched her hand away and moved back to her car as fast as she could. The door opened fully and Janet Slaughter stepped out, dressed in dark-blue jogging trousers with a pink sweat top and pink headband. She waved, called out cheerily and began a few stretching exercises on the front step.

There was no way Christine could check the bin while her neighbour was there, and she had no real reason to delay her departure. Molly would be late for school. She got in the car and drove away.

TWENTY-NINE

It was a ten-minute drive from the house to the school, but what with putting on her mask and walking Molly the last few hundred metres and then driving back again, it was nearly forty minutes later when Christine's car rolled back in through the open gates of the parking area. The bin, however, was still there.

Rodney Slaughter's white Audi was parked in its usual spot and the Slaughters' front door was shut, although Christine didn't know whether Janet was back from her run or not. She stopped the car and waited. Both houses had small windows overlooking the parking area, but they were high up, and, in her house at least, were designed to allow a little light inside rather than offering views. This meant that as long as no one came outside or arrived from the road, she'd be unseen while looking in the bin. This thought made her nervous, but she was determined.

After waiting a few seconds, she lifted the bin lid.

There was a smell. Not awful, but certainly unpleasant – the general smell of rubbish that had sat waiting to be collected. The council alternated between collecting recycling and refuse, so it would have been two weeks since the Slaughters' bin was last emptied. That probably explained why it was so full. There were tins of food and white plastic bags with plastic wrapping poking out of them, tied up by their handles. But there was nothing obviously *gruesome*. Nothing that explained the blood. She dropped the lid again and stepped back, feeling a rush of relief and – and what? Stupidity? A sense that she was losing her mind?

Something made her look again, however, just to be sure. And this time she began poking some of the bags out of the way, trying to see what, if anything, lurked deeper down. She lifted some of the items that were lying on top out of the bin completely and placed them on the floor by her feet. She panicked a little more with every bag she removed, knowing she could be discovered at any moment. But, as the little collection of rubbish at her feet grew larger, the smell grew worse. And then, halfway down the bin, she saw it.

At first it looked like the head from a broom, the bristles thick and stiff. But as she removed another bag, its side splitting slightly, the whole of the body was revealed. Its eyes were open, its mouth drawn back to reveal sharp, angry teeth. A neat cut had been made down towards the belly, and its internal organs were spilling out, bulbous tube shapes in pinks and purples. Christine stared in horror at the animal, unsure what it was. But then a snatch of a different colour caught her attention, a small piece of blue felt, and as her eyes focused on it, she saw it was a collar, the name tag still attached. *Luna*.

Christine had found Agnes Jones's missing cat.

THIRTY

Christine screamed, but quickly stifled it as she spun around to stare at the Slaughters' house. No one inside seemed to have heard or seen her. She felt her heart hammering in her chest and, before she knew it, she was scooping the bags of rubbish back into the bin, heaping them on top of the horrible corpse before anyone else saw what she'd seen. Before Rodney Slaughter knew that she *knew*.

Most of the bags held together as she stuffed them back, but one opened completely, spilling its contents out onto the gravel. Christine whimpered with fear and frustration, scrabbling to snatch up the loose pieces of rubbish.

A few minutes later it was all back inside and she flipped the bin's lid back down. She looked around, her eyes wild, her arms shaking with the adrenalin. All that was left were a few small stains on the ground, She glanced at the house – there was no sign that anyone had seen, but then she noticed something: a CCTV camera was secured high up, just under the roof line of the house, and it was pointing directly at her.

Had it always been there? If so, how come she'd never noticed it? And did it always point that way or could it have moved to show that someone inside was watching? Christine ran across the yard, but just as she was opening her front door, she heard Janet arriving back, calling out to her again. This time, Christine pretended not to hear and slammed the door shut behind her.

Inside, she sunk to the floor to catch her breath. She ran a hand through her hair, smearing it with slime from the rubbish. She let out a disgusted scream and pulled at her clothes, tearing them off on her way to the bathroom. At least here, in the lower half of the house, she wasn't overlooked. She let the hot water from the shower blast away the sticky residue from her hair and skin.

Half an hour later she poked her hand into a single rubber glove and used it to carry her clothes to the washing machine. Then she went to the kitchen and tried to decide what to do. Janet Slaughter was visible in the house opposite, sitting down, reading something on a tablet and sipping a coffee. Rodney was nowhere in sight, but Christine knew by now he was usually downstairs, in the room he used as an office. She suddenly felt how she must look, standing at her sink, staring across at their house. She reached for a glass and filled it with water but didn't trust herself to pull it to her lips; just moving it slightly sent globules of water spilling onto the tiled floor.

Murdering animals – as she knew from reading hundreds of thrillers and watching police dramas on television – was the classic behaviour of a psychopathic killer. She had to contact the police. There was no time to lose. As she was about to pick up her mobile, the doubts kicked in. What exactly was she going to do? Dial 999 and report a murdered cat? Then what? What did she think would happen? A parade of police cars coming to the house, eager to solve the crime of the decade? Was it even an actual crime to kill a cat? She had no idea. But it wasn't the cat she was worried about, it was what it *suggested* that worried her – that the internet crazies were right and the police had got the wrong man for the murder of Emy Slaughter. They'd blamed it on the homeless drifter when they should have been focusing on Emy's father, Rodney Slaughter.

There was no way to explain all that over the phone, not without sounding like one of the crazies herself. But perhaps in person, down at the police station. Perhaps she could explain it all there? And a dead cat – it *must* be some cause for concern. Surely they would take her seriously?

Without thinking further, she turned on her heel and walked to the hallway. She grabbed her keys from the table, but then stopped. She didn't even know where the police station was. Annoyed, she returned to the main room, pulled open her laptop and discovered that the closest station was in Dorchester, about ten miles away. She snatched her coat up again.

The police station was an ugly grey building on the outskirts of Dorchester. Christine parked in a visitor bay and made her way to the door. As she was about to step inside she realised she'd forgotten her mask. The irony of being arrested for not wearing a mask inside a police station added to the sudden weirdness of all this. But deciding her mission was surely more important than wearing a mask, she went inside.

A young woman police officer sat behind a counter protected by a thick glass screen. Two men stood in a socially distanced line marked out on the floor, waiting their turn. Christine felt sure her concern must trump theirs, but even so she impatiently joined the queue.

The first man began to explain his problem to the officer: a stolen bicycle. He was clearly frustrated she wasn't doing anything other than merely recording details of the crime, her face a mask of weary familiarity. Eventually the line moved forward, and Christine rehearsed what she would say in her mind.

The next man had less expectation of an actual police response. His phone had been stolen and he was simply after a crime number so he could claim for it. He was handed a yellow form and told to take his place on the other side, where a pen was chained to the counter. It seemed you couldn't even trust people not to steal a pen in a police station.

"Yes, how can I help?" The young woman gave a half decent impression of a smile as Christine moved forward. But her heart fluttered as she got a better view of her. She was so young.

"It's complicated." Christine forced herself to stay calm and launched into her pre-prepared speech. "But I want to report a crime that might have an impact upon a much bigger crime."

The smile slipped a little from the girl's – the police officer's – face. "OK. Well, try me."

Christine tried to lower her voice so that only the girl could hear. "My neighbour, I think he's..." She stopped and ran a hand through her hair. Saying this out loud sounded insane. "He's killed a cat," she said quickly, then added, rather louder than she meant to, "and I think he might be guilty of killing his daughter too."

There was a pause; she felt the eyes of the men with the stolen bicycle and phone looking up from their forms. The girl in front of her visibly swallowed. "Oh. I see." She scanned her desk, which was covered with plastic boxes containing many different forms, but clearly not one suitable for this. "Erm. I'll need you to speak to my sergeant. Could you wait here please?"

Christine nodded, relieved she wasn't being immediately dismissed as a loon. The girl got up from her seat and disappeared out of the room. There was an awkward pause while the men on either side inspected her with interest. After a while, the girl came back, an older man following her, also in uniform.

He glanced quickly at the three people in the waiting room, then leaned closer to the glass to speak with Christine.

"Madam? Would you follow me?" He beckoned her inside the police station proper. They walked a little way down a corridor, until he opened the door into a small room equipped with a table and a couple of chairs.

"Have a seat, please." She did so, and waited as he did the same. "My name is Sergeant Sinclair. Can we start with your name?"

When Christine told him, he wrote it down in a notebook.

"Now what's this about?"

Christine took a deep breath. "OK. I've just moved into a new house on the cliff-top at Lulworth Cove. In the house next to Rodney and Janet Slaughter. I'm sure you probably know them, on account of their daughter being murdered, but I didn't know anything about it. Nobody told me when I was buying the house. Not the Slaughters, nor the estate agents, nobody..."

The policeman's eyebrows began to rise at this, and Christine told herself to calm down.

"Anyway. The point is that since moving in, I've seen him – Rodney Slaughter – doing some very odd things. They've made me wonder whether he might have been involved in the murder of his daughter. And then this morning I discovered that he's killed one of our other neighbour's cats." She stopped, out of breath.

"Rodney Slaughter, you say?"

Christine nodded. "Uh huh." The sergeant had stopped writing.

"You know his daughter was murdered? Earlier this year?"

"Yes. Like I said—" Christine tried to go on, but he interrupted her.

"And the man who killed her was also killed? In a shoot-out where two police officers died?"

Christine caught the man's tone. He wasn't simply giving her information, he was admonishing her. "Yes. As I say, I'm aware of what happened, but I think maybe there's been a mistake. That Rodney Slaughter may have been *involved*."

The sergeant looked down at his notebook. "He was very much involved. His daughter was killed."

"Of course, but that's not what I mean." Christine stared at the man, her eyes pleading for him to understand.

"You think there was a mistake. Because of... what, exactly?" His tone was unchanged.

"Like I told you," Christine replied at once. "He's killed a cat."

Sergeant Sinclair breathed deeply and shifted in his seat. He was quite a heavy man. "It was your cat?"

"No! Not my cat. Look I'm sorry, I know this sounds crazy, that's why I came down here in person rather than phoning..." Christine ran her hands through her hair, then told herself to stop in case it made her look crazy. She leaned forward. "Sergeant..." – she searched her mind for the man's name, certain he'd told her, but it was gone – "*Sergeant.* My neighbour mentioned her cat was missing. Then my daughter found blood, by the Slaughters' wall, so I looked in their bin this morning. And that's where I found it. It was cut open down its middle, the insides were coming out. It was horrific."

The sergeant's expression shifted a little from clear distrust to subtle interest. He sat back, rested his thumb on his chin and tapped his nose. "It was definitely a cat?"

"Yes! I saw the collar."

"OK." He made another note, turned a page, then carried on writing.

"Do you believe me now?" she said after he'd written for a while.

"A cat is considered property under section four of the 1968 Theft Act. So if one's been killed, that may be an offence. You say you witnessed Mr Slaughter killing the animal?"

"Yes!" Christine felt a rush of relief. But not for long. "No. No, I didn't *see* him do it. I saw the evidence."

The sergeant looked up, his eyes narrowing. "You *didn't* see him?"

Christine shook her head. "No, but I've seen him doing some strange things. He gets up in middle of the night and..."

Sergeant Sinclair interrupted her with a shake of the head. "Getting up in the night isn't a police matter, Mrs Harvey. He might work nights. And there could be any number of reasons why the cat was in the Slaughters' bin. It could have been run over. Someone else could have been put it there..."

"No..." Christine stopped him. "They couldn't, and he doesn't work nights, he's an architect."

"I didn't say he *works* nights, Mrs Harvey, I said he *might* work nights. Or maybe he works at night. You'd be surprised, a lot of people do."

Christine stared at him, astonished he could be focused on such unimportant details. Then she briefly squeezed her eyes shut before trying again. "Look, it's hard to explain, but there are a lot of rumours. Online rumours, I mean, about Rodney Slaughter." She tried to give the sergeant a knowing look. "I just think they should be investigated."

She waited, continuing the look. He stared right back at her. "There was an investigation," the sergeant said after a while. "A very detailed, very thorough investigation, into the murders of Emily Slaughter and the two police officers who died that day. Who both had families by the way. And I'm afraid the presence of..." – he paused, as if searching for the right word – "internet trolls posting conspiracy theories is not unique to this case." He looked away. "In fact, it might explain the cat."

Christine stared at him, totally baffled. "Explain the cat?"

"Someone might have mistakenly thought it belonged to the Slaughters. They may have wanted to frighten them, or punish them."

"No..." Christine said. No one was trying to frighten Rodney Slaughter. He was the frightening one. She was about to say so when Sinclair interrupted her.

"*However*," he said. "I will send a car up there to take a look."

"You will?"

"Yes. And if the officers find any evidence that a crime has been committed, they'll be sure to take the appropriate steps." He closed his notebook. "Thank you for alerting us, Mrs Harvey."

For a few seconds Christine saw an image of Rodney Slaughter being escorted from his house in handcuffs. But then, without meaning to, she suddenly reached out and placed her hand on the sergeant's arm. "No. You can't..."

He pulled his arm away with distaste. "Can't what?"

"If you send a car up there to look in his bin, then he'll know that *I've* called you."

He didn't look overly concerned by this. "If the officers feel it's necessary to speak with Mr or Mrs Slaughter, they will do so without mentioning your name." He gave her a cold look.

"But he'll know! There must be something else you can do. Put him under surveillance, or..." She was going to say arrest him, but she knew how deranged that would sound.

"I think you might have been watching a little too much television, Mrs Harvey." The sergeant gave her a sarcastic smile.

"What should I do?" she asked simply, her voice sounding as desperate as she felt.

"I suggest you return home and we'll contact you if we need any more information. I can send a car now to check it out. The officers may need to speak to you, depending on what they find."

There was a form after all, just a short one, that detailed her name and address and the nature of her complaint. When she'd filled it in, Christine returned to the car and began to drive home. As she turned off the main road from Dorchester to Lulworth, towards the cliff-top houses, she noticed the familiar blue and fluorescent-yellow markings on the police car behind her. They would arrive at the house in convoy. She sighed, and her heart fluttered. Events were swiftly getting out of hand and there seemed nothing she could do about it.

But as she turned into the shared parking area, she saw at once that Rodney Slaughter's Audi was no longer in the drive. Perhaps, just maybe, it would be all right after all.

THIRTY-ONE

As she pulled into her spot, two police officers stepped out from their car.

"Mrs Harvey?" asked a female police officer. Christine looked to the house, still unsure if Janet was in or had left with Rodney.

"Yes."

"My name's PC Rose. We're responding to a complaint that a cat has been killed. I understand you reported it? Could you please show us where you saw it?"

Christine tried to breathe. What about the sergeant's promises that they wouldn't identify her? It was all nonsense. She glanced at the house, again seeing the camera mounted on the wall. The one positive was that it didn't appear to have moved. She nodded her head at the bin. "It's in there."

The two officers glanced at each other, then walked across. PC Rose lifted the lid, wrinkling her nose in distaste.

"It's about halfway down. You'll need to take the rubbish out." Christine spoke as if she barely cared any more, but the officer ignored her, holding the bin lid open for her colleague to take a look.

"I don't think so," she said, pulling the bin so that it tipped towards her. But there was no cat.

The bin was completely empty.

THIRTY-TWO

"You definitely saw the cat, Mrs Harvey?" PC Rose asked, and Christine nodded. "And you didn't think to take a photograph?"

"A photograph?" Christine thought of the cat, its mouth stuck open, little swollen tongue poking out along with its entrails. "No."

The second officer spoke. "The other bins are empty too. Guess it must be the day they get picked up."

"Well, we could put in a call to the council, ask them if their men noticed anything when they emptied this one," said Rose.

Her partner pulled out a radio and moved out of earshot. PC Rose looked at the house and drew her chest in. "You live here?"

Christine nodded.

"Next door to the Slaughters?"

Again, Christine could do nothing but nod her head.

"Terrible thing, what happened to their daughter."

"Yes," Christine replied.

PC Rose looked around, noticing the child seat in Christine's car. "You've got kids yourself?"

"Yes."

Rose said nothing, but the expression on her face communicated her feelings perfectly clearly – *and you moved here?*

The other officer returned. "Nothing. No reports of dead animals. They said if they did come across anything like that then they'd report it right away. They wouldn't just carry on. It's possible we could find it once the truck's emptied, but..."

"OK, thank you." PC Rose shrugged her shoulders at Christine, then turned back to her colleague. "Should probably have a word with the home owners. You know, just to ask them..."

"No," Christine said at once.

"Excuse me?"

"No. Then they'll know, won't they? That *I* know, I mean..."

A frown creased PC Rose's face. "Mrs Harvey, you've reported a crime, it's our duty to investigate it fully."

"They're not in."

"We can come back."

"No." Christine screwed her eyes shut. "I mean, please, no. There's no need, I think I may have been mistaken. The thing I saw, it was probably... a squirrel, or a rabbit or something. Run over I mean. They probably just threw it in the bin to get rid of it."

PC Rose gave Christine a long look, then turned to her partner with her eyebrows raised. He shrugged, devolving responsibility to her "Dave, do you want to wait in the car a moment?"

PC Rose turned to Christine. When she spoke, her voice was hesitant and careful. "My sergeant warned me about... How you think this is about more than just a dead cat." She paused, and Christine waited. "How you think it's something to do with Rodney Slaughter. His daughter..." She took a deep breath. "You have to understand, it's a really difficult subject for the guys here. The two officers who died, they both lived locally, and it's still raw. They're not going to... They're invested in the idea that those officers didn't die in vain. That they had the right man."

The woman's words seemed to offer a lifeline, and Christine held her breath.

PC Rose looked around awkwardly. "Look, there's one person, the DCI who worked the case... She's a bit of a... I don't know, she's kind of a legend in the force." She shook her head. "Look, I shouldn't be doing this, but..." She glanced at the house. "You're living right next door. I don't know, maybe she'll talk to you, explain how it was Sopley that did it. That Rodney Slaughter had nothing to do with it. And if there's anything to what you're saying, she'll find it."

Christine nodded her head. "Yes. Yes please. That would be good."

PC Rose looked for a second as if she regretted her words, but then pulled out a phone and began scanning through, looking for a contact. When she found it, she looked up. "Her name's Sands. Detective Chief Inspector Erica Sands. But she was injured in the explosion. I don't even know how she is now, let alone if she'll speak to you."

She scribbled the number on her pad, tore off the page and handed it over.

When the police car left, Christine went inside. She still had no idea if Janet was in the house opposite, but to her relief it looked empty, the living area quiet and all the lights off. She stood in the kitchen staring across into her neighbours' house, trying to work out whether she was overreacting or whether this was all real. She looked at the page from the notebook that PC Rose had given her, the numbers scrawled in childish blue handwriting. Impulsively, she typed the numbers into her phone. A few seconds later it connected.

"Is that Detective Sands? Detective Chief Inspector Erica Sands?"

PART 3

ERICA SANDS, SIX MONTHS EARLIER

THIRTY-THREE

Sands' next conscious impression was of lying on her side in the mud. Golding was shouting something, and another man – the paramedic she'd seen earlier – was leaning over her, the green of his uniform half-covered in the brown of the liquid mud. He was also yelling, telling her to hang on, to stay calm. Their voices were faint. At one point the paramedic was rubbing her chest in a circular motion, making her head roll around with the pressure of it. She felt little actual pain, only a burning sensation under his hands, and running deep within her. She blacked out.

When she next awoke she was on a gurney, travelling fast down a hospital corridor, doctors and nurses on either side of her, their faces bouncing as they ran to keep up, white coats trailing backwards. The sensation of plastic tubes in her mouth, the taste of them, running down her throat, making her gag. She reached up to pull them out, and all at once people started yelling, as if they were all different parts of the same organism. Arms shot out, holding hers back, angrily pushing the tubes back, deeper inside her. She gagged again and blacked out.

Then – it could have been any time later – the calm quiet of a hospital room, with just the rhythmic *beep* tracking her heartbeat. There were more tubes now, in her mouth, going into her arms – and when she edged her neck up a tiny bit to look, she saw more going into her stomach, which was wrapped in white like a cartoon Egyptian mummy. There was no feeling, not anywhere below her neck. Movement was impossible, even the idea of it seemed strangely alien, like it was something she knew of, but had never been able to do. For a long time she did nothing, just allowed herself slowly to become more aware of her surroundings, awaiting the return of sensation. When it didn't come, unease grew in her mind. Why couldn't she feel anything? Why couldn't she move? She tried to answer the questions in a logical way – it was the anaesthetic – but the unease persisted. If she were wrong the consequences were too large to be ignored so easily. She bit down gently on the tubes inside her mouth, still trying to suppress the growing sense in her mind that whatever had happened to her body wasn't just a temporary reaction to whatever pain killers she'd been given. She tried to move again, just to twitch her toe or raise a finger, but nothing happened. It was like her limbs had been disconnected. Movement didn't feel impossible, it just didn't feel at all.

But impossible was not a word that Erica Sands had been brought up to accept. She tried harder.

She focused instead on the fingers of her left hand; from where she was lying, they were at least in sight. She stared at them in a way she'd never done before, and slowly let her attention rest on just the tip of her forefinger. She studied it, noticing details she'd never seen before, how the fingerprint faded at the sides, how the colour changed subtly around it, from white to pink to red. She tried to feel it, the weight of it, pressing against the softness of the cotton sheet, and the coolness where it was exposed to the air. But there was nothing. No signals came back. The signals she sent down to her finger just weren't getting there. So instead she tried to imagine the tip of her finger, closing her eyes and rebuilding the image in her mind, occasionally checking and adjusting by looking. And once she had it pretty good, she added in the sensations of weight and temperature. When she was sure she felt something, she looked again, and tried to move.

Nothing happened.

There *was* a sensation, though. Not the creeping unease of earlier, but irritation. Annoyance that this process was taking so long. For a second or two it opened the door to concern again – what if this *were* permanent? What if she would never move again? And with the door open a crack, fear came suddenly bounding in. The possibility of being wheelchair-bound for the rest of her life suddenly barrelled into her, making it difficult to breathe. What would her life be like if she couldn't move? If she couldn't even use the bathroom? One particular implication nearly tore her away: she'd have no career.

She closed her eyes, choking off the panic filling up inside, forcefully, like closing a tap. *No.* She wouldn't accept it. She opened her eyes and looked around. Accepted the hospital room. Accepted reality. But she didn't accept the fear. Quietly it drained away, as if chastised.

When she was able, she changed strategy, this time allowing the questions to come at her. Facing them full on, accepting that panic would try to accompany them, but determined to reject it, calmly and surely. So what if it wasn't the anaesthetic? So what if she was paralysed? Plenty of people were paralysed. They coped. She would cope too. Clearly she was still alive. And if she hadn't been alive, that would be just fine too. But she *was* alive. So she might as well get busy sorting this out.

She closed her eyes again. The fear was still there, like a bear in a cave, but this time, instead of coming out to consume her, it stayed inside, as if ashamed of its own existence.

Again, she opened her eyes. This time she was grimly determined.

Again, she focused on the finger, trying with absurd optimism to lift it. She concentrated on it, losing track of time, but aware that it was passing in chunks perhaps hours in size. Stubbornly, the finger lay still, but it was no match for her persistence, and there was a sense, like a thread being sent down her body, down her arm, that something was reconnecting. Her face ached – she assumed from the effort of setting her jaw – but still she stared, and felt the connection inch its way slowly down from her neck to her shoulder, to her elbow, and then turn the corner into her forearm. The effort it took just to move a tiny amount was extraordinary. She had no idea if the process taking place within her was real or imaginary, but whenever doubt formed in her mind, she crushed it. She instructed her mind to obliterate the doubts, to smash them apart, to simply forbid them from existing in her mind. Eventually, she felt sensation creep from her wrist into the back of her hand.

Then she tried to move the finger again.

She stared at the tip and visualised it moving, bending into a curve, willing the muscles to contract, ordering them to obey her.

For a few seconds there was nothing. Then – a twitch. She blinked, not sure she'd seen correctly, or if the blink itself had given the illusion of movement. But when she tried again, the finger twitched, more clearly this time. She kept going and even managed to drag it slowly backwards and forwards across the cotton. She felt the nail catching on the thread, the muscles contract, the finger's weight as it lay on the sheet.

The effort left her exhausted, but the fear was broken now. She moved the finger one more time, back and forth, just to reassure herself it hadn't been a fluke, then fell into a deep, exhausted sleep.

THIRTY-FOUR

Sometime later – again Sands had no idea how many hours, or even days, had passed – she woke to find two men in her room. One of them was Detective Golding. She guessed the other man must be a doctor. Neither of them seemed aware she was awake.

"She'll need twenty-four-hour specialist care. It's not going to be easy," she heard the doctor saying. They seemed to be speaking with familiarity, as if they knew each other well, or had come to know each other well. The doctor was still wearing his surgical face mask, but what was odd – or seemed odd to Sands – was that Golding was wearing one too. Above it only half of his face was visible, his vivid blue eyes now with noticeable bags underneath, as if he hadn't slept much.

Sands tried to speak.

Whatever noise came out wasn't recognisable, but it was enough to draw both men's attention. The doctor came over at once, the plastic of his shield distorting his face.

"I think she's awake. Can you hear me, Erica?" He spoke louder. "Are you hearing this?"

Sands tried to reply but her throat was too dry, her mouth

too full of tubes. Gently, the doctor disconnected one of them and pulled it out.

"Can you hear me, Erica? If you're not able to speak, you might try blinking?"

Golding came in closer now. Sands saw his pupils dilate, the concern so clear it almost brought back the fear. She formed a word with her dry lips and somehow pushed it out. "Water," she managed to say, and she recognition on Golding's face. He nodded and poured a glass, then held it to her lips.

While she was drinking, the doctor backed away, out of sight. Sands tried to study Golding's face for more clues, but he wasn't looking her in the eye. When the doctor returned, he leant in close, his expression serious above the mask.

"Hello, Erica. My name is Dr Sangit. Can you tell me how you're feeling?"

"Shit," Sands replied, surprised at how awful her own voice sounded. "How are you?"

The sides of the doctor's face creased gently, presumably the result of a smile. "I'm very well, thank you. All the better for seeing you awake." The creases disappeared. "Now, you'd probably like to know what's happening to you?"

Sands tried to nod before remembering she couldn't. But there was a little movement in the neck, and he seemed to understand.

"Do you remember you were shot?"

Again, Sands tried the same movement.

"It was a very serious injury. The bullet was a lead ball that entered just above your right hip, traversed diagonally upward, and exited from just under the ribcage."

Sands' eyes flicked down to her white-covered torso, trying to picture the path. It felt like she was doing a fly-by inside her own body.

"You've had three operations. On the colon, the gall bladder and the bile duct."

She thought about this for a moment, then decided she didn't want to know. Not now.

"Why are you wearing masks?" Sands croaked instead, her voice slow and weak. She managed to turn her head, catching the frown visible across the doctor's exposed forehead.

"It's a new policy," he explained. "Because of a virus. I'm afraid everyone has to wear them. You didn't choose a very good time to get shot." New creases appeared in his forehead.

"I can't move," Sands managed. "Anaesthetic?" The word came out so scrambled she was surprised they understood it. But it was clear the issue was already on Doctor Sangit's mind.

He sighed, glancing at Golding before continuing. "Erica, we can have this conversation now or later, it's up to you. It might be better to wait until you're stronger."

Now it was Sands' turn to frown. "Conversation?"

The doctor hesitated again.

"What conversation?" She wanted to sit up and was frustrated that she couldn't.

"Whatever it is, I want to know." Her words partly surprised her, but she knew it was true.

The doctor looked at her for a while, then nodded.

"Maybe I should go?" Golding said, and the doctor nodded, but Sands stopped him.

"No." That surprised her too.

Finally, Doctor Sangit nodded one more time, then turned back to Erica and moved closer. His deep brown eyes widened. He took a deep breath, sucking his mask partly into his mouth, then out again.

"Erica. The operations were carried out to stabilise and repair the damage caused by the track of the pellet, and they were successful. But it was evident that it also caused significant nerve damage." He seemed to hold his breath for a second. "Damage which we've been unable to repair." He stopped again and Sands waited. "Erica, there's no easy way to tell you this, and I'm really very sorry, but the nerve damage is significant... and permanent." He lowered his head. "The problem appears to affect your whole body... over time you might get some feeling back, but we're talking about sensations." He paused again. "That's all. It won't be enough to allow you to move. I'm so sorry, so very sorry, but I'm afraid you're paralysed from the neck down."

THIRTY-FIVE

There was a silence. Sands' eyes shifted from one to the other, from Golding, who suddenly seemed to know everything about her, to this doctor – she realised she'd forgotten his name – *Sangit.*

"No, I'm not," she said.

"Excuse me?" the doctor replied, taken aback.

"I'm not paralysed. It's probably just the anaesthetic. The operations." Her voice was coming back to her now, the water had moistened her throat.

"I'm afraid not, Erica," he replied, his voice soothing but insistent. "The effect of the anaesthetic will have worn off a long time ago, and all the indications are that the damage is so severe..."

"Then the indications are wrong. I've already managed to move my finger."

She could see his jaw working under his mask, his mouth opening and closing. "I'm... Excuse me? I don't think..."

"Look." She dropped her gaze to her finger, leading his eyes in the same direction. At first nothing happened, but she had no doubts. A few seconds later she had it moving, more than before, curling and uncurling, the movements still small, but so obviously there it dragged the other fingers with it.

"Um..." the doctor said. "Um... that's... Good heavens. Could you do that again?"

Behind him she saw Golding watching too, and even with the mask she could see his smile.

* * *

Time passed. Days, not hours, but normal time now, not the jetlag-like time that started and stopped around the operations and seemed to have an elastic quality depending on how much of the painkilling drugs were in her system. She spent much of the time alone, but some of it surrounded by face-mask-wearing experts who questioned her, frowned at her and watched her as she focused on other fingers and her toes, and every time got them to move. And so the prognosis they gave her changed too. Their reality was forced to match hers. Her will became actual reality, or perhaps simply revealed it. The experts went from saying she would never be able to move anything below her neck, to acknowledging she might have some *limited* movement, but only in her extremities. And then, once she managed to move her arms and legs too, they conceded that this too *might* be possible, but that walking wasn't something she should entertain, because it was way beyond the scope of what was possible. Then she got out of bed, stood unaided and even took a few awkward steps with the aid of an aluminium walking frame. So they accepted this might be wrong too. They were split on whether she should keep doing *exactly* what it was she was doing, or whether she should slow down for fear of going too fast.

Sands mostly ignored them and concentrated on what felt right to her. The physical challenge of rehabilitating herself took almost all her time and mental energy, but she saved some space to discover how the case against Michael Sopley had been closed off. She learned that the two firearms officers had both died at the scene, along with the suspect. She learned that Golding had been kept on the case – a six-month secondment at MID under the direction of John Lindham, who'd been given a temporary promotion to fill Sands' role. She read about it in the press too. Her bed had an information console – hospital jargon for a kind of tablet-computer attached to an articulated arm – and she scoured the online newspapers for every word that had been written about the case. But there wasn't that much. For a few days after the shooting it had been national news, but almost at once the pandemic had simply overwhelmed the news agenda. It was the same within the hospital too. The virus was all anyone seemed to talk about, even more so than her miraculous recovery. Beyond vaguely supposing she would die if she caught it, Sands tried to ignore that too.

THIRTY-SIX

At some point after the shooting, Sands had received a visitor who wasn't a doctor. She was in a different room by then with the door shut, so she didn't see him coming but sensed a hesitancy in the way he knocked.

"May I?" Chief Superintendent Yorke poked his head around the door. He was dressed in his full uniform. Instead of a mask, he'd been given a clear Perspex face shield. Sands nodded and he came in, taking off his hat. Then he seemed momentarily lost. Sitting, he fingered the rim of the hat. Then he looked up. "I came as soon as I could. I'm sorry it wasn't sooner."

"The whole world's gone crazy." She glanced at the computer screen, which was on TV mode, showing a news program explaining yet again how the virus was novel to humans, and therefore could potentially infect the entire population.

"Indeed. Yes. These are very strange times."

Sands picked up a remote and turned the TV off. He watched her arm.

"They say you were paralysed. For a few days at least. Until you decided you didn't want to be."

"I was misdiagnosed." Sands gave a little shrug. "It happens."

"Well, thank Christ that's all it was." Yorke's hand went to his face, apparently to rub his jaw, but he almost knocked the shield off. "Damn thing," he said, before readjusting it. "You gave us a heck of a scare, Erica."

"Yes, sir. Sorry, sir."

"You know about Commander Roper of course? And Dean Jones?"

Sands nodded. "I wasn't fast enough, sir."

The Chief Superintendent shook his head. "Bullshit. It was a damn cock-up, but it certainly wasn't your cock-up." He stared at her for a moment without wavering, then went on. "However, that is unfortunately something to do with the reason I'm here today."

Sands frowned.

"Not the only reason of course. Actually, I wanted to come earlier, but with all the shit going on..." He stopped. "Erica, the question of blame is rearing its ugly head."

"Blame?"

For a moment his eyes flicked around the room before settling on her.

"It's a right royal mess, Erica. Multiple shots fired, two officers dead, the suspect killed as well. And your actions..." He stopped.

"What about my actions?"

Yorke fingered the lining of his hat again. "Erica, for a day or so it looked extremely unlikely that you were going to survive, and I suspect that gave an opportunity for certain individuals to claim that your actions precipitated the firefight. Statements were prepared in a way that removes any blame from the firearms squad."

"I didn't precipitate the shots sir. I responded to them."

"I don't doubt that, Erica."

"Then who does?"

He didn't answer. "There'll be an independent investigation, of course, and the truth will come out, the problem..."

"Who says I caused the shots?"

His eyes flicked onto her face again. "Some members of the Armed Response Unit are saying that you running out caused Sopley to fire."

"That's not true." She shook her head as forcefully as she could. "I saw Sopley was preparing to fire so I attempted to get Commander Roper down out of the way."

It took him a few moments to answer. When he did so, his voice was soft. "Even so Erica, you entered a live scene at a highly critical time, where you had ceded control, and without securing authorisation."

Sands felt the blood rush to her head. "There was no time to secure..."

"I know. *I know*. And that's what I believe the evidence will show once the panel examines it."

Sands felt her heart rate soaring and forced herself to calm down. "OK. When will that be?"

Yorke was still shaking his head. "Soon. I hope. But... In a way, that's the problem." He touched his face shield. "Right now there's a new priority, and it trumps everything. Literally everything. This virus... *everything* has stopped, they're talking about locking the country down. Literally, people shut up in their homes, not allowed to go outside. I don't know when it'll get back to normal. I don't know *if* it will get back to normal." He toyed with his hat again. "But until it does, I'm sorry to say you're suspended."

"Suspended?" Sands' mouth fell open.

"Pending an investigation by the IOPC, which I'm sure will clear you, Erica, just as soon as you're better and able to give evidence." He shook his head. "You know how these things work. It happens automatically in any serious incident where officers have died. It doesn't indicate any blame on your part."

"They were wearing body cams, the firearms squad. Get the footage, that'll show what happened."

"I've tried. Unfortunately several of the devices malfunctioned, and no one's been able to recover the files. The ones that did work are inconclusive."

"How could they malfunction?"

"I don't know. But it's going to come down to who saw what. Look, I'm sure it won't be a problem, but a bigger issue is the time scale. I have simply no idea when it will happen."

"Which means I'm suspended indefinitely? That's not..." She was going to say 'fair' but it sounded childish. "That can't be right."

"I'm sorry, Erica. It's out of my hands."

Sands tried to think. "I'd still like to be involved in finalising the Sopley case."

Yorke shook his head. "That won't be... I'm sorry, but that's not going to be possible. John Lindham is wrapping it up."

"Lindham doesn't have the experience..." Sands began, but he cut her off.

"John Lindham is a perfectly capable detective. But I'll make sure the bulk of the credit goes where it's due, Erica, if that's what you're worried about."

"That isn't what I'm worried about," she snapped back, suddenly angry. But Yorke didn't take offence. He took a deep breath.

"Erica, you're facing a hearing on your conduct in that case. I cannot allow you to have any further involvement until it's cleared up."

"But you can't tell me when that is? You can't give me any timescale?"

Through the Perspex mask she saw him bite his lip. “No. I can’t.”

She looked away, frustrated.

“I’m sorry, Erica. I know this is a blow, but it will give you the time and space to focus on your recovery. Take that as a positive. That’s going to take time as well. Use it.”

Sands’ jaw was locked as she muttered her reply. “Yes, sir.”

THIRTY-SEVEN

Not long after Yorke's visit, Sands phoned Lindham to check how the case was progressing and particularly to ask if certain aspects were being followed up, particularly the forensic examinations of the girl's bedroom and Sopley's room at the shelter. And while Lindham did, reluctantly, provide a summary, he also told her that Yorke had warned him she would likely make contact, and to report this to Yorke personally. Lindham promised to let it go on this occasion, but made it quite clear he wouldn't do so again.

The next day, the hospital was put into lockdown. Visitors were banned, and patients were ordered to remain in their beds at all times, due to a nationwide shortage of protective equipment. Front-line hospital staff – people treating Covid victims – were already going without. They were beginning to fall ill too. And they were beginning to die. In Sands' case it made little difference – no one was likely to visit her, and she couldn't move anyway – but the sheer magnitude of what was happening suddenly became clear.

Sands watched the country, and most of the world, descend into the full disaster-movie craziness of the pandemic. Shops and offices were closed and the streets emptied as millions of people were told to stay in their homes. The news was full of nervous-looking presenters discussing with virology experts about just how many millions might die.

Even so, some aspects of life somehow kept going. The coroner's office finished its report into the death of Emy Slaughter, concluding that she was most likely killed by Michael Sopley after he broke into her house and abducted her. Sopley was also recorded as being officially responsible for the deaths of Commander Mike Roper and ARO Dean Jones. There could be no charges from the CPS, since Sopley was dead, but the police inquiry was effectively shut down. There was still no date for the investigation into the events at the farm.

Sands had no alternative but to follow Yorke's advice and focus on her rehabilitation, Although it soon became clear that her recovery was going to more closely resemble a marathon than a sprint, she did at least make progress. She was allowed access to a water-treatment room – and because the pandemic had put a halt to most non-emergency treatment, the room was hardly used. She was there every day, far exceeding the time recommended by the doctors. She set milestones – walk upright halfway across the pool, walk the full way across the pool, walk there and back – and quickly knocked them off, even if the exercise hurt more than she let on.

After seven weeks in hospital, she discharged herself. She was partly being selfless – she wanted to free up her bed, and the staff who were looking after her, to be redeployed to the rapidly worsening crisis. But she had more selfish reasons. It seemed self-evident that the longer she stayed in hospital, it would be only a matter of time before the disease found its way to her.

She returned to the privacy of her own flat. As the weeks following the shooting turned into months, and as the pandemic ground on, she found herself alone, and, for the first time in her life (excluding the four hours of rehab – twice what the doctors had recommended for her), she had absolutely nothing to do.

The first idea she had to solve this problem was to focus on researching open criminal cases.

She knew that of the approximately 1,000 murders committed each year in England and Wales, around forty percent were never solved. In some cases, the police knew full well who'd committed the crime but hadn't been able to accumulate enough evidence to convince the CPS to file a charge. All murder cases generated reams of paperwork – maps, photographs and forensic reports from the crime scene, witness statements, CCTV footage – the list went on. It was likely that most unsolved cases contained, somewhere within these information treasure troves, a piece of so-far overlooked evidence which might allow the case to move forward if properly identified. And seen in that light, her injury and rehabilitation presented a unique opportunity to carry out a thorough review of some of these cases.

The problem? Since she'd been suspended from duty, she wasn't allowed access to any of them. She did her best to get around this by putting in a request to Chief Superintendent Yorke to make an exception on the grounds that her suspension was far longer than it should be due to the Covid pandemic. When this request was officially denied, she phoned Yorke at home to argue the point, but he wouldn't budge.

This failure didn't particularly surprise her, so she changed tack. Instead of studying unsolved cases, she decided to study murders that *had* been solved. While police files aren't available to the public, or to suspended officers, criminal trial transcripts are a matter of public record, along with all documents and information entered into court records. Every couple of days she would download and print out upwards of 600 pages of court proceedings for every murder trial she could find. She would sit and read through the entire thing, front to back, and when she'd finished she'd go right back to the beginning and start again, this time with a yellow highlighter in her hands to pick out any aspects that seemed important.

On the third reading, Sands would make copious notes in a separate file, drastically reducing the case to its constituent parts which she'd enter on a computer database. She wanted to be able to quickly compare cases, to qualify and quantify which factors had been important in both identifying the suspects and proving their involvement. It was a labour-intensive process, and soon her living room began to resemble an incident room, albeit a rather chaotic one. Her kitchen and bedroom were soon covered with piles of paper as the cases spread out from table-tops and across the floor. But it was an entertaining and useful way to fill the hours. At least, that was how Sands saw it.

So it was that on one warm spring day, she sat in her lounge, chair angled so that she faced the sparkling water of the harbour, but looking instead at the transcripts for the trial of a man named Joshua Jones. He was a twenty-nine-year-old man from south London who'd been charged with the murder of an elderly lady, Ada Adewole. Mrs Adewole, who was of Nigerian descent, had been raped and killed at home in Wimbledon. As she lived alone and received very few visitors, it had been several days before her body was found, meaning the pathologists had been unable to even give a precise date of death. From almost all the forensic data gleaned from the house, it seemed her killer had been careful – there were no fingerprints or DNA found at the scene. But a single glass was found in the sink with a small amount of water. It was as if the killer had been thirsty after carrying out his work, and momentarily forgotten himself. The glass was found to contain a full set of fingerprints, along with DNA traces from saliva on the rim. A match lit up on NCNAD – the UK National Criminal Intelligence DNA

Database. The name? One Joshua Jones. Everything else had quickly dropped into place. Jones lived just a few streets away from the victim, and he had a history of sexual violence towards older women, having been caught abusing residents at a care home where he'd worked for several years. His online history also showed he was a habitual racist, with a particular hatred towards black African peoples. The evidence was sufficient to convince the jury, and he was sentenced to fifteen years in prison, despite his continued protestations of innocence. It was a simple yet effective piece of police work, which had earned the lead investigator a commendation. But for all that, there was something about it that troubled Sands. She couldn't decide what it was.

THIRTY-EIGHT

Sands was busy with her highlighter when her phone started ringing.

Annoyed at the interruption, she considered not answering, It had been a long time since she'd received a call that wasn't from someone trying to sell her something or scam her, but old habits die hard, and she'd been unable to leave any of them unanswered.

"Yes?"

"Is this Erica Sands?" The voice was wrong for a sales call, much more anxious.

"Yes."

"Detective Chief Inspector Erica Sands?"

"Yes." She frowned. "Who's speaking please?"

"Erm..." It was a woman's voice. "I heard... I was given your name by... well, originally by one of the WPCs at Dorchester, but then someone at MID, the Murder Investigation Department, they passed me on to someone else, and I left a message but no one got back to me for ages, so I didn't know what to do and..."

"What's it regarding?"

There was a pause. Sands could hear the woman's rapid breathing on the other end of the line.

"Take a deep breath and tell me what you're calling about."

"OK... OK. It's about Rodney Slaughter. I think it was him that killed his daughter, not the other guy."

For a second, Sands was adrift. Then time caught up with her. "*Rodney Slaughter*? Emily Slaughter's father?"

"Yes."

She felt herself zooming back to her last case. Almost instantly she was able to picture Rodney Slaughter, his black, black eyes. She remembered the coldness of his reaction when he learned of his daughter's death.

"Who gave you my name?"

"Erm. I'm not... I'm not sure I should say."

"You said it was a PC at Dorchester? A woman?"

"WPC Rose..."

"That term's no longer used. Who are you?"

"Erm..."

"You need to identify yourself, right now."

There was a pause. It sounded like she was crying. "Look, you don't know me. My name is Christine Harvey." A half-sob. "I've moved next door to Rodney Slaughter, and I've been watching him, and I think... Well, I think you made a mistake. That it was him who murdered his daughter."

Sands blinked in surprise. For a few seconds she had no idea what to say. "What mistake?" she said eventually.

"I live next door. To Rodney Slaughter," Christine said again. "I've got a daughter the same age as Emily was, Molly. And I'm scared. Scared he's going to do something to her. To Molly." She was in floods of tears now, the sobs clear down the phone line.

"Why would you be scared?" Sands asked. "The man who killed Emily Slaughter is dead."

"I know you think that. But what if you're wrong?"

Sands' brain, still filled with dates and data from the trials, was taking longer than usual to respond, and the woman ended up answering her own question.

"Because he looks at her funny and..."

"I'm not..."

"...He murdered a cat."

Sands, who had been about to add the word "wrong", instead stayed quiet.

"And he gets up in the night. He does weird things," Christine went on.

"That's not a crime." Sands' brain supplied the phrase before she was sure whether it was really what she wanted to say.

"I know, but the police won't listen. They say it was this homeless man, but what if it wasn't? What if the police got it wrong, and it wasn't him, but Rodney Slaughter? And now I'm living next door to him?"

Sands started to think properly. The woman was clearly a crank. In normal circumstances she'd pass her on to a junior detective. But she was suspended. She couldn't do that. At least, not easily.

"If you have any concerns about the case you should go to the police," she said finally. "Call your local station."

"I did," Christine replied. "I went to the police and they wouldn't help. But one of the officers, Constable Rose, she gave me your number. She said you would help. That there was something about you. That you would help. Please. I'm desperate."

Sands listened, her eyes on the court transcripts surrounding her chair. Serious crimes. Human beings stabbed and strangled in explosions of emotion or as the result of sadistic, horrific plans by dark and dangerous souls. Crimes that she was predestined to spend her life trying to solve. She noticed how desperately she yearned to get back to it, not deal with a woman and her dead cat. And yet. Combined with Slaughter's odd reaction to his daughter's death, it was just enough to keep her on the line.

"You say he killed a cat? What do you mean? How was it killed?"

"I don't... I don't know. Its neck was all floppy, and its insides were coming out."

"Floppy? As in extended?" That could indicate it had been strangled.

"I don't..." The woman was sobbing again. "I don't know."

"The insides, *how* were they coming out?"

"It looked like it had been cut open."

Erica felt more alert now. "Was it definitely a cut, or could it have been the result of an animal attack, or being hit by a vehicle?"

"I don't... I don't know. The bin men took the body away before the police could see it."

Sands sighed, momentarily disappointed. What this woman was talking about had absolutely nothing to do with the murder of Emily Slaughter.

"I found blood, and then the body was in the Slaughters' wheelie bin, but it was emptied before the police could..."

"I'm sorry, Mrs Harvey," Sands interrupted. "But whatever this is about, I can't get involved. If you have a problem you should see your local police. Goodbye."

She ended the call. And then Sands stood in the silence of her kitchen and tried to remember what she'd been doing before.

THIRTY-NINE

The same number rang again a few moments later, but she didn't answer. Instead, she put the device on silent, and drank a glass of tap water. As she put the glass down, she pictured Joshua Jones doing exactly the same thing.

Why did he take his gloves off?

It bugged her. Forensics indicated that the killer had been extremely careful throughout the murder, and yet when he'd got thirsty, he'd not only failed to wash the glass he'd used, but he'd also taken off his glove to pick it up. Why? She went back to the court papers, searching for something that might explain, or at least mention, that this was odd behaviour. But there was nothing. And what about the obvious inconsistency? To Sands it seemed self-evident that, if there were fingerprints on the glass, they should also appear on the handle of the tap. But Sands found no reference to that at all. No indication that this had even been checked.

As she pondered this, and how to file it in her database, she found her mind wandering more than ever. She could picture the house next door to the Slaughters, a large traditional building that she guessed was used for holiday lets. Her detectives would have visited in the days after the killing. They would have interviewed this Mrs Harvey... no. The woman hadn't said she lived next door, but *moved* next door. So the house must have come onto the market? No surprise there. Who would want to holiday next to a house associated with such a horrible crime? Perhaps it came onto the market cheap? Or maybe the woman had bought it at a knock-down price, not even knowing why it was so affordable?

Yes, that might explain her sense of uneasiness. The woman had moved her family a little too close to tragedy to be comfortable. And now she was regretting it. Rodney Slaughter had nothing to do with the girl's death. He couldn't have: they had Michael Sopley for that, and that was a certainty. Or at least as much of a certainty as you can get when investigating serious crime.

Not for the first time, she regretted not being able to interview Sopley. It would have been a rare chance to witness first-hand the mannerisms and characteristics of a killer, rather than just reading second-hand reports. She wondered if she could have got him to confess. The evidence was already overwhelming, and the follow-up work only added to the case against him. Would he have known there was no chance, that his efforts to conceal his actions had failed? Or would he have been like Joshua Jones, denying reality, even in the face of overwhelming evidence? She thought back to the words she'd exchanged with Sopley, shouted through the loudspeaker across the farmyard. Hadn't he nearly confessed?

She stopped, suddenly puzzled at two points. Firstly, why she had nearly misremembered his words as a confession, when they hadn't been anything of the kind. And secondly, *why* he hadn't confessed. If he knew he was about to die in a blaze of bullets, why not admit what he'd done? Wasn't that odd? Preferring to die without ever admitting his guilt?

She didn't know. But now it felt like a jigsaw piece that

didn't quite fit. She shook her head. She'd spent too much time in this damn flat, reading about murders and the thousands of tiny puzzles that accompanied them.

She went back to the Jones case, but something had shifted. The systematic evaluation of evidence, motive, and statements from each crime felt pointless now. Even stupid. She tried to calm her mind, to breathe deeply and concentrate, but she couldn't. She kept glancing at the phone, perhaps hoping it might light up, but when it didn't, she found herself checking the volume in case she had inadvertently put it on silent. Finally she gave up and embarked upon the remaining two hours of rehabilitation exercises for that day. After that, she took a shower. She made a sandwich and watched the quay below her window while she ate it. And then, about six hours after Christine Harvey had first rung her, Sands gave in to the inevitable. She rang her back.

"Tell me again. Why do you think Rodney Slaughter had something to do with the murder?" She listened as Christine listed her concerns, and almost immediately regretted her decision. They were all insane, lacking in evidence. Almost laughable. The only thing that kept her on the line was that the woman was clearly deeply upset.

"Well?" Christine spoke into a growing silence. "Can you help? Please?"

Sands considered. Technically she was still suspended from duty, and therefore should have nothing to do with the case. She should write a (brief) report and pass it on to John Lindham, trusting he'd follow it up if he deemed it relevant. But then technically, there *wasn't* a case, at least not an open one. Sopley couldn't be put on trial. Furthermore, and perhaps less of a logical stretch, this woman had nothing to do with it. She hadn't even lived there when the crime took place. Therefore, you *could* argue there was no actual conflict in Sands looking into it. That would be a generous interpretation, but Sands decided she was in a generous mood.

"When did you move in?" Sands checked.

"A month ago."

"It's the big house, right? Red roof tiles?"

"Yes— No. We've moved in..." Christine Harvey seemed to understand the mistake. "The Slaughters had to split their house in two. I bought the other half."

The picture Sands had in her mind of a large, traditional house next to the Slaughters' ultra-modern building was shattered as she recalled the empty shell opposite the rooms the Slaughters had been living in.

"I see."

"My husband died. From this virus. He was a doctor. I don't know, I thought it would be good for the kids to move down here. I had no idea where I was taking them..."

"Why don't we meet?" Sands said suddenly. "You can tell me about it then. I'll come to you."

Sands dressed in a suit she hadn't needed for a while. She noticed it hung on her differently. She'd lost weight, even if it wasn't weight she'd needed to lose. She threw a notebook and pen in a bag and limped out to the car.

She'd done so little in the six months since the shooting that the Lulworth address was still on the list of recent destinations in the vehicle's GPS. Driving back down the coast road, she recalled her emotions the last time she'd made that journey. Horror at the death of a child, but also excitement. The confusing lump of guilt or relief or fear – or whatever it was – about her own father's illness. It all seemed a lifetime away, the world of today entirely changed.

When she arrived in the village, she found it far busier than in the winter. The huge car park on the side of the hill was nearly full – the lockdown of earlier in the year was now over and people were making up for it. The lane down to the cove was packed with families carrying buckets and spades and picnic hampers. She took a moment to park and follow them down to the edge of the cove itself. Nothing looked the same. The water looked inviting instead of cold and slate grey. The green of the cliffs was vibrant, their chalk sides white in the late summer sunshine. She turned to the right and saw the modernist block of the Slaughters' house up on the top of the cliff. It looked even more out of place today than before.

She passed a few people as she walked back to the car. They glanced at her in the awkward way she'd grown used to, curious about her limp, but seemingly unsure whether to give some sympathetic acknowledgement of it or pretend they hadn't noticed. She gave them her own look back. A mind-your-own-business glare that put them right in no time.

She climbed back into the Alfa and drove the final few hundred metres to visit Christine Harvey.

FORTY

There was space to park in front of the Slaughters' house – Christine had already told her that. But she'd decided not to in case the Slaughters remembered her car. Instead, she turned right at the top of the hill, away from the Slaughters' house, and pulled the car off the road where it couldn't be seen. Then she walked back, noting two cars in the driveway, a white Audi 4x4, and a red Fiat estate. She remembered that the Audi belonged to the Slaughters.

Christine Harvey had explained that she now occupied the right-hand side of the house, and Sands saw that a second door had been added since she was last there. She walked up to it, noting a CCTV camera positioned above the original front door – which presumably still belonged to the Slaughters. She rang the bell, stepping back to take another look at the camera. It hadn't moved. Then the door opened and a woman beckoned her in. She was younger than Sands had expected. Not much older than herself.

"Detective Sands? Come in quickly please."

Technically Sands wasn't working as a detective at that precise moment, but she chose not to correct her.

The alterations inside had been well done. The house had been split in half, down the centre of its U-shape, so that the inside courtyard now formed two small garden areas, separated by a low wall and some bushes, not yet properly established. Christine Harvey led her to the right, and, just as before, the corridor opened into a large, open-plan living area, the front wall looking out over the ocean. Even though her own flat had a view of the water, the effect here was much more dramatic.

"Hmmm?" She suddenly realised Christine had been speaking to her.

"Did you want tea? Coffee?"

"Tea. Please." Sands smiled. She came back into the kitchen and watched the woman as she moved around. There was a sadness about her, she decided. She moved around the room as if defeated.

"I came here because I wanted to explain the case against Michael Sopley," Sands said as Harvey made the tea

"He can't see us," Christine said suddenly. "We were completely overlooked when we first got here, but I finally got the blinds installed, thank God. They only came this week. I keep them closed the whole time."

Sands looked, taking a moment to understand what she was talking about. The room had large side windows that would have overlooked the courtyard – and the Slaughters' half of the house – had they not been closed off with white blinds. Sands suspected this was overkill, but she nodded and waited until Christine indicated where they should sit, at a small table that looked a little cheap for such a beautiful room. She refused milk, then settled the tea in front of her.

"You must realise, there's no doubt that Sopley was responsible for the murder of Emily Slaughter. As I explained on the telephone, I led the case up until the point where he was killed."

Christine nodded and sipped her own drink. But it was obvious she wasn't really taking it in. Sands kept going.

"First of all, he had a history of similar offences. He was arrested several times for breaking into homes, and once he was caught inside the bedroom of a young girl. Arranging her dolls." Sands kept her eyes on Christine Harvey, frowning at her lack of proper attention. "When Sopley broke in..." – she glanced across at the blinds – "...next door, he didn't only take Emily Slaughter, he also took her doll. We're not sure exactly why, but he arranged the doll with her body." As she spoke, she saw the image of the doll burrowing inside the cavity in the girl's chest, its feet sticking out. She let the thought linger a moment, as if to examine it anew, but then pushed it away. "We don't know exactly why, but it was an important part of the crime for him."

Christine Harvey took another sip and Sands decided to shock her just a little, to see if that would bring her into the conversation more. "He butchered her, he opened a hole in her torso, so he could place the doll there." She was about to go on, to say it would have been part of a fantasy playing out in his head while he committed the murder – but Christine suddenly surprised her.

"Just like with the cat."

"What?"

Christine sniffed. "Like with the cat. I told you, its organs were everywhere."

Sands paused for a second. "No... I'm talking about Michael Sopley, Christine. Sopley. *He* did it."

"That's what you say. But what if you're wrong?" She didn't say it in a challenging way, but in a completely flat tone. As if stating a simple truth.

Sands tried again. "There's other evidence. A lot of other evidence. Would you like to hear about it?"

It took a while, but Christine's shoulders twitched in what was probably a shrug of acceptance.

"The bedrooms in this house, are they downstairs? With sliding doors, secured by Bullion three-point locks?" She pulled out her phone and held it up for Christine to see the photograph. Again she half-shrugged, half-nodded.

"They're very secure locks. But Sopley had worked as a locksmith, so he knew exactly how to break into them. It would have been one of the reasons he chose the Slaughters. He picked Emy because he knew he'd be able to break into her room."

Christine didn't reply. After a while Sands clicked her phone off and put it down on the table.

"We found DNA evidence on the girl's body linking Sopley directly to the crime. The chances of the material we found on the girl coming from someone else are hundreds of millions to one against, Christine. It's as close to certain as we can be." She stared, but sensed the power of the mathematical proof wasn't as convincing to Christine as it was for her.

"He was seeing a specialist, a man who works with paedophiles. Sopley told him he was going to try a therapy to relieve his urges. It was based around swimming, going into cold water every day. That's why Sopley moved down here, to the refuge. To be near to the ocean to try and cure himself. The problem is, it's not real science. There's no evidence it works, at least not for the problem Sopley had. But if he *believed* it did, and therefore stopped taking the medication which was actually supressing his urges, then it may have allowed them to build up until they were too strong to resist." She stopped. It was clear by now this wasn't working. Nothing was going in. It was like the woman had built up a wall around her, a defence against anything that challenged what she already believed. Then Christine started to cry. Fat, glistening tears, that rolled down her cheek. She made no effort to wipe them away.

Sands watched, but did nothing to comfort her.

"You don't believe me," Christine said, after she'd cried for several minutes. Finally, she wiped her face and stared, looking almost defiant.

"It's not that I don't believe you," Sands replied. "It's just that you're wrong. You're not accepting the truth. What the evidence shows."

"The evidence could be wrong." Christine looked up suddenly, her eyes momentarily clear. "It is wrong. It *has* to be wrong."

Sands shook her head. "No. The evidence is the evidence."

The woman screwed her eyes shut, squeezing out the last of the tears. When she opened them again, she wore a haunted look on her face. "You're not going to help me?" It was half-question, half-statement, and Sands nearly agreed with it, but something about the woman in front of her generated some degree of compassion. She took a deep breath. "There's probably a simple explanation for this..." she began, then realised she didn't have one, so fell silent again.

"Do you have children, Detective?" Christine asked suddenly.

"No."

"I have a daughter," she went on, her eyes red and puffy. She looked up at a photograph of a girl beaming down from the wall. "She's nine now. The same age Emy would have been if she hadn't been killed."

It took Sands a while, but she looked at the photograph and nodded. "I expect that's what's concerning you," she said. "You've moved in the house next door to where a girl the same age was taken and murdered. I assume you didn't know beforehand? You weren't aware when you bought the house?"

Christine shook her head.

"That's unfortunate. You should have been informed."

Christine nodded this time.

"I expect it's quite normal that you're going to worry,"

Sands said stiffly. She took a sip from her tea. "But it doesn't change the evidence. It isn't wrong."

Christine was crying again, and Sands watched her sniffle for a few moments before she turned away to look out of the wide front window at the sea. The view today looked so different to when she'd been in the building before. Clouds floated over the water, casting shadows interrupting the blue-white sparkle.

"But what if you've understood it wrong?" Christine asked.

Sands said nothing as she looked around, the mirror image of the Slaughters' room. "You could move," she said quietly. "There's no need to do so, but it might help you. To get away."

Christine shook her head.

"A place like this would sell easily, even if..." She didn't finish the thought.

"I can't." Christine sounded stubborn.

"Why not?"

Now the mother took a deep breath, and on the surface she seemed more focused, more rational. "I've moved the children once. They seem settled. I don't want to move them again." Sands waited, already she'd seen through the excuse.

"You paid too much for the house. A study I read about found that buildings associated with murders are valued an average of seventeen percent lower than otherwise similar properties, with an even bigger reduction for high-profile cases. You didn't know about the murder so you overpaid." Sands shrugged. "Just accept it. Take the loss and move on. Your well-being is more important."

Christine looked shocked and angry for a moment, but then she nodded. "I paid one and a half million. I don't know what it's really worth." She sniffed, and Sands thought to herself, *Not that much.*

Christine's next words surprised her. "Besides. If we sell the house he'll know. He'll *know* that I know."

Although she didn't quite understand why, a cold shiver ran down Sands' back at the way Christine said this. "He won't *know,* Christine. He won't know, because he didn't kill his daughter, so there's nothing *to* know. At worst, he might come to believe that you suspect him – and that might make relations difficult until the move goes through. But he won't *do* anything, because he's *not* a killer."

There was a long silence while Christine appeared to consider this. But by the time she spoke again, she was adrift on her fears once more. "What about the cat? If he's not a killer, why did he kill the cat?"

Sands couldn't answer this. At least, not yet. But it occurred to her that she could change that.

It was a hell of a step down from her last case, but on the other hand, it was quite a step up from what she was currently doing, reviewing dusty old cases that had already been settled. And since there was still no word on the investigation into her conduct, not even a date for the hearing, how much harm could she do by helping put this woman's fears to rest?

"Perhaps I could look into what happened to the cat for you? Did anybody else see it? Anybody I could speak to?"

"No. It was gone by the time the police came, the council had emptied the bins."

Sands nodded slowly. "Well, perhaps I could speak to the men who emptied the bins. It's likely they'd have noticed if a dead animal had been dumped that way."

She watched as Christine thought this through. "No, the police asked them. They said they didn't see anything."

"Did you think to take any photographs?"

Christine shook her head.

"So no one saw it? Only you?"

The woman nodded. Sands considered. "Christine, did you notice my limp when I walked in here?"

Christine looked up in surprise, but nodded again.

"I was shot, when Sopley was killed. In the crossfire. I can walk, but at the moment I can't run or move fast. But I have dreams. Dreams where I'm running, loose and free. And they seem incredibly real. Sometimes I wake up and simply cannot believe that it's not real, that I still can't move properly. And sometimes Christine, sometimes those dreams happen in the daytime. But every time I try to move quickly, do you know what happens?"

Christine shook her head.

"My legs yank me right back to reality. That's what." Sands paused. "You don't have that, Christine. You don't have that link to reality, bringing you back."

Christine just watched, her chest rising and falling quickly.

"But that's not your fault. You've been put under tremendous pressure. We all have, with this pandemic. It's been the craziest year ever. On top of that, your husband died. You've moved. All of these events have put pressure on you. There's no shame in letting all that get to you."

Christine just stared.

"Are you quite sure, one hundred percent sure, that there was a cat? A cat that no one else saw?"

Christine's mouth fell open. "You think I imagined it?"

Sands sighed. "I don't know. But as an investigator, it's a possibility I have to consider. Because I know that people under pressure do imagine things."

"But the blood where he killed it. I saw the blood as well."

"Can you show me?"

"No. It's gone. It was washed away..." She stared out the window towards the sea. When she looked back, her lip was quivering. "I have to get my daughter from school."

"OK." Sands nodded. There was no help she could give here, nothing to investigate, but perhaps she'd done some good anyway. Either way, this was the moment to extract herself. Gently and carefully.

"What about his alibi?"

This threw Sands. "Whose alibi?"

"The guy, the homeless guy you keep talking about. Michael Sopley. He had an alibi."

For a second, Sands' mind spun, searching through what she'd been able to piece together from the file, referenced and sorted in her mind, but she came up blank. "What alibi? What are you talking about?"

"The alibi!" Christine's face was twisted in annoyance. She got up suddenly and began lifting envelopes and children's colouring books, eventually recovering an iPad. "Here." She focused on the screen for a while, swiping and tapping, and looking increasingly worried when she failed to find what she was searching for. But then her expression changed again.

"Here," she handed the device over. "What do you make of that?"

FORTY-ONE

Sands read a few lines on the iPad, then stopped.

"What is this? The local paper?" She asked. She'd been shown a list of comments, and scrolled up the page, trying to reach the top and see who owned the webpage.

"No! It's in the comments. Read through the comments." Christine snatched the iPad back and frowned at the screen as she scrolled back down to the same place.

"It's there somewhere." She passed it back and Sands read again:

You can tell that Slaughter guy is guilty just by looking at him.
What kind of parents let someone break into your house when your actually there?
Rodney Slaughter is guilty as sin. End of. I hope he rots in hell.

There were more. Plenty more. "Christine, you shouldn't read this kind of thing. It won't help..."

"Read the one about the alibi. You have to find that one."

Reluctantly Sands kept reading.

"I have to go get my daughter," Christine said again. Sands looked up to see she now had a set of car keys in her hand. "Don't go anywhere. I'll only be half an hour."

"*What?* No, I can't stay..."

"Don't be silly. Read it. I'll be thirty minutes."

"Christine, I can't stay in your house, not while you're not here."

"*Read it.* Please." Christine flashed a strange, desperate smile. "I have to go or I'll be late for Molly." Then, before Sands could refuse again, Christine took off at a faster pace than Sands could match with her injuries.

Sands stood and took a step forward, wincing at the pain that shot up her side. After sitting for even a short while, the damaged muscles in her hips tightened. She heard the front door open and close. In the end, she sat down, sighed heavily and began to read.

Sands scrolled back to the top to see the comments related to an article in the *South West Star* written a few days after Emily's body had been discovered. The article was mostly accurate, focusing on Sopley's shooting, the deaths of Commander Roper and ARO Jones, and her own involvement. But the comments below were clearly open season to lunatics. The site was unmoderated – there was a disclaimer to this effect, setting out that any views posted below the line were not of the journalists nor the newspaper they represented. They were obviously lies and nonsense. But as she read down, Sands reached the part that Christine was interested in.

TruBrit_Truegrit: Michael Sopley is an evil scumbag. Hell is to good for him. End off!!!

LindaBear87: that ain't true. Michael Sopley was murdered by police to cover up their false accusations about killing that girl. He didn't do it.

*TruBrit_Truegrit: Oh yeah? And you know more than the police do you? *scumbag**

LindaBear87: Yes. I do know more than the police, as it happens.

TruBrit_Truegrit: How come?

Then the same poster had replied to their own comment.

TruBrit_Truegrit: Gone quiet have you? I knew you was full of it. #pedoscum.

LindaBear87: I know because he was my boyfriend. And he was with me the whole entire time. So he had an alibi. So he couldn't have done it. Could he? Freakin' Genius.

Other posters had waded in at this point, though their comments and replies didn't seem relevant. Sands searched the rest of the comments section, but couldn't find any more messages left by the LindaBear87 account.

She considered what this meant. None of this would bear any weight in an actual investigation, but at the same time, it did make her ask one question. Before she could stop herself, she grabbed her mobile and dialled John Lindham's number. They hadn't spoken since he'd warned her he wasn't able to give her any updates.

"Ma'am." His voice was wary.

"I have a question about the Sopley case."

There was a pause, an audible sigh. "You know I can't..."

"Do you still have the file? I know it's closed."

Another pause, and when he spoke again, he sounded frustrated. "No. It's all wrapped up. There is no case..."

"Did you find anything about an alibi for Sopley?"

Lindham stopped. "An alibi?"

"Yes."

A pause. "Ma'am, he was *dead*. How was he going to give us an alibi?"

Sands bit her lip in irritation. "So you didn't look? You didn't ask around, find out if anyone else claimed to have been with him when the Slaughter girl was taken?"

She could almost hear his confusion through the phone line. "Why would we?"

"Why would you?" she repeated, failing to keep the surprise and irritation from her voice. "Why the hell wouldn't you?"

"There was no need. Forensics placed him at the scene, his background was a perfect match to the crime, and his fleeing confirmed his guilt..."

"Not if he had an alibi it didn't."

"He didn't have an alibi."

"How do you know, if you didn't even look?"

There was another pause as Lindham caught up with the logic. When he came back his voice was angry. "Look boss, *you* gave us Sopley. I only got the case after the whole thing was blown to shit in that farmyard. So if you've got a problem with it now, perhaps you should be having this conversation with the Super?"

Sands didn't reply. She knew that was never going to happen. Lindham went on, more conciliatory this time. "I'm sorry, ma'am, but you need to understand how it was. Two men died. And people said that only happened because of the way you went charging in. I don't know if that's true, I wasn't there. But I'm damn sure you questioning whether Sopley was our man or not isn't going to help anyone. It's better to just keep things simple. A lot better."

"I think it's better if we discover the truth," Sands replied coldly. "Isn't that our job?

"It's my job, but it sure isn't yours. Not while you're suspended. So whatever it is you're doing, you shouldn't be doing it. And if you keep doing it, I am going to report you."

Sands took a deep breath. For a few seconds she visualised what was happening in MID without her influence. She didn't like the thought. "Just tell me one thing. Did Sopley have a girlfriend? Anyone he might have spent the night with, or did anyone come up with the name Linda?"

Lindham took a long while to answer. When he did so his anger had changed to resignation. "I don't know, ma'am. I don't think anyone even checked."

FORTY-TWO

Sands lowered the phone in slow contemplation. Lindham was right, of course. She shouldn't be looking into this, and if he carried out his threat of reporting it, she was in big trouble. But at the same time, his words troubled her.

She got up and stretched, massaging away the pain in her muscles, before slowly walking to the window and lifting the blinds a little. Across the other side of the courtyard she could see into the Slaughters' house. It was mid-afternoon, and after a few seconds she was able to confirm no one was there. She lifted the blinds a little more for a better view. The room didn't look too different from when she'd last been there, informing the couple of their daughter's death. It had the same minimalist look; she could see the same giant green-glass dining table.

She dropped the blinds. Considering. It occurred to her that Christine Harvey's actions in covering the windows were slightly excessive. The two houses did overlook each other, but was it really any worse than her own neighbours being able to see into certain rooms of her flat?

She went back to the kitchen table to take a closer look at

the papers and envelopes that had been left there. There were electricity bills, water bills, a letter acknowledging a change-of-address request from a bank. Nothing out of the ordinary. She glanced through the pictures, which the child had presumably drawn – female figures with wings that she guessed were supposed to be fairies. She turned the paper to identify an animal drawn on the side: a giraffe, maybe? It didn't look very happy, whatever it was. She pulled open the kitchen drawers to reveal cutlery, table mats and napkins, nothing particularly revealing. She clicked her tongue. Christine and her family had just moved in, there hadn't been enough time to leave their stamp on the place.

She remembered how the Slaughters' house was arranged upside down. Rodney Slaughter had kept a small home office down there. Perhaps Christine had done the same. She wasn't after anything in particular, she just wanted to get a feel for this woman who'd brought a genuine concern to light. And while she had no right to search the house, she'd been invited in, so there was no legal barrier. She checked her watch. She still had ten minutes before Christine returned. She doubted she'd be early: she presumably already had a routine to picking up her child, and knew exactly how long it would take. So Sands set out down the stairs and along the lower corridor, identical but opposite to the one she'd seen in the Slaughters' house.

The first room was a child's bedroom, eerily similar to Emily Slaughter's. The same light pink colour on the walls, so Sands presumed the Slaughters had had it painted themselves, perhaps once they knew a family with a child was buying the house. The same sliding French doors, with the same brand of lock, though the handle here had been tied crudely with rope so that it couldn't be opened. Sands looked around quickly, seeing nothing else unusual, then backed out and continued down the corridor.

The door to the next room was shut. Sands hesitated slightly. She considered slipping on a pair of forensic gloves to avoid leaving any fingerprints, but dismissed the idea. Instead, she pulled her sleeve over her hand, using the material as a barrier between her skin and the handle. She pushed the door open and looked into what must be Christine Harvey's room. She hadn't unpacked yet. There were boxes on the floor and black plastic clothes bags on hangers, stretching the thin material of the bags tight, tearing holes in places.

The decoration here was neutral, a blank canvas that Christine hadn't yet done anything with. Sands backed out and moved to the next door. This room was also full of cardboard boxes. A bare bed suggested it was an unfinished guest room. Presumably that meant the final room on the corridor belonged to Christine's other child, the teenage boy, which in turn meant there was no home office to snoop around in. A little disappointed, Sands moved to the last door to see if her reasoning was correct.

It was. It looked like the boy had spent time making the room to his liking. There were posters on the walls – some gothic-looking band that Sands didn't recognise, and a young model posing in her underwear. The room itself was neat and tidy. There was a laptop and a stack of papers on a desk by the window. Her eye was drawn to something hanging from a shelving unit, but before she could identify what it was, she noticed that the laptop was on – its screen reflected in the window. Seconds later she heard the flush of a toilet from what must be an en-suite bathroom. They saw each other at once, and both stopped, stunned. Sands had one foot in the boy's bedroom, the other still in the hallway.

"Who are you?" He was clearly scared. She saw his eyes slide down to the floor, coming to rest on a sports bag that was near her feet. The handle of something poked from the top – a tennis racket perhaps – though the shape was wrong. Whatever it was, he eyed it as if it might be needed to defend himself. Sands felt her heart beat hard.

"It's OK. I'm a friend of your mum's," she replied, lifted her hands in a reassuring gesture.

"Mum went out," the boy said, nervously. "To get Molly."

"I know. I was... I'm just waiting for her. I was just looking for the bathroom."

It was obvious the boy didn't believe her, and Sands realised she'd have to give him something else. His eyes dropped to the bat again. "There's a bathroom upstairs. Off the hall."

Sands nodded and smiled, mostly at the thought that she'd nearly put on her forensic gloves. That would really have freaked the kid out.

"I'm sorry, you're right." She stopped. "Actually, I'm not being completely honest with you." Sands paused and tried to smile at him conspiratorially. But the fear on his face only shifted a little, into confusion.

She kept smiling. "Your mum popped out to get Molly, but she hasn't shown me the house yet. And I got... nosy." She wrinkled her nose up. "It's such a beautiful house. I'm a bit jealous."

The boy was staring at his feet now.

"You must be Ryan?" Sands continued. "I'm Erica."

"I was just doing my homework," the boy said somewhat unconvincingly, and then, when his words prompted Sands to glance towards his laptop, he reddened suddenly. Sands couldn't see the screen directly, but now she realised she could see the gist of it reflected in the window. Another young model, this time without her underwear and her legs spread considerably wider than Sands could currently manage.

The boy quickly crossed the room and pushed the screen closed. She smiled again and backed further out of the room. "Well, I'll let you get on with it. I'm sorry to have disturbed you." She glanced at him, expecting his face to redden further. Instead, she found him watching her.

"What's wrong with you?" he asked.

"What's *wrong* with me?"

"Yeah. You've got a limp."

Sands considered for a few moments. "I was in a car accident. A drunk driver."

The boy considered this. "How do you know Mum?"

Sands opened her mouth to answer, but was saved by the sound of the key in the front door. "I'll leave you to it," she said again, and limped back up the stairs.

"Did you read it? Did you see about the alibi?" Christine asked once she'd installed Molly in front of the TV in her bedroom.

"Yes." Sands worked out quickly what she wanted to say. "It's interesting, but just because someone posts something on an internet site, that's a long way from being actual evidence." She hoped this would be enough to settle the point, but Christine came right to the same issue that was bothering Sands.

"Did someone check it out then? Track down this 'Lindabear' and find out what she meant?"

Sands hesitated enough for Christine to sense the answer.

"Oh," she said. "Well, shouldn't they have? I mean, isn't that the least they should do? Wouldn't it prove... that Rodney could have done it, after all?"

Sands shook her head. "It probably isn't true. It's just an anonymous person on the internet."

Christine took a deep breath and dropped her head. She looked like she wanted to believe, desperately so, but didn't.

"There might be something I can do," Sands said eventually. This time, Christine's eyes filled with hope. "This Linda-Bear – it's almost certainly someone making up rubbish, just to wind people up online, or appear more important than they really are. But I could try to check it out."

"Really? You'll do that?"

Sands felt a little awkward at the desperate look on the woman's face and nodded as she got up to go. "No promises. It's a long shot, but I'll try."

FORTY-THREE

Driving away, Sands refused to consider whether any of this was a good idea, and thought instead about Christine and her two children – all of them, living so close to where Emy Slaughter had been abducted. No wonder they needed help.

She took the same Wareham road she'd driven down all those months before. She didn't even know if the St Austells centre was still open. It might have closed for Covid reasons, or perhaps because one of its residents had turned out to be a killer. But as she pulled through the entrance in the red-brick walls, it looked exactly the same. The minibus with St Austells stencilled on the side was parked in the same place, the car with its wheels removed was still up on bricks, though the weeds growing around it looked considerably bigger.

The front door was open, just as it had been before. She was about to push her way inside when she stopped, remembering that because of her suspension, she ought to tread carefully. So she knocked and waited, until the door was opened by the same woman as last time.

"Hello. It's Wendy, isn't it?"

The woman stared back. "I remember you. You're that policewoman. The one who got shot."

Sands nodded. "That's right. Is your boss in? I just need to ask him a couple of questions." She felt her hand reaching automatically for the badge that wasn't currently there, and stopped herself with a private smile. She hoped the woman wouldn't ask to see it.

"I thought you lot were all done?"

"Almost," Sands replied, trying to offer a smile. "I've just got a couple of loose ends to clear up."

Wendy didn't ask for her ID. Instead, she led the way back along the corridor to the office where she and Golding had met Julian Pink six months earlier. The place still smelt unpleasant, but less so. Wendy knocked but then opened the door and leaned in, whispering so that Sands couldn't hear what she said. Then she stepped back. "Mr Pink will see you now." She watched as Sands limped past into the room.

Julian Pink continued typing something on his computer for a while before looking up. "You know, I'm pretty sure I've answered every question at least five times. The centre cannot be held responsible for the actions of one man—"

Sands was quick to interrupt him. "I'm sorry to bother you again, Mr Pink." She tried to give a reassuring smile, but it wasn't a look that felt very natural. "I'm sure this whole business has been incredibly disruptive."

He frowned at her, clearly not expecting this change in her attitude. "Where's the other one?"

"Excuse me?"

"The last time you were here there was a local plod with you? And the other lot all came in pairs too."

"I'm working independently of Detective Golding, if that's what you mean. I'm just following up on a few small points."

"I thought it was all done. Sopley should never have been allowed to come here. That was all your fault."

Sands smiled again to show she didn't doubt it. After a while, he sighed.

"Go on then." He held out his hand, inviting her to sit. "What is it this time?"

Sands settled herself before speaking. "I understand that Michael Sopley had a girlfriend while he was here at St Austells? A woman named Linda."

Pink scratched his head for a second, then shrugged. "I don't know. Maybe he did."

Sands remembered the woman's username, and specifically the date. "She'd probably have been early thirties, I think. Her date of birth is 1987. I'm just trying to track her down, I have a few questions for her."

Pink still looked blank. "I don't know. I never saw him with anyone." His annoyance seemed to have morphed into boredom.

"You don't have anyone who meets that description staying here? Or did have? When Sopley was a resident?"

"Nope." He didn't seem to have anything to add.

"Well, perhaps it's possible Arthur might remember something? Arthur Josephs, the man we spoke to in the wheelchair?"

"I doubt it, Detective." Pink gave her a smug, self-satisfied smile. "Arthur's dead. Gangrene got him, just like I told you."

Sands cursed inwardly. She'd feared that might be the case. "Were any of the other residents close to Sopley? Anyone else still here who might have known if he had a girlfriend?"

It took Pink a while to decide whether he was going to answer or not. In the end he chose the latter, his expression leaving no doubt that he was delighted not to be of any help. Sands stayed quiet for a moment, wishing she were working officially and could force him to take this more seriously. But in the end she decided it probably wouldn't work anyway. She got up. "Well, that's everything. Thank you for your time."

He also stood. "Not at all." He grinned at her. "Happy to help."

Walking back out through the centre, Sands felt her face glowing a little hot. It was partly that the meeting had been somewhat humiliating, but it had more to do with irritation that she hadn't found the information she wanted. The only other way she thought she could get it was to visit the newspaper offices and persuade them to reveal the contact details of whoever had posted under the name LindaBear. Under normal circumstances they'd have the legal right to refuse her, never mind her suspension.

But as she reached the front door she found Wendy standing there, blocking the door, indecision on her face. Sands stopped, unable to continue without physically moving her out of the way. "I was just leaving," she prompted. The woman barely reacted. "Wendy? Is there something you wanted?"

Wendy looked behind Sands, as if expecting to see Julian Pink looming behind her, but the corridor was empty. "I probably shouldn't have been listening," she said eventually. "But I was. And I know who Linda is. Or who she was."

FORTY-FOUR

They went outside, so that if Julian Pink emerged from his office he wouldn't be able to see them.

"Who?" Sands asked.

"She never stayed here. But sometimes we do meals for non-residents. People who need food and can't get it anywhere else. Linda came a few times. I think that's where she met Sopley."

"You said you knew who she *was*? Past tense?"

A pause. Wendy's eyes wobbled. "She killed herself."

Sands nodded slowly. "When?"

"A few weeks after the Sopley thing. Guess she couldn't take it. All the hate he was getting, after what happened."

Sands fished in her bag for a notebook. "Do you have a surname?"

Wendy shook her head. "I'm not sure, it was Cole or Collins or something like that. But I know someone else who knew her better. She'll know."

Sands glanced up, waiting.

"Local girl called Kelly O'Reilly. They shared a house together. Over in Poole."

"You know the address?"

"I got it from the computer when you was with Mr Pink."

Sands' lips curled into a smile as she wrote it down. "Thank you."

She plugged it into the car's GPS and was there in twenty minutes. O'Reilly lived in a small, terraced house in an ugly estate on the outskirts of Poole. It looked a million miles away from the picture-postcard beauty surrounding St Austells. Sands got out of the car and locked it, but when she looked at the house – dark inside, even with the fast-approaching night – no one seemed to be home. She knocked on the door anyway, just to be sure, and to her surprise she heard noises, then angry shouts. She knocked again.

The door opened and an unnaturally skinny, pallid woman with dirty black hair stared back at her.

"What?" Sands noticed her tongue was pierced. Behind her, the dingy hallway was illuminated by a single candle that twisted and flickered and was nearly extinguished by the breeze from the door.

"Kelly O'Reilly?"

The woman looked Sands up and down, her face twisted into a sneer. "Depends who's asking, and why are you making such a racket?" Her whole body was tense, her fingers flexed on the edge of the door, the nails chewed and cracked. She seemed about to slam it shut. Sands abandoned her plans to ask about Sopley. "Why are you in the dark?" she said instead.

"*What?*" The anger changed to confusion on the woman's face. "Who are you?"

"Did they cut your electricity off?"

"What business is that of yours?"

"When did they do it?"

"*I don't know.*" She looked perplexed. "Last week sometime. Who the hell are you?"

"Have they told you they'll reinstate it?"

The woman stared for a moment. "*No.*"

"Because they have to. By law. If your income is less than sixty percent of the national average, and you suffer from a recognised disability, such as substance abuse, then it's against the law to leave you without power or water. I can help you draft a letter. If you send it, they'll be forced to reconnect you within forty-eight hours. They'll also compensate you financially for the time you've been cut off. It'll be a significant amount, several hundred pounds per day."

A range of emotions seemed to flow over the woman's face, first fury, presumably at the accusation that she was a drug addict, but then a more pragmatic look. She *was* a heavy user of heroin, after all. "Is that true?" she said. "About the law'n all?"

"Yes."

"How do you know? Who are you?"

"I'm a police officer. It's my job to know."

The sneer came right back onto the woman's face. "Police?"

"That's right."

"I knew it."

Sands said nothing, and after a while the woman shrugged. "And you're here about my electricity?"

"No." Sands shook her head. "I'm here because I'm investigating the circumstances around Michael Sopley's death. I came to see you because I believe you may have known him, or known someone who knew him. A woman named Linda. Linda Cole, or Collins."

For a few seconds the woman didn't answer. "Kline. You're talking about Linda Kline. And I don't suppose anyone's gonna investigate *her* death, are they?"

"I don't know. Should they?"

Kelly glanced at her then looked away, disgust written all over her face.

"Are you hungry?" Sands asked suddenly. "Can I get you something to eat?"

"What?"

"I'm hungry, and you look like you should eat something too. Would you like to get some food? I'll pay."

"Are you for real?'

It took a bit of convincing, but Sands got her to leave the house and climb into the car. Then she drove a few miles away to a more affluent suburb of the town and an Italian bistro she knew. Sands took them inside, where Kelly wouldn't be stared at, and no one else could hear them speak.

"Don't know what this town's coming to," Kelly said after she'd looked at the menu. "It's all vegan this and hummus that." When the waitress approached, she ordered a lasagne and chips. Sands asked for the same.

"And two salads too," she added as an afterthought. "You should probably eat something green," she said by way of an explanation.

"You can. I ain't going to," Kelly replied.

While they waited, Sands pulled a page from her notebook and wrote out a paragraph quoting the regulations regarding household electricity supply. When she was finished, she tore it off. "Copy that onto a proper sheet of paper and add the dates you were cut off. They'll have to compensate you."

Kelly read it and eyed Sands. "You know all that, without having to look it up?"

"Yes."

Kelly folded the paper up and slipped it into her jeans pocket. "I know who you are," she said a moment later. "From your limp. You're the one what was shot. When Mike was killed."

Sands nodded. "That's right."

"So what is it you want?"

"I'm following up loose ends. About Mike and Linda."

Kelly snorted. "Loose ends? Is that all Linda is to you people?"

"I don't know yet. I'm hoping you can tell me."

Kelly shook her head. She paused while the waitress returned with their food, and they were both silent as the plates were put in front of them. Sands waited until the waitress had left and Kelly had eaten a little. "Linda left a post, on a newspaper article. She said that she was with Sopley the night the girl was taken."

Kelly chewed and swallowed. "Did she?"

"Yes. Do you know anything about it?"

"About Linda posting on some internet site? No."

"About her being with Michael Sopley on the night of Emily Slaughter's death?"

Kelly cut off another corner of the pasta and pushed it into her mouth. "Better late than never, huh?" she said when she'd swallowed again. "You bastards were in such a rush to arrest Mike, you forgot to check if he even could have done it."

Sands breathed slowly, remembering that day, and even considering there was some validity to what this woman was saying. But they *would* have checked. Once they'd arrested Sopley, they would have checked then. At least, they would have, had she been in charge. "Did she tell you about it?"

"It doesn't hardly matter, does it? What I say now. It's not going to change anything. Not now they're both dead."

Sands took a bite of her own food and chewed thoughtfully. "I don't know if it'll change anything," she said when she'd finished. "Or not. Not until you tell me what you know." She took another bite.

Kelly looked away, but when she looked back her eyes were glistening. "So you want to hear at last. Someone suddenly gives a shit."

Sands chewed and waited.

It took Kelly a few moments to compose herself before she

went on. "Linda died from an overdose." She set her head on one side. "I found her. Dead in her bed, with sick all over the sheets." Her face shuddered again, and she wiped away tears that weren't there.

"Heroin?"

Kelly nodded, and Sands watched her.

"Accident or deliberate?"

"I dunno. Normally we shot up together, you know?" She glanced up at Sands, as if she might understand. Sands held her gaze until Kelly looked away. "But maybe she wanted to be alone. After Mike. Or maybe she wanted... out." Kelly looked away, then back. "I dunno. She didn't tell me, and she was my friend, you know?"

"Did she tell you about the night Sopley died?" Sands asked after a while. They'd both stopped eating now.

Kelly hesitated, but then answered. "Yeah she told me. And I told her to go to see you guys, but she wouldn't. She was so... confused by it all."

"Confused?"

"That's right."

Sands frowned. "I don't understand, Kelly. What was she confused about? Can you tell me what she told you?"

Again, Kelly looked away for a few moments before turning back. "They were together. In his room in the shelter. She weren't meant to be there, but it was easy to get in. His room was right at the end of the corridor, and you can sneak in up the fire escape. That's where she saw him. Where she was that night."

"The night that Emily Slaughter was abducted?"

Kelly nodded.

"Did she say what time she got there? It's important, Kelly."

"I dunno. The afternoon sometime. About four I think."

There was no need for Sands to remind herself of the time-line. The Slaughters putting their daughter to bed at about

7pm, the pathology report concluding she'd been killed between 10pm and 3am. "And what time did she leave?"

"Next morning. About eight."

"Could he have left? Slipped out, sometime in the night?"

"That's what I asked her. Cos I didn't believe the cops could get it so wrong, but she swore blind he was there the whole time. And she..." Kelly looked away.

"What?"

Defiance and despair were both evident on Kelly's face.

"What is it, Kelly?"

"Look, I don't necessarily want to give Mike an alibi, right?" she said suddenly. "He was a scumbag, and I'm not sorry he's dead. And I ain't getting dragged into court or whatever."

"It's unlikely this will get to a court," Sands replied at once. "Not with Sopley dead. You may need to give a statement under oath. But that's probably as far as it'll go."

Abruptly, Kelly pushed away her plate. She gulped down the rest of her Coke and sat there, breathing hard from the effort. Of what, Sands didn't quite understand.

"What is it Kelly?" Sands said, seeing the knuckles on Kelly's hand turning white where she held the glass. "If she was with him, what don't you want to say?"

Finally, Kelly set down the glass. She turned to Sands again. "You wanna know why Linda didn't know what the hell to do? After Mike got shot? But how she knew one hundred percent he didn't kill that kid? Alright. Here you go. She said she didn't sleep one wink that night. But Mike did. He slept like a little baby. Right after he raped her."

Kelly turned to Sands and her defiant face finally cracked as a tear rolled down her cheek.

FORTY-FIVE

The words sent a wave of shock through Sands' mind, but she recovered quickly, pushing it down and instead observing the woman opposite her. She watched her carefully, looking for the common signs of lying – hands covering her face or vulnerable body parts, such as the throat or chest. She glanced down at Kelly's feet to see if they were shuffling nervously. And she waited, giving the woman every opportunity to add unnecessary layers of detail to the story. She didn't see any of the usual tells. Instead, Kelly sniffed loudly, looked back at her food and began eating again.

Sands considered what she'd heard. If Kelly wasn't lying, then it might explain why Sopley had run on the morning of the murder. He might have felt guilty or scared about what he'd done, or feared that the rape would be discovered when the police came to ask questions at the refuge. And once he'd been told about the death of a young girl, he'd have known the police *would* come – with his history of breaking into houses, his interest in children and his record on the sexual offenders' register. He would have known he'd need to rely on Linda for an alibi. In those circumstances it was little wonder he panicked –

if it was true. But if it was true that Michael Sopley didn't kill Emily Slaughter, then *somebody else did...* Sands' mind spun. Was it possible that Christine Harvey was right? Everything Sands thought she knew about the case suddenly felt completely uncertain. She reached out for a sip of water, felt her whole arm trembling, and set it down again, cursing the nerve damage.

"I need to be quite sure about this," she said, a moment later. "You couldn't be making a mistake about the day this happened, or what time Linda told you she arrived and left?"

Kelly's jaw jutted out in response. "It really ain't that hard to remember, given how you killed him the next day." Then her face softened and she shook her head. "No, I'm not making a mistake."

It felt like a huge hole had opened up in Sands' mind. "When did she tell you?"

Kelly shrugged. "A couple of weeks later. She locked herself in her room for about a week. Eventually I got her to come out. That's when she told me."

"Why didn't you go to the police? You must have known it meant he couldn't have killed Emily Slaughter."

She shrugged again. "Dunno. Guess we thought you lot would come to us. But you never did, did you?"

Sands just stared at her.

"And then it was too late, because a few weeks after that she killed herself."

Kelly finished her food while Sands found she'd lost her appetite. But she paid the bill and drove Kelly back to her house. As they pulled up outside, Sands noticed the graffiti-covered walls lining an alleyway just opposite, She stopped the engine. "Send that letter, Kelly. Get your power back."

Kelly nodded. "What happens now? With Mike?"

Sands was trying to make sense of that question, trying to force the conflicting pieces of evidence together, and each time she came up short.

"Write that letter."

She watched Kelly disappear into the dark interior and sat for a while, letting her mind range further. If she hadn't been suspended, she could have petitioned to have the case re-opened. She would need to convince her superiors that new evidence had come to light, in a previously solved case involving the deaths of two officers. She smiled wryly at the thought of how popular that would be, and she considered *how* she might present that evidence – one now-deceased drug addict had told another drug addict she'd been with Sopley the night the murder took place. She might get a hearing, but there would be significant objections raised.

The first problem was evidential. They might get Kelly to give a statement putting on record what Linda had told her, but it was second-hand testimony. If they were then able to arrest someone other than Sopley for the murder, the weakness of Kelly's statement would be a huge problem for the prosecution. Any decent defence attorney would use it to undermine their case, showing how the police had considered Sopley guilty until the second-hand, hearsay-alibi came up. With such an enormous element of doubt, it would make it extremely difficult to build any convincing case.

Secondly – and far more importantly – either Kelly or Linda could be lying. True, there had been no obvious signs that Kelly had lied to her just then, but body language only ever gave a rough indication. Some people were such poor liars that you could easily spot the signs; others lied so often they'd mastered the skill of hiding it. In Kelly's case, it was more likely that she believed she'd been telling the truth, but that didn't actually make it true.

All of this was moot, however, because Sands was

suspended. She shouldn't be anywhere near this case, which left her options extremely limited.

She came to two possible conclusions. She could drive home and wait for the results of the investigation into her conduct in the hope she'd be found to have acted professionally, and be reinstated. At that point she could submit a request to reopen the case. In the meantime, she could continue to work on her physical recovery and her paper study of solved murder cases from court-case files. Or...

She thought about the fear in Christine Harvey's eyes. If Sopley hadn't killed Emily Slaughter, then *somebody else had.* And that person was still at large. Scarier still, according to the published statistics of child killings, the most likely explanation was that he lived next door.

She thought of Rodney Slaughter with his thick, black hair, how he'd reacted to the news of his daughter's death, the gaps in the timeline when he could have taken her to the beach and killed her.

Sands left the estate where Kelly lived and drove back towards the main road. She came to a roundabout. One exit would take her back towards the Purbeck Hills and the village of Lulworth, the other would lead back to her flat. Since no one was behind her, she went around again.

Finally, she indicated right and pulled the car out onto the road back towards Lulworth.

FORTY-SIX

The white Audi was still in the driveway when she got back to the two cliff-top houses. Again, she pulled her car out of sight a little way down the lane and approached on foot. It was getting dark and a downlighter cast a little pool of white LED light over the doorstep.

Christine answered, glancing nervously around and noticing the Slaughters' car. "Come in. Quickly."

Sands stepped inside. "Where are the children?"

"Molly's asleep. Ryan's in his room. Did you find her? LindaBear?"

Sands nodded. "After a fashion."

Christine led the way into the main room. The kitchen showed the remains of a meal, plates piled on the work surface. Christine misinterpreted her look. "I did save some dinner if you want to eat?"

"No. Thanks."

Sands sat down and waited for Christine to do the same. "So you found her?" she prompted, clearly nervous.

Sands explained what she'd learned, and stressed the problems – that the information was second hand and that the woman had since died. She didn't mention the alleged rape. When she'd finished, Christine asked, "Well? What does that all mean?"

Sands pulled out her notebook and opened it to a new page. "Tell me everything. Every reason you have to suspect Rodney Slaughter of killing his daughter."

She listened as Christine unburdened herself, giving her drips of information, and revealing just how tangled and fragmented her thinking was. It was a challenge to connect the different threads, but by noting the details down under several headings, Sands eventually built up a more complete picture. She heard again about the cat's body, although she learned this time that another adult had seen the blood before it was washed away by the rain. This was something she could check, although she doubted whether she'd be able to ascertain if the blood had come from a cat or another animal. She heard how, in Christine's opinion, Rodney Slaughter looked at her daughter in a weird, or unsettling way. She heard how Christine suspected him of having an affair with a teaching assistant at the local primary school, a woman who now taught Molly Harvey, but who'd also taught his own daughter. Sands had her doubts about this, but when Christine told her she'd seen him at the teacher's home, and that he'd hidden this fact from his wife, she accepted it sounded like a fair conclusion. And she heard about Slaughter walking naked around the house in middle of the night and taking part in some kind of martial arts practice. As she listened and wrote, she racked her brain for anything that might help the two seemingly certain yet incompatible pieces of evidence to come together: the near certainty that Michael Sopley had committed the murder, and yet the impossibility of him being there to do it.

"Well?" Christine said when she'd finished. "What happens now?"

Sands drew a deep breath. She'd hoped for something she

could follow up on, or something that indicated a mistake had been made, but if it was there, she wasn't seeing it.

She was already shaking her head. "We could open an investigation into Rodney Slaughter. But realistically, it's highly unlikely there'll be anything to find."

"Why not?"

"Because, if he was involved—" She stopped again, trying to stress that from what Christine had told her, this was by no means certain. "*If* he was involved, then it's been six months. We found nothing on Emily's body to indicate he played any part in her death." She thought again, ticking off the points in her mind before saying them out loud. "He had an alibi for the night she went missing, albeit there is space within it for him to have carried out the murder, but only just."

Christine listened in silence, her face white.

"And the other accusations you've made against him – the possibility that he's having an affair, the odd way you say he looks at your daughter, his nocturnal activities. None of those are evidence of murder. Or indeed of any other crime."

Christine bit her lip. "You don't believe me, do you? You don't believe he did it?"

"I believe I have a duty to keep an open mind until the evidence is clear, one way or another. I thought it was, now I'm not so sure."

Christine stared at her, breathing hard. "Stay tonight," she said suddenly. Her hand shot out and gripped Sands' arm. "It's Friday night. He always does it on a Friday. The weird night-time stuff. Stay here and see for yourself. Then you'll believe me."

Sands didn't answer.

"Please. You can sleep on the sofa, or in the spare room downstairs. I'll wait up and wake you when he does it. You can *see* him for yourself, see the way he stares at Molly's room. The weird look in his eyes."

The idea was ridiculous. It occurred to Sands that the look in Christine Harvey's eyes was of absolute desperation. But it was enough to make her hesitate. She drew in a deep breath to give herself time to think. It would be unusual, even in normal circumstances, to conduct overnight surveillance on a suspect, unless there was a very specific need to do so. There didn't appear to be one here, but then again, these weren't normal circumstances. She wasn't officially working this case. Indeed, if her actions were discovered, her career would be at risk. But then again, it was already hanging in the balance.

She stared at the shuttered window, thinking of the Slaughters' house just beyond it. And she caught something, some sense, or feeling, that there was *something* here. Something that felt, in some weird way, familiar.

And while she didn't think for a moment that watching Rodney Slaughter's night-time exercises would help her understand what that was, it would buy her time. And *that* she might be able to use.

"Please, Detective Sands. Please don't leave me here next to him. You have to believe me."

Sands stared at Christine. She looked like a woman begging for her life. A woman trying to escape from a violent and ruthless killer. And a memory came to her, of herself, when she was a child, in exactly the same position.

"I'll stay tonight," she said.

FORTY-SEVEN

"We need to decide what to tell your children," Sands said after a while. "It's better they don't know about your suspicions."

"I'll say you're an old school friend. I'll say you're having issues at home, boyfriend troubles. Ryan'll know not to dig, and he won't really care."

"I already met your son. When you went to pick up Molly."

"Oh." Christine barely seemed to register this. "He's OK. And Molly will be pleased to have you here. I think she likes you."

Sands strode over to the window facing the Slaughters' house and lifted one of the slats. She could see Janet Slaughter working in the kitchen. Rodney Slaughter was nowhere to be seen.

"Could you not do that?" Christine asked from behind her. "It's just that they'll see the light. I only ever watch with the lights off."

Sands let the slat fall back into place.

. . .

Sands asked Christine to bring her a blanket and put it on the sofa. Not that she intended to sleep, but she wanted Christine's excuse to be believable if the children found her there. She went back to her car to collect a pair of prismatic binoculars. And then, at eleven o'clock, Christine switched off the lounge lights and lifted the blinds an inch or so, making a gap at the bottom where they could watch the Slaughters without being noticed. Sands set the focus on the binoculars, bringing details in the Slaughters' house into sharp relief, and she spent a full five minutes intently scanning the room. Both Janet and Rodney Slaughter were in the main room, him sitting and apparently reading, her cleaning the kitchen after their meal. At one point, Rodney appeared to call out to her; she stopped what she was doing and opened a cupboard, taking out a bottle of whisky and pouring a measure into a glass before carrying it over to him. He did nothing to acknowledge her, but when she was back cleaning up in the kitchen area, he very carefully took a sip. Eventually she sat down too and picked up a book. Sands couldn't see the titles of either book, but Janet's appeared to be a softback novel, whereas Rodney was holding a hardback. Neither of them paid any attention to the house opposite.

At 11:25, Janet rose from the sofa, said something to Rodney and waited; when he again seemed to ignore her, she left the room. A few seconds later, two lights went on in the rooms below, one in Emily's former room, Sands noted, the other one presumably in the Slaughters' bedroom. Both rooms had their curtains drawn. Immediately afterwards the light in the dead girl's room went out. Five minutes later, the other bedroom went dark. Rodney Slaughter didn't move.

Sands kept her glasses trained on Rodney Slaughter's face. Her feeling from earlier had come back and was growing stronger. Something about the situation here was wrong. But she still didn't know what it was that troubled her quite so much.

"Could I have a look?" Christine's voice surprised her as she'd been quiet for so long. Sands bit her lip as she watched Christine Harvey scanning the room opposite.

Just before midnight, Rodney Slaughter placed a bookmark in his book and set it aside, pushed up from the chair and walked across the room. He switched off the lights in the main room, throwing it into darkness. This time, only one light went on downstairs – presumably in the room the couple were using as their bedroom. After a further four minutes, that light also went off and the entire house fell dark.

"I'm going to check on Molly," Christine whispered a short while later, before padding off out of the room and down the stairs. Left alone, Sands continued to think. She replayed her entire conversation with Kelly O'Reilly, trying to test the certainty of the alibi she'd provided for Michael Sopley, who was surely still the most likely killer of the child. But after a while her thoughts shifted, unbidden by her conscious mind. They moved to her own memories. Her father, and her childhood house. And her mother who was no longer here.

She jumped a little when Christine suddenly returned, slipping down onto the floor beside her at the window. There was still nothing to see. "He usually comes back between two and three in the morning," Christine whispered. Sands nodded, and they stayed quiet for several minutes. Eventually, Sands rose and went back to the sofa. "We may as well wait here," she said. "We'll see if the light goes back on." When Christine joined her, they sat for a while in silence. Eventually she turned to Sands again.

"Thank you, by the way," she said. "For staying with me. It's the first time I've not been alone since Evan died."

Sands still didn't reply, but turned to Christine and watched her in the dim light of the room.

"I read about you being in hospital as well. After the business with Sopley. That must have been awful," Christine said. "In the middle of the pandemic."

"It wasn't too bad."

"Are you still injured? The way you move..."

"It's getting better."

Sands broke the ensuing silence. She sensed she was expected to return the sentiment. "I never said, about the loss of your husband." Sands' voice was stiff. "I'm sorry..."

"Thank you." Christine gave her a grateful look. It was obvious she wanted to talk about it. "He was working in the ICU – the intensive care unit – where they put the patients with the disease. He caught it before they understood how dangerous it was. He shouldn't even have been in there. He wasn't that sort of doctor, but he volunteered. He just had to help people. That's what he was like."

Christine smiled at Sands in the low light, the front windows still open to the night and the sliver of moon.

"You know, I suppose if he hadn't died, then none of this would have happened. Moving here I mean. We'd still be in London. You wouldn't need to be here." She gave Sands another sad smile, just visible.

"Rodney Slaughter would still be here though," Sands replied.

Christine's face stiffened, and her eyes darted to the side window and the Slaughters' house beyond. It was still dark beyond the glass.

"Yes. Yes, I suppose so."

Sands lasted longer than Christine, who dozed on the sofa and eventually fell fast asleep. Using her binoculars, Sands was able to see the name of the book that Rodney Slaughter had been reading, a literary work which had been long-listed for the Booker Prize. She downloaded it to her phone and read the first chapter, but wasn't impressed. Her mind turned to possible scenarios allowing Sopley's DNA to be found on Emily Slaughter's body, without him being present to abduct or murder her. The only ones she could come up with were so convoluted they were surely impossible. She gave up and mused on her own case for a while, coming up with a scenario she hadn't considered before. Could it be possible that all this – her being here, going *rogue* – was just a distraction from the frightening possibility that they'd find her guilty? If that was the outcome, then given that two officers and the suspect had been killed in the incident, the sanctions would be severe. She would lose her job, certainly, and perhaps even be open to a civil prosecution case by the deceased officers' families. She tried to dismiss this as impossible, but failed: there were more and more such cases these days. And her certainty that the officers' body cameras would prove her case had been dashed.

A light snapped on in the Slaughters' house opposite. Sands sat up at once to see Rodney Slaughter crossing the room. She shook the sleeping figure of Christine beside her until she woke. Then she went over to the window. Slaughter was still striding purposefully, his chest bare, but the rest of him hidden behind the kitchen cabinets. Christine, still not quite awake, was mumbling something, so Sands padded back and roused her again. Then the two women went back to the window and stared.

Slaughter was completely naked now, standing by a cabinet on the far wall, his backside pointed towards them. He opened the cabinet and pulled out a pair of trousers. He bent over and pulled them on, turning once he'd done so. He seemed to glance at Christine's house, but if he was aware of being watched, he gave no sign of it. Instead he turned back, this time pulling out a mat from the cabinet. He shook it out and laid it down on the ground facing the large window that looked out over the sea. Sands watched through the binoculars as he went back to the cabinet a third time and pulled out a strange-looking object. It was long and thin, and it seemed so incongruous, it took her a few moments to accept that it was what Christine had warned her it would be – a curved sword in a scabbard. As she watched, he carefully withdrew the sword and laid the scabbard down on the table. Then he held the sword in both hands and studied the blade.

"Is this what he did before?" Sands asked, trying to keep her growing sense of anxiety out of her voice. It was one thing to be told about this, another to see it first-hand, and she could really understand now why this had scared Christine Harvey.

She heard Christine's reply beside her, a breathless *yes*, and she turned to see the shine of something in her eyes, perhaps hope that she'd finally be believed.

Slaughter returned to the mat and stood at one end, using both hands to grip the handle of the sword in front of him. Then he slowly began to move, a programme of what looked like choreographed movements, blocking and parrying an invisible enemy. As he warmed up, his moves became more attacking – lunges and strikes as well. Sands and Christine watched in silence.

Slaughter was obviously skilled. He moved quickly from one movement to the next, and at times the blade of the sword flashed brilliantly quickly through the air in front of him, but always seemingly within his control. Yet at the same time, something about the way he moved seemed to frustrate him. As if he expected better from himself.

"What's he doing?" Christine asked.

"It's a samurai sword," Sands answered, but with no idea of its relevance

"He goes on for almost an hour sometimes," Christine said. On this occasion she was proved wrong, as he suddenly stopped. It seemed as though he had mis-stepped, or lost control of the flying sword for a second, breaking his poise and concentration. He put a hand on his hip and Sands watched as his chest rapidly moved up and down with the effort of what he'd been doing. Then he turned suddenly, dropped the sword carelessly on the table and strode to the kitchen. He yanked open the fridge, pulled out a glass bottle of mineral water and drank straight from it. Then he came right up to the window overlooking Christine's house.

Both Sands and Christine instinctively shrank back, though there was no way he could see them, not with the light on in his house and off in theirs. But he still seemed to stare, out into the darkness, and then Sands thought she saw his gaze dropping to Molly's bedroom.

"This is what he does. He stares at her room." Christine's voice was right in her ear again, and Sands moved a fraction away. She picked up the binoculars and focused again on Slaughter's face. He had only turned a dim side-light on, so it was hard to see exactly where he was looking. But the set of his eyes was clear. He was grim-faced. Suddenly, he turned to face another part of the courtyard, towards the sea. In a sudden move he swapped the water bottle for the sword and left the room. It happened so quickly, Sands wasn't sure what she'd just seen. But the sword was clearly gone. Sands waited a second, then whispered to Christine. "Is that it? Is he done?"

Before Christine could answer, a new light shone from the downstairs part of the house. Not an internal light this time, but an illuminated rectangular shape that could only come from an external door opening. For a second, Rodney Slaughter's figure was silhouetted against it before it shut behind him.

It was harder to follow him outside, in the darkness, but they could see his shadowy shape. It looked like he was waiting for something or trying to keep himself hidden. He then pointed a small flashlight into some bushes that had been planted as a border between the two properties. He didn't seem to see anything so clicked the light off, but not before Sands saw that he was still holding the sword out in front of him.

After that he crept back along the boundary, and, at a point where the bushes were low, he stepped over into Christine's half of the courtyard. Sands heard Christine catch her breath. She sensed that he hadn't done this before, that this was an escalation. Instinctively, she put her hand on Christine's arm, feeling how tense her muscles were.

"What's he doing?" she murmured, more to herself than Christine.

A second later he was out of sight, underneath the upper part of Christine's house, which, like the Slaughters' house opposite, overhung the lower part. Sands moved at once, but Christine was quicker. They both went to the stairs.

"Stay quiet, and don't turn on any lights." Sands hissed the order since she didn't want Christine's children to wake. Her injuries still left her slower than the other woman, but Christine did as she was told and waited for her at the bottom of the stairs. When Sands caught up, she took Christine's arm and, moving as one, they came to Molly's room.

Christine had left the door open with the curtains drawn against the French doors, just as Molly liked. She went to the bed to check on her daughter, nodding to Sands that she was OK and still sleeping. Sands moved to the external glass door. Moving her hand slowly, she reached out and grabbed a corner of the curtain that covered the door, quickly pulling it away to see outside.

And at the exact moment she did so, she found herself staring eye-to-eye with Rodney Slaughter, just an inch or so away, standing on the other side of the glass.

FORTY-EIGHT

He ran, just as Sands let out an involuntary gasp, nearly falling backwards into the room.

"What is it?" Christine asked, terrified, and much too loudly. Molly stirred but didn't wake. Sands scrambled the curtains shut, breathing hard, not knowing what to say.

"What's he doing?"

"He was..." Sands didn't know whether to speak or not. "He was right there." She fought to calm herself down.

A panicked sound escaped from Christine's lips, but she quickly found the presence of mind to speak. "Is he still there?" Her voice was pure misery.

"No. He's gone." Sands reached out again and pulled a corner of the curtain away, just in time to see the light from the doorway opposite and Rodney Slaughter disappearing back into his own house.

"He's gone back inside."

"What was he doing? He was trying to get in here, wasn't he?" The tone of Christine's voice was rising fast. "He was trying to get to Molly."

"Calm down. You can't wake your children."

"Oh my God. He was. *He was...*"

Sands didn't answer. But she was shaken. She checked, as quietly and inconspicuously as she could, where Christine had wedged and tied the door shut, making sure that even if the lock was picked from the outside, it couldn't actually be opened, and then she led the way back upstairs. She went straight to the window and stared out across the courtyard into the Slaughters' house. But now all the lights were off so that the inside was dark, the interior invisible.

"What happens now? Can you do anything? Now that you've seen?"

Sands didn't reply.

"Can you call the police? The other police? Make them *do something*?"

"I think he saw me," Sands said instead, speaking more to herself than to Christine. "My face, I mean. I think he recognised me."

Christine stayed a few minutes longer, asking the same questions over and over, demanding that something be done, but when Sands either wouldn't or couldn't answer her, she went back downstairs to be with Molly. Sands was grateful for the space to think.

What *had* Slaughter been doing? Had he really been trying to break into the house to attack Molly? The idea seemed inconceivable. For one thing, how did he think he'd get away with it? He certainly couldn't blame Sopley anymore. She felt the unresolved conflict in her mind: all the evidence pointed to Sopley, except that his alibi made his guilt impossible. Frustrated, Sands tried to reset.

He *had* seen her. She was certain of that, but she didn't know whether he'd recognised her. They'd only met the one time, when she and Detective Golding had come to the house to tell them their daughter was dead. Would that have locked the image of her forever into his mind, or would he have been so distracted and distraught that his memory had been affected? Sands didn't know. She was a similar age and height as Christine. It was possible – perhaps even likely – that he thought he'd seen Christine at the window. What did *that* mean? She didn't know. She glanced at her watch – it was 3am now – and although she felt wide awake from the adrenalin still flowing around her body, she could also feel the tiredness making her thoughts drag At the same time, she felt more strongly than ever that *something* was happening here, something she wasn't fully grasping.

She tried to focus on what to do, right now. Slaughter had certainly seen someone. This surely meant that if he had been planning to break into Molly's bedroom, for whatever reason, he would at least have put those plans on hold for now. She could sleep, and she would need to sleep if she were to make sense of what was happening here. She took the blanket and lay down on the sofa, closing her eyes and waited with a firm stubbornness until sleep finally came.

FORTY-NINE

The sun, rising up from the land behind the house, was blocked from Christine Harvey's windows by the bulk of the Slaughters' side of the house. They'd made sure they'd kept the better half.

Perhaps Sands was slow to wake because of the late rising of the sun, or perhaps the activities of the night before had simply left her tired. Either way, when she did open her eyes, she was unable to place where she was for a few seconds. And then another few seconds before she registered she wasn't alone.

"Hello."

The girl, Molly, was dressed in pink pyjamas, a motif of a unicorn subtly outlined on the chest. She stood in the middle of the room looking uncertainly at Sands, as she lay under the blanket on the sofa.

Sands winced as she pushed herself upright. Her injuries still hurt first thing in the morning. "Hello, Molly."

"Why are you still here?" she asked, tipping her head to one side. She wasn't smiling as she asked the question. Sands finally managed to sit up and blinked her eyes. "Didn't your mummy tell you?"

"No."

"Oh." Sands felt annoyed. She didn't want to lie. "Well, I stayed late last night. I had to talk to your mummy." She wondered if Molly had woken up at any point, or sensed the drama in her room, but it seemed not.

"Like a sleepover?" Molly tipped her head to the other side now.

"I suppose so."

"Mummy doesn't let me have sleepovers."

"No?" Sands glanced at her watch. It was past seven o'clock. She'd meant to rise earlier and leave before Christine's children got up.

"I want to have a sleepover with Daisy. She's got a horse."

Sands turned back to look at the little girl. For the first time she realised something obvious which she'd missed before. Molly was very similar in appearance to the Slaughters' girl. The same height and hair colour.

"It's a girl horse. It's brown and white. Do you know what that's called?"

"What?"

"A brown and white horse. It's called a pinto. That's not her name though, she's called Holly."

"I have to go now," Sands said as she got up off the sofa, but she spoke quietly and the girl didn't seem to hear.

"Do you like horses?" Molly again tipped her head on one side, as if this were a matter of great importance to her. Sands paused. "My mother did. She kept a horse when I was about your age."

The girl's eyes widened. "Really? Did you ride it? Daisy says she rides hers, but Mummy says it's too dangerous for me."

"Sometimes. For a little while."

"Why only a little while? Did it die?"

The question surprised Sands. In fact, the whole conversation surprised her. "No," she said. "My mother did, so I had to move away."

"Oh. That's a bit like me," Molly replied. "Except it was my daddy who died. That's why we moved here." She suddenly looked earnest, as if she felt she was sharing something important with this stranger.

"Yes, your... mummy told me. I was sorry to hear that."

"It's alright," the girl went on, shrugging slightly. "I suppose. I hope I can have a horse, now we've come to live here."

The conversation was interrupted at that point by Christine arriving breathlessly in the room. She saw Molly, gave a little gasp and ran over to her. "Molly, *there* you are." She enveloped the girl in a tight hug. "I was worried about you."

"I was talking to your friend."

"I can see that." Christine put on an unconvincingly happy voice and didn't look at Sands. "Yes. She decided to stay over last night."

"OK," Molly replied easily. "What's her name?"

For a second, Christine hesitated, and Sands realised she was about to make something up. She briefly considered letting her, but decided she didn't want to tell a complete lie.

"I'm Erica."

Molly held out her hand and offered a beautiful smile. "It's nice to meet you, Erica."

"I should go," Sands said after shaking the girl's hand, but Christine said, "You must have breakfast." She smiled. Everything about her mannerisms was obviously fake, hiding an anguish she refused to show in front of her daughter, and it swept Sands along. Christine got Molly gathering up bowls and cereal packets from the cupboard, and after a while Sands began to help too.

Sands found herself sat at the breakfast table while Molly talked more about horses, and what she liked for breakfast. Then Ryan stumbled in, yawning, his hair messed up from where he'd been sleeping on it.

He stopped when he saw Sands.

"Ryan, this is my friend Erica," Christine explained again quickly. "She used to work with me, but she's been..." – She overplayed the sadness in her voice – "...she's been having a bit of a difficult time at home, and she stayed here last night."

Ryan still didn't move until Christine mouthed at him, "Relationship. Don't ask." After that he sat down at the table at the opposite end from Sands, and pretended he wasn't taking furtive glances at her whenever he thought no one was looking.

"I'm going for a playdate with Daisy," Molly told her brother when Christine had sat down too. "I told you Daisy has a horse. I think I might be allowed to ride it."

"Yeah?" Ryan kept buttering his toast, uninterested.

"Erm. I don't think so," Christine interrupted. "I told you it's too dangerous."

Molly looked disappointed by this, but she didn't insist.

"And how about you Ryan?" Christine seemed to be enjoying playing the happy family. "What are you up to today?" She glanced at Sands as if to indicate they were like this all the time. But Ryan wasn't joining in.

"What d'you mean?" He looked up, an angry, uncertain look on his face. "Have you forgotten?"

"Forgotten what?"

"I'm going to Simon's house. You said you'd take me. You said I could drive."

Christine's face fell at once. "Oh, yes. I forgot. Of course." She smiled again quickly and explained to Sands. "Ryan is taking his driving test next week. It's very hard to get any lessons at all, with the pandemic, so I'm doing my best to teach him myself."

When they were done, Molly and Ryan went downstairs to get dressed. Sands helped Christine load the dishwasher.

"Thank you for that." Christine spoke quietly so there was no chance of the children hearing. "For playing along."

"That's OK."

"I've got to go with Ryan now. I'll take Molly as well. But please don't leave. We really need to talk. When I get back?"

Sands nodded.

Left alone again in the house, Sands accepted the offer of a shower, using the en-suite in the spare room. The room was being used more as a store: boxes were lined up against the wall. She opened one of them and discovered a man's shoes. Size ten and a half. Many of the others were filled with tissue paper, which confused her at first. But when she dug deeper she found it was protecting little metal figures, soldiers in full battle dress with muskets and swords, each one painted with meticulous detail, even down to the medals on their chests. She studied them for a while, guessing they were the work of Evan Harvey before his untimely death. She wrapped them back up and went into the bathroom.

Afterwards, she went back upstairs and made another cup of coffee. As she was drinking it, she lifted the blinds covering the window facing the Slaughters' house. Rodney Slaughter was standing by his own coffee machine. For a second their eyes met, and it was clear to Sands that he knew it had been her he'd seen last night. She put down her coffee, went out of the front and knocked on the Slaughters' door.

FIFTY

"What are you doing here?" Rodney Slaughter answered the door.

"You remember me then?"

"Of course I remember you. What are you doing on my property?"

"It's not your property. You sold it to Christine Harvey, and I came to ask what you were doing last night, on her property?"

Rodney hesitated, and Sands simply stared at him. After a while, he looked left and right. "Maybe we should have this conversation inside?"

"If it helps you tell me what's going on."

Slaughter stepped aside, letting her into the house and leading her into the kitchen. Sands noted that Janet Slaughter was nowhere to be seen. There was a laptop on the glass table, an Apple Macbook Pro, but instead of using the inbuilt mouse, Slaughter had attached a complicated and expensive-looking pointer. Plans were unfurled on the table, blueprints for a building.

"Well?" Sands turned away from the table to face Slaughter, who was leaning against the worktop, his chest slowly rising and falling.

"You were injured when Michael Sopley was killed?" he asked eventually. He raised a hand to smarten his gelled hair; she noticed it was shaking slightly.

"That's right."

He didn't offer any condolences. But then neither had she.

"Is your wife here?"

"No. She's out." His eyes glanced up to a clock on the wall. "She runs."

Sands noticed the calculation in his eyes, as if he were working out her route, and where she would be on it.

"Can I ask what you're doing here?" Slaughter asked, interrupting her thoughts.

"No. But you should tell me what you were doing last night, in Christine's garden."

Sands turned to the coffee machine. "Would you like coffee, Detective Sands?"

"OK." She shrugged.

Rodney Slaughter collected two black cups from a cupboard, ground the beans and poured two thick, dark espressos, the whole procedure feeling like a performance put on for her benefit. Perhaps to demonstrate how calm he was. But if so, Sands was more than prepared to watch it. There was something interesting about the way his hands continued to shake, just a little, as he worked.

He handed a full cup to Sands.

"I don't understand what's happening here. Are you spying on us?"

"Should I need to spy on you?"

Slaughter looked away, frustrated. But then he looked back. "No. You don't. And I'd like to know why you are."

"And like I said, I'd like to know what you were doing last

night when I saw you outside a nine-year-old girl's bedroom window."

Slaughter looked away as if wounded. When he turned back, he was clearly trying to adopt a reasonable tone. "Look, Detective Sands, I..." He dropped his shaking hand below the tabletop where she couldn't see it. "If you must know, I thought I heard a noise."

"What kind of noise?"

"A perfectly normal noise I expect." His voice flared briefly with anger. "The normal noises of the night. A fox perhaps? It could have been anything. It could have been nothing."

"And what does that have to do with Christine Harvey's daughter?"

After a few seconds, when Slaughter finally looked at her, his face was dark. "Because I was scared, Detective. I was up, because I can't sleep, not anymore, and I thought I heard a noise, and I thought it was happening all over again. I thought that Michael Sopley was outside, breaking in. I failed my own daughter, I didn't want to fail another child."

Sands watched him for a few seconds. "Michael Sopley is dead."

"I know. *I know that.* Of course I know..." His face twisted with pain. "Do you have children, Detective?"

Sands gave the slightest of shakes.

"Then you've never lost a child either. You can't possibly know what it's like."

Sands contemplated this. Strictly speaking it was true, but she was certainly familiar with loss. "Why come to her window?"

"To check the door. I wanted to make sure it was locked." He drank his coffee, hand still shaking.

"You were carrying a sword."

He waved a hand as if to dismiss this. "I thought I heard someone in the courtyard. Sopley, another Sopley. The truth is,

I hear them all the time. I see them everywhere." He looked away, frustrated.

Sands listened, taking a sip of the jet-black coffee. It was fiercely strong. "You have trouble sleeping? That's why you get up in the nights?"

Slaughter's nod was so slight she barely registered it.

"And the sword?"

He glanced at her, then looked away. "Just a hobby I picked up in Japan. We lived out there for a while."

"You're good at it."

"I used to be, until..." he stopped suddenly, and she followed his eyes as they drifted to the kitchen worktop. The Slaughters may have tried to keep their house looking like a showroom, but not everything was kept out of sight. She noticed a bottle of medicine, fixed the name in her memory and looked back at him.

"I'm sorry if I scared her," Slaughter went on. "The girl, I mean."

"You didn't. Fortunately she didn't wake. You scared Christine though."

Slaughter stiffened. "She doesn't like me. I've not..." He glanced at the side window and across to the Harveys' part of the building. "I've not been the most welcoming. I realise that, but at the same time..." His voice faded away again.

"At the same time what?"

"It takes two, doesn't it? My wife made a real effort to get to know her. We both did. We invited her over for dinner, and she's been... Let's just say she's hardly reciprocated. We've had no invitations back. And the way she looks at me... I assumed..." He stopped.

"You assumed what?"

"I don't know," he sighed, and tried again. "I assumed she must have her doubts. About us. She must have heard some of the rubbish that people say about us. Read the rubbish online."

"What do people say?"

"What do you think they say? A man broke into our house and took our daughter from under our very noses. They say we're negligent. That it was our fault."

Sands thought for a second. She considered telling him about Michael Sopley's alibi. It would be interesting to see his reaction, but she knew she couldn't do that; he'd go straight to John Lindham, demand to know more. As things stood, he felt guilty and was unlikely to tell anyone she'd been there.

"You didn't answer my question." Rodney Slaughter interrupted her thoughts, but he was on the same wavelength. "Why are you here? Is this an official visit, because it doesn't feel like it?"

Sands used the same excuse as Christine, but delivered it so it wasn't quite a lie. "I know Christine," she said, not specifying when they'd met. "She didn't know about the murder before she bought the house. Then when she found out, she was distressed. I came to reassure her that the man who killed your daughter is dead. That Molly isn't in any danger."

He seemed to accept the explanation, and the two of them watched each other without speaking. Sands tried to use the time to think. Was his answer plausible? Did she believe it? She had seen none of the tell-tale signs that indicated Slaughter was obviously lying. But then, she wouldn't expect him to. If he really had killed his own daughter in such a hideous way, then he must be a very pure kind of psychopath. And she knew from personal experience just how convincingly they could lie. Indeed she knew what an attractive opportunity it would *be* to lie, a chance to play the role of the victim. Sands knew enough to not trust an excuse he'd had time to concoct. She considered quickly, looking for an angle he wouldn't be ready for. She could confront him with how Christine had found the dead cat in his bin. She could ask him about the schoolteacher, Miss Juniper. Either might catch him off guard. But in her unofficial capacity, she knew that pursuing either of these questions would be going too far. In the end, it was Rodney Slaughter who caught her off guard.

"I'd like you to leave now," he said. "My wife will be back very soon and I'd rather you were gone before she gets here."

For a moment, Sands felt like a little girl again, outmanoeuvred by a father who was smarter than her and who better understood the rules of the game.

"It isn't good for her to be reminded of what happened," Slaughter continued. "It upsets her."

Sands nodded. Unconsciously, she reached for the locket that hung around her neck, her fingers falling easily to its sides, where over many years they had worn the silver thin. Realising what she was doing, she pulled her hand away, as if burned by the touch. She didn't meet Slaughter's eyes but got to her feet.

FIFTY-ONE

"He says he was worried someone might try to break into her room," Sands explained half an hour later. Christine had dispatched Molly to watch cartoons in her room when she returned from dropping Ryan off, and they'd sat down to talk.

"But surely you don't believe him?" Christine wouldn't accept it. "You saw what he did. You saw that he tried to take Molly."

She shook her head. "I saw him come over to your side of the courtyard. He didn't actually try to break in."

"Only because you stopped him. He stopped when he saw you. Otherwise, God knows what would have happened. He's an animal. A monster."

"We don't know that."

"He killed his daughter. He murdered her."

"We don't know that either."

"But it's possible. You have to admit it's possible," Christine pleaded with her.

"It's possible."

Christine seemed grateful that Sands at least accepted this.

She was quiet for a moment. "So what do we do? Can you arrest him?"

Christine took Sands' silence as answer enough. She laughed bitterly. "So, what? We have to wait until he actually breaks in, *actually* takes Molly. Is that it? Is that how it works?"

Sands kept quiet, watching the other woman. And Christine wouldn't let it go

"That woman, the one who knew Michael Sopley's girlfriend. Doesn't what she said prove it wasn't him?" Christine's voice was rising again and Sands closed the door.

"I don't know. I've no way of telling whether she was telling the truth or not."

"You said you believed her yesterday."

"I said I believed *she* thought she was telling the truth. But it's possible I was wrong. Or that she was lied to, or mistaken in some way."

Christine's face crumpled in confusion. "I don't understand. If it wasn't Sopley then it must have been Rodney Slaughter, and I'm living next door to him. Molly's living next door to him. Can't you interview him? Get him to confess?" Christine was pleading with her for help.

Sands was silent for some time, trying to decide what she should do. There was no easy answer. She decided to come clean. "Christine, I haven't fully explained my situation here, and I think you ought to know."

"What?" Christine's eyes widened.

"I came here because I felt you deserved to know the facts about Michael Sopley. So that you'd feel safe living here. I didn't come in an official capacity, and... I wasn't able to either." She grimaced as she spoke, still annoyed at what her words meant. "Technically, I'm not a serving police officer at the moment. I'm suspended from duty." She waited a moment for this to sink in.

"I don't understand. What does that mean?"

"When Michael Sopley was shot, two officers died. I tried to intervene and help them, which is when I was shot as well. When something like that happens there has to be an official inquiry, and until that takes place, I'm suspended. That means I can't be seen to be pursuing any case, much less *this* one."

Christine was silent again. Sands went on.

"Unfortunately there's more. Since the coroner has ruled that Sopley was responsible for Emily Slaughter's murder, there *is no case*. The investigation was closed. And that means that even if I wasn't suspended, I still wouldn't be able to look into it. It would need to be reopened first. And there isn't enough evidence for that. All we have is Kelly O'Reilly claiming that Sopley's girlfriend told her he was with her on the night of the abduction. It's hearsay, third-hand testimony. I wouldn't even be able to interview Slaughter on that basis, let alone investigate him."

Although Christine seemed to be taking this in, her response suggested otherwise. "So you're not going to do anything?"

Sands sighed, frustrated. The simple truth was that no one had properly examined the case against Slaughter, perhaps because Sopley had been killed, perhaps because of the pandemic, perhaps it was Lindham's fault, but one thing was clear: at that point there was zero chance of any official investigation into Rodney Slaughter. But there was an opportunity for her to investigate, given her enforced non-official status. Yes, her career would be at risk if anyone found out, but it was already under threat. And... she looked around the house again, once more feeling that something, *somehow* here was wrong. Just like that, the decision was made.

"There is one delicate path I can tread," Sands began. "*You're* not part of the case. You weren't even here when Emily was murdered, you just happened to move next door afterwards. So, if we continue this charade – that we're just friends –

then technically I'm not getting involved in any case. I'm just staying with a friend. I'll at least have a vantage point to observe Slaughter from, and if there is anything to discover about him – and I do mean if – then perhaps I can collect the evidence to prove it." She paused. Her plan sounded mad, even to her.

"And once I beat the hearing, I may be able to make the argument that the Slaughter case needs a second look."

Christine stared. She nodded. And then she began to sob.

FIFTY-TWO

Christine was absurdly grateful. She rushed downstairs to move the boxes from the spare room, piling them up against the wall in her bedroom so Sands wouldn't have to spend another night on the sofa. Then she explained to Molly that Sands would be staying a few more days. After lunch, Christine announced she and Molly were going to pick up Ryan, who would then drive the car home as practice for his test. She suggested that Sands accompanied them, in her role as a friend of the family. Sands agreed.

When they picked Ryan up from Dorchester, he glared accusingly at his mother. She gave him the same explanation as Molly, embellishing the story with some imaginary problems Sands was having with her made-up boyfriend. Sands was almost impressed by the level of detail, but noted it did little to improve the way the boy looked at her. It was clear his attitude could prove an obstacle to the plan they'd put together.

And the situation was made worse by how bad Christine was as a driving instructor. Before Ryan had even started the engine she was anxious, pointing out potential dangers everywhere and telling him off for not checking his mirrors. They drove slowly across town, then drove out into the countryside and back towards Lulworth. But on the way, Christine decided she needed a rest and told Ryan to stop in a layby. Sands got out of the car with Molly, and then watched as mother and son sat inside arguing. Christine finally wound down the window and announced that they were ready to set off again. When Ryan pulled away, he was heavy on the throttle, spinning the tyres in the dirt.

FIFTY-THREE

Sands ate an evening meal with the Harveys before Christine took Molly downstairs to bed. When Ryan went back to his room, Sands was left alone as the light began to fade over the ocean. She watched it, thinking. Once again she felt there was something she wasn't seeing, wasn't quite grasping. But her confidence was growing that the pieces of this puzzle would fall into place, if only she stayed observant.

When Christine returned, she opened a bottle of white wine and poured one large glass. Sands watched her curiously and Christine misinterpreted the look. "Did you want some? I'm sorry, I wasn't thinking." Without waiting for a reply she produced a second glass, but only filled it half way, as if Sands were not yet old enough for a full glass. It felt like another piece of the puzzle, though she didn't know yet where it would fit. The thought was like a shadow, shifting, dancing away from her.

"What are we going to do now?" Christine took a large slug from her wine. "Maybe we should stay up again to see if he tries to break in? Or, I was thinking when I was putting Molly down, maybe we could record him? Evan bought Ryan a video camera and it's still here somewhere. I thought we could set it up pointing through the window, then we could record him and get some evidence?" Christine's face took on a pleading look. Sands realised she needed to see some sort of action, no matter whether it helped or not.

"OK."

Christine began rooting through a cardboard box. "If we wait until it's properly dark, we can lift the blinds a little and point the camera at his house; if he turns the light on it'll record what he's doing."

Sands nodded and watched. This time she took a sip from her own wine.

Christine mounted the camera on a small tripod and pointed it at the window, still insisting on waiting until it was fully dark before lifting the blinds. And so they waited, while Christine told Sands about her life in London with Evan, and their struggle to conceive until Molly came along. She talked of the work she'd done, and how she'd never quite had her own career because of all the financial support she'd received from her husband. Eventually darkness fell upstairs in the Slaughter's house, and Christine lifted the blinds. Sands hit record on the camera, then checked it was working correctly. The whole idea was stupid, but if they were to do it, they might as well do it properly.

"What was I saying?" Christine asked when they were done. She looked eager to continue her story, but by now Sands had heard enough. It felt like she'd been bombarded with information and now needed space to process it. She needed to get out. To walk.

"Actually there's something I need to do," Sands interrupted her.

"Oh?"

Sands spoke slowly. "The investigation identified Michael Sopley very early on, and after he was killed, there was no chance of a prosecution. That meant some very basic questions were left unanswered, one of which was how long it would have taken for Rodney Slaughter, or anyone else for that matter, to take Emily Slaughter from the house to the murder site. I'm going to do exactly that now. I'll time it to see how long it takes."

Fear etched itself on Christine's face. "*Now?* It's dark..."

"Emily Slaughter was taken in the dark."

"I don't think I can... I don't want to leave Mol—"

"I'm not asking you to," Sands said. "You stay here with the children."

Christine looked relieved. She nodded. Then, a few moments later, her eyes lit up. "So it's like a reconstruction? Like on TV?"

Sands glanced at Christine, surprised by her reaction. There was a childishness to her character. She seemed overly happy at any progress towards confirming her view of Rodney Slaughter's guilt, but was plunged into fear whenever the opposite happened. Perhaps that made sense, in the circumstances, but then again perhaps it was rather odd.

"If you like."

"I get it." Christine suddenly looked around the room. "If only we had a mannequin or something to carry, to recreate taking the girl. You know, like the ones they have in shop windows. They have children-sized ones sometimes." Christine bit her lip, thinking. "I could grab a gym bag? There're loads of rocks outside, we could fill it up with them and you could carry it. It wouldn't be the right shape, but we could make it the right weight. That's important? Right?"

Sands glanced at the video camera, pointlessly recording next door, and now there was this. But she flashed a quick smile.

"Sure. Good idea."

. . .

Ten minutes later, Christine had dug out a yellow and black gym bag and told Sands several times where she could find a pile of bricks and rocks left over from the building work. Sands somehow found herself swept up in the exercise. The two women went out together to fill the bag, Christine making care she picked suitable rocks to make the bag an accurate representation of an eight-year-old girl. Several times she glanced around into the darkness, and finally said what was on her mind. "Are you sure this isn't dangerous?"

Sands nodded, seizing on the excuse. "It might be. You should go inside, check on Molly. And then go to bed. I'll take a key and see you in the morning."

Even in the dark she could see the look on Christine's face. "I'll sleep in her room tonight."

"Good idea."

It was like the air had suddenly cleared. Sands took a few moments, drawing in lungfuls of cool, moist air, then she got to work. First she started a stopwatch on her phone before emptying the heavy bag of rocks, dumping them in a ditch where Christine wouldn't see them. It was useful to check the timeline, but Sands appreciated she'd be a lot slower: the killer probably hadn't been shot six months previously, as she had.

She needed to leave enough time for however long it took to break into Emily's room and drug her. The girl's autopsy had revealed traces of chloroform, which would have rendered her unconscious within seconds. That part of the equation was relatively simple. It was more complex to work out how long it would have taken to pick the locks. In theory this could have been anywhere from a few seconds to half an hour, depending on the level of skill. But if it was Slaughter, then he could have picked the lock in advance to make it look like someone from outside the house had taken Emily. It was an unsolvable problem, and Sands only pondered it briefly before giving up and getting on with it.

She took the cliff path that led down from the houses towards the cove. Although the Slaughters' house was the last of the cliff-top homes, there were others set slightly further back from the edge. The way the cliff fell away, gathering steepness as it dropped towards the sea, meant that the path Sands took was below the line of sight of their windows. On the night of the murder, whoever took this path would have been hidden from view.

The walk would have been easy enough had it not been for her worsening limp. The moon appeared and disappeared between clouds before the path cut inland, passing through a small wooded area. The moonlight here couldn't penetrate the trees, and it looked as though the path plunged into total darkness. Sands felt no fear, but considered a detour, as her injury made her less than agile. She could easily trip on an exposed root and put her rehabilitation back. But the only other possible path would take her near the other houses, an unlikely route for the killer. She pressed on.

As soon as she stepped under the canopy of branches, the ambient lighting went to almost nothing. She had to feel her way forward with uncertain steps. her hands held out in front of her. The light breeze whispering through the trees sounded like voices, and there were other noises, eerie and strange, as animals moved around her. Gradually her eyes adjusted, and soon she saw the light change as the wood thinned up ahead. Then there was a different noise, a sudden scuffling sound from quite close behind her. She froze, and then turned to peer into the darkness.

It was probably an animal. There would be foxes, badgers, perhaps even deer in the little wood, but an uncomfortable, irrational thought also occurred to her. What if they'd been wrong about Rodney Slaughter? What if, instead of going to bed early, he'd been waiting in his house, watching them as they'd set up the video camera? And what if he'd seen her leave, and decided to follow? For the first time, she felt a chill of alarm.

She stayed there for a while, listening to the black night around her, but the only sound was the whisper of the leaves in the trees. She began moving again, her senses more alert this time, and it wasn't long before she was out of the wood, back in the moonlight. At once, she breathed easier, and descended quickly down a series of short interconnecting paths to the cove itself.

She checked her phone. It had been less than nine minutes since she'd set off, allowing for the time taken to abduct the girl. At no point had she been visible, and she was now walking away from civilisation towards the deserted part of the beach. She slipped her phone away and set off along the curve of the shore, hearing the small wavelets lap against the pebbles. The going was easier here and she looked ahead, trying to judge where the murder had taken place. But then there was another noise, sounding a little like a sneeze. She whirled around at once. There was no one behind her. Nowhere to hide. Not on the beach at least. But the chalk cliff rose up in steps, and at the top of the first one, perhaps ten meters above her, there was a second path. Had the sound come from there? Sands thought about the powerful flashlight stored in her car and cursed her stupidity for not taking it. She could use the light on her phone, but it wouldn't reach that far, serving only to identify her position.

She squinted into the darkness, trying to make out the route of the path above her, realising now how it offered an advantage over the path she was on. Anyone taking that route could easily duck down out of sight, protected by the lip of the small cliff. Could Rodney Slaughter have followed her? And if so, why?

The noise came again from the water's edge. And when she

looked, she saw a slightly larger wave breaking onto the pebbles of the beach, moving them with a whooshing sound. She turned again, studied the cliff, but all was still. Keen now to get this over with, she hurried forward as best she could – her limp was getting worse, she realised. She felt a knot of anxiety growing inside her.

She considered the bag she was still carrying. She'd emptied the rocks, but the truth was, she'd walked a significant distance, and it would have been very difficult to carry an unconscious child this far. Unbidden, her mind returned to the view she'd had six months earlier of Rodney Slaughter's broad, strong back as they'd descended the stairs of his house to check the dead girl's room. If the girl had been abducted by a lone criminal, they'd need to be built like Slaughter. Then another thought replaced it, another option. They knew the killer had used chloroform, but not *when* they'd used it. If Rodney Slaughter was the killer, then Emily would have trusted him enough to walk willingly to the murder site. An exciting night-time adventure. Sands looked around at the cove, trying to picture it. It was such a picturesque spot that even at night it looked appealing. The cliffs loomed in the semi-darkness, and half a dozen yachts lay at anchor in the clear water, their running lights glinting in the night. It hadn't been like that in February, of course. It would have been colder and emptier. Hard to imagine the girl willingly leaving her warm bed.

Sands had nearly reached the place where Emily Slaughter's body had been found. She set down the bag and considered how long it would have taken for the killer to complete their macabre work. It wasn't difficult to remember how the girl's body had looked, her chest hacked open, the doll stuffed inside the cavity. She considered again her lack of a flashlight, and realised the killer must have had some form of lighting. Sands remembered she'd forgotten to check how light it would have been that night. She made a mental note to correct this and slipped out her phone again to check the time. She would allow ten minutes for the murder to take place, then head back. The screen's bright light suddenly cut off her night vision.

This time, she was sure. Not a sneeze, but a cough, and close. Five, ten metres away. She cut off the phone and peered around, all her senses flaring in alarm. Her phone would have given away her position. She moved sideways up the beach but her foot snagged on something and a second later the air was split open by a horrible scream right in front of her. She heard panicked voices, and then a light switched on, pointing directly into her eyes. Sands was blinded, her heart nearly busting out of her chest.

Whoever held the torch swung the beam off her and out over the water of the cove.

"I'm sorry. We're just camping." It was a boy's voice. He sounded young and absolutely terrified. "I'm sorry if we're not allowed."

Sands' brain screamed to makes sense of what was happening. Her heart pounding, she'd been expecting to have to fight Slaughter off, but in the torchlight she made out the shape of a tent ahead of her; her foot had clipped the guy-rope holding it up. The boy holding the light played it around, and she noticed a girl with him, her own eyes wide and white with fear.

"Our parents are on that yacht. They're probably watching," the boy went on. His voice trembled as he spoke, but he was trying to force an implication into his words. Sands began to understand, but for a moment still couldn't find the words to explain her sudden interruption.

"You're just kids?" she asked at last. "Camping on the shore for the night?"

"Yes."

Sands felt her pulse rate slow. She took a couple more breaths to calm herself further. Freaked-out kids wouldn't help her. And if Slaughter *was* here, scared off by the noise... She made up something fast. "I'm from the warden's office. You better tell your parents to come get you. There's no camping here."

"OK, we're sorry." The boy hurriedly agreed and Sands saw the light from his mobile phone as he quickly dialled his parents' number. A few seconds later the saloon lights flicked on in one of the yachts in the bay

Sands moved away, out into the darkness, but she knew it was futile. If Slaughter had been there, he would have had ample opportunity to sneak away. But if he had been there, then why? Had she pissed him off so much that he wanted to harm her?

"They're coming now to pick us up. We're really sorry. We thought it was OK to camp here." Sands turned again to see a new light on the yacht, and then the silence of the bay was broken by the buzzing sound of a small outboard motor.

Sands waited with the children until the parents' dinghy was ashore, then moved away. There was nothing to be gained from a confrontation with the adults. Instead, she limped quickly back along the beach, looking around the whole time for any clue that Slaughter was following her. If he was, he managed to stay out of sight.

Eventually she made it back to the two Slaughter houses and let herself inside Christine Harvey's side of the property before slumping down against the front door and breathing out.

The stopwatch on her mobile phone read fifty-two minutes.

She thought back to the timeline Rodney and Janet Slaughter had given them for the night of her abduction. Janet Slaughter had put the girl to bed a few minutes after seven. The Wades had arrived just before eight, and had been there the entire evening, until nearly midnight. At that point Janet Slaughter had gone to bed, while Rodney had spent between forty minutes and one hour cleaning up before joining her.

Janet had woken when he came to bed, remembering the time as just after 1am.

It was tight, but Rodney Slaughter just about had time to kill his daughter, assuming he'd either managed to pick the lock incredibly quickly, or he'd picked it earlier.

Sands stopped, examining that thought more carefully. And suddenly she was surprised – and annoyed as well – that it had taken her so long to consider something so obvious. *The lock to Emily Slaughter's room had been picked.* The forensic locksmith had said so in his preliminary report. This had directed all the attention to Michael Sopley, the former locksmith. But if Rodney Slaughter was guilty, then the picking of the lock took on a new significance. Perhaps he'd picked it before the night of the murder, when his wife and daughter were out and he could work unobserved. But even so, he would have needed to be capable of doing it at some point. A memory triggered – the medicines on Rodney Slaughter's kitchen worktop and the special pointer he'd attached to his computer. The picking of the lock, she suddenly realised, had always been the key to this crime.

And now, she needed some help.

FIFTY-FOUR

Sands set an alarm to wake her at six. She went upstairs, removed the video camera and tripod from the window overlooking the Slaughters' side of the house and lowered the blinds. She made coffee and carried the cup downstairs. She might as well watch the video through.

There was no TV in the spare room, so she had to watch on the tiny screen attached to the video camera. It had kept running all night, but since it had only recorded darkness most of the time, she was able to fast forward and simply wait until any light appeared on the screen. She sipped her coffee slowly, watching fuzzy darkness, and then set it on the floor so she could work through her exercises. Finally, the screen began to lighten slightly, not because a light had come on, but because the camera had recorded the beginnings of dawn. She switched it off, yawned and checked the time. 8am. She picked up her mobile.

There was a moment, as the line connected, when she wondered if he would help, or whether he would threaten to report her, as Lindham had. But she pictured the young detective who'd shadowed her on that first day – and then appeared in hospital after her shooting. She hoped he would help.

"Hello boss." Luke Golding sounded out of breath. "How are you feeling?"

"Fine. Are you in the office?"

"Um... Not yet, no. I'm on the way."

Sands glanced at the time again, but made no comment. "When you get there, I need the forensic report on the Slaughters' lock. But you can't let Lindham know what you're doing." She heard a car horn in the background.

"Why not? And why do you need it?" There was another sound, the hiss of air brakes, then Golding talking to someone else.

"There are loose ends. Where are you?"

"I'm on a bus. What loose ends? And what about your hearing? I thought you were still suspended?"

"I am, but... Why are you on a bus? Where's your car?"

"I left it somewhere last night. But why do you need the file, the case is closed?" For a moment Sands was distracted by the scenario of Luke Golding and colleagues from the department out drinking. Luke deciding not to drive home and ending up... where exactly? A bus ride away from work. She swept the thought away at once. She didn't even know where he lived. And there was certainly no reason to care.

"I know it's closed. Can you get it for me?"

"I'd... I'd have to put a request in. And Lindham would need to authorise it, so..."

Sands clicked her tongue. "That's no good. Did you read it? Do you remember what it said?"

"Um... I glanced through." Golding paused, as if thinking. "It confirmed that the lock on the girl's room was picked."

"I know that. What else did it say?"

"I don't know. The lock had been picked, and Sopley was a former locksmith..."

Sands interrupted him. "I need to meet the forensic locksmith who examined those locks. You'll need to set it up, and you can't tell Lindham." She thought a moment then added, "You should come too."

Golding drew out the first word of his answer. "Sure... OK, yeah, I can do that. It would kinda help if you told me what this is about?"

"I did. Possible loose ends."

"You can't be more specific?"

Sands hesitated. "I'm not exactly sure myself yet. I'll fill you in when we meet. Today if you can."

"Alright. I'll get back to you."

"Good." Sands ended the call. She remembered to add the words "thank you", but by then the line was already dead.

FIFTY-FIVE

Sands went up to join the Harveys. It was a school day, so the leisurely breakfast of before was replaced by a more rushed affair. Sands largely stayed out of the way, and was pleased when Golding texted to say he'd arranged an appointment for later that day. She left as soon as Christine took Molly to school.

But with time to kill, she called in first at her flat, finding an interesting letter and taking it upstairs to open in the kitchen. After waiting months for the disciplinary panel to figure out its social-distancing protocols, they now wanted to get through their backlog. Her hearing would be in just two weeks' time. The second part of the letter summarised the situation, rather unnecessary in her case. It reminded her of the seriousness of the charge, and warned that her suspension would become permanent if she were found guilty of misconduct. The thought left a dry taste in her mouth.

She put the letter away and looked around. She'd only been away two nights, but it felt longer, and she saw the mess in her flat through new eyes. Every surface was covered with piles of court transcripts covered in coffee-cup stains and yellow highlighter. Her laptop computer was where she'd left it, a kind of epicentre to the mess. When she switched on the screen, her database was still open.

She still had an hour before she was due to meet Golding, and she set to work, trying to create some order, but there wasn't really enough time. She looked in her fridge for something to eat and found nothing, so she grabbed her keys again and got on her way.

She arrived in a drab-looking industrial estate on the outskirts of Southampton. When she located the relevant unit, she saw Golding waiting for her, leaning against his unremarkable Vauxhall. She lowered the window.

"Boss." He nodded, a smile on his face. "I don't suppose I'm going to get an explanation for all this, am I?"

Sands raised the window, but spoke before it shut fully. "After."

The forensic locksmith laboratory was deliberately discreet. A buzzer system led you into a small waiting room, complete with well-thumbed copies of *Locks and Key* magazine and a water cooler in the corner. There was no receptionist. Instead, the man who'd answered via the intercom introduced himself. "Detective Golding? I'm Dr Bland." He was a short man, slightly overweight, with a thick black beard flecked with grey.

"That's right." While Bland checked Golding's police ID, her former colleague introduced her. "This is Detective Chief Inspector Sands. She led the Sopley investigation." Bland didn't seem to notice that Sands never offered her own ID.

"I thought that case was closed?" Bland said instead, wiping his hands carefully on a rag. "Is there a problem?"

Sands smiled briskly as she took over. "Not a problem, no. We just need to check a couple of things."

"Alright. What exactly?"

"Do you still have the actual lock that was recovered from

the house where Emily Slaughter was abducted? Or do you just keep photographs?"

"Both."

"Good. Can we see them?"

"Why? I wrote a full report, you won't see anything that's not in there."

Sands smiled awkwardly. "Sometimes it helps to see things in person."

Bland took a deep breath, but then he shrugged. "Fine. If that's what you want. Come on through."

He took them through to a larger room – part metal-shop, part computer-lab and part storage area. It had the high ceilings of a warehouse and several rows of industrial shelving, mostly stacked with opaque plastic storage boxes. Another part of the room was furnished with desks, large machines and a microscope. Bland rolled a stepladder halfway down one of the aisles, locked the base into place and climbed up to fetch a box labelled with the case name and number. Inside, the locks were stored in heavy-duty clear plastic evidence bags.

"Here you go. The locks from the Slaughter house. That top one is from the girl's room. What exactly did you want to see?"

Now she was here, Sands wasn't completely sure herself. She thought for a moment, then replied. "Perhaps you can summarise what you put in the report?"

The man didn't look happy. "It was pretty clear. What exactly didn't you understand?"

"Just assume it's everything," Sands said. "You gave a preliminary report saying that the lock on Emily Slaughter's bedroom door had been picked. How could you tell?"

Bland glanced at both of them, but then shrugged. "When I took them off the door, I could see the marks."

"What do you mean?"

"Marks from the pick that was used."

"Explain. Imagine I don't know anything about picking locks. But I need to understand exactly what happened here."

Bland frowned but seemed to approve of the question. It wasn't often that the police took quite so much interest in his work. "OK," He put the rag down. "When you pick a lock you need two tools, a tension tool, which applies tension to the lock, and a pick, which positions the components of the lock so you can open it. And because these tools need to fit through a very small entrance – the keyhole in most cases – they have to be very thin. Therefore, they also need to be made of extremely strong material. You follow me?"

Sands nodded, then looked at Golding. His eyebrows raised a notch.

"And when you use a pick tool it requires a certain degree of force to actually move the internal components of the lock against the springs. Even more so on a lock like this, which secures the door in three places. As a result, the stronger pick tool will usually leave some kind of a mark on the softer brass or nickel-silver of the mechanism."

"OK, and that's what you saw when you took the Slaughters' lock apart?"

"That's right. I found evidence that the lock had been picked."

Sands looked in the box again. "Can you show me?"

"Not with this. I'd have to scrub up and get it clamped up on the electron microscope. I can show you the photos though." Opening a folder from inside the box, he showed them a dozen large colour photographs of what looked like a metal ball bearing in extreme close-up.

"These here are the pin heads."

Sands leaned in, but then shook her head. "And what do they show?"

"Look here." He pointed to a series of shallow lines scratched into the surface of the metal. "You can see where the tip of the pick scraped against it as they pushed it into position."

Sands took the photograph from his hands and studied it more closely. "That there? They couldn't have been made by the key?"

"The key doesn't touch here."

Sands frowned. "And these markings will always be present if a lock is picked?"

"Oh yeah." Bland seemed to be warming to his explanation. "It's the nature of the beast. A hard pick tool against softer components."

"What if you had someone who was really skilled? Could they pick a lock without leaving these marks?"

Bland shook his head. "Someone *really* good, using extremely light tension, and a very steady hand, that might not get noticed by every investigator, and certainly not with the lock in situ. But once I get it back here and under the electron microscope, I'll always pick it up."

"There'll always be marks?"

"Hard pick tools against the soft metal of the lock. Nature of the beast," he repeated.

Sands stared at the photos for a while. "So what you're saying is, you can make a judgement about the... skill level of the attacker from how deep the scratches are?"

"Uh huh. That's right."

Sands thought for a while. "Could you show me what a lock picked by an amateur would look like?"

"Sure." Bland turned to a nearby computer terminal. After a few clicks, an image came up on the screen. Another ball bearing image. Sands and Golding moved closer to see.

"These are 250x images of the same type of pin. You can see here..." – he pointed at the screen, and a series of significantly deeper scratches on the metal – "The attacker who did this was a lot less skilful."

Sands held up the photograph of the Slaughters' lock for comparison. "How would someone learn how to do this? Would they need to be a professional? And how do actual locksmiths learn?"

Bland half-shrugged. "Anyone could learn really. There are plenty of amateurs out there in the community."

"Community?"

"Online. On the forums." Bland scratched his beard absently. "There's a whole scene. Basically, every time a manufacturer announces a new model of lock, there's a race, professionals and amateurs. Who can be the first to break it. The first to publish proof."

"What proof?"

"Video showing the lock being broken, and how it was done."

"And that exists for this lock? Published proof that shows how to break it?"

"The Bullion three-point? For sure. Let's have a look." He clicked the photograph on the screen away and opened a web browser. Band typed "Bullion three-point" in a lock-picking forum search box. It returned around fifty posts. Bland clicked one which loaded step-by-step instructions, with photographs, of how to break the lock.

"So *I* could learn to break this lock? Anyone could learn?"

Bland chuckled a little, "Well not just *anyone*..." but then he caught sight of Sands' face and nodded instead. "Anyone who's prepared to put in the time learning the basics."

"And this lock." Sands held out the photograph again. "Is this basic? Is this a particularly difficult lock to break?"

The locksmith frowned, as if he wasn't keen on being pressed to be too specific. "It would depend on your skill level. A total amateur wouldn't be able to break the Bullion, they'd need to work up to it. But someone like me could do it fairly easily."

"How long would it take?" Golding asked.

"To build up to it?" said Bland. "Depends how long and how often they practised."

"No, to break it," Golding corrected. "How long would you take?"

"Oh right. Ten? Fifteen?"

"That's minutes?" Golding checked.

"Seconds." The locksmith's face was deadpan.

Sands brought the conversation back to what she wanted to focus on. She tapped her finger on the photograph of the Slaughters' lock. "Can you say how many times this lock has been picked?"

"Once or maybe twice. No more."

"How can you tell?"

"The number of scratches. Each time you push the pin with the pick you'll leave a mark. There are two here, showing it was done twice at the most, but more likely it took two goes to get it open. That also suggests a decent level of skill. Not professional, but they knew what they were doing."

"Did you examine the other locks on the Slaughters' doors?"

"Yes."

"Were they picked?"

"No."

"Thank you, Dr Bland." Sands handed the photograph back to him. "Oh, and one more thing, you mentioned the need for a steady hand? How important is that?"

Bland smiled broadly before answering. "That's just about the most important thing." He chuckled. "Good luck trying when you've had a few."

FIFTY-SIX

"You know, I'm really looking forward to hearing what all this is about," Luke Golding said when they were back outside. Sands had barely spoken since Bland's last response, and it had been left to Golding to thank the forensic locksmith as they left.

"Are you hungry?" Sands replied instead, looking around. There was a burger van in the industrial estate, advertising its wares with the smell of fried food, but she acted as if it wasn't there. "Follow me. I'll treat you."

Sands led the way. She drove past several open restaurants and cafés, but instead joined the motorway to Poole, where she finally stopped at a small Japanese restaurant called Oshiki. She slid the Alfa into the only parking spot outside, meaning Golding had to drive on and search for a space. He found her sitting in the restaurant studying the menu and sipping at a glass of sparkling water.

"So?" he asked, sitting down. "Are you going to tell me now?"

Sands glanced at him but ignored the question. "What do you like? The Yaki Udon is good here. Or the Mimigaa."

Golding sighed. He picked his own menu up, but she didn't

give him time to read it, instead raising her hand and clicking her fingers. The waitress, a middle-aged Japanese lady who had been watching Sands carefully, padded over and smiled politely.

"We'll have Korokke and Harumaki to start, then I'll have the Wagyu." Sands looked expectantly at Golding. He glanced at his own menu, but gave up at once. "Um, do you do..." He turned to Sands. "What was the second thing you said?"

"Mimigaa."

"Yeah, I'll have that. Thanks." He smiled at the waitress, who nodded and hurried away.

"What did I just order?" Golding watched her leave.

"It's a traditional dish from Okinawa. Boiled pig's ears."

"Oh. Great." He rubbed a hand across his face. "I love pig's ears. So, are you going to tell me?"

"I've been investigating the Michael Sopley case."

"I gathered that. I was wondering why?"

"Loose ends, like I said. Some new evidence might have come to light."

"What evidence?"

But Sands didn't answer. Instead she sat frowning, as if deep in though. Golding gave up again, and not long after the food arrived. The Korokee turned out to be little breaded rolls, deep fried and filled with vegetables, meat and crab. The Harumaki were more familiar, Japanese spring rolls served on a green salad. Sands expertly lifted the food with the chopsticks while Golding unapologetically used a fork.

"What new evidence?" Golding asked again, once the starters were gone. "And how come you have it, when you're meant to be suspended?"

"I hope I soon won't be. My hearing is in two weeks."

His eyebrows rose a fraction. "Well, that's something. It sucks how long they've left you hanging on."

"Yes." She pressed down a flutter of anxiety.

"So what's the new evidence?"

Sands set down her chopsticks. She took a breath.

"Did you know the Slaughters split their house in two? After the murder? That they sold half of it?"

Golding shook his head. "No. I hadn't even looked at the case until you called. It's not as if we haven't been busy, what with the pandemic. And what's the point if there's no trial?"

The waitress returned with the main courses. The Wagyu was a steak, an inch thick, pink on the inside. Even the pig's ears looked better than they sounded.

"A few days ago," Sands continued, cutting into her steak, "I had a call from a woman named Christine Harvey. She and her children moved into the other side of the Slaughters' house. She's concerned there might have been a mistake, and that Rodney Slaughter was responsible for Emily's death. And that he might now pose a danger to her own daughter. Her girl, Molly, is about the same age as Emily was when she died."

"OK," Golding said, trying to eat his food without looking too closely. "Rodney Slaughter seemed like a heartless bastard, but he didn't kill the girl. We have Michael Sopley's DNA on her body."

Sands continued, ignoring his input. "Christine Harvey showed me an online post under a newspaper article from someone who says they were with Sopley when the abduction took place."

"*With* him?" It was Golding's turn to hesitate. "As in, an alibi?"

"Yes. For the entire timespan of when the killing could have taken place."

Golding opened his mouth to protest, but then changed his mind. He considered for a few moments. "You said a posting under a newspaper article?"

"Yes." Sands glanced at him as if daring him to challenge the authenticity, but then she backed off. "I didn't believe it either, so I tracked it down, and it was his girlfriend. She's now dead, but I spoke to her friend, and she says..."

"Hold on, hold on." Golding had his hands up. "Slow down a second. You really are *actively* investigating this?"

A look somewhere between confusion and irritation appeared on her face. "Yes."

"But you can't be. I mean, you're *suspended*. If anyone finds out you're investigating a case, especially *this* case... they're gonna fire you." He looked around, fearful they might be overheard.

She frowned at him. "I'm not prepared to be responsible for a serious miscarriage of justice, especially if it means a dangerous killer is still at large." She softened suddenly. "It's also why I'm speaking to you. I need someone who can continue the investigation on my behalf. Make some checks that I can't make while I'm suspended." Sands raised a hand to attract the waitress's attention and ordered something called Agairi, explaining to Golding that it was a type of Japanese tea. The waitress left and Sands composed herself.

Golding slowly closed his mouth, which had dropped open. He scratched the back of his neck, pulling the collar away as if it were suddenly too tight. "You know they might fire me too if I help you?"

Sands didn't reply, letting a silence hang in the air until Golding went on.

"You said she was dead, this woman who was Sopley's girlfriend? How'd she die?"

"An overdose. It may or may not be suspicious – that's one of the things I want you to check out. But before she died, she told her friend that Sopley raped her on the night of the murder, which might explain why he ran when he saw all those police that morning."

The tea arrived in white porcelain cups. Golding was silent while the waitress poured it for them. He went on when she left. "It might. It could also be because he murdered Emily Slaughter. We found his DNA on the body, remember? How do you explain that?"

"I can't explain that. At least, not exactly. But the girl I spoke to. I believed her. I don't think she was lying."

She stayed quiet for a moment, giving him time to take things in. "So what are you saying?" he asked in the end.

"It's simple. If Sopley had an alibi, then he couldn't have abducted and killed Emily Slaughter. Which means someone else did. And in that case, they might have tried to frame Sopley using his DNA." Sands waited for a response.

"And... you told me that day that when young girls are killed, it's usually the dad that does it? Like, seventy percent of the time?"

"Sixty-six percent."

"You think it might have been Rodney Slaughter after all?"

Sands didn't answer directly. "Christine Harvey certainly thinks so. She told me he often wakes up in the middle of the night and stares at her house. I stayed over and saw him coming right up to the girl's bedroom at around three in the morning. He was carrying a sword."

"*A sword?* Holy shit. What the hell was he doing?"

"He'd been practising Kenjutsu. Of course it might have been an accident that he took the sword with him, something he didn't think through."

Golding shook his head and blinked. "Kenjut... what?"

"Japanese swordsmanship. The Slaughters lived for a while in Japan, it's a popular hobby there. Not uncommon."

"Are you serious? An actual sword?"

Sands raised her hand again and the waitress came over to them, a questioning look on her face.

"How popular is Kenjutsu in Japan?" Sands asked her. The woman frowned deeply, clearly thrown by the question. But when Sands kept her eyes fixed on her face and waited, she eventually answered. "Many people... Many people enjoy this. All over Japan."

"And they use a sword? When they practise?"

"Yes... many sword. Tachi, Katana, Wakizahi, many different sword."

"Thank you." Sands nodded and turned back to Golding, as if dismissing her. The waitress hesitated a moment, and then retreated, clearly still confused.

"OK." He shrugged. "So now I get why you took me to a Japanese restaurant. But even if having a sword is common over there, it's kinda weird here. And what actually happened?"

"I'm not sure. He saw me, then he went away."

"Did he try to break in?"

"No, but he might have been about to. I can understand why Christine Harvey is concerned."

Golding considered again "So you want me to speak to him? Since you're suspended?"

"I already spoke to him. He told me he was worried the same thing might happen again. That someone might try and break in and abduct Christine Harvey's daughter. He said he thought he heard something, but he knew it was really in his head."

Golding thought about this. "Maybe. But if he's the sort of man who could kill his own daughter, he'd certainly be capable of lying about it."

"That's what I thought," Sands went on, then changed the subject. "After I was injured, was there a scoping exercise, an effort to find any other murders that Sopley might have been responsible for?"

"Yeah," Golding replied, thinking. "I mean, it could have been more exhaustive. It all went a bit crazy as the pandemic hit."

"Why?"

"Why? Because the whole country pretty much shut down with the virus..."

"No. *Why* was there a scoping exercise?"

Golding looked at her as if she were crazy. "There always is. It's routine when we find a murderer's identity, to check if they could have committed any similar unsolved crimes."

"But not in *all* murders. Not if it's obvious that it's a first-time killing?"

"Obviously not."

"So, was it judged likely, or at least plausible, that this wasn't a first-time killing? That Sopley might have killed before?"

Golding nodded. "Yeah. Lindham thought so."

"OK. Did you find anything?"

"No."

"Where did you look?"

"The usual places. Unsolved cases in the area. And then nationwide."

"Did you look at solved cases? With other convicted killers?"

Golding made a face. "No. Why would we?"

Sands steepled her fingers and sat back, thinking. Eventually, she spoke again. "Most murders that come along, they're kind of simple. But every now and then, one comes along that isn't simple at all. What if Emily's killing was one of those? And that's where we've gone wrong?"

Golding frowned, deep creases lining his face. "I'm sorry boss. I'm not sure I follow where you're going here."

Sands looked away, thinking how best to clarify. Then she turned back. "The single strongest piece of evidence against Michael Sopley is that one of his pubic hairs, with a conveniently intact follicle, was found on the body, directly linking him to the crime. Correct?"

"I guess so."

"And there was no way we *weren't* going to find that hair. And no way, once we did find it, that we wouldn't process it and come up with Sopley's name. He was on the sex offenders' register. We were always going to find him."

Golding nodded.

"So if Sopley *didn't* do it, how did the hair get there?"

Golding soon gave up trying to answer.

"The only possible answer is that *someone else* put it there. If it wasn't Sopley, then it has to have been someone who framed Sopley, by planting a very specific piece of his DNA on the body."

Golding hunched forward at this point. "Well how would they get it? It's kinda a personal thing."

Sands waved away the question. "Not really. It could be a sexual partner, could be a roommate who found it in his bed sheets or laundry. It could have been done at the lab, swapping one hair for another, falsifying the results..."

"That's pretty far-fetched..."

"It doesn't matter. What's important is that it *could* have been done. And if it *was* done once, it could have been done before. Many times perhaps, different people being framed each time. Which means we wouldn't find anything by looking at unsolved cases, because the relevant cases here wouldn't *be* unsolved. They'd be solved."

Golding thought about this for a moment. "OK. So let me guess, that's the second thing you want me to do, search solved cases to see if Rodney Slaughter comes up anywhere?"

Sands shook her head. "No. Not Slaughter."

"But I thought you said..."

"I said Christine Harvey thinks he did it. She's wrong."

"OK... And why?"

"Because of what the locksmith said." Sands held up her hand and clicked her fingers, calling the waitress again.

"OK. What exactly did the locksmith say?" But Sands didn't answer, instead asking respectfully for the bill.

Golding tried again. "So if not Slaughter, do you know who did it?"

"I think I might know where to look. By the way, where did you leave your car?"

"My car? In the NCP car park."

"That's good, you can leave it there, we'll go in mine." Sands paid the bill with her credit card.

"Where are we going? What are we going to look at?"

"My place." She turned back with a smile.

FIFTY-SEVEN

Sands zapped open the Alfa and climbed in. Golding shot a glance at the nearby multi-storey car park where his own vehicle was parked, but did the same. She waited until he'd plugged in the seatbelt, then fired the engine.

"While I've been injured, I've been reading through trial transcripts of solved murder cases. Mostly where the prosecution was able to secure a conviction."

Golding frowned. "Trial transcripts?"

"Yes. Yorke denied my original request to review unsolved cases to see where something might have been missed. But trial transcripts are a matter of public record, along with any documents submitted in evidence, so I was able to download them and go through them."

"What for?"

"I wanted to identify which factors were most important in securing convictions, statistically speaking. So I tried to reduce each case to its key elements. Location, cause of death, age of victim, hair colour – things like that. And then I built a database to cross-reference all these factors." She paused. "I thought it would be interesting."

Golding's eyebrows rose up his forehead. "And you did all this while you were recovering from being shot?"

"Well there was a pandemic on. I wasn't allowed out." Sands looked confused.

"How many did you download?"

"All of them. From the last ten years."

"All of them? How many is that?"

"About eight hundred."

"Eight hundred trials?"

"Yes. But that's just England and Wales. I haven't got round to Scotland yet."

"Alright." Golding looked a little car sick. "Did you find anything?"

"I didn't think so at first. I mean, I hadn't finished, and I'd found several interesting cases, but then I was interrupted by Christine Harvey's phone call. And it was only then that I realised other cases had a superficial similarity to Sopley's. In that they hinged on just one piece of actual evidence, and everything else was purely circumstantial."

They came to a stop outside Sands' apartment building. She limped slightly as she led the way into the lobby and, ignoring the lift, up three flights of stairs to the top floor. Her apartment was still a complete mess, with papers piled up high on every surface.

"This is where you live?" Golding asked. Sands ignored him, trying to find her computer. "It's nice. Or it could be. If you had a bit of a clear up." He looked out the window over the harbour.

Sands continued to ignore him, pointing to her computer screen instead. "This is the database. I didn't have time to finish it before we were due to meet, but I should be able to run a search for the cases we need." She sat down and began to type, scrolling through pages of data, occasionally asking Golding to hand her one of the documents scattered on the desk. Then suddenly she got up, looking thoughtful, and walked over to a pile of papers next to the window seat. She flicked through them quickly, eventually pulling one out.

"This one." She read as she spoke so that her voice was distant and vague. "It involves a guy called Joshua Jones. He was convicted for the murder of an elderly lady in south London." She turned the page, running her finger quickly down the lines.

"He's in prison now. Fifteen-year stretch, but he always denied any involvement. I remembered he had a therapist. I made a medical contacts field on the database. I didn't think it would mean much at the time, but..."

She stopped suddenly. Stared, blinking at the paper in front of her. Then she turned to Golding. "Remember the name of the woman who lives next door to Rodney and Janet Slaughter?"

Golding had to search his memory, but he got it. "Christine something. Christine Harvey?"

Sands handed him the paper, and he read it for a few moments before reaching the relevant part. "Oh shit," he said. "Does that... what does... Does that mean what I think it means?"

PART 4

FIFTY-EIGHT

CHRISTINE

Christine sat with a plate on her lap watching TV. The gameshows and dramas that filled the daytime schedules were like old friends to her. For many years they'd helped her to forget the troubles in her life. Right now, the thoughts they helped crowd out were why the police wouldn't arrest Rodney Slaughter, why Erica Sands, who'd promised to help, and had even moved in with them temporarily, didn't seem to be doing anything. And now – where on earth she was. After saying she'd protect them from Slaughter, she'd now disappeared, not seen for almost a fortnight. And when Christine phoned her – repeatedly – she'd only say she was "investigating leads". The procession of thoughts that chased each other endlessly around her mind was suddenly interrupted. She thought at first it was a new sound effect on the gameshow she was watching. Then she realised it was the doorbell.

"Who's that?" she shouted as she made her way out into the hallway, where she squinted through the spyglass fitted to the front door. Immediately, her heart bounced inside her chest. It was a group of people, one of whom was Erica Sands, her serious face distorted by the curvature of the glass. Beside her was an older man, and behind *them* another man and a woman. What did they all want? For a glorious, hope-filled second or two, she wondered if they'd come to help – to arrest Rodney Slaughter, to let her live her life in peace.

"Yes?" Christine asked, swinging open the front door.

"Christine Harvey," Sands began. She paused, just enough to offer Christine a look of respect, a nod, but she spoke slowly. "This is Chief Superintendent Yorke." She motioned to the older man standing next to her, and then stood back to reveal the others.

"This is Detective Luke Golding, and this is Helen Emmerson. Helen works for the child protection service here in Dorset." She stepped forward again as the other officers nodded sternly. "May we come in, Christine?"

Christine stared at them, briefly unsure whether this was real, or just a dream. "Why? What for?"

"Please." Christine felt Sands' eyes fixed on hers. "We need to do this inside."

Christine wanted to say no. She wanted to go back to her world, however horrible, where she could withdraw just enough into *Countdown* to keep everything pressed down and hidden. But it was obvious she couldn't send them away. She'd started this, and now she sensed that it was, after so many years, finally coming to an end.

"OK." Her voice was tiny, hoarse.

Sands led them into the main living space. Without asking, she opened the blinds to let some light in, then switched off the television. Sands and the younger man, Golding, cleared the dining table, piling the dirty bowls in the sink. Christine just watched until Sands was done. Then she asked Christine to sit down. The others all did so too.

"What is this?" Christine asked. "Have you come to arrest Rodney Slaughter?"

There was silence.

"No Christine, that's not why we're here," Sands began. Christine glanced at the woman – the *child protection officer*. That was the title that scared her, far more than the detectives, or the Chief Superintendent. Christine risked a glance at the woman's face. Impassive, superficially kind, but what lay hidden beneath?

"Are your children here?" Sands was asking. "Your daughter Molly?"

Christine felt a sudden burning in her chest at the mention of her daughter, as if her heart had suddenly stopped and her lungs had collapsed. Were they here for Molly? She took in a few hacking breaths. Managed to choke out a word. "W-why?"

"Please just answer the question."

Christine tried to pull herself together. "No. She's at a play-date. With Daisy... And Ryan's out with friends. He passed his driving test!" For a moment she was back living the lie that this woman was a friend of hers. A friend of her family. But then the thought faded. "He'll be back soon." She tried to crack a smile, but it turned into something ugly. "Please, what's this about?"

"Daisy Reynolds?"

"Yes."

Sands turned to the child protection officer and spoke in a low voice. "She's a school friend. See if you can get an address, and we'll pick her up afterwards." The woman moved to the other end of the room, pulling out her mobile.

Pick her up? And after *what*? "Erica, what's going on? *Please?*"

"Christine, look at me," said Sands, a harsh edge to her voice. "This is a very unusual situation Christine, but we're here because it's also a very serious one. We need to talk to you, and it's important that you're honest. More honest than you've been so far. I hope you're ready for that, Christine. Are you ready to be honest?"

Christine stared at Sands while she talked, then swivelled

to look in amazement at the two men. The thought passed through her that they were staring at her as if *she* were the criminal. She felt her head go light, the familiar survival mechanism beginning to churn, stirring the pot of old excuses. But the way Sands was looking at her, the way the two men were staring, she found herself nodding. "Of course."

"Good. Thank you, Christine," Sands replied. Her voice was calm, almost sad. "Now, you asked me here because you thought we'd made a mistake and that it was Rodney Slaughter who killed Emily."

Hope flared up again within Christine, but Sands didn't give it a chance to take hold.

"We've come to explain that you're wrong about that."

Christine immediately began shaking her head again, wanting the light, needing the flare. "No. *No,* you have to believe me. You've *seen* the way he looks at Molly... You saw him, he came to her window. He tried to break in."

"He didn't try to break in, Christine." Sands was firm now. "I did see Rodney Slaughter outside Molly's bedroom window. But I didn't see him try to break in, and when I asked him why he was there, he told me he thought he'd heard a noise, and came outside to investigate. He says he lives in fear of what happened to his daughter happening to other children, including Molly. I think that's a reasonable excuse under the circumstances."

Christine made a noise suggesting this was anything but reasonable. "He's a liar," she told Sands. "You know it. He's a murderer and a liar. You can't possibly trust him."

"We're not trusting him, Christine. We've examined the evidence, and it doesn't support the idea that Rodney Slaughter could have done it."

Christine was still breathing deeply, not listening to what Sands was saying.

"When the lock on Emily Slaughter's bedroom door was

examined, it showed clear signs of being picked from the outside. That strongly indicates that Emily was abducted by someone who broke into the house, not someone already on the inside. Why would Rodney pick the lock, Christine? Why would he do that?"

Christine almost laughed. "Is that it? Is that all you've got? Isn't it obvious?" For a moment she couldn't believe the stupidity of the woman in front of her. Her own stupidity in trusting her. "He *wanted* to make it look like someone from outside took her. Oh my God. That's *why* he did it. *He* picked the lock, so it would look like there was an intruder. There never was, it was him all along." She turned to the other men, the older one and the good-looking one. She nodded frantically, willing them to see the truth. But they didn't respond.

"I thought that might be a possibility too," Sands replied. Her voice seemed to pull Christine back to her like a magnet. "But when a lock is picked, we can tell something about how skilled or otherwise the perpetrator is. And whoever picked the lock on Emily's door did a good job. Most importantly, it was opened by someone with a steady hand."

Christine tried to listen, but the words made no sense. "I don't understand. What are you saying?"

"Christine, I've spoken to Rodney Slaughter about this, and he's given me permission to tell you, although he's asked you don't repeat it, for obvious reasons."

"What? Repeat what?"

"You've spent time watching Rodney Slaughter through this window. You've seen his habits, you've seen him at work on his computer. You've seen the pointing device he uses." Sands paused, and Christine was baffled.

"So?"

"You've also said you've witnessed outbursts of anger. Once, when he was kite-surfing, and again when practising with his sword. These outbursts stem from his own frustration at his physical decline."

"What?" Suddenly this was too much. "*Practising with his sword?* What kind of a person practises with a sword in the first place? In the middle of the night."

Sands ignored her and kept going, her voice maddeningly calm. "Christine, Rodney Slaughter is suffering from Parkinson's disease. That's why his hands always shake. That's why he has a special pointing device on his computer. It's one reason he's angry. I've spoken to his doctor, and to several other specialists. They all confirm there's simply no way he could have been responsible for opening the lock on Emily's bedroom door. It wasn't Slaughter."

"But... No." Facts quickly rearranged themselves in Christine's mind. Different strategies appeared, fully formed. "Parkinson's disease? He's faking. He's pretending to have it. Or maybe it comes and goes? Or what if he got someone else to pick the lock for him. When he took poor Emily. It must be something like that. Because *he* did it. I *know* he did."

No one spoke for a while, so Christine tried another tack. "And sword-fighting. What about the sword-fighting? You saw him, in the middle of the night." The older man, the Chief Superintendent or whatever he was, shifted uncomfortably in his seat.

"It doesn't mean anything, Christine." Sands voice stayed calm. "It is an unusual hobby here, but it's common in Japan, where Rodney Slaughter picked it up. He lived out there for several years." She paused for a moment. "He's also grieving and traumatised by the murder of his only child. Perhaps in those circumstances it's understandable that he wants to keep a weapon in the house and practise with it when he's unable to sleep."

Christine felt herself glimpsing the void, but she wasn't ready yet to face it. "Then the lock, you're wrong about the lock.

He could pick it, or he didn't need to – why would he need to? He had the key. He was already inside. So he took her, and he faked the lock, or you're wrong about it being picked." It took Christine a few seconds to become aware of how much she was shaking her head. She forced herself to be still.

Sands was silent, but Christine felt the way she was being watched, by all of them.

"No. *No!* This is insane. You can't *believe* him. He's a *liar*. He's not ill – *Parkinson's*," – she wanted to spit the word – "And who would he be protecting? Himself, look at the size of him! Or do you mean his wife, because he sure as damn doesn't want to *protect* her. He's probably going to kill her..." Christine swung to look directly at one of the men – Yorke she'd called him – he was the senior one, surely he'd listen? "He's having an affair. Rodney Slaughter is having an affair." There was a brief silence. "Did she tell you that? Did she tell you I *saw* him, sneaking off with Molly's teacher, *his own daughter's teacher?* Disgusting, both of them. They weren't even trying to hide it."

Sands answered. "Having an affair is not a police matter, Christine. Although it may be a disciplinary one for the teaching assistant. But that's a matter for the school."

Christine opened her mouth then closed it again. "So you admit it? That he's having an affair."

"It seems a plausible explanation for what you described, but it has no possible bearing on what happened to Emily Slaughter."

"So it doesn't... It doesn't *matter?*"

"It has no bearing on this case."

"It doesn't matter. He still took his daughter..." she murmured, wanting it to be true.

"No, Christine, he didn't," Sands answered gently. "Someone else broke in that night. Someone else abducted and murdered Emily." She paused, and when she spoke again her words carried the weight of the world. "And I think you know that."

Christine glanced down. She saw the fear that she lived with suddenly swell up inside her. A blackness, that began to spin, and make her dizzy. Thoughts were sucked down into it, lies and cover stories were spat out.

"Wait, what!? You still think it was Sopley?" She laughed, aware that she sounded like a lunatic, but not able to stop. "I told you about his *alibi*. You spoke to that *woman*..." She managed to steady her head so that she was staring at Yorke. The fear dimmed a little – could she close it up? Could she yet force it back in the dark place of her mind where it mostly hid? "Has she told you about *that*? How it couldn't be Sopley because he was with someone else that night?"

"Yes," Yorke replied, but so calmly that Christine didn't hear him properly and kept up her rant.

"It *has* to be Rodney Slaughter. It just has to be."

"Christine, how did you come to buy this house?"

"*What?*"

"*This house*. How did you find it?"

"What?" She sensed the trap in the question, but couldn't see where it was. "I... I saw it on the internet. I thought it looked nice. I didn't know there was a *monster* living next door..."

"And this area? How did you come to know about this area?"

"We used..." Christine stopped. Her neck suddenly cricked sharply, pulling her head to one side. Then it relaxed again. But it was OK. None of them saw it. "We used to come here for holidays. Years ago."

Sands replied by picking up the tablet on the table. "May I?"

Christine felt cold, and Sands had to repeat herself.

"What for?" Christine snapped, suddenly breathing hard. "What do you want it for?"

"Please Christine, it's time for the truth." Sands held out the tablet for Christine to unlock. There was no other option.

Sands found Christine's Facebook account and scrolled back in time through her feed.

"You don't post too much these days, but you did when your husband was alive. Is that right?"

"I suppose so."

"And it wasn't ages ago that you came here on holiday, it was more recent than that. It was actually this year. February half term. Isn't that right?"

Christine didn't dare glance down. She knew the fear was back. The swirling black clouds that concealed everything. She wondered if she were strong enough to push them away again. It was so tiring to do so.

"Isn't that right, Christine?"

"Perhaps. I can't remember."

"The very same week that Emily Slaughter was murdered?"

Christine breathed hard. Still she didn't look down. "So what?"

Sands held up the tablet, showing a photograph of her family. Her beautiful, wonderful family, before dear Evan had been taken from her. It showed the four of them, Christine with her arms around Molly in a protective embrace, Evan and Ryan side-by-side. Evan had lodged his phone in a rock and set the timer to take the photograph. In the background you could see the headland overlooking the cove.

"You posted this two days before the murder."

"So what if I did?"

Sands ignored her. Instead, she flicked back a few images on Christine's Facebook page, finding one that showed Evan on his own, painting one of his model soldiers.

"I saw these downstairs." Sands smiled again, sadly. "Beautifully detailed. Such intricate work."

"*So*? What are you saying? What is this?"

The fear was roaring now. Like an enormous dark whirlpool trying to drag her down. And nearly succeeding. "I don't understand."

"You were here, Christine. You were here when Emily Slaughter was taken. And not just you."

"No. You're wrong. Whatever you're saying, you're wrong. It was Rodney Slaughter. It was the homeless man, Sopley..." Her words were like lifebuoys, just about keeping her afloat.

"Where did you stay, Christine?"

"Just down in the village. Evan found a place on Airbnb, but..."

Her fingers gripped the edge of the table. She noticed a kitchen knife on the work surface, just within reach. If she made a lunge for it... But just then the male detective, the younger one, took a step forward and gently removed it. She heard herself whimpering.

"Detective Golding has been looking into your husband's work," Sands said. "You told me he died working on the Covid wards, but that wasn't his usual place of work, was it?"

Christine breathed hard, trying to focus. "No."

"He was both a medical doctor and a specialist in psychiatry. When the pandemic hit, he volunteered to work on the front line, helping critically ill patients. Is that right?"

She nodded.

"An unusual decision."

"He was a very unusual man. Brilliant. Brave."

Sands took a deep breath and let it out slowly. "In his normal work, before Covid, he treated patients who had a range of problems, including convicted paedophiles and the like? Is that correct?"

"I don't know. He didn't discuss his work. He wasn't allowed to."

"You never knew anything about his work?" Yorke asked this question. He sounded surprised.

"I know he worked with difficult people."

"Christine." Sands took over again. "Did you know that Michael Sopley was a former patient of your husband?"

Christine froze. Her eyes were the only thing left moving, glancing in stops and starts around the room, as if unsure where it was safe to rest. "Sopley? The homeless man?"

"Yes. He had several therapy sessions with your husband. It was a requirement in a court order against Sopley following his conviction for burglary. Because Sopley wasn't a typical burglar. He broke into houses to arrange children's toys in their bedrooms. He had a particular interest in dolls. Sopley was required by law to discuss this with your husband. Your husband would also have known that Sopley had worked for many years as a locksmith. In short, he had all the information he needed to frame Michael Sopley for this crime."

"But why would he...?" Christine's hand was on her chest. She suddenly felt strangely calm. "And Evan's *dead*, Detective. Evan *died* five months ago."

"I know that Christine. And I know that you chose to move here after that. Next door to where Emily Slaughter was abducted and murdered. And I think we'd all like to know why you made that decision."

There was silence in the room, everyone waiting for Christine to answer. But she didn't. In the end, a look, almost of contentment, appeared on her face.

"Detective Golding has also done some research into some of your husband's other former patients, Christine. A surprising number of them have gone on to be convicted of murder."

"I told you, he worked with some difficult people."

Sands reached into the bag she was carrying and pulled out a file. "This is the court report for the trial of Joshua Jones. Another of your husband's former patients. He was convicted of killing Ada Adawole. The crime very precisely fits Jones's history, the problems he was required to discuss with your husband. Adawole was a black woman, and Jones was an open racist. She was old, and he had a history of abusing elderly patients in a care home. But most convincing of all, fingerprints on a glass placed Jones at the scene of the crime. It's quite possible he drank from that glass while undergoing therapy with your husband. Evan could have saved it and planted it at the scene of the crime."

Christine shook her head, and Sands pushed the file aside to reveal another. "And this is the court report from the trial of William Harris, another former patient of your husband. He was convicted of strangling a man named Daniel Cox. A single tissue was found in Cox's flat that placed Harris at the scene, although he denied ever being there or even meeting Cox."

Christine stared at her.

"Again, Harris could have used that tissue during one of their therapy sessions, and your husband could have planted it at the scene. Again, he had all the information he needed to choose a victim that would have been a typical target for Harris."

In response, Christine covered her face with her hands. The fear had filled her mind fully now. Sucked her down. But unlike the raging torrent it had always seemed to be from above, actually being in it was strangely calming. Almost peaceful.

"Just what are you saying? My husband sacrificed himself to work with these people. It wasn't popular, but somebody had to do it."

"I don't think your husband sacrificed himself at all, Christine. I think he preyed upon these people. I think he set them up for murders he committed himself."

Suddenly, Christine burst out laughing. "That's absurd. That's the most ridiculous thing I've ever heard. It's much more likely that these..." She looked away again, her neck jerking to the left. "These people did it themselves. Vermin." She muttered the last word almost under her breath.

"People like Michael Sopley?" Sands asked quietly.

"Yes." Christine rounded on her. "Exactly like Sopley. If Rodney Slaughter didn't kill his daughter, then it must have been Sopley after all."

"But as you yourself said. It couldn't have been Sopley, because he had an alibi."

A part of Christine yearned to give in, now she'd been sucked into the black hole that had stretched underneath her mind for so long. Someone handed her a glass of water, and she took a shaky sip.

"There hasn't been time for a detailed investigation," Sands said. "But we've looked into how many Covid patients died while your husband was working on the ward, and it's higher than the average. Significantly higher. We suspect your husband chose to work there for the opportunity to kill those patients."

Christine laughed out loud. The water spilled from the glass and pooled on the tabletop.

"We think there are more, Christine. We think we'll find other people that Evan treated who've gone on to be convicted of murder. Murders that your husband committed. We think you know that's the truth, and now we want you to help us. To tell us what you know."

For a long time, Christine kept her eyes on the spilled water. Then slowly she turned her head to face Sands. Her eyes were red and wide and trembling from the thin film of water that now coated them. "I thought you were here to help me."

Sands looked away, then glanced at Yorke again. He took over the questioning, his voice soft and measured. "We think it *will* help you, Christine. Why did you buy this house? It can't have been a coincidence. Was it guilt? Did you want to try to make things better, perhaps at some subconscious level?"

"I thought coming to the country would help. Everyone was dying in London. From Covid..."

"But why *this* house? Why next door to where Emily lived?"

"And the animals. They were starting to turn up again, and I couldn't cope with all that again, so I thought if we moved away... I don't know..." Christine looked up now, crying, her face open for the first time. "And anyway, *I* didn't find the house, Ryan did. He wasn't even keen on moving at first, but then he found this house on Rightmove and suddenly, he liked the idea."

There was a noise – the squeak of shoe rubber on a hard floor – and moments later the sound of the front door shutting.

Christine's head jerked up at the sound. "That's probably Ryan now. I said he could take the car to pick Molly up. Did I tell you he passed his driving test? He did ever so well." She looked at Sands, but the detective looked quite different now, her body frozen, her face suddenly white.

"That was your son leaving?" Yorke asked. "You told us he was out with friends?"

"Did I?" Christine gave an apologetic look. "He must have been downstairs. You know what it's like with teenagers, I never know what he's up to these days."

The two men looked at each other – they seemed concerned – but Christine was more interested in Sands. She was still white, and then her eyes had widened. Slowly she rose to her feet. The other two policemen looked questioningly at her. Christine was looking too.

"The *animals*," Sands said. "The cat. The cat in the bloody bin. With all the madness about Evan Harvey, we forgot about the *bloody cat*."

FIFTY-NINE

ERICA SANDS

Sands ran to the front door, her injuries dragging at her hips, but the signals not reaching her brain. She found it had been shut and double locked – presumably from the outside, since the key was missing from where Christine usually kept it hanging by the door. It took her a frustratingly long time to return to the living area, snatch the second set from the kitchen worktop and return to the hallway. When she finally got the door open, Christine's car was nowhere to be seen. She breathed hard.

"*Shit.*" She turned to see Golding and Yorke behind her, staring, not understanding.

"The cat," she said again. "Christine said the animals started again, in London." She waited a beat, but they still weren't with her. "She found a murdered cat a few weeks ago. *Here.* Unless he came back from the dead, it wasn't killed by Evan Harvey."

She was paralysed by inaction, but only for a second. She ran back inside to where Christine was waiting with Emmerson, the child protection officer.

"Have you got the address for Daisy Reynolds? Where Molly Harvey has her playdate?"

"I've just got it."

"Good. Go."

"*Now!*" Sands added when no one moved. Then she spun to see Golding behind her. "You too. You need to get to Molly before he does."

"What's going on?" Yorke asked from behind her. "What's happening? Are you saying everything we said in there is wrong?"

Sands spun around, shaking her head. "Not wrong, incomplete. We didn't properly account for the boy. Ryan is the same as his father. Or maybe he's getting that way, I don't know. But if he's been here all this time, he could have heard everything we said." She felt sick as she spoke.

Still neither Emmerson nor Golding had gone, and Sands suddenly yelled at them both. "Move! *Go.* Get the girl." She hurried them outside to the parking area. They had arrived in two cars, her own red Alfa and Chief Inspector Yorke's silver Mercedes, which was blocking her in so she turned to Yorke. "Give Golding your keys, it'll be quicker."

If Yorke minded being given orders by someone he outranked, he did nothing to show it. Instead, he tossed his keys to Golding, and watched as the detective and Emmerson quickly ran to the silver Mercedes.

"Phone me when you have her," Sands called out. "The moment you get her." Golding nodded before slamming the car door closed.

They all watched as the tyres kicked up grit as they gripped the road, and the car disappeared down the hill. All the while Christine was making a noise – a quiet whining sound that reminded Sands of Janet Slaughter, when she'd first heard about her daughter's death. It had the same note of hopelessness and terror.

"Let's go and wait inside." Yorke said; obviously he could hear it too. But Sands wasn't listening. Instead she was staring at the front right tyre of her own car, the only one now left in the parking area.

"Oh shit," she said. "He knows."

SIXTY

"How do you know?" Yorke asked, before noticing that the tyre was completely flat. Something was protruding from the side-wall, a short shaft of aluminium, on its exposed end the stabilising vanes of a crossbow dart.

"What the hell is that?"

Sands replied, her stomach twisted tight. "I think it's a crossbow bolt."

Christine Harvey's whimpering grew louder.

"Does Ryan own a crossbow?" Sands asked, but as she spoke she remembered the sports bag on Ryan's bedroom floor, when he had had caught her snooping in his bedroom. She hadn't expected to see a weapon, so she had missed it. She glanced at Christine now, but it was obvious the mother wasn't going to reply.

"We need to warn Golding," Yorke said, and Sands nodded. But then she had an idea. "I think I know where he might have gone."

Yorke was quiet, waiting.

"The cove. Where the murder happened." Sands turned to look down the lane to where the cove glittered in the late afternoon sunlight. It looked innocent, appealing even from this distance. She turned again to Yorke. "Take Christine inside." She barely heard his answer as she started jogging, as best as she could with the pain in her side, down the hill and towards the little beach.

When she reached the end of the lane at the top of the beach, she wasn't at all surprised to find Christine's car there, parked illegally, the passenger door hanging open. She checked it quickly, but Ryan Harvey was nowhere to be seen. She pulled out her phone to call Yorke, but it rang as she did so.

"Golding. Tell me you've got Molly?"

"Negative. Ryan got there just before us. There's no sign of either of them."

"*Shit.* I'm with his car now. They're at the murder site. Get over here and get some back-up." She killed the call.

She ran along the beach as best she could. It was a weekday, and late enough that the only people left were a few tourists, already heading back to their cars parked in the village behind her. Sands' feet sunk into the loose sand and pebbles, and her hips hurt as she pushed herself to keep running. Eventually, the rocks at the far end of the beach were close enough to make out. But there was no one there. Nothing to see. Sands slowed, out of breath now, and beginning to doubt, hoping she might be wrong. But not for long. She heard a weird noise – or more of a sensation of noise – like a tiny bird had flown past her ear. It stopped her dead.

"Best not come any closer." Ryan Harvey stepped out from behind the rock where he'd been hiding. In his hands he held a crossbow, painted in browns and camouflage greens, its string wound back and another bolt already in place. He held it up to show her. "That one was a warning. I'm pretty good with this. Been practising on the local wildlife. And a couple of cats." He grinned. Then, as Sands made to step forward, his face became serious.

"I'm not going to miss again."

"Where's Molly?" Sands asked. She felt completely exposed, stuck halfway between the water's edge and the top of the beach. There was nowhere to duck for cover if he fired again.

"Oh, she's here. She's sleeping. I was supposed to just pick her up, but then I heard you guys talking to Mum, and I decided to bring her here instead. Told her there was a special surprise." He grinned again.

"What do you mean she's sleeping?"

"I mean I hit her with a rock. But she's OK, she's just knocked out. For now."

"What are you doing? What's this all about?" Sands asked. .

"You seem to know. You're the one with all the answers." Ryan casually aimed the crossbow at her face. He was close enough that she could see directly down the shaft of the arrow. He mimed firing the device, pretending to allow for the recoil to kick up his arm.

"*Pow,*" he said, sniggering. "You know, I haven't shot an actual person with this yet, I'm kinda curious..."

"It's over, Ryan. We know all about your father. We know what he did."

Ryan rolled his eyes. "Don't be stupid. You don't know shit. Dad had you totally fooled. You thought it was Sopley. You all did."

"We made a mistake. But we know the truth now."

"Yeah, maybe." He grew suddenly serious again, steadying the crossbow. "Or maybe not."

Sands took a step forward.

"*Stop!*" His voice was suddenly commanding. "You want me to shoot you?"

"I want to know where Molly is. I need to check she's alright."

"I told you she's fine. You wanna see? Come take a look."

Sands stepped forward and he grinned widely.

"*Slowly!*"

She did what he said, moving slowly forward, feeling her increasing vulnerability to the crossbow. When she was within five metres of him, the scene he had created came into view behind some taller rocks.

"*Oh Ryan.*"

Molly was lying face down on the stones, a stain of blood matting her fair hair.

"She's fine. She was screaming so I had to shut her up." He said it contemptuously, like it was pathetic of his sister to have been scared. Then he put his foot under her stomach and used it to turn her over. As her body rolled, Sands noticed her arm move to protect herself. The girl was woozy, but alive.

"See? And the best part is, now you're here, you get to watch her die."

"She's hurt. Let me check her over."

"Fuck you." Ryan suddenly angered. He pointed the weapon at Sands. "Maybe I should shoot you first, for screwing everything up?"

He suddenly screamed, like the roar of a wounded animal, and his eyes turned wild. For a second, Sands thought he'd actually fired. She could almost feel the arrow penetrating her chest. He laughed hysterically.

"It's over, Ryan," Sands recovered fast. "I have back-up coming. Nobody has to die here."

"It's not over." He was completely calm again. "Not until *I* say it is. And if I want people to die, then they're gonna die." He suddenly swung the crossbow back towards his sister and steadied his arm, as if preparing to fire.

"*No!*" Sands thought desperately. "Come on Ryan. She's your sister. What did she ever do? What did she do to hurt you?"

Ryan paused, then laughed and turned back to stare at Sands. "Oh, she's done plenty." His arm relaxed a little, though the arrow was still pointed at Molly. "Ever since she was born it was *Molly, Molly, Molly.*" He screwed his face into a sneer. "Even *before* she was born. Before she was even *conceived.* Mum never gave a *shit* about me."

"That's not true."

"Oh, you don't think so? You've seen what my mother's *like.*"

Sands didn't have a proper answer for this and immediately regretted her next words. "But your dad did care for you?"

There was a long silence. Finally, Ryan grinned. "Yeah. I guess he did. And you think that helps? Dad loved me to bits. My dad the *serial killer*. Do you know what that's like? Do you have any idea what that's like? To have an actual *serial killer as a father*? It's no wonder I'm here with a crossbow, shooting my spoilt, dumb bitch of a sister."

What happened next seemed in slow motion, at least to Sands. Ryan tightened his grip on the crossbow, moving it down her body until it pointed at her stomach before loosing the bolt. There was a snap, a thud, and her body jerked.

Ryan roared again, aggressive and victorious, as Sands gagged. Both sounds were animal, guttural. Ryan moved over to his sister and tried to roll her over, but she was pinned now, the arrow's head embedded into the sand.

"Whoa – can you believe that? *It went right the way through*!" Sands was stunned, speechless. She felt her head going light. She wondered if she might pass out.

"Well, I guess you'll take me seriously now." The only

sign that Ryan was affected by his actions was his rapid breathing. He took another bolt and fitted it to the bow, before drawing back the string. Shaking her head to break free from the shock, Sands desperately forced herself to concentrate. Ryan aimed the crossbow at her, but she noticed there was no barbed head to the arrow, it was just a sharpened point. The previous bolt had been the same. What did that mean? Maybe it would do less damage? Maybe if the arrow he had fired into Molly had missed her major organs, then she might yet survive? If Sands could get her to a hospital, fast...

"I don't doubt you've got back-up coming," Ryan interrupted her thoughts. "I knew this was over when I heard you talking to Mum. That's why I came here. My last chance. I'm not going to prison. I'd rather go out with glory, you know what I mean?" He smiled and rocked the weapon from side to side, as if savouring its balance. "Take out a few of you pigs while I'm about it." He bit his lip, enjoying the insult. "So how about it? You want a go, or shall I put another one in my little sister?"

"Actually, I do know," Sands answered. Her words cut through Ryan's grin.

"Know what?"

"I do know what it's like."

He screwed up his face, not understanding. "What are you talking about?"

"I do know what it's like growing up with a serial killer as a father. In fact, I'm probably the only person you'll ever meet who does."

He stared at her, more confused now. "I don't get what you're saying."

"Oh, I know." Quelling the fury within her at what he had done, she went on, her voice strangely calm now. "Do you have your phone here?"

He hesitated. "Yeah."

"Do a search for Charles Sterling. Put 'Maths Murderer' after the name."

"Maths... What the hell?" Ryan laughed suddenly, bitter and dry. "What is this? A trick, right? I get my phone out, you rush me and grab the crossbow? Nice try, but it's not gonna work..."

"It's not a trick." Sands voice was sharper, cutting. "I'll lie down. You know I'm injured. I can't move quickly anyway. And you're going to want to know about this."

Ryan hesitated again, but she could see he was intrigued. After a while he said, "OK then. Lie down. But do it *slowly*. Very slowly." He kept the crossbow trained on Sands as she dropped to her knees, watching her all the time, much more distrustful now. Finally, she was lying face down on the beach.

"Hands behind you."

Again, she did what she was told, twisting her neck up so that she could at least see him. When he was satisfied she posed no threat, he let the crossbow hang from his belt and pulled out his phone from his jeans pocket. What was that name?"

"Charles Sterling."

She watched as his fingers tapped on the screen. Then he began reading aloud.

"Charles Sterling, known as the Maths Murderer, was arrested in 1999 for the murder of seven woman, including his wife and youngest daughter." He stopped reading out loud, and seemed to continue silently. "So?" he asked a moment later. "He was some loser who got himself caught. What's it got to do with you?"

"He was my father."

"Bullshit."

"I was twelve years old when he got caught. The day after he killed my mother and sister. He could have killed me, but he left me alive."

"I don't believe you. You're just saying it, so you can seem like me."

Sands shook her head slowly. "No. I *am* like you. I know what it's like."

Ryan's head twisted from side to side, as if he were looking for a way out of this unexpected situation. "You could just know *about* him. You could have read the same Wikipedia page I'm reading. Doesn't mean you *know* him." Ryan shook his head, his confidence returning. "I don't know what you think you're doing, but it's not gonna work." He slipped the phone away and wrapped his hand again around the handle of the crossbow. His eyes narrowed in determination, as if he wanted to get this done as soon as possible. He aimed the weapon at Sands and breathed steadily to try and steady his hands.

"Susan Barker." Sands' voice was still deathly calm. "Search for her now. She was murdered by Charles Sterling in 1996. There's a famous picture that the police used when she went missing. Find it and look closely. Zoom in and look at her neck."

Ryan breathed hard for several moments, but then he dropped the crossbow a second time and pulled out his phone again. "Is this really the last thing you wanna to do before you die? Make up some shit about some dude you don't even know?" But he ran the search. Moments later he shrugged, looking up from the screen. "OK. I see her neck. So what?"

"You see the pendant? The little frog?"

"Yeah."

Sands began to twist around.

"What the...? What are you doing? Stop moving!"

"I'm *showing you.*" Sands pulled out the silver chain from around her own neck. On the end of it was a locket. "Look again at the photo. Barker had a golden frog pendant, with one of its legs broken off. She was wearing it when she went missing, but it wasn't found when her body was recovered. Look at it. Look closely."

His fingers pinched the screen to zoom in. Then he approached her carefully, staring at her clenched fingers. "Open your hands. And no tricks." The screen showed a grainy photograph, a golden frog hanging around the neck of a smiling young woman. One of its legs was missing. Sands opened her fingers to show him her locket.

She'd opened it, with practiced fingers. Inside was a tiny golden frog, one leg broken off. Exactly the same as the frog on the screen.

"My father gave me this locket on my eleventh birthday. He woke me up after I'd gone to bed and told me I had to keep it secret. Not even tell my mother. He said it would bind us together."

Ryan stared at the frog, then at his screen.

"Go on. Take it." She held it out to him.

Sands tried to brace herself for an opportunity, but her position – lying down on the rocky ground – was hopeless, and Ryan was far too quick. His hand shot out and grabbed the pendant. She was watched him examine the frog in detail, turning it over and over in his hands, then comparing it again to the image on the screen of his phone.

"I kept it secret even after he got arrested. I've worn it ever since."

"Wow. You're actually telling me the truth?"

She tried to nod. "Charles Sterling is my father. He murdered eight women between 1985 and 1999. The last two were my sister and my mother, while I was sleeping over at a friend's house. I found the bodies the next morning. He was still there, cooking breakfast."

Ryan's eyes were wide now. He stood up, took a few steps back and started striding up and down the beach. "Shit!" he said, at last. "That's wild!"

"So shoot me, Ryan Harvey." Sands' voice rose now, stopping him again. "But don't tell me I don't know what it feels like. Don't you *dare* do that."

Ryan jumped closer and handed the golden frog back to her. Almost reverentially. He immediately skipped backwards again, keeping himself out of her reach.

"May I sit up?" Sands asked.

"Sure." Ryan nodded enthusiastically. His whole demeanour seemed to have changed. "This is cool!" He was smiling widely now. "I'm still gonna kill you, you understand that, right? But this is freakin' cool."

Sands nodded and rolled over onto her side, then sat cross-legged on the gravelly sand.

"How did you find out about your father?" she asked.

"Huh? Oh." Ryan crouched down, like he was getting ready now for a comfortable talk. He was still shaking his head at what she'd told him. "I dunno. I just..." He stopped. "OK..." He rocked back on his heels. "So I was about eight or nine, and I guess I'd sort of known for a while, but not really known, you know?" He stopped. "I guess you do know." He grinned suddenly. "I guess you really do."

"Anyway, it was bonfire night, and Dad had killed a dog. He did that sometimes, back then. He had it hidden in some wood we were storing to burn. But the thing was, I found it, and I wrote about it in my diary. Only what I didn't know was, Dad liked to read my diary." Ryan grinned at this. "So then Dad sits me down, he's worried I'm going to tell someone, but I thought it was cool. I was more interested than shocked. And after that he very slowly let me in. We made traps, catching mice and squirrels, and just hurting them at first, not even killing them. But gradually he got me into it." He laughed suddenly. "It was a wild way to grow up."

"When did you know he killed people? As well as animals?"

"I dunno. It took a while. Maybe when I was twelve, thirteen?"

"And you watched that too? He got you involved?"

"Yeah. I was up for it by then." He grinned again.

"And Emily Slaughter?" Sands asked. "You were there when he killed her?"

There was a long silence, which Ryan Harvey finally broke by chuckling lightly to himself. "You know, you've got a lot of this wrong." His head fell to one side as he watched her, but Sands didn't reply. Eventually he went on. "*Dad* didn't kill her." His mouth opened into a grin, waiting for her to catch on.

"So who did?" As she spoke, Sands already knew the answer.

"*I* did. She was mine. I mean, Dad helped and that, but I was the one who stuck her." His lips twisted into a boastful sneer. "Stuck her over and over until all her guts came out."

Sands looked away, not wanting to see the images that came to her mind.

"How did you do it? How did you frame Sopley with the DNA?"

Ryan kept grinning for a moment, but he didn't answer the question. "How long have I got? Before your back-up arrives?"

Sands twisted around to look up the beach towards where the road met the water a long way around the cove. There were a couple of figures there, but they weren't police, and they were clearly too far away to see or hear what was happening. They weren't going to offer any help.

"With the roads around here, probably half an hour at least."

"OK. Let's take that as fifteen minutes, shall we?" He gave her a knowing sneer, but he seemed content with this. "What did you want to know?"

"How did you get Sopley's DNA? We found one of his pubic hairs inside Emily's underwear."

Ryan shook his head, enjoying the question. "The thing you don't understand, Dad was a *genius* at what he did. A proper genius. If you don't get that, you're not going to understand any of...." He broke away. "We were going to do so many... so many more, and you'd never have caught him. And the best thing, he was gonna teach it all to me."

"Go on. I'm interested." There was genuine interest in her voice. Sands knew she was probably going to die there, but she wanted to know the truth.

"They *paid* Dad to give those losers therapy. That's the beauty of it. That's how we targeted them. Dad would find out all their dirty little secrets and fix up a target that fit them just right. Sopley was just a mark. The fall guy, he could never have done what we did."

"I know. I get that. But I don't see how you did it. The pubic hair..."

Ryan smiled. He waved a hand dismissively, as if the detail was unimportant. But he explained it anyway. "Sopley had a thing for little girls and dolls, right? So Dad told him about this swimming therapy. It was supposed to manage how screwed up he was. Anyway, he had to go twice a week, to a local pool. I just followed him there and broke into his locker. Found a hair in his dirty kegs. Disgusting, but well worth it. We kept it in a bag until we killed the girl, so it wouldn't dry out. And you fuckers assumed it couldn't be anyone other than Sopley. Just like Dad said you would."

Sands nodded. It made sense. And it would almost certainly have been enough to convince her.

"But there were other ways that could have worked. We could have broken into his house. It's really not hard." He stopped, and grinned. "But then you know that too."

Suddenly, Sands noticed a movement on the headland, behind Ryan, and out of his eyeline. She was quick enough to not follow it with her eyes, but through her peripheral vision she identified Detective Golding slipping quietly down the path that led towards the beach.

"That's clever." Sands forced her voice to stay level. She kept her eyes on Ryan. She calculated. Golding might be able to get near to the beach without being spotted, but the final twenty metres of the path down from the little cliff were more of a scramble, and then he would have to cover another twenty metres of the rock-strewn beach. There was no way he could get to Ryan before the teenager shot her, or turned and shot him. Sands had to keep Ryan distracted, and hope for something to change.

"How did you get the crossbow? You're underage."

"*What?* Are you patronising me? You know what we've done? You know *how many* we've done, and that's what you wanna ask me? There's like a million ways I could get this." He twisted the device on its axis, casually aiming it at Sands again now.

"So which way did you use? I'm interested." Sands said.

It seemed like Ryan wasn't going to answer, but then he shrugged his shoulders. "My mum's credit card. I told her I wanted a wetsuit, so I could go surfing with some guys from school." He laughed. "It's actually legal. Just in her name."

Behind him there was another noise, this time coming from Molly. She still hadn't fully regained consciousness, but a moan had escaped from her lips. Sands glanced over at her. Blood soaked her shirt around her stomach, but it wasn't pumping out. Her chest was still rising and falling.

"She's still alive," Sands said. "Molly isn't dead. This doesn't have to end the way you see it ending."

Ryan said nothing, and Sands went on, still hoping to distract him from Golding creeping further forward, making his way down the steeper part of the cliff path where it met the beach. "I can tell them it was your father who killed Emily Slaughter. That he forced you to come with him. People will understand."

"No, they won't."

"They will. They will if I tell them that."

"And what if I don't *want* you to tell them that? I killed that girl, she was mine."

"So what do you want?" Sands asked. "Why are we here?"

He turned a little to better show her the tight-fitting shoulder bag he was wearing. It was full with more of the crossbow bolts. "So I can put one of these through my sister's skull. And then another one through yours. After that I'll still have ten bolts left. So I reckon I should be able to take out a few more of you before I get taken down." He smiled, calm. "I know they'll take me out, but I don't care about that. I'll be back with Dad. That's where I want to be." He looked around suddenly at the surrounding landscape, as if he'd heard something. Golding saw him, just in time and managed to drop down behind a gorse bush.

"Pretty perfect place for a siege, don't you think?" Ryan said, the unchanged tone of his voice telling Sands he hadn't noticed Golding.

She took a breath, raising her voice so that Golding could hear her. "Suicide by cop? That's your plan?" Sands shook her head. "You don't have to. You don't have to die."

Ryan seemed to lose any remaining patience. "You know what? Fuck you, Detective *Sands*. You didn't even keep his name. You should be called Sterling. Were you embarrassed about where you came from? Who you really were?" Behind Ryan, Golding began edging forward once more. Sands didn't let her eyes move from Ryan. "Because I'm not embarrassed. I'm proud of my dad."

"I wouldn't have changed it," Sands said at once. "I was twelve years old. They took me into care when he was arrested. They wanted to protect me."

"You could have changed it back." Ryan swung round towards her now, agitated again. "Oh, you know what? Shut up. You're *boring* me now, with your life story. We're not alike. You think you're like me but you're not. You're *no one*. Your dad might have been someone, but not you, so *shut the hell up*."

With that, he turned back to Molly, who was lying a few feet away from him. This time he carefully aimed the weapon at her face. He held his arm steady for a few moments. "Head shot. Watch this."

Golding was still far too far away to do anything, and Sands knew she had to act, otherwise he'd shoot the girl, then likely her, long before Golding or anyone else could stop him.

"Stop, please," she called.

"Fuck you. You asked how it ends. Now you get to see."

"*No!*"

"Bye bye, little sis," Ryan ignored her. "No Mummy here to save you this time."

He took a deeper breath, concentrating on his aim. She saw the muscles in his wrist contract.

"No!" Sands shouted. "*Let me.*"

Ryan froze. For a long time there was silence, neither of them moved. Then he turned his head back towards Sands. "Let *you*? Let you what?"

"Let me kill her."

"You what?"

"You're going to kill us both anyway, so let *me* do it. I've always wondered."

A range of expressions passed over Ryan's face. Suspicion. Disbelief. Interest. "*You* want to kill my sister?"

"Yes."

"Whoa!" He laughed out loud. "That I did *not* see coming."

"Me neither." Sands meant it, but now she went all in. "Your father *taught* you, everything he showed you, how to kill? That was a gift. I could have had it too, but I was too scared, too weak. But you know what? I *always* wondered. Always. Ever since it happened I thought, what if...? What if I'd helped my dad that day instead of screaming for help? What if he'd taught *me*." Sands breathed fast. She had no idea if this was working, but he hadn't loosened the bolt yet. "So let me find out. Let me put it right, before you kill me. Let me know how it *feels* to be a killer."

She was silent. Her breath still coming hard. "Let me, Ryan. It's my birthright. Just like you."

Ryan lowered the crossbow again and ran his fingers through his thick, dark hair. He seemed to be marvelling at how this was turning out. "Well, you're full of surprises, aren't you?" He scratched his chin. "I thought that, when you came into my room that time... I was looking at porn – you know that? And you walked in, and I thought, I'd do you. I mean you're too old, and you move like a cripple, but..." He shook his head. "I kind of got the idea you might be up for it too."

Sands didn't reply.

"And now you want to kill Molly?" Although he seemed on the verge of agreeing, he suddenly said, "Uh-huh. I'm not falling for it."

He shook his head a second time, more firmly. "No. You want to do it with the crossbow right? Then you'll use it against me. Just how dumb do you think I am?"

"You can keep it." Sands heard herself speaking, though she was barely in control of what she said. "You cover me, with the weapon, the whole time. I'll do it with a rock. I'll smash her brains out. I really want to. I *need* this." This time she could see Ryan was tempted. "Are you frightened? Is that it? You're scared I'll overpower you?"

He didn't reply, but he looked insulted. She went on. "You think I'll outsmart you. You're scared I've got some plan you haven't figured out yet. And I'll beat you because your daddy was the smart one and you're too dumb to do this." She smiled, almost laughed, and was about to go on when he turned on her.

"Shut up!" Ryan aimed the crossbow at her face again, his arm quivering.

"Go on," Sands said, not thinking at all now. Not even caring. "Shoot me. If you're so brave, so smart. Shoot me, then finish off Molly." She laughed now, freely and easily. "And then see what happens. I lied about my back-up. It could be an hour before anyone else turns up here. You reckon you can wait that long for your glorious siege? My bet is you'll be so scared you'll turn that thing on yourself." As she said it, she knew she was right. Or at least that he feared she might be.

"You want infamy? You want people to know you were serious, like your Dad? Let *me* kill Molly. Think what the forensics will make of that? Because they'll know. I'll have her blood, her brains under my fingernails, so they'll know what happened. And think what your *dad* would make of it Think what *my* dad will say!" She paused, and a strange look came unbidden onto her face. "Because he'll find out."

"We're both gonna die today, Ryan. We both know it. So let's make it count. Let's put down a marker. For history."

He was still for a long time, then he spoke. "I'm keeping the crossbow." He took a couple of steps back. "Crawl over to her. *Slowly.*"

He pointed the weapon at her as she did so. As she crawled, she selected a fist-sized rock. She wondered if she might be able to throw it at him, but from her crawling position she'd never generate enough force.

"I'm watching."

She gripped the rock harder and continued to crawl.

When she reached Molly, she checked quickly for signs of life. Up close, the arrow's shaft was just a narrow aluminium rod. As Ryan had said it went all the way through the girl's body, but at the edge of her chest. And somehow she was still breathing.

"What are you doing?"

"I'm making sure she's still alive." Sands moved her hands carefully over the girl, all the time willing Ryan to come closer so she could turn and try to attack him. But he stayed a safe distance back, cautiously watching. She couldn't see Golding now, but all that meant was he wasn't close. Not close enough to save her. She hesitated.

"She's alive alright," Ryan answered. But one of us is gonna kill her. So you're either gonna do it or I am. Get the hell on with it."

Sands moved her hands to the girl's face, closing her eyes. She was unconscious, but even so Sands didn't want her to see this. She lifted the rock above the girl's head.

Then, in one swift movement, and before Ryan could say another word, she brought it down, hard.

SIXTY-ONE

At the very last moment she let her weight fall to one side so the rock missed Molly's head and cracked onto the ground beside her instead. She continued to twist, picked the rock back up and launched it towards Ryan. He let out a cry and sidestepped so that the rock went flying by.

There was no time for either of them to speak as she rolled onto her feet and launched herself towards him. As she did so he released the crossbow bolt.

But Sands anticipated it, having already shifted her weight to change direction, not coming for Ryan after all but throwing herself off to the side. It wasn't enough for the bolt to miss altogether, but it meant it struck into her side rather than her middle, and her momentum meant it didn't penetrate through, but twisted away. Even so, the impact spun her around three hundred and sixty degrees, so that she was again facing Ryan. It wasn't clear which of them was more surprised, but Sands was fastest to react. She charged at him again.

Her body knocked the weapon from his hands, sending them both tumbling to the rocky ground. He was, however, able to roll away, and then his advantage began to pay off: he was bigger and uninjured. He made to grab her and managed to get his hands around her throat. She found herself on her back, sharp rocks digging into her as he scrambled to mount her, applying more and more pressure to her throat.

"Bitch," he snarled, his breath strong and sour on her face. "I knew it was a trick." She tried to get her hands between his to pry them off, but he was strong, and now her side lit up with pain where his thigh jerked the crossbow bolt embedded in her.

"Oh, you like that?" He saw it hurt her, and did it again, harder, and then leaned into his stranglehold. Sands realised that he knew what he was doing, he knew how to cut off the air supply and give his victim no chance of survival. He eased off just enough, as if sensing she was already losing consciousness and he wanted to bring her back so she'd see how much he was enjoying it.

There was no way to loosen his grip. He was killing her, coldly, calculatedly. She was gagging and choking, each second agony. She knew she was dying.

"Damn bitc—"

He didn't finish the curse, since at that moment the flying figure of Detective Golding hit Ryan Harvey hard from behind, and the two of them went sprawling. Sands tried to ready herself to intervene, to try to sit up, but it was all she could do to lie back and force her lungs to start working again. When she finally managed to turn her head, she saw there was no need. With the element of surprise, Golding had been faster to react. He now had both Ryan's arms pinned viciously high up behind his chest and handcuffed together. Golding made the teenager kneel, then Sands heard his adrenalin-filled voice reading Ryan his rights.

It wasn't over, not quite, Sands realised a few minutes later. She was still lying on her back, now unsure if she could move at all and craning her neck to see how deep the crossbow bolt had penetrated into her. Golding and Ryan were arguing, bickering almost, like children.

"Are you alright, ma'am?" Golding asked. He'd managed to get the handcuffs on both of Ryan's wrists, but, with nothing to secure him to, he was still holding on to him.

"I couldn't get down any quicker."

"Help the girl. I'm fine."

It wasn't true, but Sands didn't care. She lay on her back, staring up at the sky. She tried to lift her head, to see whether she could help Golding, or even move to where Molly lay, but she couldn't.

In the distance, a car moved slowly onto the beach, a Land Rover, a blue light flashing on its roof. Somehow they'd driven it over the boulders. She let her head drop back and stared upwards at the deep blue of the sky, brushed here and there with the lightest strokes of clouds.

It was, she thought. A beautiful day to die.

SIXTY-TWO

But it wasn't her day to die. Instead, she was left on the beach with Golding's jacket pressed up against the base of the crossbow bolt until a rescue helicopter landed just a few metres away. She was loaded onto a stretcher and lifted aboard, and then flown to the hospital in Poole. And then, pumped with painkillers, the murky, milky and now almost-familiar descent into the unconsciousness of emergency surgery.

"Hey." Golding's voice interrupted Sands' thoughts as she lay recovering, thirty-six hours later. It was the same building, but a different room from six months earlier.

She lifted her mouth into a brief smile and he took it as an invitation to sit down. His usual good humour was absent and he seemed deflated. He didn't say anything for a long time. In fact, almost two minutes passed before either of them spoke.

"How'd you feel?"

"Like I look."

"Mmmm." Golding nodded, glancing at the bandages

covering Sands' right side, the bruises on her neck. "So what hurts more? Getting shot by a shotgun, or with a crossbow bolt?"

"It's not really a true comparison. This one was only a flesh wound."

He seemed to consider this. "Fair enough. Maybe tell me next time then?"

The very beginnings of a smile formed in the corners of her mouth. "I'm hoping I've learned my lesson." He nodded, agreeing, then fell silent.

"The kid, Molly, she's just come out of surgery," Golding went on eventually. "She's alright." He paused. "Considering. I mean, they say she'll be alright, physically at least. Mentally, who knows?" He shook his head now. "How do you even do that? How do you do that to your *own sister*?"

Sands had to look away as an image of Molly's body came to her mind, jerking backwards as the arrow entered her. It was a few moments before she was able to speak. "Is he talking?"

"Ryan? Oh yeah. Little shitbag won't shut up. He's actually proud of what he did. Can you believe that?"

She could, but didn't say so. "What's he saying?" she asked instead.

"It's like he was on some sort of apprentice course following what his dad did." He shook his head again. "I don't get it. I really don't get it. He's *seventeen* years old and now he's gonna spend his whole life in prison." He grimaced. "I just don't get it."

Sands watched him, blinking slowly but not replying.

Golding broke the silence. "Listen, ma'am..." He stopped, puffing out his cheeks. "Everything you said to him, on the beach. About your father. About how you... I don't know, I was thinking you might be wondering how much I heard?"

He looked away and rubbed his hand across his face. He

hadn't shaved, and the movement made a loud rasping sound in the quiet room.

"It was a still day. You were close enough. I assumed you heard everything."

Golding was quiet, then he nodded. "I haven't said... I haven't told anyone what *you* said. I didn't think it was relevant, and I didn't think it was anyone's business... I mean, I don't even know if it's true. You could have just been saying that..." He paused again, his eyes searching hers almost hopefully.

"Saying what?"

"About who your father is? Maybe you said that to distract him." He waited a beat, but Sands didn't reply. She didn't look away either. "I mean, shit – obviously you didn't mean the last bit. You were never going to bash the girl's head in... but he actually thought you might – that was clever. That saved her life."

Again there was silence.

"*Is* it true, though? Everything else? I mean, if you don't mind? If you don't want to talk about it, that's..."

"Yes." She cut him off. "It's true. My father is Charles Sterling. The so-called Maths Murderer. He was caught when I was twelve years old. His last victims were my mother and my sister. But I didn't know. I had no idea what he was until I walked in that morning. He was making scrambled eggs, my mother was lying dead on the floor."

Golding stared at her, his mouth slightly open, then his expression changed. "He was dying." His eyes widened. "Your father. The night we first met? In my sister's gallery. Your father was in a hospital? You didn't want to visit him."

Her eyes flicked over to him, but she said nothing.

"And then he pulled through? So he's still alive now?"

She nodded now, slowly. "He was never ill in the first place. He likes to play tricks. He enjoys messing people around."

Golding didn't seem to know what to say. He opened his mouth and shook his head.

Sands found she didn't want to look at him. Instead she stared blankly forwards.

"So what happened?" Golding went on at last. "How did you escape?"

"I didn't need to escape. He let me live."

Golding didn't reply. She heard him swallow.

"He told me he didn't want me to die, because I was just like him." She drew in a deep breath. "I called the police, and he just let me."

"Then what? After he was arrested? Did you have other relatives or what?"

Sands took a long time to reply. "No relatives close enough. I went to foster homes, but they... didn't work out. I was angry, confused, for a long time. Eventually I was old enough to live on my own, so I did. I always had plenty of money. My father was wealthy; when he was convicted it was signed over to me."

Golding listened. "I'm so sorry," he said, his eyes downcast. Then they flicked back to her face. "Does anyone else know? In the force, I mean?"

Sands shook her head. "Only Yorke. I reported it when I joined, he decided it would be better if it wasn't widely known. Now he acts as an intermediary. There are still... legal issues. Yorke helps me to deal with them."

Golding considered for a few moments. "How long's his sentence?" he asked.

"Whole life. He won't ever be released."

Golding nodded as if this was something. "And nobody else knows. At the station?"

"They *didn't*. Not till now."

"They still won't." He was quick to reply. "If you want to keep this quiet – and I get why you want to – you still can. I'm not going to tell a soul."

Sands was quiet a moment, then she smiled softly. "It's not you I'm worried about. You've already told me that Ryan Harvey can't keep his mouth shut."

Golding opened his mouth to protest. "There's no proof. No one will believe him."

She gave him a look then turned away.

Golding seemed to consider this for a few moments, then he pulled something out of his pocket, lifting it up and down a couple of times, as if considering what to do, then he opened his hand to show her. It was the locket she'd shown to Ryan. He used a fingernail to prise it open, and the golden frog fell out into his palm.

"I picked it up from the beach. Maybe you should decide what to do with it."

Sands' eyes widened when she saw it, and she felt an urge to reach out and take it, to keep it close, keep it hidden. Like she'd done for so many years.

"Take it," Golding said. "Without this, no one's gonna believe him."

Sands stared at the frog, seeing how the break in the leg had been worn smooth by her fingers over time. She wanted to touch it again, to trace its familiar contours. But then she shook her head. "It's about time it went back to her family." She swallowed. "It's time for me to deal with people knowing the truth." She lifted her eyes from the frog, more firmly this time. "Bag it up please, detective."

Golding stared at her but eventually nodded and slipped both parts back into his pocket.

"Jesus." He shook his head a third time. "And you still have your misconduct hearing coming up."

Sands' face was expressionless. Then she nodded very slightly. "Yeah. I do."

SIXTY-THREE

Exactly one month later, Sands drove past the building that housed MID looking for somewhere to park. The staff car park was still off limits to her; even if it hadn't been, she wasn't sure if leaving her car there was the right thing to do. Instead she drove up and down several side streets but found nowhere. Eventually she headed to the NCP car park and left the Alfa there.

She walked back to the police station, but hesitated outside. It didn't look much from the outside, but it had been her life, her everything, until the suspension. And now there would be a hearing to determine whether that part of her was over. The closer it came, the less sure she became that it was even something she wanted anymore. Maybe today would answer that question? She walked up the steps to the public entrance. As she opened the door, she tried to swallow her nerves.

Inside, the female PC who took her name insisted upon accompanying her upstairs where the senior officers were based.

"There's no need," she insisted. "I know the way."

"I'm sorry ma'am, but you don't have a building pass, and I'm required to take you."

Sands let it go, allowing the woman lead her to the bank of lifts.

"Actually, would you mind if we take the stairs?" Sands changed her mind. Any opportunity to delay things.

They climbed the stairwell together, the woman puffing from the effort. Sands felt it too, even though her body was healing fast. On the fifth floor they reached a quiet recess where a middle-aged woman sat behind a computer.

"DCI Sands." Her mouth sounded dry as she spoke. "I'm here to see Chief Superintendent Yorke. He's expecting me."

"I'll let him know." Yorke's PA smiled politely, but when she tried the phone there was no answer. "He's on a call. I'll try again in a moment."

Sands nodded, then turned to the woman who had accompanied her. "You can probably go now," she said. The PC looked uncomfortable, but did as she was told.

It was a long phone call. Several times the PA tried the line again, but shook her head sadly. All the while, Sands tried to not to think too much. She'd been discharged from the hospital a fortnight earlier, but since she was still suspended, she'd been unable to play any further role in sorting out the mess of the Harveys' crimes. And then, last night, she'd received the message from Yorke asking her to come in and meet him. He hadn't said whether it was good news or bad news. He'd have said if it was good. Which meant it was bad.

The PA tried the line again, and this time it must have connected because she spoke into the line, then listened and nodded.

"You can go in now."

Sands got up and limped towards the door.

. . .

"Ah – Erica, thank you for coming in."

"Sir."

"Have a seat." Paperwork was piled high on both sides of Yorke's desk, and as she sat down he removed a pair of reading glasses and folded the arms away, placing them in his desk.

"I shouldn't complain, but you've created a mountain of work, trying to figure out who's in prison that shouldn't be."

She didn't reply, but he smiled anyway.

"How are you?"

"Fine," she lied.

"Good. Good." He didn't seem to expect a more fulsome answer. Instead, he opened a drawer behind the desk and pulled out a plastic-bound report.

"Well, here we are. Hot off the press, as they say." He tossed the report onto the desk, then slid it over to her.

"What's this?"

"It's an advance copy of the IPCC report into your actions on the afternoon of 11th February."

Sands stared at it. "What about the hearing?"

"There isn't going to be one." He smiled again. "It's all in here." Again, he gave no indication whether this was good news or bad.

"What does it say?"

"If you read it, you'll find out."

Sands glanced at Yorke, confused, then picked up the document. She flicked through, unsure where to start.

"You can read the whole thing of course, but the recommendation is probably what you're most interested in. Page three."

Sands turned to it and began reading.

"Oh come on, Erica! Where's your sense of drama? Read it out loud. Second paragraph."

Sands did what he asked.

"'Although this investigation considers a large amount of evidence, it can be reduced to a simple question. On the afternoon of 11th February, when Detective Chief Inspector Erica Sands attempted to assist Commander Michael Roper in pulling Gunnery Sergeant Dean Jones to safety, did her actions precipitate, or cause Michael Sopley, to fire upon the three officers? It is the finding of this investigation, backed up by video evidence from the body cameras worn by several of the firearms officers, that they did not. Indeed, the evidence clearly shows Sopley coming into view and preparing to fire before DCI Sands made any move to assist."

Sands slowed, but kept reading. "Therefore, this report concludes that DCI Sands was not at fault, and in fact displayed outstanding bravery."

She stopped. "I don't understand. What about the hearing? It's supposed to start next week."

"Not anymore it's not. It's been dropped. I told you not to worry."

"But how? How's it been dropped?"

Yorke got up from his seat and went to a corner cabinet. He took out a bottle of whisky and two crystal glasses. "I know you're not a big drinker, Erica, but I'm going to have one." He smiled at her as he poured a generous amount into each glass. Then he handed one to her and sat back down. "You remember I told you that the firearms unit had submitted statements? Saying you moved before Sopley, which prompted him to fire?"

"Of course."

"They've chosen to rescind them. I wouldn't like to speculate unduly, but I'd say a lot of people have been scrabbling very hard once they worked out they're on the wrong side of this. You demonstrated Sopley was innocent, and you've given us Evan Harvey. You're about the only one who comes out of this well. You'd have to be brave or stupid to want to testify against you after all that." He shrugged. "Once all the statements began to line up, it became clear there was little for a hearing to discover."

"What about the body cameras? You said they malfunctioned, there was no footage?"

"The two cameras which failed, which also just happened to be the ones best-placed to capture what actually took place, both made a miraculous recovery. Both clearly showed your version of events was correct." He tipped his glass to the report. "It's all in there."

Sands said nothing.

"Of course, whether this is actually over is another matter. I think there's clear evidence the unit tried to set you up as the fall-guy for this. I think you can prove it, and I think you should."

Sands blinked. Several moments from her career flashed through her mind. The pushback she'd received as a female officer. The old boys' network, which had expected to recruit John Lindham into its ranks when the opportunity to lead MID became vacant – until Sands' relentless drive made it impossible for her not to be selected instead. The shame she'd always felt because of her father and what he'd done. And worst of all, the fact that her team now knew who her father was. Where *she* came from. Along with everyone else in the entire force.

"I think you should file an official complaint." Yorke was still speaking.

Sands stared at him. Was that what she wanted, to kick up a fuss? With all the baggage she carried? Or was this another moment? The push to do something else, to start again. She looked around Yorke's office. Her eyes took in a photograph of his wife, another with his two daughters, they'd be in their early twenties now. Was that why he'd taken to her when she'd joined. Did he see something of his own children in her?

"I won't pretend it'll be easy, but I can promise you my full backing." He seemed to read her thoughts.

"I don't want to submit a complaint," she said quietly.

Yorke was slow to reply, he smoothed one of his eyebrows

with a finger. "Are you sure? This is your career. Had this gone the other way, you would have likely been fighting a civil case for wrongful death. You could have lost everything."

"I'm sure."

Yorke nodded. "Of course. Well, I can't say we don't have enough to do." He gestured again at the pile of papers.

"What about the Sopley case?" Sands asked suddenly. "Will I face any sanction for investigating while suspended?"

He looked surprised. "The Sopley case was closed. I don't see how anyone could have been investigating a case which wasn't even open." His eyebrows rose a fraction, and he smiled knowingly. "Detective Golding tells me that was how you justified it to him as well?"

Sands swallowed. "Yes."

"Well, I can see the logic." The smile deepened.

Yorke lifted his glass and rolled the amber liquid around. "There's no appetite to heap blame on you here, Erica. Your suspension is over. You're back." He lifted his glass in a toast, but when she failed to lift hers, he finally he seemed to catch on.

"If you want to come back, that is."

Sands couldn't meet his gaze. She looked around the room again, before letting her eyes come to rest on her glass, which was still untouched on the desk in front of her. She opened her mouth to speak, but struggled to find the right phrasing.

"Ryan Harvey... Is he still talking?" She glanced up, catching Yorke's expression change.

Yorke sighed, and very lightly he nodded.

"So everyone knows?"

Yorke was careful with his words now. "The Commander and I had a discussion about whether it was practical, or even possible, to prevent the information about your former relationship with Charles Sterling coming out. But..." he shook his head now. "They're detectives, Erica. You know it would never work."

Sands herself nodded now, it was nothing less than what she already knew, but it surprised her how much it cut to have it confirmed.

"What do they think?"

"No one's going to think anything. They know who you are. He's just a scumbag in a high security cell, deep underground. A scumbag who's never getting out. Nothing's going to change because of where you came from. Something you had no choice in." He had a terrible poker face, but Sands left it. It wasn't his fault.

Still Sands hadn't touched the drink, and Yorke set his down now. Instead he unlocked and opened the top drawer to his desk. He poked around inside, and finally pulled out a black leather case, he opened it and turned it to face her, so she could see what it was. Her warrant card. Then he placed it down on the desk, and slid it forward, over to her side. She stared at it, seeing her own unsmiling face in the photograph, beside it the metal badge, its curves smoothed by use.

"It's your call Erica," Yorke said.

Sands glanced around the room again. On the bookshelf, next to a golfing trophy, was another photograph. This time of Yorke with his brother, both carrying fly fishing rods, a grey-green mountain looming behind them. Each of them wore wide, relaxed smiles. She thought of her own office, entirely absent of photographs, of any kind of personal effects. She thought of her flat, where the same could be said – unless you counted the scene-of-crime photographs that still littered the dining room table. Did she want this? Could she still do this? Now that everyone knew?

Or perhaps the real question was, was there anything else she could do?

She reached forward and touched the ID badge. At first she didn't pick it up, just traced her finger around the swirls in the cool metal. But then she did pick it up, folded the wallet closed, and then she shifted on the seat so that she could slip it into the pocket of her jeans.

"I want to go back to work." Sands said.

And Yorke nodded.

"Welcome back, Erica. Welcome back."

A LETTER FROM THE AUTHOR

Dear reader,

Huge thanks for reading *The Cove*. I hope you enjoyed following Erica Sands as she uncovered the clues – and that you'll want to know what comes next. As I write these words I'm just finishing up book two in the series, *The Pool*, and I'm full of ideas about book three.

If you'd like to join other readers in keeping in touch, here are two options. Stay in the loop with my new releases with the link below. You'll be the first to know about all future books I write.

Or sign up to my personal email newsletter on the website at the bottom of this note. You'll get bonus content, a free novella, and get occasional updates and insights from my writing life. I'd be delighted if you choose to sign up to either – or both!

www.stormpublishing.co/gregg-dunnett

If you enjoyed this book and could spare a few moments to leave a review that would be hugely appreciated. Even a short review can make all the difference in encouraging a reader to discover my books for the first time. Thank you so much!

Join other readers in hearing about my writing (and life) experiences, get a free copy of my bestselling novel, and other bonus content. Simply head over to my website at www.gregg dunnett.com

facebook.com/greggwriter

Made in United States
North Haven, CT
20 August 2023

40552564R00243